Hey — I found your stuff while I was
shelving. (Looks like you left in a hurry!) I read
a few chapters & loved it. Felt bad about
keeping the book from you, though, since you
obviously need it for your work.
    Have to get my own copy!
        —Jen

SHIP of THESEUS

HERE — IF YOU LIKED IT YOU SHOULD
FINISH IT. I NEED A BREAK, ANYWAY.
(LEAVE IT ON THE LAST SHELF IN
THE SOUTH STACKS WHEN YOU'RE FINISHED.)

Thanks! Read the rest in one sitting — wow.
    Haven't liked a book so much in a long time
        (& I'm a lit major!) — Loved all the
    mystery — the book, Straka, all of it.
    I really needed an escape, I think.

DEAR UNDERGRAD LIT MAJOR:
IF YOU THOUGHT IT WAS AN "ESCAPE",
THEN YOU WEREN'T READING CLOSELY ENOUGH.
WANT TO GIVE IT ANOTHER SHOT?

Dear ~~Arrogant~~,
    I made some notes in the margins so you can
see how closely I read. But what do I know?

I CAN'T BELIEVE → I'm just an undergrad.
YOU WROTE ALL OVER
MY BOOK.   I know. It was so
                    presumptuous of me.

Don't bother leaving it for me
again. Good luck with your work. Oh, and by the way,
    you've totally missed something important
        about F.X. Caldeira. — IS IT THAT HE'S A COMPLETE
CRANK? BECAUSE PRETTY MUCH EVERY SERIOUS STRAKA SCHOLAR
EVER HAS THOUGHT SO. AND IF YOU THINK "CALDEIRA" WAS
STRAKA PRETENDING TO BE HIS OWN TRANSLATOR, THAT'S →
BEEN PRETTY WELL COVERED, TOO.

ALSO BY V. M. STRAKA

I know the
footnotes are really strange—
but what if they weren't
~~supposed~~ to be informative?
What if they were signals
or messages to someone—
like Straka himself?

STRAKA WAS DEAD BY THEN.
Just saying: I don't think
we should assume Caldeira
was stupid/insane. There's
got to be more to it.

"WE" ??
OK, that was a mistake.

DO YOU STILL THINK SO?
Absolutely.

STILL?
You really need
to ask?

SHIP OF THESEUS

by

V. M. STRAKA

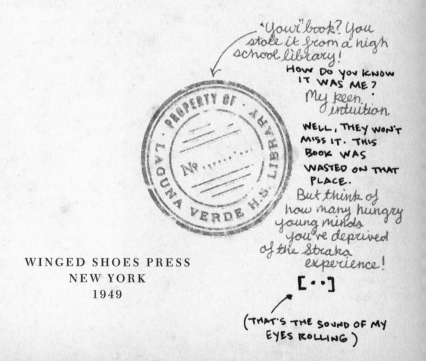

"Your" book? You stole it from a high school library!

HOW DO YOU KNOW IT WAS ME? My keen intuition.

WELL, THEY WON'T MISS IT. THIS BOOK WAS WASTED ON THAT PLACE.

But think of how many hungry young minds you've deprived of the Straka experience!

[··]

(THAT'S THE SOUND OF MY EYES ROLLING)

WINGED SHOES PRESS
NEW YORK
1949

TRANSLATOR'S NOTE

AND FOREWORD[1]

by

F. X. CALDEIRA

I.

WHO WAS V. M. STRAKA? The world knows
his name, knows his reputation as the prolific
author of provocative fictions, novels that toppled
governments, shamed ruthless industrialists, and
foresaw the horrifying sweep of totalitarianism that
has been a particular plague in these last few
decades. It knows him as the most nimble of writers, one whose mastery of diverse literary idioms
and approaches was on display from book to book,
even chapter to chapter. But the world never knew

---

[1] This book was to have been published by my former employer, Karst & Son—as all of Straka's previous books were. However, that firm has shut its doors abruptly and without notice to
its employee. I have—at considerable personal expense (financial and otherwise)—begun my
own publishing venture so that Straka's capstone work can be appreciated by the public.

Straka's face, never knew with certainty a single fact of the man's life.

Predictably, though disappointingly, the mystery of Straka's identity has become more intensely studied than his (body of work.) Interest in his life story is understandable, certainly, as he is widely acknowledged as one of the most idiosyncratic and influential novelists of the first half of this century.[2] His appreciative readers wanted to know the man who created the stories they loved, and his enemies wanted to know who he was so he could be silenced.

The furor over Straka's identity is particularly intense due to the rumors about his activities and affiliations—rumors that are fairly bursting with tales of sabotage, espionage, conspiracy, subversion, larceny, and assassination.* If there is a category of skullduggery to which Straka's name has not been linked in the popular press (and in some infuriating articles passed off as "literary scholarship"), I am not aware of it. Perhaps this is to be expected, as Straka's work itself often included secrets, conspiracies, and shadow-world occurrences. The author's

---

[2] Ernest Hemingway expressed his admiration for Straka's books in a 1935 interview in *Le Monde*. It is well-known that Hemingway later became one of Straka's harshest critics. What is less-well-known is that Hemingway's about-face came shortly after he begged for a personal audience with Straka and his request was met with indifferent silence.

{ vi }

Handwritten annotations:

So why'd you have to leave the library in such a hurry the other night?
I DIDN'T WANT TO BE SEEN.
By...?
BY ANYONE.
Nice evasion.
Letting it slide — For now.

So how long have you been studying Straka?
SINCE HIGH SCHOOL, I GUESS. SO, 14-15 YRS.
Ever wonder if you should be doing something else? NO.
This is where an empathetic person might ask "Why?"
OK, WHY?
I'm graduating in May. No clue what to do next.
FIND WHAT YOU LOVE. THEN FIGHT LIKE HELL WHEN PEOPLE TRY TO TAKE IT AWAY FROM YOU.
That sounds like great advice — but I wish it didn't. Isn't it supposed to be easier than that?
DEPENDS ON WHAT "IT" IS.

* How much of this stuff can be true?
DEPENDS ON WHO YOU ASK. MANY PEOPLE (+ GOV'TS) DID THINK HE WAS DANGEROUS. LEAKED/DECLASSIFIED DOCS SHOW IT.
I love this word.
PLEASE TELL ME THAT'S NOT THE BEST YOU CAN DO. IF YOU'RE GOING TO HELP, HELP.
Are you always this charming?
SORRY — JUST FEEL LIKE I'M RACING THE CLOCK HERE.

EVIDENCE? THERE'S NOTHING IN THE ARCHIVES — STRAKA'S OR HEMINGWAY'S.

This is one place where a reasonable person would've suggested we meet instead of passing the book.
I NEVER CLAIMED TO BE REASONABLE.

personal reclusiveness was perhaps the grandest and most provocative of these.

[But the focus on the Writer and not the Work dishonors both.] Only in the author's private life—which was and is nobody's business—might it matter "who" he "was." (The few verifiable public statements Straka issued) confirm that he, too, believed the authorship controversy was misguided—not to mention a pernicious threat to his safety, liberty, and peace of mind.

Nineteen novels are attributed to Straka, the first being the satirical adventure *Miracle at Braxenholm*, which was the toast of Europe in 1911, the final one being the book you have in your hand. [Herein you will also find extensive annotations that I have contributed for the benefit of Straka's devoted readers and the responsible scholars who study his work.]

SEE BOLTON (1957) — ARG. THAT FXC'S ANNOTS. SUGGEST HE'S SCHIZOPHRENIC

II.

While I do so with trepidation, I shall encapsulate the most common arguments over "candidates," lest readers seek such information from unreliable sources.

Some believe that V. M. Straka the author was the factory worker Vaclav Straka (born 1892 in South

No middle name? ^

{ vii }

Handwritten marginalia:

WHY, WHEN THE Q. OF IDENTITY IS ESSENTIAL IN THE BOOKS THEMSELVES? (ESP. SOT, WINGED SHOES, CORIOLIS)

What are they? Do you have copies?

ATTACHED. MY FAVORITE: LETTER TO GRAHN RIPPING FILM ADAPTATION OF SANTANA MARCH.

Hilarious. Makes me feel bad for Grahn, though.

→ I read it. Idiotic. Guy thinks strong emotion = mental illness.

WENT BACK + REREAD. YOU'RE RIGHT — IT'S SO 1950S. FUNNY NO ONE HAS GONE BACK TO QUESTION IT. YOU'D THINK I WOULD HAVE.

Why you?

B/C I'VE HAD PEOPLE MAKE JUDGMENTS LIKE THAT ABOUT WHO I AM.

Wait — recently?

IF I SAY YES, ARE YOU GOING TO STOP WRITING?

Apparently not.

NO.

Wondering. what does the "F.X." stand for in Caldeira's name?

F = FRANCISCO OR FILIP (DEPENDS ON SOURCE)
X = XABREGAS

Bohemia), although this argument must strain to account for a newspaper item about the suicide of a man by this name in Prague in 1910. Others—including many *soi-disant* "literary experts"—dispute the theory for a different reason: as with the Shakespeare authorship controversy, they argue that these works could not have been written by a man with little formal education. No, they say, it must have been someone else writing under the Straka name, someone with more sterling credentials, such as:

- The Swedish children's author Torsten Ekstrom; or
- The Scottish philosopher, novelist, and *bon vivant* Guthrie MacInnes; or
- The once-revered and now-much-out-of-favor Spanish novelist and memoirist Tiago García Ferrara; or
- The aptly-initialed American pulp novelist and screenwriter Victor Martin Summersby; or
- The Canadian adventurer C. F. J. Wallingford; or
- The German anarchist and polemicist Reinhold Feuerbach; or
- The noted Czech poet and playwright Kajetán Hruby; or even

Prof. Moody did a guest lecture on this in my Elizabethan Lit. class last year.

I HOPE YOU IGNORED EVERY GODDAMN WORD

Just a guess: you're not a fan.

HE WAS MY DISSERTATION ADVISOR. IT ENDED BADLY.

Why?

IN PART B/C HE'S A LIAR + A THIEF.

So the clock you're racing—it has to do with Moody?

HE'S ABOUT TO CASH IN ON MY WORK.

Sign-in log says Moody was in the archive yesterday with "Esme Emerson-Plum."

BIG NY EDITOR. MEANS HE'S CLOSE.

Should I read that one next?
NO. GO BACK TO BRAXENHOLM
(THE FIRST) AND WORK
CHRONOLOGICALLY.

• The French archaeologist-suffragist-novelist Amarante Durand.[3] AB + VMS MUST'VE KNOWN EACH OTHER. DETAILS IN PAINTED CAVE HAD TO COME FROM HER.

Some allegedly-serious people have suggested occult origins (A little girl receiving messages from a fourteenth-century nun! An ancient Nazca king, originally from a distant planet! Grand Duchess Olga, writing both before and after her murder!) and other absurdities (A murderous Serbian nationalist known only as "Apis's Amanuensis"! The almost-certainly-fictional "Last Spanish Pirate" Juan Blas Covarrubias! The proverbial million monkeys!), which merit mention only to be scoffed at.

I'd mention that this is also a very cool word but you'd probably flip out again. So I won't.
YEAH, IT'S GOOD THAT YOU DIDN'T.

I have little interest in arguing about which "candidate"—plausible, fantastic, or otherwise—for Straka is the strongest. I do not know his birth name, his birthplace, or his native tongue. I do not know his height, his weight, his street address, his work history, or the paths of his travels. I do not know if he committed any of the illegal, subversive, or violent acts of which he has been accused. I do not care who other people think he was or what they thought of him.[4]

Examples?
1920 WALL ST. BOMBING;
"SANTORINI MAN" MURDER(S);
MANY LABOR RIOTS; SPYING FOR LEFT-WING ORGS;
MY FAVORITE: HE WAS PART OF THE GROUP THAT SHOT THE ARCHDUKE IN SARAJEVO + THUS STARTED WWI. SEE INTERLUDE (OBV.)
And in The Black 19 — reads like a confession to lots of Black Hand killings.
YOU'VE READ B19 ALREADY?
Yup. Finished last night.

→ MORE FOOLISH THAN PIRATE THEORY? ＊
(THAN GHOST-OF-MEDIEVAL-NUN THEORY?)

[3] Durand is a particularly foolish suggestion. All available evidence indicates that V. M. Straka was a man.

[4] Do I think he was a dangerous man? Perhaps, if you posed a danger to _him_.

↳ FXC = sexist? The great writer _has_ to be a man?
MAYBE FXC WAS.
BUT THERE'S JUST { ix }
NOT MUCH EVIDENCE
FOR DURAND.

＊Sounds like me 3 yrs ago—to anyone who didn't like Jacob (the ex, BTW).
DID IT END UP MATTERING WHAT PEOPLE THOUGHT OF HIM?
Yeah, b/c they were right 3 years wasted.
I'VE BEEN AT PSU 2 YEARS—AND I'LL NEVER GET MY PH.D. B/C OF MOODY. →

I care about the artistry of his words and the passion of his convictions. I feel no urge to *identify* him because I *knew* him. I saw the world through the eyes of his characters; I heard his voice in his letters and in our discussions in the margins of his typescripts; I felt his gratitude for my efforts to bring his stories to a wider audience. His mysteries, his secrets, his mistakes? These are not, have never been, and will never be, my concern.

III.

I confess: it is my most fervent wish that someday my morning mail will contain another one of those creased and ink-stained manila envelopes with a smudged postmark and no return address, that inside it will be one of Straka's customary onionskin typescripts—(written, as usual, in a language I was not aware the author knew)—and that this twentieth novel, provocative and delightful, elusive and revelatory, will prove to be a worthy addition to the author's *oeuvre*.

But this will not happen. V. M. Straka is dead. By whose hand, I cannot say.[5]

---

[5] I shall not speculate in print as to who might want Straka dead. Suffice it to say that there are several possibilities—individuals and organizations—and that they all have a long reach.

Handwritten margin notes:

What happened? TOO MUCH.
Can't you work w/ another prof.? Or at another school?
NO ONE IN THE STRAKA WORLD WILL TOUCH ME. ONE GUY IN PARIS, MAYBE, BUT HE'S TOO OLD + SENILE TO TAKE ON STUDENTS.

IS JACOB THE REASON YOU NEEDED AN "ESCAPE"?
A big reason. Not the only one.

IT'S PROSE LIKE THIS THAT SHOWS FXC WAS A HACK.

So Straka knew many languages too? Why use a translator, then?
SEE DESJARDINS (1982) — SUGGESTS VMS WASN'T TRULY FLUENT. NEEDED SOMEONE TO CLEAN UP.
Why not write in the language you actually know? It's crazy.
ECCENTRIC ≠ CRAZY. CAN'T STAND HOW EVERYONE EQUATES THE TWO.
Sorry. Bad choice of words. Really not what I meant.

Paranoia? Or for real?
BOTH. SECRET POLICE DOCS (FROM FRANCE, US, USSR, GERMANY, NORWAY) SHOW {x} THEY ALL WANTED HIM DEAD. SAME WITH BOUCHARD + A FEW OTHER BIG CORPS.

*!!! *But some still exist, right?*

SOME. LOTS OF HOAXES/ FRAUDS, THOUGH. CAN'T TAKE ANYTHING AT FACE VALUE.

TRANSLATOR'S NOTE AND FOREWORD

IV.

Three years ago, in late May 1946, I received a telegram from Straka summoning me from New York to the Hotel San Sebastián in Havana. Here, it read, he would hand me the manuscript of the tenth and final chapter of his new novel, *Ship of Theseus*.[6] I'd had the honor and pleasure of working with Straka for over two decades, translating thirteen of his novels (each of them into several languages),[7] but though our partnership was profound and productive, it flourished through correspondence only;[8] we had never, to my knowledge, met face-to-face. The telegram hinted that he was, finally, prepared to reveal himself to me, fully trusting that I would never reveal anything that would compromise his anonymity and security.[9]

Impressive for one person. BUT A LITTLE HARD TO BELIEVE, RIGHT?

WHY THE QUALIFICATION?

CZECH → HRUBY?

---

[6] I had spent the better part of a year working on my translation of the first nine chapters from the original Czech but felt I could go no further even on these without knowing how the novel would end. I had sent him a telegram that urged him to complete the book, as I (and, of course, his entire reading public) was desperately awaiting it. His response, in the message referred to above, hinted that he could not write the final lines without the two of us discussing them in person. HARD TO IMAGINE ANYTHING VMS WOULD BE LESS LIKELY TO DO.

[7] The finest of these, in my opinion, are *The Spotted Cat* (1924), *The Black Nineteen* (1925), *Washington & Greene* (1929), *The Night Palisades* (1934), *Wineblood's Mine* (1939), *The Winged Shoes of Emydio Alves* (1942), and *Coriolis* (1944). No translator has ever been credited with work on Straka's first six novels.

[8] Those who would seek to read or acquire our letters should know that they no longer exist. (A condition of correspondence with Straka was that the recipient burn all materials after reading them.) *

[9] Certainly I have been tested enough. No amount of money could remunerate me for all the threatening encounters, harassment, burglaries, break-ins, pursuits, and surveillance (both stealthy and overt) to which I have been subjected.

So FXC arrived in NYC between 1924–1929.

You don't believe FXC here?
I DON'T BELIEVE FXC ANYWHERE.
He sounds sincere to me.

Why go through all this? What makes someone so devoted?

COMMITMENT TO ART? POLITICS?

{ xi }

I've got time to kill at work + access to all kinds of databases. Might be more available about FXC these days. Gonna look.

▷ I THINK I WAS CAREFUL ENOUGH.

So what's in the photo? What's everyone looking for?

DIDN'T GET A GOOD ENOUGH LOOK.

TRANSLATOR'S NOTE AND FOREWORD

YUP. PARIS — AT HOTEL LA GRANDE HORLOGE.
◁ ACROSS THE STREET FROM THE DEUX MARTRES — WHILE EKSTROM
WAS THERE IN 1931.

I arrived as planned at the hotel on the morning of June 5. At the front desk, I asked for him by the alias under which he was traveling (which I will not specify here, even though he will use it no more). I was told by the desk clerk that "Señor F—" had gone out and requested that any visitors wait in the hotel restaurant until he returned. I waited until the restaurant closed at midnight. Sick with worry, I persuaded the night clerk to take me up to the room. What we found inside was a scene I shall never forget: evidence of a terrible struggle—chairs splintered, a table overturned, holes and slashes in the plastered walls, clothing strewn, a Wanderer typewriter upside down on the floor, blood on the windowsill—and the window open to a three-story fall into an alley. Below the window? Two men in police uniforms, loading a blanket-rolled body into the back of a truck and carting it away. And after that? Nothing except for the truck's exhaust and a few sheets of onionskin paper fluttering about.

(Should I have followed the truck?) Perhaps. But in my shock and grief, I acted on instinct. I ran down to the alley and collected the papers. As I had both hoped and feared, they were part of Straka's manuscript for the tenth chapter of *Ship of Theseus*. These,

"S. FORTUNUS" — DID VMS USE THIS ANYWHERE ELSE? CHECK FOR VARIANTS, ANAGRAMS, ETC.

I assume Serin is paying...? Be careful.

JUST GOT WORD THAT A PHOTO OF THE SCENE IS UP FOR AUCTION. APPEARED OUT OF NOWHERE. I'M OFF TO NYC.

MUNICH + PRAGUE ARCHIVES BOTH CLAIM TO HAVE THIS TYPEWRITER. (PSU CHOSE NOT TO ACQUIRE — B/C MOODY THINKS HAVANA STORY IS BS.)

Why would FXC make it up?

(A) FXC WAS SCHIZOPHRENIC
(B) DISINFORMATION TO THROW PEOPLE OFF VMS'S TRAIL
(C) FXC WAS VMS HIMSELF
(D) BOTH (B) AND (C)
(E) ALL OF THE ABOVE.

And down the rabbit hole we go.

* *So all FXC saw was a body in a blanket.*

TRUE. BUT VMS NEVER WROTE ANYTHING AFTER THAT + WAS NEVER HEARD FROM.

IF HE DIDN'T DIE, HE DID A CONVINCING JOB OF ACTING DEAD.

Could've been the whole point.

UM, YES.

Why? If they killed Straka, they'd kill FXC. Then they're both dead and there's no book.

along with a few additional pages that a maid found stuffed under the mattress in Straka's room, are the basis for the version of Chapter Ten that you will soon read.[10] I have used my best efforts to reconstruct the chapter and to fill in the gaps in ways consistent with Straka's intentions.

HE NEVER EXPLAINS/DOCUMENTS THIS!

So this ending is FXC's, not Straka's.

NO ONE KNOWS. THERE ARE A FEW VERSIONS OF CH. 10 OUT THERE. A COUPLE ARE OBVIOUS HOAXES. INTERNET RUMOR SAYS MOODY RECENTLY GOT HOLD OF ONE THAT SEEMS V. CREDIBLE. THAT'D KILL ME.

Whoa, there. A little perspective.

V.

"If Straka is dead," some have asked, "then where is his body?"[11] Why does it matter? If his remains are in the ground anywhere, then they have become part of the earth in its entirety. If they are in water, then they fill our oceans and rain down from our clouds. If they are in the air, then we breathe them as surely as we draw breaths of life from his fictions. V. M. Straka was not just a storyteller, he was a story. And story is resilient, protean, eternal.

What else do we know about FXC?

NO OTHER WRITINGS, NO CORRESPONDENCE, NO INTERVIEWS. VMS NEVER LET FXC SPEAK FOR HIM. THAT'S WHY PEOPLE THINK HE MADE UP FXC ENTIRELY.

So — assuming FXC existed — we know... what? Brazilian-born. Knew at least a few languages. Anything else?

VI.

No book of Straka's has ever included a foreword, a translator's note, footnotes, or any other additional

LEFT NY + WENT BACK TO BRAZIL IN THE LATE 50s. DIED IN 60s.

Assumptions...

---

[10] It should be noted that, unfortunately, the very last page—the one containing the true ending of Straka's masterwork—was not among the pages that were retrieved.

[11] In the most mundanely literal sense, the answer to this question is probably "in an unmarked grave in or near Havana." But no discerning reader of Straka's work would be satisfied with the mundanely literal.

I'VE ALWAYS BEEN IMPRESSED THAT YOU COULD DRAW THIS SO WELL.

S

Wait — I always thought you drew it. Tell me you're joking...

WHY DO IT, THEN? WHY ADD FNS THAT FOCUS ON IDENTITY QUESTION IF YOU THINK READERS SHOULDN'T CARE? MAKES NO SENSE!

text; the author was adamant that only his writings should appear between the covers of his books. Am I then violating his authorial wishes now? Doubtlessly so. But if these words of mine were, somehow, to reach Straka, he would understand my motivations and find them sound and sincere. He saw me as someone who cared deeply for his work, who helped his words reach millions of readers, and who zealously guarded the anonymity upon which his artistic integrity—and, indeed, his survival—depended.[12] He understood that my allegiance to him was and is unwavering, from first to last. It is in the fondest regions of my heart and mind that my connection with V. M. Straka began, and it is there that it shall end.

CLICHÉ. BRUTAL.

This phrase is in Coriolis (p. 464). And in Winged Shoes (p. 268).

HOW HAVE YOU HAD TIME TO READ ALL OF THIS?

Recently dumped, senioritis, etc.

YOU'RE NOT READING THEM IN ORDER...

Never been much for following directions.

What if these lines are meant as a kind of signal phrase? A hint about what to look for? If so, why not use a familiar line? It'd stand out.

KEY TO A CODE?

Maybe one that's in the footnotes?

SIMPLER EXPLANATION: IT'S JUST AN HOMAGE TO HIS WRITING.

Simpler isn't always better.

— F. X. CALDEIRA
October 30, 1949
New York

---

12 Let me reiterate: I possess no personal information about Straka. I have made tremendous sacrifices and put myself at grave risk by collaborating with him, and I am disinclined to invite more of these foul attentions.

AGAIN, WHY PUT UP W/ ALL OF THIS?

I think it's love.

FUNNY.

I'm serious.

{ xiv }

AND YOUR SUPPORT FOR THIS IS...?

A feeling.

YOU NEED MORE THAN THAT.

SHIP OF
THESEUS

So: I don't know *your* name!→ THOUGHT YOU'D JUST CHECK WHO WORKROOM B19 WAS ASSIGNED TO.

I *could*. I'd prefer you tell me yourself.

Hey, you can't reply to all the other stuff and leave this hanging. Not fair.

OK—You left me no choice. but to check the workroom assignments, Mr. Thomas Lyle Chadwick (PSU ID# 3946608)!!

WELL, YOU FOUND ME OUT.

Oh, you thought you were *so* clever.

CHAPTER 1

So: I've been reading up on what your scholarly homeboys have said about who wrote this book. Looks like 5 main args : ① FXC's story is true: VMS wrote it, FXC filled in where necessary. ② Same as above, but FXC overstepped.

WHAT BEGINS, WHAT ENDS

ONLY VMS BOOK TO USE CHAPTER TITLES

③ It's all VMS's work, + FXC lied about reconstructing Ch. 10.

④ Doesn't matter, b/c VMS + FXC were the same person.

⑤ The whole book is a hoax—someone (maybe FXC, maybe not) imitating Straka's style.

COMPLICATED BY THE FACT THAT NO ONE KNOWS WHO "VMS" IS, ANYWAY. MOST PEOPLE DECIDE WHAT THEY THINK EARLY ON + DON'T CHANGE THEIR MINDS.

What do you think?

I'M PRETTY MUCH A (2).

DUSK. **THE** Old Quarter of a city where river meets sea.

A man in a dark gray overcoat walks the Quarter's streets, a tangle of cobblestone passages that spin from the harbor and thread themselves through neighborhoods where the smells of cooking spices vary but the sad decrepitude is shared. The buildings, black with the soot of centuries, loom over him, blocking out most of the sky and making it difficult to know at any given moment whether he is heading toward the water or away from it.[1]

But re FXC overstepping: where do you draw the line? At what point does the book stop being Straka's alone + become theirs?

---

[1] A sense of spatial disorientation afflicts characters throughout Straka's body of work—most notably in *Coriolis*, which features a character afflicted with a fictional ailment called "Eötvös Syndrome." The illness causes his sense of disorientation to intensify as his travels take him closer to the equator.

The Eötvös Wheel is the key to decoding the puzzles in Coriolis, right? Maybe it would work here, if these FNs are coded?

I'VE ENCLOSED A {3} WHEEL. YOU'RE GOING TO HAVE TO PLAY AROUND TO FIND THE REFERENCE LATITUDES. GIVE IT A SHOT IF YOU HAVE TIME. *You don't need it?* I MADE ONE BY HAND WHEN I WAS IN HS. I LIKE USING THAT ONE. *That is so not what I was doing in high school.*

The man suspects this is a city in which even life-long residents find themselves lost. He does not know whether he is such a person, though. He does not know whether he has ever been here before. He does not know why he is here now.

As the sky darkens, the buildings appear to list precariously. In the oily luminescence of the occasional streetlights (new-looking and polished to a high gleam incongruous with their surroundings), they cast shadows at odd, seemingly random, angles that suggest that light behaves differently here; this is a city of ancient and flawed geometries.

A steady drizzle falls. The man in the overcoat passes people taking cover under awnings and overhangs, plodding forward with heads down and hats low, huddling under rags in alleyways. Though this is a city of watchful eyes, gazes wash over him and roll away. This is a man who does not attract attention. He turns a corner...

A wide-hipped woman stands outside her home— a narrow brick building, four stories tall and covered with a black layer of lichen—and she hangs a sign offering ROOMS. She is the wife of a sea captain who left four years ago on a ship bound for a remote land

[Handwritten marginalia:]

And I don't know why I'm scribbling in a book with a stranger.

WELL, YOU SAID YOU LIKE MYSTERIES.

CF. SPOTTED CAT:
NAZCA LINES = "ANCIENT GEOMETRIES".
(P. 33)

Painted Cave, too
(p. 144)
(WAIT: YOU'VE READ THAT ONE NOW, TOO?
Yup. Feels good to be interested in something again.

Unlike you, that night in the library.
Was it Moody who saw you?
ALMOST AS BAD. IT WAS ILSA DIRKS. MOODY'S OTHER GRAD STUDENT.
She's my TA in 20th Century Poetry.
Seems nice enough.
EMPHASIS ON "SEEMS." SHE SOLD ME OUT— DID MOODY'S DIRTY WORK FOR HIM?
BTW: DON'T TELL HER THAT YOU'VE TALKED TO ME.
I haven't talked to you. — YOU KNOW WHAT I MEAN.

I just checked last year's P.S.U. directory. If you worked with Moody, why are you listed as a grad student in geology??? How can I believe you're who you say you are?

I DIDN'T SAY I WAS ANYONE. YOU SAID I WAS CHADWICK

Dear Mr. Not-Chadwick—
———— See p. 10 for my
response.

JEN?

I WISH YOU'D WRITE BACK.

YOUR NOTES ARE REALLY HELPING ME.

where the hills were said to be bursting with silver, the valleys teeming with exotic fruits and game. His return is eight months overdue, and the bank account is empty, so she has begun taking in and feeding poxy and gnat-gnawed sailors in addition to her three ravenous sons, who are all dreaming of following their father and shipping out into the unknown. None of them yet knows that her husband's bones are lying under a mile of water, some beneath a stack of cracked timbers just off Cape Fortuna, a place they have never heard of, and some scattered for miles by pelagic scavengers. (This is what happens, of course: men get lost, men vanish, men are erased and reborn.)

PLUS, IT'S REALLY DISAPPOINTING TO PICK UP THE BOOK + FIND NOTHING FROM YOU.

FIRST OF MANY DETAILS RE: SUCCESSION/ NEXT GENERATIONS. (REF. TO THE BOUCHARDS?)

CF. HAVANA: "S. FORTUNUS"

POSS. A REF. TO VMS HIMSELF—FLUID IDENTITY. ALSO: ERASABLE

The woman steps back, eyes the sign, tries to determine whether it is hanging true. She tips it back and forth, dissatisfied, and she wonders whether perhaps it is the building that is crooked, or the city itself—she has heard whispers that it is sinking. Regardless of the cause, she will not abide a crooked sign—why, that man in the overcoat plodding her way might be looking for a room, and if she wants a higher class of lodger, she must give a good impression—and she tips the sign one way, then the other, then back again. The man walks past. She glances up just in time to see one dripping gray

Hey— I just sent an email to your PSU address. It bounced.

DON'T BOTHER TRYING THAT AGAIN. I DON'T USE EMAIL. DON'T TRUST IT.

Paranoid???

GOT HACKED A FEW TIMES LAST YEAR. SOMEONE WAS TRYING TO STEAL MY WORK. MORE THAN ONE PERSON, ACTUALLY.

IMPOSSIBILITY OF BALANCE

I didn't think you were ever going to leave the book again after this.

[How do you know I'm not?]

{ 5 }

I ALMOST DIDN'T — IT FELT LIKE IT WAS THE BIGGEST, DUMBEST RISK I'D EVER TAKEN.

It probably was.

coattail disappear around a curve in the street. He will never cross the threshold into her home.

She sighs and turns her thoughts to that pot of miserably thin brown soup bubbling in the kitchen, and to how she can make it last for an entire week.

Why is the man in the overcoat so wet? Perhaps he has been walking in the rain for hours. Or perhaps he has been wading through the maze of half-submerged tunnels that underlie the twisted city. Perhaps some anonymous onlooker fished him from the waters beneath the wobbly bridge that spans the river, connecting the Old Quarter and the New. Perhaps he simply crawled up out of the brackish river like some amphibian ancestor from the Old Red Age.

A mystery to himself, he has only three connections to an earlier life. One is in his coat pocket: a sludge of ink-stained paper on which he believes something important was once written, though all he can make out clearly is an ornate S-shaped symbol. Another is in his trouser pocket: a tiny black orb that might be a pebble, or perhaps a piece of ancient and petrified fruit. The third runs through every cell in his body: a vague but terrifying sense-memory of falling from a great height.

That's me in a few months. (M + D) said they won't help out at all if I turn down the marketing job D arranged in NYC. — (Mom + Dad)

DO YOU WANT THE JOB?

Not really—but having a plan seems better than not having one.

TURN IT DOWN. FIND SOMETHING YOU'RE PASSIONATE ABOUT.

No offense, but that doesn't seem to be working out so well for you right now.

YOU'VE GOT TOO SHARP A MIND TO WASTE ON SOMETHING SO CRASS + MANIPULATIVE.

It's what D does for a living. *

FORGET "D." WHAT DOES J. WANT??

JUST RUMORS.

You've heard the rumors about steam tunnels under the campus, right?

LIKE VACLAV STRAKA?

(Except he NEVER got OUT of the RIVER.)

DEATHS BY FALLING:
VACLAV STRAKA (BRIDGE);
EKSTROM (BALCONY);
SUMMERSBY (OVERBOARD);
FEUERBACH (IN HOME)

Durand, too. — NO — SHOT BY FRANCO'S TROOPS NEAR MADRID.
That's what Hemingway + Gellhorn { 6 } said. But Dos Passos hinted that she was thrown from a roof first, + they finished her off b/c she was still breathing. (Yes, I've been researching.)
NOTE: SAID VS. HINTED. NOT SAME THING.
Just saying it's possible. Either way, there has been way

too much death-by-falling in the world of Straka.

Can't believe how flippant I was about this. It's so easy not to think about how the bad things that happen to people are bad things that happen to PEOPLE.

SHIP OF THESEUS

But falling from where? And into what? And why?

He pauses at the edge of a puddle, and perhaps this is a trick of the light or a trick of the shadows or a trick of this tilted city, but for a curious moment the light reflecting on the surface shapes itself into an image of a woman's face. And then, just as quickly, the image is gone, and the puddle is simply a puddle again, one with a few streaks of light and a rainbow sheen greasing its surface.

"Flowers!" a voice calls from an alleyway. "Flowers! Going out of business!"

He turns another corner…

…onto a still-narrower street, where a malnourished cat laps eagerly at a puddle, pausing to arch and hiss as the man in the overcoat passes close. Several hundred yards ahead, a recent immigrant who speaks the language only haltingly enters a storefront to return a rented barrel organ. The owner, who wears a yellowed undershirt with a greasy stain on the belly, rises from the desk at which he has been sawing at a grayish sausage on a plate, takes the organ from the immigrant, and leans it against a wall along with the eighteen other organs that he rents each morning to other just-as-recent

REF. TO FLORENCE STONEHAM-SMITH? FLORIS OF BRUGES?

And they are...?

THE LITTLE GIRL WHO CLAIMED TO HAVE WRITTEN STRAKA'S BOOKS, AND THE LONG-DEAD NUN SHE CLAIMED TO BE CHANNELING.

That's my favorite one so far!

A LOT OF PEOPLE TOOK IT SERIOUSLY AT ONE POINT. IT'S AMAZING WHAT PEOPLE WILL BELIEVE.

You're not from here, right? California, maybe?

HOW'D YOU GUESS?

The name of your high school. Totally Cali.

WHAT ABOUT YOU?

I'm as in-state as you can get. Six generations.

THE QUESTION REMAINS: WHAT DOES J WANT??

If J. knew, J. probably wouldn't be writing in a stranger's book @ 3am. {7} — SHE MIGHT BE, THOUGH.

SERIOUSLY — IF NOT MARKETING, WHAT? I have no idea. For 4 years I've done what I'm supposed to do (with, OK, more than a few late-night exceptions). Go to class, work, study, hangout. I don't even remember what I like.

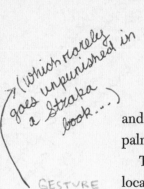

→ (which rarely goes unpunished in a Straka book...)

GESTURE
OF TRUST

and just-as-tone-deaf immigrants. He holds out his palm for his half of the organ-grinder's take.

The organ-grinder does not yet understand the local currency, so he hands his cigar box of coins to the owner, asks him via hand gestures and sentence fragments to do the stacking and splitting for him. The owner makes two piles. He pushes the taller stack across the table to the organ-grinder. The shorter stack, which is worth much more (this, apparently, being a city of ancient and flawed arithmetics as well), he sweeps into an open drawer.

The organ-grinder, who understood when he rented the organ that this unscrupulous man would cheat him at any opportunity, has anticipated such a trick and has stashed away a portion of the day's take. Those coins, wrapped inside a handkerchief, are snug in the pocket of the tattered red coat worn by his capuchin monkey. The monkey sits grimly at the end of a thin piece of rope that is knotted through the organ-grinder's belt loop, giving away nothing.[2]

E.G.: MOODY. (HE KILLED MY FUNDING. I EVEN HAD TO PAY BACK SOME GRANT $$.) *Wow. So what are you living on?* NOT MUCH. I'VE SOLD SOME THINGS. IT'S NOT A BAD WAY TO LIVE, ONCE YOU LET GO OF THE IDEA THAT YOU DESERVE MORE. CF. VMS IN THE BOUCHARD NOTE: "YOU SEEK A WORLD POPULATED BY TRICK-MONKEYS WHO DANCE TO YOUR TUNES FOR THE EMPTY PROMISE OF COINS."

what do you know about Hermès Bouchard?

---

[2] Given the public's fascination with Straka's refusal of the "prestigious" Prix Bouchard in September 1912 (sending a tufted capuchin monkey to Chamonix to accept the award in his stead), I should clarify an element of the story. The note pinned to the monkey's jacket was not, as the newspapers reported, a gentle declaration that the author found no joy in receiving such prizes, but rather an accusation that the Bouchard family had routinely arranged for the murders of syndicalist agitators in order to protect their vast and varied business interests, and in fact orchestrated the brutal massacre of striking factory workers in Calais in early 1912. (I have seen, but am no longer in possession of, a carbon copy of the note.) Why the confusion in the news accounts? Because the newspapers printed what Hermès Bouchard told them to.

NOT MUCH. COMPANY DISSOLVED AFTER WWI, AND HE (+ FAMILY TOO?) BECAME RECLUSIVE. HE WAS DEF. THE MODEL FOR WINEBLOOD IN WINEBLOOD'S MINE — THE MOST PURELY EVIL OF STRAKA'S CHARACTERS. *il know. il read it.*

Have you ever seen the note?

NO— IT WAS IN THE MUNICH ARCHIVE. LAST SEEN IN 1983— PROBABLY STOLEN.

{ 8 }

OF COURSE YOU DID.

SHIP OF THESEUS

The owner, of course, suspects that the organ-grinder has done this. It's not a new trick to him. Once the immigrant leaves the shop, the owner will direct his slow-witted but strong-armed sons to follow the man through the night, as long as it takes, until he gives himself away—perhaps when he ducks into an alley beside a tavern and empties the monkey's pockets, at which point the sons will hold him down in the street and crush his wrist bones to dust with lead pipes. They will catch the fleeing monkey by its rope and try to sell the beast inside the tavern. No one will want it, of course, so they will try again and again at the increasingly disreputable watering holes closer to the harbor. Eventually, the brothers—now quite drunk—will go out to the docks, tie something heavy to the other end of the rope, and test how well monkeys can swim.

Yet none of this will happen for hours. Right now, as the owner slams the drawer shut and the organ-grinder pockets his meager take, the man in the dark overcoat passes by outside. (The men do not notice him, but the monkey, sprawled in the doorway, bares its teeth and hisses.) The owner and the organ-grinder part with a handshake that both conceals and codifies their mutual distrust,

> (NEXT GENERATION)
> You seem a little fixated on this.
>
> MY THEORY: VMS WAS DROPPING HINTS THAT THE S HAD RECONSTITUTED ITSELF. IT'S A REACH, BUT IT'S POSSIBLE.
>
> Wait—totally confused. The Character?
>
> NOT THE CHARACTER. DESJARDINS—THE OLD GUY IN PARIS—THEORIZED ABOUT SOME KIND OF SECRET ORG (IN THE REAL WORLD) CALLED "THE S."
>
> Does he think Straka was a member? Or a target?
>
> IT'S NOT CLEAR.

SHIP OF THESEUS

and the man in the dark overcoat disappears around another corner, leaving these two to their commerce of song, coin, and bone, with his soles squishing softly on the stone and the sky darkening into true night.

...then another corner, and another, and the man in the overcoat finds himself on an unlit street. From far ahead come a few sharp, percussive sounds—stone on stone, it sounds like—but here, around him, the street is deserted, quiet but for the rain's soft patter, so quiet that he imagines he can hear the whispering voices of people who have met their ends in this place where river meets sea, in this city and in the maze of tunnels running just below its streets, in the former trading-post village buried beneath the maze, in the catacombs below that, and in the mud-hut settlement buried still deeper, all through the strata of civilizations. The sounds come at him in a sonic Möbius of whispers; the words are indistinct, but the tones—of rage and lament, of burden and cataclysm, of dissent and vengeance and grief—are as sharp as blades.[3]

---

[3] Straka was attuned to the histories of places; he mentioned in a letter to me that he often had dreams that took place on several archaeological strata simultaneously. }

THAT'S YOUR RESPONSE?? UM, THERE'S NOTHING THERE.
Astute observation.
OK — HERE'S THE TRUTH. I FOUND CHADWICK'S ID + I'VE BEEN USING IT — BUT ONLY B/C I NEED ACCESS TO THE LIBRARY.
aren't you a student?
I WAS. I GOT "EXPUNGED" IN JANUARY.
Wait, they really do that? Thought it was a myth. What did you do?
SEE: THE DAILY PRONGHORN, JAN. 8 (P. 1).
The flood in Standefer Hall?
I WASN'T MAKING GREAT DECISIONS AT THAT TIME.
Name please. For real. And you'd better not lie to me.
ERIC HUSCH
You're sure???
YES. PROMISE.
Pleased (provisionally) to make your acquaintance, Mr. Husch
I (PROVISIONALLY) LOVE THAT LINE.
(Provisionally) get bent.
ARCHAEOLOGICAL SENSIBILITY → DURAND'S INFLUENCE?
Or Durand herself?
FXC WOULD SAY THAT'S PARTICULARLY FOOLISH OF YOU.
What do you think?
I THINK THEY KNEW EACH OTHER. MY GUT SAYS THEY WERE CLOSE.
Mine, too.
That would be so cool.
We are brilliant.
LET'S NOT GET AHEAD OF OURSELVES. HAVE TO BE ABLE TO PROVE IT.
I thought we had to beat Moody...
BEATING HIM IS MEANINGLESS IF WE'RE NOT RIGHT.
This FN doesn't seem as random as the others in Ch. 1.
{ 10 } AGREED. WHAT TO MAKE OF THAT, THOUGH?
That FXC was a lot craftier than anyone thought.

_____

He wonders now if he should be feeling fear rather than the numbness of body and mind that has dampened his senses since he awoke—from what? a dream? a fugue state? a borrowed life? —and began wandering the Quarter. He tries to listen more closely to the voices, but the rain drives harder against the street, drowning them in a wash of sound, and then the *placks* of stone against stone come again—nine sharp reports, in three groups of three—and his feet carry him around another corner…

…onto a well-lit stretch of road. The three boys who have been hurling chunks of brick at the glowing glass domes tuck themselves into an alley when the man in the overcoat comes into view. Struggling to stifle the giddy laughter of transgression, they wait for him to pass. None of the three bothers to look at his face, for who is he to them? He is an adult, and thus merely a faceless representative of order and judgment. He is the conk from a policeman's cudgel; he is the blow that awaits them at home; he is the end of all possible thrills; thus he is to be avoided. Beyond that he is not to be taken seriously; he is to be scoffed at and then forgotten.

_____

{ 11 }

CF. CH. 6 IN BRAX.
(HUGE CELEBRATION
OF THE CITY'S FIRST
STREETLIGHTS).
IMAGE ECHOED HERE,
BUT SUBVERTED.

Did you flag
this because you
think that's how
Moody sees you?

YOU'RE GOOD.
No—just dealing
with similar stuff.

The sodden man passes them—his head cocked as if he is listening for something, the fool—and they wait as he shuffles, as his shadow passes over the brick-fronted buildings, they wait, and finally he is gone. They dart back into the street, take aim, and sling rocks at one of the city's new streetlights. The very first throw finds its mark, sending a cascade of broken glass and sparkling magnesium down to the street. The boys laugh and scurry off. White smoke rises from the wet street.

As the man in the coat approaches the harbor, one of the city's voices re-emerges, intoning one phrase over the fading rustle of whispers: *What begins at the water shall end there, and what ends there shall once more begin.*[4] *What begins at the water shall end there, and what ends there shall once more begin. What begins at the water…*

The harbormaster is on the docks, looking through his spyglass and through the murk and rain at a dark shape in the distance, just inside the mouth

---

4 (Endings and beginnings were particular preoccupations of Straka's.) After I made this observation, he scoffed. "Beginnings and endings are the preoccupation of every serious storyteller," he wrote, "whether man or woman, prodigy or elder, Briton or Turk or Zulu or Slav."

{ 12 }

of the harbor. All of those ships cleared to anchor or berth are already accounted for, and no more vessels are scheduled to arrive tonight or tomorrow or even the next day—not until the behemoth liner *Imperia* departs. The shape on the water looks vaguely shiplike, but unwieldy and strange; it is either heeling steeply in the wind-sheltered bay, or it is the product of an inept craftsman, afloat only by means of Neptune's fickle grace.

He lowers his spyglass and shrugs, concluding that the dark shape must be a cloud formation, maybe some optical trick of troubled air conjured by the strengthening storm as it tumbles itself off the sea and into the harbor. Time to get himself home to a fire, a hot meal, a dry bed, and the tick-ticking of his mother's knitting needles in the tidy home they share on the river side of the Quarter. He turns up his collar, hunches his shoulders against the rain, and begins his walk along darkened streets, the shattered glass of streetlight globes crunching under his shoes. He grits his teeth in irritation; such times are these!

He nods a greeting to a drowned-looking man in a dark overcoat and a homburg; the man ignores him and sloshes past, which angers him further. *What ever happened to comradeship and civility,*

So: a city of flawed physics, too?

Appearance vs. Reality — Another preoccupation for pretty much everyone, don't you think?

Are you close to your family?

NOT REALLY.

Care to elaborate?

NOT REALLY.

I'd better make a list of your sore points... There's no way I'll remember them all.

the friendly hello, the small talk of a shared city? That man is bound, doubtlessly, for one of the waterfront taverns that serve as gathering places for the most dubious characters, morally bankrupt tosspots, and societal scourges, people with whom the harbormaster would never think of associating. He shakes his head, irritation with the stranger's snub still gnawing at him. *Yet another drunk who'll end up with the rest of them. A waste of a life.*

The tavern is a low brick building on the corner of two streets that must form the nexus of the city's stink, a powerful mixture of dead fish, low tide, and human, canine, and feline effluvia. Painted on the brick, illuminated by a single intact streetlight, is a familiar symbol: the ornate twist that remained visible on the paper in his pocket.

5

This is it, he thinks. He may not know what the symbol means, but its reappearance makes a kind of sense. This is where he is supposed to be.

What begins at the water shall end there, the voice tells him, *and what ends there shall once more begin...*

{ 14 }

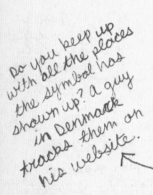

Margin notes (left):

JUDGMENT

Do you keep up with all the places the symbol has shown up? A guy in Denmark tracks them on his website.

Margin notes (bottom left):

NOT REALLY. THAT'S THE STRAKA WORLD'S VERSION OF CROP CIRCLES. ALL EASILY FAKED.

Sure. But how cool would it be if even just a few are real (esp. the really old ones)? And how much did Straka know about them?

IT'S NOT MY THING. THE BOOKS, DOCS, ARTIFACTS... THAT'S WHERE I THINK THE ANSWERS ARE.

Don't forget PEOPLE, Eric. People have answers.

ANYONE WHO KNEW VMS IS PROBABLY OVER 100 BY NOW.

Margin notes (bottom right):

But why? It turns out to be a hostile place.

MAYBE VMS IS SAYING THAT NOTHING IN THE WORLD IS ENTIRELY ONE WAY OR ANOTHER.

Or maybe it's about Sola. She's there, so he's supposed to be — for good or bad.

I JUST DON'T BUY THAT SOT IS FUNDAMENTALLY A LOVE STORY.

I think you're wrong.

SHIP OF THESEUS

Inside, the tavern keeper sniffs an empty glass,
his long mustache trailing over the rim. His face
pinches, as if the smell brings back an unpleasant
memory. A dozen blind-drunk rascals are calling his
name, shouting and beating their own empty glasses
on the bar, so the tavern keeper takes note of the
wet man in the overcoat only long enough to snap
up his money, fill the offending glass, and thump it
down on the bar in front of him. This establishment
sees its share of waterlogged men; twice a night
some sailor staggers out to the harbor, falls in, and
comes back for another drink to warm up; twice a
day some poor bugger is flung from his ship into the
shallows and swims in to seek a drink, a whore, and
a new employer, almost certainly in that order. The
man in the wet overcoat turns away, drink in hand,
and the bartender forgets him immediately, turning
to serve the next needy sonofabitch.

The man in the overcoat finds an opening on a
wooden bench that runs the length of the room, and
he settles himself down with the weary sigh of a
man who believes himself to be at the end of a long
journey. He glances around the room, at the stumbling, shouting, laughing, back-slapping, cursing,

{ 15 }

and shoving groups of sailors, and at the solitary patrons, like this curly-haired man with a waist-length orange beard, who for some reason is carrying a claw hammer and twirling it idly. And that man, there, sallow and heavy-lidded and dressed in mortician's black. And that man, wearing a brown duster, sitting on a barstool, scanning the crowd and jotting occasionally in a notebook. Are these his people, these malcontents, this assemblage of the strange and suspicious? Is he in his homeland? The coin he handed over for this glass of beer was foreign to him...but then perhaps he simply has no memory of his native currency.

At a table along the far wall sits a young woman of no more than twenty, alone.[5] She is reading a book—a large volume, as thick as *Don Quixote*—in the light from a sconce on the wall behind her, as if this chaotic, drunken hovel were a library. She reads with one elbow on the table, her thumb cradling her chin, one finger resting thoughtfully over her lips. Her olive complexion and black hair, which is pulled back and tied into a long braid that hangs nearly to her waist, suggest that she hails from a part of the

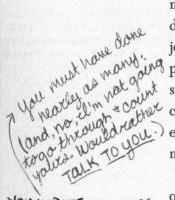

---

[5] Every critic of this book, I suspect, will offer one hypothesis or another about what this character represents and/or whom Straka may have used for a model. I doubt any of these guesses will prove to be more credible than any other.

Did Straka ever marry/have affairs/etc.? Any rumors of them, at least?

SURPRISINGLY FEW. ONE WOMAN CLAIMED TO HAVE A PHOTO OF HIM, BUT CONSENSUS IS THAT IT WAS JUST SOME SALESMAN WHO TOLD HER HE WAS VMS.

SHIP OF THESEUS

Lying about himself — seems appropriate.

POSS. THE SAME WOMAN THE NARRATOR DESCRIBES IN THE FUGUE SCENE FROM CORIOLIS? VERY SIMILAR, ANYWAY.

FUNNY TO THINK OF SOMEONE WHO DISTRUSTED THE ENTIRE CAPITALIST SYSTEM AS A SALESMAN. MAYBE HE WAS PLANNING TO TEAR IT DOWN FROM THE INSIDE.

... OH, WAIT — YOU WERE TALKING ABOUT ME THERE, WEREN'T *For a Boy* YOU... *Genius, you're pretty slow sometimes.*

world where the sun shines more warmly and more often than it does in this city, which has the feel of the gray northern latitudes. Odd that she is by herself here; there are only a handful of other women about, all of them with commerce on the mind, winding through the groups of sailors, seeking trade. Odder still that none of these men, roaring with uncorked courage, is foisting his attentions upon the bookish young woman. (She appears to enjoy her public solitude; there is an easy grace in her square-shouldered posture) and the neatness of her attire (a finely-tailored dress of emerald green), in the unhurried manner with which she turns a page, in the way she lays a finger over her lips and stares off, right through the commotion, presumably contemplating a line she has just read. Comfortable alone and easily overlooked. A kindred spirit? Perhaps—if not kindred to the man he is, or was, then to the sort of man he wouldn't mind being.

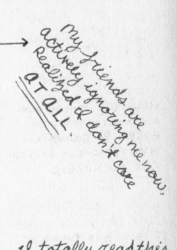

My friends are actively ignoring me now. Realized I don't care AT ALL.

He wonders then what he looks like to others. They might assume that <u>he is waiting for something or someone but is not sure what, or who, that might be.</u> Or that he is an informer for the police or for a ship's captain. Or that he simply is a lonely traveler. He sips his drink, he hunches forward on the bench,

I totally read this as Straka talking about himself — waiting for someone (in a romantic way).

Maybe I'm reading it that way b/c I'm just sitting around, cluelessly waiting for somebody.
THAT'S THE BREAKUP[17] TALKING.
Note, again, that condescension tends to irritate people.

CAREFUL RE: LINKING EVERYTHING IN A BOOK TO THE AUTHOR PERSONALLY. SOMETIMES FICTION'S JUST FICTION.
I could point to a dozen examples of you doing the exact same thing.
NOT SAYING THAT I DON'T — JUST SAYING ~~you~~ WE NEED TO BE CAREFUL ABOUT THE CONCLUSIONS WE DRAW.

moody at the café again.
He was worse this time — I was at the
counter + his breath just about knocked me over.

Doubt it. He was
~~probably too~~ baffled about
why he was seeing 3 of me.

he watches as the drops of water fall from him onto the uneven floor and wend along it in a rivulet, snaking over and around and between the warped boards. He steals unanswered glances at the young woman now and again. He watches the door, lets his gaze drift across the crowd, waits—hopes—to be recognized. He must have some history in this establishment, or some other purpose for being here. (The symbol must mean something; his intuition must have a basis.

A sailor with a freshly split lip and a bloody chin sloshes by and bumps knees with the man in the overcoat.) The sailor stops, looking flummoxed that something solid has impeded his progress, and gradually his bloodshot eyes focus on the man, who braces himself for an insult, a threat, or a fist. Instead the sailor wobbles there, shifting his weight erratically from one foot to the other. "You're—" the sailor says, searching for words, "—wet."

"You're bleeding," the man in the overcoat replies.

It takes a moment for the sailor to understand the words. Perhaps the man in the overcoat has an accent quite foreign to the sailor's ear. Finally, the sailor nods. "'S the truth," he slurs. He pushes himself

Has anyone ever
complained about
how good S.'s
intuition is?

HELL, YES. THERE WAS
A CRITIC NAMED
EDSEL B. GRIMSHAW
WHO FAMOUSLY RIPPED
SOT TO SHREDS.

What do
you think?

Isn't it a little convenient?
IT IS ... BUT THERE'S
SOMETHING OTHERWORLDLY
ABOUT WHAT S. IS GOING
THROUGH, + I'VE ALWAYS
THOUGHT THE MOMENTS
LIKE THIS HAVE A
SURREAL, DISORIENTING
DÉJÀ VU QUALITY THAT
FITS. EVERYTHING HE
EXPERIENCES AS INTUITION
MIGHT BE SOMETHING HE REMEMBERS
FROM PRE-AMNESIA LIFE,
BUT HE CAN'T KNOW FOR SURE.

POSS. VMS SAYING THAT THE S IS
REAL? AND/OR REPRESENTS THE TRUTH?
Ilsa would say "that's a
reach" if you wrote that in a
paper.

SHE SAYS THAT A LOT,
PERIOD.

{ 18 }

away from the man and staggers down a narrow channel of open space, listing hard to port, then thrusts himself into a circle of seamen, all of them clad in filthy canvas doublets, all of them showing the marks of violence upon their faces. They will spend the next hour speculating in half-sentences about the origin and purpose of the hulking ship at the harbor's edge and about the wages the owner of such a foul vessel might be willing to pay to coax a crew on board. The man in the overcoat will not be a subject, much less a part, of their conversation. The sailor forgot about him immediately.

The man stares into his glass, sighs, contemplates. How *did* he come to be so wet? Why does his body ache, especially his right knee and hip? The entire right side of his body, in fact, feels deeply bruised. There is a raw, burning sensation behind his right ear, and now that he has begun to dry, he recognizes a feeling of stickiness down his back. *Did* he fall from a significant height? Perhaps he is simply engrossed in the catalogue of his injuries, or perhaps he has grown too complacent with being overlooked—such gifts do not last forever, of course—but he is slow to notice that the young woman is now regarding him from across the room.

Her look might be one of recognition, but it might not; his intuition tells him nothing. Still, every other part of him agrees that it would be shrewd to investigate further.

He stops several steps from her table and gestures toward the empty chair opposite her. "Might I ask if you're waiting for someone?"

"It depends on what you mean," the young woman says. Her voice surprises him. It sounds as if it belongs to a much older woman.

"I mean, here, now, this evening, are you expecting someone to join you?"

"I thought *you* might."

"May I sit?"

"You're awfully wet."

(("I know," he says. "It appears to be my most salient characteristic."

"Surely there's more to you than that. You must be *someone* when you're dry."))

"I can't remember the last time I was dry."

"Why don't you take off your coat?"

"I would prefer not to," he says. He hopes she won't ask why. He doesn't have a reason, just a fear.

"Perhaps you're the sort of person who often has to leave places quickly," she offers.

{ 20 }

Handwritten margin notes:

No one ever describes Straka as being funny, but I think he is. Here + there, anyway.

I·VE ALWAYS THOUGHT SO. Imagine Katharine Hepburn saying Sola's line here. She'd nail it.

YOU LIKE OLD MOVIES?
YES!
Been going to the Varsity a lot — another way of filling the nights. They just had a Bogart festival. Awesome.
I WAS THERE FOR TO HAVE + HAVE NOT.
I was, too!

Hey... I know someone like that!

Ship of Theseus

He is unsure how much to reveal about his state of being—physical, mnemonic, philosophical, or otherwise. "I find myself, currently, in uncertain circumstances," he says. "Tell me, have we met?"

She sighs. "That's a tired line. And one that usually serves as a prelude to an equally tedious proposition." She closes her book and sets it on the table. The embossed lettering on the cover is flaking away, but he can make out the title and author: [*The Archer's Tales*, by Arquimedes de Sobreiro.] Neither is familiar to him.

"Do you live here? In—this city?"

✱ "I am traveling," she says. "I travel frequently. I arrived on the liner. The *Imperia*."

"Do you always travel with such cumbersome books?"

"I don't trust anyone who wouldn't."

He purses his lips, nods. "So," he says, "I trust you know the name of this city?"

She tilts her head and regards him slantwise. Then she laughs. "You're making sport of me. What's your game?"

"I'm curious," he says, "as to whether you know who I am."

"Are you someone I should know?"

{ 21 }

Handwritten margin notes:

JUST FOR FUN: THERE'S A WEBSITE W/ A LIST OF ALL THE FICTIONAL BOOKS + AUTHORS VMS EVER REFERRED TO IN HIS WORK. (YOU CAN SEE IT'S SOMETHING HE REALLY LIKED TO DO.)

Do you know for sure that this one's made up?

THERE'S NO EVIDENCE AT ALL THAT ARCHER'S TALES (OR SOBREIRO) EXIST(ED) OUTSIDE OF SOT.

Clearly you lit scholars aren't the best researchers. See attached!

WOW. BUT HOW DID VMS KNOW ABOUT IT? (AND WHY USE A REAL BOOK HERE, WHEN HE'S ALWAYS MADE THEM UP?)

✱ I had the chance to study in Paris last year. Won a prize from the French Dept. that would've covered room + board. And I didn't go. I can't believe I didn't go.

WHY DIDN'T YOU??

Felt like I had too much going on here. Think I was just scared to do something different.

THAT'S TOO BAD. I was hoping you'd say something uplifting.

THAT'S NOT REALLY WHAT I'M GOOD AT.

"Probably not," he says. "I can't say for certain."

The look she gives him invites further explanation, and he decides—though it's more an impulse than a decision—to offer the closest thing he knows to the truth. "Something happened to my memory," he says, and he waits, tensed, for her response.

She reaches for her drink—a vein of dark liquid in a tall, narrow glass—and sips thoughtfully. Something about her in this moment strikes him as being familiar. The motion of her arm? The shape of her hand? The wrinkle of her upper lip? He does not know. Nor does he have any way to tell whether what he is sensing is a fragment of memory, a fragment of the *idea* of a memory, or something his mind, desperate for connections, has created on its own.

It is an agonizingly long wait before she returns the glass to the table, blots her lips dry with the corner of a handkerchief. "You should be very careful whom you tell that to," she says, indicating the entire room—or perhaps the world—with a sweep of her eyes. "Many people would take advantage."

"Undoubtedly."

"Do you know your name? Where you live?"

"No."

{ 22 }

Handwritten margin notes:

I'm asking straight out: Who do you think was Straka?

SUMMERSBY. MAYBE SUMMERSBY + EKSTROM TOGETHER. YOU?

Today Shimizu is my favorite.

HE'S A LONG SHOT. SCHOLARS ARE PRETTY UNANIMOUS THAT VMS WAS EUROPEAN OR NORTH AMERICAN B/C OF HIS SETTINGS, CONCERNS, APPARENT LITERARY INFLUENCES, ETC.

Blah blah blah. That's the Shakespeare argument. TOTAL BS.

OK. WHY SHIMIZU THEN?

He's an underdog I like underdogs. Even more now than I used to.

HE'S NOT THE ONLY ONE.

That's fine. I'll feel good about any of them... Singh, Massoud, Durand, even García Ferrara. The nun + the pirate, too...

REMINDER: THE PIRATE IS FICTIONAL.

Yeah, that's just what They want you to think.

I THINK THEY DON'T CARE WHAT WE THINK, AS LONG AS WE DON'T KNOW.

Ending with a preposition?? Bad translator, FXC! Bad!

(★) SIMPLEST EXPLANATION IS THAT VMS MADE IT UP, AND PEOPLE HAVE BEEN HAVING FUN PUTTING IT UP EVERYWHERE THEY CAN THINK OF.

I don't think you really believe that.

I HAVE A FEW IDEAS. NOT READY TO SHARE YET.

SHIP OF THESEUS

I DON'T LIKE BEING WRONG IN

This is public?   PUBLIC.

Notes written by 2 people who've never met?

SOUNDS DUMB, I KNOW. BUT THAT'S WHAT IT FEELS LIKE.

"Do you have anything in your pockets? Anything that might—?"

He thinks about the wet mash of paper in his overcoat pocket, but he decides not to show it to her just yet. Not until he discovers (what the symbol means,) or what else used to be written on that page—or, for that matter, who she is. He shakes his head.

REF. TO SANTORINI MAN?

(★) *So the Danish guy's website has about 50 theories about what the symbol means.*

"Ah," she says with a playful smirk, "you do have something. What is it?"

This sends unease creeping through him—her knowing, or sensing, his thoughts—and he finds himself searching for a way to shift the conversation smoothly, searching so intently that he fails to register the piercing *screak* of the tavern door opening, fails to notice the heavy footsteps making their way toward them over the warped floorboards. *You haven't given me your name*, he is about to say, when he notices a change in the young woman's expression: her eyes widening slightly, her mouth reshaping itself from that smirk to a tense pinch. What is this look? Disapproval? Resignation? Surprise does not seem to be part of it.

FEAR/ANXIETY/AVERSION TO BEING KNOWN (AND/OR SEEN THROUGH)

ANXIETY → FREEZING UP. GETS LOST IN HIS HEAD.

Been there, done that

ME, TOO. AT THE HEARING, I COULD BARELY GET A SENTENCE OUT.

I couldn't say anything when Ilsa accused me. I wanted to spill everything, tell her what we know about her and about Moody, but I held back. She prob. took it as an admission.

"What—?" he asks, just as a filthy handkerchief is clamped over his face from behind. He struggles, but the grip that holds him is like iron. He tries not

YOU'LL GET A HEARING. I CAN HELP YOU PREPARE SOMETHING TO SAY.

No, thanks. That's exactly how I got into this.

to inhale—for a moment—and then two—but of course he cannot stop himself, and his vision begins to shimmer and blur as a smell, sweet but scorched, fills his head, reminding him of the holiday cakes he enjoyed as a child. Panicked, he inhales again, involuntarily, and all the sounds around him turn metallic and indistinct—in the center of this cloud is her voice, saying words that sound as if they're in a language he does not know, but the warp of the air in the twisting, bending room strips these words of inflection, so that he cannot understand the words or what she means or even to whom she is speaking. Another voice, male, answers her in a grunted, bilabial reply. Then, as the last ember of his consciousness is extinguishing itself in this dark corner of this dark bar on this dark night in this dark city, he glimpses the larger man's face and is struck by its familiarity (it resembles a face that his mind pictures as his own) only with scars running down the center of the forehead and diverging wildly just above his brow—a river-delta of cicatricose tissue. Not a twin, not necessarily a brotherly resemblance; more like that of a cousin whom life has treated most cruelly and who has learned cruelty in return. Or perhaps it's all just a trick of the fumes.

{ 24 }

CHECK— ANY REFS TO THESE IN EARLIER BOOKS/DOCS?

Did you ever find any?

ONE — IN CORIOLIS. BUT IT'S TO GINGERBREAD NOT CAKE.

Translation issue?

PROB. NOT. FXC DID THAT ONE, TOO.

What's the one thing you'd most want someone to know about you?

SOUNDS LIKE A QUESTION FOR A JOB INTERVIEW. OR AN INTAKE ASSESSMENT.

Explain?

I WOULD PREFER NOT TO.

Quoting Melville doesn't make the evasion any less irritating.

MAYBE THEY ARE TEACHING THE UNDERGRADS HERE SOMETHING.

See: previous notes re: condescension

I'm getting creeped out by Straka's world (and/o not sleeping enough). Got home last night, when I turned on the light I saw myself in the mirror. Jumped out of my skin. Totally thought someone else was there.

He would scream if he had any control over his mouth.

No one remarks upon the man in the dark overcoat as he leaves the bar, even though he is being carried over another man's shoulder, limp as a sack of beets. Just another traveler overcome by drink, not worthy of a shout or even a cynical chuckle. Gazes, as we have seen, wash over him and roll away.

Outside, the shock of the cold and driving rain pounds one last flicker of awareness into the man in the overcoat. He opens his eyes just as a monkey wearing shreds of velveteen darts across the street, trailing a rope that slaps softly over the street-stones. He hears curses and heavy breathing and sees two brutish men chasing the creature. His final thought, before the world turns a flat and absolute black, is *Run, monkey. Run.*

Motion. His mind does not sense it, but his body does. It is yanked and tugged, a piece of unwieldy freight. It bounces along with the cadence of someone else's footsteps. It is hoisted, swung, dropped, dragged, and dropped again.

BETTER THAT...

Than what?
THAN BLOWING UP AT
YOUR PROFESSOR IN
FRONT OF EVERYONE
AT THE ENGLISH DEPT.
HOLIDAY PARTY.

...which you
painted on the
wall in Standefer.
(You can see it in the
newspaper photo)
MY MESSAGE TO MOODY.
IT'S SUCH A TERRIBLE
FEELING TO FIND OUT YOU'VE
BEEN DUMB ENOUGH TO TRUST
THE WRONG PERSON.
Well, you can never
know ahead of time.
That's what makes it
I KNOW. IT'S   trust.
EASY TO FORGET, THOUGH.

Radical idea: what
if we were to actually meet
one of these days? As fun as all
of this is, it doesn't feel real,
somehow.
I'M BEING REAL. AREN'T YOU?
Of course. I've been nothing
but honest with you.

VMS USED PSEUDONYM
"S. OPICE - TANCE" —
"THE MONKEY DANCES" IN CZECH

Note: this
ended up being not
exactly true.
I'm still not sure
if you wanted me to {25}
push you more here or
not. You're *really*
hard to read
sometimes.

CAN'T RIGHT NOW. TOO MUCH WORK TO DO
(+ SOME OTHER THINGS I CAN'T EXPLAIN).
BUT I LOVE DOING THIS, AND I REALLY
APPRECIATE YOUR HELP.
Fine. Forget I brought it up.

(Rest.) *If only. Don't know how long I can keep this going.*

Then, slowly building from the stillness: a gestational rock and bounce. Fluid transverse and longitudinal sways. Gradually, his consciousness returns, presses against the walls of its dark, pinhole-sized cell, expanding and expanding, and his other senses resume function. A curious dankness in the air. A wash of sound: a baritone sweep of tidal spirants, a percussive roll of wind-snapped linen, a mezzo-soprano note of creaking wood[6]—all of which lets him know before he opens his eyes that he is at sea, that he has been stolen from land and deposited on water.

What begins at the water…

He is in a hammock that smells as if it has been marinating for decades in saltwater stink. His overcoat, dry now, is spread over him like a blanket. He blinks—once, twice—then rubs his eyes.

He is in a small, dim cabin that is the length of a ninepin lane and just wide enough to accommodate the hammock that has been tied to both walls. At the far end, a ladder leads up to an open hatch that

---

6 Young Straka was a violin prodigy, and musical references abound in the novels. (He quit the instrument, he told me, after he performed in a competition and the judge told him that, in the field of nineteen entrants, he had come in 19th.)

NO EVIDENCE OF THIS AT ALL!

Funny that FXC writes out "nineteen" once + uses "19" right after.

{ 26 }

YOU'RE RIGHT. FXC MIGHT BE AN IDIOT, BUT HE'S NOT SLOPPY. SO IF WE'RE LOOKING FOR THINGS THAT MIGHT BE SIGNALS…
Exactly what I was thinking.

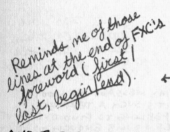

REBIRTH — Isn't that what college is supposed to give you? A chance to reinvent yourself?
YOU DON'T THINK IT DID, DID THAT? I wasn't paying attention.

Reminds me of those lines at the end of FXC's foreword (first/last, begin/end).

AND THERE'S THE TITLE OF CH.1. (+ REMEMBER, VMS DIDN'T TITLE HIS CHAPTERS. SO THERE HAS TO BE A REASON FOR IT HERE…)
Assuming that Straka did, in fact, write this book.
HE DID. I HAVEN'T SPENT MY LIFE STUDYING A FAKE.

admits a rectangle of deep-orange sunlight. He has a terrible headache and feels feverish and slow. That sweet-scorched smell still haunts his nostrils, only now it reminds him not of the holidays he enjoyed as a child but of the ones he will never enjoy again, now that he does not know who he is or where—if anywhere—is home.

He eases himself from the sling—his legs wobble like a newborn fawn's—then wraps the overcoat around himself to fight off the chill. He has just stepped onto the first rung of the ladder when he notices the knife-cuts wounding the dark wood of the bulkhead, just above where his head was when he was in the hammock: a crude, jagged version of that same *S* symbol he saw outside the bar and on that paper. This time, though, he understands its meaning much differently. *This place,* it seems to say, *is the last place you ought to be.*

At the top of the ladder, he peeks out cautiously. The hatch opens directly onto the forecastle, which strikes him as odd; his cabin, apparently, is unconnected to any other part of the ship, as if it is used for quarantine—or as a brig. But if he is a prisoner, why would the hatch be open?

MUTABILITY
OF MEANING

ERIC – Check this out!
First + last "letters"
in Ch. 1 footnotes gives you:
{ 29 }
[AR GO SY EV ER yo(19th) (1900)H RS]
And there was an Argosy Hotel on East 38th St. !!

My theory: FX (did I believe VMS was alive + or wanted to
was telling him how/when/where they could meet.
GOOD CATCH. You know, for an undergrad,
you can pretend to be cool all you want, but I know you're jumping
up + down, wherever you are.
The question is: was he alive?? → THAT'S ONE QUESTION, ANYWAY.

The ship itself is an archaic-looking vessel. He recognizes it as a xebec design, sleek and shallow-drafting, (a three-master favored by the pirates of previous centuries,) but an anachronism on the modern seas—and it is improbable-looking as well, in a state midway between decrepitude and tidy renovation, albeit renovation performed by a shipwright working against reason. The deck is freshly re-planked in some places, while in others the wood has rotted away, leaving holes big enough to catch and break a sailor's ankle, if not swallow him whole. Two of the three lateen sails look fresh from the nearest sail loft, while the third is torn and frayed, a discolored banner of neglect flying from a mizzen-mast whose top third appears blackened, as if by a lightning strike.

[A revelation: he is someone who knows at least a few things about ships.] He counts nineteen crewmen on the main deck and the quarterdeck, none of whom is moving with the urgency he associates with even the most undisciplined and resentful crews. Instead they trudge from task to task, grim and oxlike, somehow keeping the ship afloat and smoothly on the move. He cannot see their downcast faces clearly, but their varied

---

Handwritten marginalia:

Oh, of course.
Everyone
recognizes a "xebec design."
I WOULD.
How? More importantly, why?
MY UNCLE WAS INTO SAILING.
HE LIKED TO TEACH ME THINGS.
And you were interested?
IT WAS STUFF TO KNOW, + I WAS INTERESTED
IN KNOWING STUFF. DIDN'T MATTER WHAT IT WAS.

Teasing about the pirate myth here?
COULD BE... ALTHOUGH THIS SHIP SOUNDS A LOT LIKE THE ARIADNE IN BRAXENHOLM (EXCEPT HERE IT'S FALLING APART). Or turning into another ship entirely.
RIGHT—HENCE THE TITLE OF SOT—NOTE THE MYTHOLOGICAL CONNECTION B/W ARIADNE + THESEUS, TOO.
Confession: I had to look those up.

SOMETIMES I WONDER IF VMS EVER HAD AMNESIA HIMSELF.
God, could you imagine if he survived Havana but ended up amnesiac? So, if you include Maelstrom.
THAT'D BE THE CRUELEST IRONY EVER.
MAELSTROM IS DIFFERENT. VMS IS CLEAR ABOUT THAT.

19 SAILORS, 19 BOOKS

skin tones and builds suggest a heterogeneous crew drawn from all corners of the globe. He watches them for a long time, his ears full of the rushing wind catching the sails and slapping at the rigging, of the churn and wash of the waves and their watery smacks against the wooden hull, before he realizes how strangely quiet the crew is. There are no shouts of command, there is none of the rough repartee of the briny, there are no grunts or cries or complaints. Somewhere overhead, a few birds call out, (but the crew is silent as the dead.) *

He assumes he is to join them. After all, isn't that why people are shanghaied? For labor they would not give voluntarily? He's in no hurry to start, though, unsure of his surroundings and drowning in a sense of threat, still woozy from the chloroform and with what he can tell are a landsman's unsteady legs and stomach.

Dark clouds map the sky, their edges illuminated by the orange sun, streaky and low on the horizon. Has he slept through an entire day? At first this surprises him, but he slowly realizes that he feels as if he has been unconscious far longer than that. Until now, he has felt fairly calm—at the very least, calm for someone who has been abducted by unknown

{ 29 }

Handwritten marginalia:

* Unlike the crew of the Ariadne — one big party until the wreck. (Yes I've read Braxenholm. You can stop being bewildered by the fact that I can read.)

So cool that you're getting to immerse yourself in VMS all at once. Just don't forget to graduate, okay?

I won't screw it up. I am so ready to get out of here. But thanks for caring.

CF. THE ARCHER'S TALES? CREW AS COMPOSITE OF TRADITIONS?

Did you go sailing when you were a kid? NOW + THEN. Your family had boats? ARE YOU KIDDING! WE HAD ONE CAR — A '74 PINTO. MY UNCLE HAD A BOAT — A PIECE OF SHIT 28-FOOTER THAT HE FIXED UP HIMSELF. HE WAS REALLY PROUD OF IT.

Eric!! — I tracked down passenger manifests for every ship that arrived in NY from Brazil b/w 1923–1929. There's no Francisco Filip Xabregas Caldeira... BUT: There was a Filomela Xabregas Caldeira who showed up often on the crew of the Imperia — as a translator. And on 5/15/24 there was a passenger on the Imperia named S. Opice — Tance.

WOW. I MEAN, WOW. SO: MAYBE LOVE? So: maybe love.

YOU REALLY FOUND THIS? YOU'D BETTER NOT BE KIDDING. CHANGES EVERYTHING. Not kidding. MARRY ME. OK — even as a joke, that's a little creepy. At least until we meet. Probably after, too. SORRY. TRYING TO EXPRESS EXTREME GRATITUDE + EXCITEMENT + RESPECT. NOT USED TO DOING THAT. Your personal warmth just leaps off the page. SO NOTED.

persons for unknown purposes—but this, this sense that large swaths of time have gone by, time in which the world may have shifted in some fundamental way without his noticing, makes his skin crawl. He can feel dread weighting his insides; his stomach feels as dense as mercury. He looks at the sun and thinks: *Setting. To starboard. Which means we're headed south*. He exhales. What a relief, to know one thing, however vague, about one's direction.

A burst of reedy, high-pitched trills—those sea-birds, he thinks, looking up, though he still doesn't see them—snaps him back to the moment. He scans the ship and the water, thinking of escape. No land in sight. No ships to signal. In one corner of the main deck is a tarp covering what might be a dinghy, but he'd never be able to launch it himself. His only option, it seems, is to hurl himself into the waves and put his faith in water, and something in the back of his mind tells him that he has tried that sort of thing before without success.[7] He shivers in a gust of cool wind and hugs the overcoat around himself more tightly.

Then: a scratchy voice comes to his ears. At first it startles him, because he thought those voices

---

[7] 1900 saw the anonymous publication of a poem called "La Foi en Eau" (or "Faith in Water"). It is possible that Straka was making a reference to it, but there is no clear evidence of such.

Handwritten annotations:

VACLAV / BRIDGE? *It was a suicide attempt— weird to talk about "faith" there.*

DEPENDS ON WHAT HE WAS HOPING THE WATER WOULD DO.

THIS POEM DOES NOT EXIST! NO WONDER VMS DIDN'T WANT ANNOTATIONS. THIS IS ASININE.

I double-checked on the poem. I think you're right.

I KNOW I'M RIGHT. YOU DIDN'T HAVE TO WASTE YOUR TIME.

Hey, you've missed a few things. More than a few.

belonged to the Old Quarter, but he realizes that
the sound is coming from the main deck below him.
He ducks, hopes he has escaped notice, but the
voice continues—it's more of a wax-cylinder hiss
than a voice, really, but it is *there* on the ship, and
real—and it repeats a word over and over as it
approaches him. *S*—, the voice says. It is not a word
that means anything to him. He hears feet climbing
rungs up to the forecastle. *You*, he hears. *S*—.

There will be no hiding. And so he arranges himself into a stolid posture, standing tall on the forecastle to face what is coming his way.

The owner of the voice is a behemoth of a man,
clad neck-to-shin in sailor's osnaburg. One arm of
the shirt is full of sags and rips and is discolored in a
hundred tones of brown and black; the other is a
perfect shade of bone, with a ring of pristine white
stitches attaching it at the shoulder. (A quick glance
aft shows that the rest of the crew is also dressed, to
varying degrees, in such nautical motley.) The sail-
or's head is bald and sun-blistered; his beard is a
maelstrom of black hair. He does not appear to be
wearing a sidearm, but this does not leave the man
in the overcoat feeling any more secure about his
current situation or his future prospects.

INTERESTING FOR A
CHARACTER WHO WORRIES
ABOUT COWARDICE. HE
DOESN'T SHOW ANY HERE.

S. is his own worst
critic, el guess.
LIKE MOST OF US.

CF. MAN IN PHOTO FROM
THE SANTANA MARCH
FILM SHOOT.
Wow—that's
uncanny. who is that?
"UNIDENTIFIED CREW"
You'd think someone who
looked like that
would be pretty
memorable.

"Me?"

You. S—.

"That's my name?"

The sailor nods.

S—. He runs the name through his mind and over his tongue. It continues to mean nothing to him. Just a word. Still, he feels calmer suddenly; it is much better to have a name than not to have one.

He knows two facts now: *I am on a ship heading south. My name, at the moment, is S—.*

The sailor says something that sounds like *beggars* or maybe *bears*, but S. can't hear it clearly, as it is masked by the rushing breeze. There is more important information to be gathered, anyway.

"What's the name of your vessel?" S. asks.

Int mine, the sailor says.

"What's the name of *this* vessel?"

Dunt ten' a name. His voice is surprisingly insubstantial—more noticed than heard.

"No name?"

Dun once, haps. Dunt n'more.

"What's your name?"

Ridden o' mine, the big man says. He nods toward the shuffling crew to the aft of the ship. *They ridden o' tharn. Names's trouble.*

Handwritten marginalia:

MIX OF DIALECTS INTENTIONAL? TRANSLATION ISSUE?

Tell me about it. ← People won't stop calling me "Jenny." Even my alleged friends, who are supposed to understand why I want to change.

PEOPLE GENERALLY FIND WAYS TO DISAPPOINT YOU.

Seriously, I think you're the only person who calls me Jen.

WELL, THAT'S HOW YOU INTRODUCED YOURSELF.

I still appreciate it.

"And yet I have one. Apparently."

The big man smiles. His teeth are rounded, like little yellow tombstones set irregularly into gums the color of earth. *Trouble,* he says. His accent is a strange thing—it seems not to issue from a specific place but instead is ladled up from a transoceanic stew of dictions and impediments.

"Why was I brought here?" S. asks. "Where's the man with the scar?" He traces a line down the center of his forehead, then jerks his hand away, disconcerted to find that the skin there feels raw and tingly. A chill slowly descends his spine.

We've 'structs, the sailor says, *to take y'.*

"What do you mean, take me?"

Take y'.

"Take me where?"

No where.

"I need to speak to the captain. Where is the captain?"

Int na captain.

"How can there be no captain?"

Int na captain. 'S us. We viv the ship. He pauses. *Do what's needin.*

The big sailor seems calm, but the *wrongness* of him, of his silent comrades, of this crazy-quilt of a

---

Handwritten marginalia:

Don't you think we should get together and talk? At least to figure out what to do with the Filomela info?

YOU'RE PROBABLY RIGHT.

Good. Tomorrow @ 9 pm. coffee at Pronghorn Java. OK?

OK.

A WORLD W/O CENTRALIZED POWER / AUTHORITY

WHERE WERE YOU???

I'M SORRY. I WANTED TO. BUT I COULDN'T.

Well, you are the one who said people find ways to disappoint you.... I'm wondering if I'm being used.

THAT'S NOT IT. I SWEAR I'M NOT LIKE THAT.

Except you just showed me you are. So either you're lying, or you just don't know who you really are.

ship and S.'s own presence on it, sends a stab of panic through him. He feels his heart thudding faster, feels his spine turning to ice. He—this alleged S.—has no control over who or where or why he is. He feels as if he is falling again, falling through the dark, with nothing to believe in but the cruel efficiency of gravity.

His knees buckle, and he collapses to the deck. The wood feels damp and cool on his cheek, and it offers a sort of relief. He hears the big man whistle sharply, hears many sets of feet crossing the deck toward them, feels himself tugged back up to standing and supported on the shoulder of another sailor. He scans the lineup of faces in front of him[8] while the big man addresses them in his scratchy, eerily insubstantial voice, and he notices something odd: except for the big man, all of the sailors have dark blemishes around their mouths. He is still trying to understand what sort of dietary deficiency or tobacco habit might account for this when the crewman holding him up turns to face him—he's so close, their noses nearly touch—and S. sees thin, dark threads crisscrossing his lips and ending in a tiny knot at one corner. Tiny pink spots mark where

---

[8] Readers will note that, as the book continues, each of these sailors' faces will be described in such a way that it resembles one of the authorship controversy's most popular candidates.

{ 34 }

I like this, too.

Another FN that at least makes some sense.

I DON'T THINK IT'S TRUE, THOUGH. GO THROUGH THE BOOK + TRY TO MATCH UP THE DESCRIPTIONS WITH EKSTROM, MACINNES, GARCÍA FERRARA, FEUERBACH, SUMMERSBY—EVEN DURAND— ET AL. IT DOESN'T SEEM TO WORK.

_____

the stitches enter and exit the skin. S. gasps audibly, and the crewman's lips stretch to the side, straining the threads and turning the pink spots blood-red, and S. finds himself wishing that he could unwind time so that he could live his life without ever seeing up close what passes for a smile on this nameless, monstrous vessel.

Regret— maybe hinting about some regrets of Straka's own.

AGAIN: YOU HAVE TO BE CAREFUL. NOT EVERYTHING A WRITER WRITES IS ABOUT THE WRITER.

I'd ask you to say that 10 times fast, but it would just be 10 times as condescending.

aHEM...

I'M SORRY. JUST FEEL
SAFER DOING IT THIS
WAY FOR NOW.

I swear I'm not as
scary-looking as those sailors.
(But maybe you know that? Maybe
you've stalked the stacks?)

So we have a
"spirit of things"
DON'T YOU THINK?

HAVEN'T. I WON'T LIE — IT'S TEMPTING.
BUT IT SEEMS UNFAIR + NOT IN THE
SPIRIT OF THINGS.

I do. It's why
this feels fun (and not totally creepy).

CHAPTER 2

THE DRIFTING TWINS

So which book is this chapter based on? I haven't come across anything close yet.

THE SANTANA MARCH

TWO **DAYS** and two nights pass aboard the ship. S. spends long hours in his cabin feeling nauseated by the ship's lurching as it rises and falls, smacked about by the busy seas. Sometimes he is able to hold his food, sometimes he is not. He is fed adequately, though not well: tooth-cracking ship-biscuits and petrified salt pork, both of which possess a vaguely bluish hue, and fresh but rather marshy-tasting water. Silenced sailors bring him his food on a tin plate, his water in a tin mug, and (though he knows he ought to try to communicate with them, he cannot bring himself to look them in the face.) Those black threads revolt him, terrify him, raise questions he is not yet willing to ask, even to himself.

That whole book takes place in a __desert__.

DIFFERENT CONTEXT, BUT THE PLOT/ACTION IS SIMILAR. THE ESCAPE ATTEMPT, ESPECIALLY.

E.G., HOW DO THEY EAT?

And eg: "Who's sending Eric S, and why?"

AND:

"IS JEN ACTUALLY GOING TO GRADUATE?"

And: Who is that guy in the suit? What the hell does he want from me? And what the hell did Ilsa tell him??

On the afternoon of the third day, the big, unsewn sailor—whose beard has inspired S. to dub him *Maelstrom*—appears at the hatch, looking down at him. The beard hangs far enough to brush the topmost rung of the ladder.

POE REF. ? →

"Please clarify something for me," S. calls to him. "Am I a passenger? You don't seem to expect me to work—"

Ye'll work t' lapsin an' yond. Creed on't.

"I notice that—that you're not—that, whereas the crew has—" How do you ask such a thing? "—that you are, ah, free to speak."

Maelstrom raises his hands to his face and pulls the thick hair away from his mouth, revealing lips blighted with sores. But that's not what the big man is trying to show him. No: it is the ghastly pattern of pinpoint scars that encircle his mouth. Further explanation, though, does not come.

"Tell me this," S. says. "Am I being taken to someone who wishes me well or ill?"[1]

Int no spondin' tha'.

"Why not?" S. asks him.

---

[1] The character's question here echoes one that the author often asked about his publishers. The adversarial relationship between them is one of the few elements of Straka's life about which there is universal agreement. (After the second disappearance of Straka's agent, Lewis Looper, in 1930, I was the one most often asked to play the role of go-between.)

{ 38 }

Handwritten marginalia:

First-and-last doesn't work for Ch. 2 footnotes or any other chapters.

BUT, LIKE CH. 1, SOME SEEM TO MAKE SERIOUS COMMENTS + SOME DON'T. (AND FOR THE RECORD: I THINK WE SHOULD TECHNICALLY BE CALLING THESE CIPHERS.)

I think you should technically get over it.

He disappeared twice?

NO — JUST ONCE. LOTS OF PEOPLE THOUGHT HE WAS VMS, SO A 2ND DISAPPEARANCE DEF. WOULD'VE BEEN NEWS. NO CLUE WHAT FXC IS TALKING ABOUT.

So Looper + FXC both worked w/ VMS from 1924–1930? Were they ever seen together?

NEITHER WAS SEEN, PERIOD.

BUT WHAT IF VMS WAS HIS OWN PUBLISHER? KARST DIDN'T PUBLISH MUCH ELSE

Something about 2nd is important, then. It's not the 2nd letters or 2nd words (of the FNs or the text)...

MAYBE THE 2ND FN OF THE CHAPTER? IT'S A STRANGE ONE.

<< BINGO >>

SHIP OF THESEUS

_____

Maelstrom looks at him as if he is a fool. *Cause cant nobod spond it.* He pauses, dragging a hand through his dangling beard and appearing deep in thought. *Landways voxin tha' Sola gotter shine wi' ye.* His words, such as they are, sound carefully considered.

"I don't know what that means," S. says. "Can you please ex—?" But the unsewn sailor's face disappears from the hatchway, and S. hears the decking groan under his weight as he walks aft and descends to the main deck. S. jumps up with a mind to pursue him, but the ship lurches and sends his stomach and its contents spinning. He sits back down on the floor, pressing himself into the solidity of a wall. Doubling over, he begs an array of gods in which he does not believe to let this spell of sickness pass quickly.

Throughout these days and the nights, S. has heard the sounds of the sailors tromping over the deck as they've gone about the business of sailing the ship. Occasionally Maelstrom barks orders and observations in some particularly inscrutable dialect of nautical language, but more often the crew's communication takes the form of birdlike whistles, fluttering and trilling in a wide range of pitches, rhythms, and tempos that send the men into action.

_____

{ 39 }

It sounds as if S. is being held captive in a sanctuary for deranged passerines.

The reason for this, which he confirms with a morbidly-fascinated glance at the tar who brings his next meal, is that mouth-sewn sailors wear whistles on lanyards around their necks, thin-bored wooden whistles that they can fit into a gap between stitches and blow. This sailor looks to be about thirty-five; he has sleepy eyes and center-parted hair, the two waves of which are sharp-crested and look like bat-ears atop his head. S. tries to get his attention, hoping for a response—any response, even just a whistle. The man ignores him.

The voice he hears most frequently, then, is his own, as he mutters to himself, trying to draw out any streams of memory that may still run inside him. He says whatever words and phrases come to mind, following trails of associations to their invariably dead ends. He pounces on the few images that come to mind—a black sheep on a green hillside; a trout on a hook, dripping and jerking and flopping; a cold, dark room with a valise on the floor at its center; a coop full of burbling, pacing pigeons; a wall of fog rushing down a dark street—but these images are merely individual frames from a film

{ 40 }

Handwritten marginalia:

ILSA PUBLISHED A PAPER ABOUT HIS BIRD METAPHORS.
Any good?
PRETTY SHALLOW.

Creepy (above "they can fit")

ARTIFACT IN PRAGUE ARCHIVES: WOODEN WHISTLE W/ S SYMBOL BURNED INTO IT.
People think it was Straka's?

SOME DO. LOOPER PUT IT UP FOR AUCTION IN '25 (ALONG W/ 19 PIECES OF OBSIDIAN ETCHED W/ THE S). SAID IT WAS ALL PRECIOUS TO VMS, ALL CENTURIES OLD, FOUND IN A SHIPWRECK NEAR THE AZORES.
Straka must have been pissed (if he wasn't Looper).

UNLESS HE NEEDED CASH.
Wondering: if Straka ever played the whistle, ALL OF THESE ARE IMAGES FROM EARLIER VMS BOOKS *maybe, there'd be DNA on it? Could it be tested?*

GOOD QUESTION — I'LL ASK PRAGUE. I'VE HAD A GOOD RELATIONSHIP W/ THEM. ——— *Guess what's missing from Prague now...*

NOT LOOKING GOOD. NEED TO APPLY FOR PERMISSION TO REMOVE ARTIFACT. PROCESS TAKES A YEAR, AND "PROBABLY WON'T BE APPROVED."
Thought you had a good relationship...
I DID, TOO.

I AM DISINCLINED TO TRANSCRIBE THE WORDS THAT JUST CAME OUT OF MY MOUTH.

Lot's of newly-found S symbols on the Danish kid's site. From totally far-flung places. ANYONE CAN MAKE THEM.

There's one painted on the side of the Varsity now. Was it you? Messing with me? WASN'T ME. YOU'RE SAYING YOU DIDN'T DO IT?

SHIP OF THESEUS *yeah, i'm saying that.*

WELL... A LOT OF PEOPLE READ VMS'S BOOKS...

——————

Varsity is showing <u>Santana</u> *tomorrow night. Last-minute change. Coincidence? Tell me it is.*

that no longer exists. He describes aloud what he

sees, hoping that some word, any word, will coax his

memory into the light.

PROBABLY. BUT WE DEF. SHOULDN'T GO. *You couldn't pay me to go right now.*

He scrutinizes his face in the surface of the turbid water that is handed down to him. He studies
the contours and shapes of his features, <u>tries to</u>
<u>assemble an image of himself.</u> He catalogues the
bruises and scrapes and old, whitened scars over his
body, theorizing about each injury's possible cause.
He studies the stains that darken his overcoat. He
studies his shirt, his trousers, his shoes, looking for
tell-tale blemishes, names of manufacturers, anything. He even studies the wood-grain Rorschachs
that present themselves in the deckhead above his
hammock. (And all the while, that strange symbol
gouged into the wood looms over him.*) He studies it,
too, but it remains a cipher to him.

ATTEMPT TO RECOGNIZE/ DEFINE SELF—EXTERNAL EVIDENCE TO DRAW INTERNAL CONCLUSION. (MORE DIFFICULT, THOUGH, TO ASSEMBLE ONESELF FROM THE INSIDE + PROJECT OUTWARD (ACC. TO DR. BRAND)—

who's Dr. Brand? GUY WHO HELPED ME MOST WHEN I WAS IN THE HOSPITAL. *When were you in the hospital?* OVER THE WINTER. I DIDN'T EXACTLY HANDLE THE MOODY SITUATION WELL.

The next day he awakens exasperated and angry,
irritated with his passivity. Enough. He can't simply sit around feeling ill and rummaging uselessly
through a <u>defective memory</u>, not when each minute on this ship brings him closer to a fate he cannot fathom, or farther from the life he wishes he'd
retained. As weak as he is, he's got to start looking
for a means of escape. Leaving his overcoat in the

ISN'T ALL MEMORY? *Remind me to tell you about the day I disappeared.* TELL ME NOW. *It'll take too long. Not enough room either.*

DON'T WE ALL...

——————

{ 41 }

cabin,[2] he ascends the ladder and clambers onto the forecastle.

The sky is overcast, the seas calm. A swift breeze blows from starboard, and the ship cuts swiftly through the water, sailing on a beam reach. From the stern comes the sound of one sailor banging on wood with a mallet. S. looks out over the deck and counts the crewmen—again, nineteen, not including Maelstrom. A few of the crewmen notice him watching but turn back to their tasks without any response. There is a similar lack of concern, or regard, when he descends to the main deck and walks among them, with the exception of one sailor—a middle-aged man with sunken, scowling eyes and mere wisps of lank hair ornamenting a vast white dome of forehead—who grumbles in his throat when S. treads too close to the area of the deck he is scrubbing with a holystone.

Even with the wind, the air at deck level is heavy, clotted with the smells of unwashed men—to which S. himself is strongly contributing. He looks away

Speaking of... one of those pieces of obsidian is missing from the archives.

---

[2] Several commentators of limited acumen have pointed out that overcoats figure prominently in many of Straka's books and have argued in favor of one grand metaphorical interpretation or another. (I humbly observe that an overcoat, most often, is simply an overcoat. Its function is to keep its wearer warm.) This sort of pedantic nonsense set Straka's teeth on edge, particularly when its purveyors were strident critics of his work and/or politics who steadfastly refused to play fair, as it were. Among the worst offenders—Oskar Heilemann, Herbert Uhler, Bolingbroke Wadkins, Helmer Aasen, Martin Gonçalves, and Sydney Youngblood.

AND A FN IS USUALLY JUST A FN. BUT NOT HERE B/C NONE OF THOSE PEOPLE EXIST.

Playfair Cipher — creates a string of paired letters—like initials. (OH, HU, BW, etc.) Need to figure out the keyword to decipher it.

SOMETHING IN THE CHAPTER TITLE? DRIFTING TWINS? THE DRIFTING TWINS? TWINS? Gemini. { 42 } Which gives us:

"Looper agent." So she's warning him about Looper?

DOESN'T MAKE SENSE. VMS WAS LOOPER.

That's what you assumed. ME, AND THOUSANDS OF OTHERS. — How nice that you all got to be wrong together.

whenever a crewman reaches for the whistle around his neck to plug it between his lips. The last thing a man without memories needs is terrible new ones.

Emboldened by his apparent <u>freedom to wander,</u> S. walks—with steadier legs now—to the aft end of the main deck. Above, on the quarterdeck, Maelstrom is taking a turn at the ship's wheel. S. is tempted to assail him with more questions, even if the answers will be infuriatingly opaque, but he restrains himself. Instead, he approaches the door to the cabin beneath the quarterdeck, which he guesses would be the chart-room, or perhaps the captain's cabin, if there were a captain. He tries the knob, and it turns. He glances around. <u>No one moves or shouts or whistles</u> to stop him. He opens the door.

The space is roughly twice the size of his own area below the forecastle. Light from the starboard-side porthole bathes the austere space in the fiery glow of sunset, but the air inside is dank and close. The only furnishing is one rickety wooden table that must be a hundred years old. On it are a <u>sextant crusted over with verdigris and a pilot chart so blackened with mold as to be unreadable.</u> If any acts of navigation are being performed on this ship, they are not occurring in this room.

For someone who's banned from campus, you seem to move around pretty freely.
IT'S A BIG CAMPUS + I'M GOOD AT NOT BEING NOTICED. + I'VE GOT A FEW TRICKS I CAN USE WHEN I NEED TO.

Like the steam tunnels?

IT'S FUNNY. IN HS, I GOT LEFT OUT OF THE YEARBOOK COMPLETELY.
Were you one of those kids who ditched school all the time?
NO, I WAS THERE — IT JUST NEVER OCCURRED TO ANYBODY TO RECORD MY PRESENCE. I EXISTED ONLY ADMINISTRATIVELY. (OK, I'M IN THE BACKGROUND OF ONE PHOTO— BACK TURNED, A SPIKY-HAIRED BLUR. VERY VMS.)

Did it bother you? Being left out?
ONCE I REALIZED I WASN'T GETTING NOTICED, IT FELT LIKE MORE FUN TO TRY TO STAY THAT WAY.

Did you get into Straka before or after that?
Which— and I'm just making an observation here— was around the time of the boat trip.
I DON'T REMEMBER. ABOUT THE SAME TIME, I GUESS.

CF. RUINED MAPS/ COMPASS IN SANTANA MARCH

He is in the doorway, about to step into the open air, (when the deck comes alive with whistles—really, it sounds like a flock of alarmed barn swallows)—just as one of the sailors is emerging from the hatch that leads to the lower decks—two of them, S. surmises from his glances over the rail, and below them, the orlop and the hold. The sailor, fifty if he is a day, is a man with a blue watch cap crookedly on his head. He has jug-handle ears, a broad nose, and wide, round eyes with a look of alarm in them. The crazed look, however, is belied by the way the (man hauls himself slowly toward mid-deck, moving as if he is exhausted. The exposed skin around his neck and on his hands appears lightly mottled with blue-black—a shade darker, perhaps, than a fresh bruise.) Arriving at the mainmast, he lifts one arm shakily, fits his whistle into his mouth, and blows an enervated squeak of a note. Immediately, another man climbs down out of the ratlines and descends into the ship through the same hatch. The sailor with the jug-ears pulls himself aloft in the ratlines and disappears into the jungle of canvas and rope.

A curious ritual, this: an inverted changing-of-the-guard, with the spent man replacing the

{ 44 }

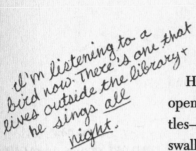

I'm listening to a bird now. There's one that lives outside the library & he sings all night.

THE MOCKINGBIRD, RIGHT? HE'S BEEN THERE EVERY SPRING THAT I'VE BEEN AT PSU.

Sounds like me every finals week.

SOUNDS LIKE ME NOW. NO TIME FOR SLEEP THESE DAYS. LOST 2 MOS. IN THE HOSPITAL. GOT TO CATCH UP. CAN'T LET MOODY WIN.

Be careful—I mean, you're still recovering, right?

I'M RECOVERING BY GETTING MY WORK DONE.

Maybe that's what I'm doing too.

OBSERVATION: YOU'RE DOING OUR WORK, BUT YOU MIGHT BE AVOIDING YOURS.

I've been wondering: am I really getting this degree for myself? or is it for my parents?

GOOD QUESTIONS, BAD TIME TO ASK THEM. YOU'RE SO CLOSE...

fresher one.[3] This makes no sense to S.; a stiff gust of wind might just blow a fatigued man of that age right out of the rigging. He finds himself looking upward as he walks the deck, half-expecting a heavy body to come falling down at him.

((Night brings fewer whistles, between which reigns an almost funereal silence. There is no evidence of drinking, music, dancing, any of the sorts of pastimes one expects)to encounter in a cohort of sailors confined on the waves. S. walks the deck, taking in his surroundings discreetly, no closer to an escape plan than he was the moment he awoke on this vessel. He watches as one sailor—slim and boyish, even feminine in build, with shoulder-length dark hair framing a narrow face of sepulchral mien—refills the masthead lamps from a tin of kerosene and relights them with a flint. Another sits with his back against the bulwark, whittling a whistle from a thin stick of wood, his unruly thatch of straw-colored hair shivering stiffly in the wind. S. prays that the whistle is not meant for his neck. A shudder

Reminds me of my apartment. I've suddenly become a 40-year-old (acc. to my super-awesome roommate, anyway).

I'VE PRETTY MUCH ALWAYS BEEN ONE.

That's kind of sad.

I USED TO THINK SO. NOW I THINK: YOU'RE BORN A CERTAIN WAY. LATER YOU GET TO DECIDE HOW MUCH YOU WANT TO FIGHT / CHANGE THAT.

I missed this the 1st time through.

You must mind. If you didn't you wouldn't be doing this with me. (And you probably wouldn't be so mad at Ilsa.)

I'D BE MAD REGARDLESS.

SEWN-UP → WHISTLING (FORCED INTO STANDARDIZED / LIMITED MODE OF COMMUNICATION)

3   Often in our correspondence, Straka would lament how exhausted he was and enumerate his physical ailments. (For example: chronic ear infections left him unable to hear sounds in the frequency range of 2710 Hz. to 2760 Hz.) Although staying ahead of creditors, state organs of repression, covert operatives, and would-be exploiters of his work, reputation, and identity obviously took a toll on him, the prolificacy and vitality of his writing demonstrate conclusively that he was a man of uncommon vigor and perseverance.

I'd call you pretentious if that hadn't been a note to yourself.

→ That's weirdly specific.

PART OF ANOTHER MESSAGE TO VMS, THEN?

I'm not having any luck w/ codes here. Are you?

IF IT DOESN'T HAVE ANYTHING TO DO W/ THE CH. 2 CODE, WHAT'S IT DOING HERE?

Part of another code?
Or a reference to something else entirely.

— OR FXC TRYING TO THROW PEOPLE OFF? RANDOM DETAILS THAT SEEM MEANINGFUL BUT AREN'T?

{ 45 }

passes through him, and as it does, the two sailors share an amused, knowing look. S. hurries away from them.

Eventually, S. collects his uneaten ship-biscuit and the rest of his water and ascends to the forecastle. He sits at the foremast and studies the starry sky before him, searching for familiar constellations. He won't be able to pinpoint the ship's position—he knows he's not well-versed in astronomy—but even a tiny scrap of information is better than nothing. More than anything, he wants to see something *familiar*, something that connects him, however tenuously, to the world he must have known before he lost his memory, his identity, himself.

There: Aquila. There: Cygnus. There: Gemini. He dips his biscuit in the water, holds it there awhile so it can soften, then works his teeth against it. He manages to tear off a few shreds before he has to dunk the ancient bread again.

When he looks back up to the sky, it's as if the stars have shifted; he can still make out the constellations, but their shapes are different. The stars that made the eagle's wing-tips have spread out over the sky, leaving the bird unfinished, eternally spilling itself out into the black. The swan's neck is bent, as

{ 46 }

This is hitting me hard. everything in my life feels like it's changing too quickly.

IT'S HOW I FELT IN THE HOSPITAL.

Did you find your "something familiar"?

IT'S IN YOUR HANDS.

Surprised they didn't want you to take a break from work.

I DID. I JUST READ THE BOOK. DIDN'T THINK SO MUCH. I LOVED THIS BOOK BEFORE PSU, BEFORE MOODY. GOT BACK TO LOVING IT IN A SIMPLE WAY.

Here's where you might ask, "What's changing for you?"

WHAT'S CHANGING FOR YOU?

Um, the stuff you know: relationship, parents, school (being in it + also being about to leave). But it's *me*, too. I'm not interested in what I thought I was interested in. I don't want what I always assumed I wanted. And my mood, too; I'm on a total short fuse. Everyone + everything is on the verge of pissing me off hugely all the time.

I ASSUME I'M ONE OF THEM.

if wrung. The twins have detached from one another. But stars can't independently drift into new positions without regard to their former arrangements, can they? Surely this is a phantasm conjured by an overwhelmed mind, by an exhausted and dehydrated body. Or perhaps it is an ophthalmic problem he does not recollect having? He closes his eyes, tries to shake his head clear—but gently, so as not to trigger another rush of nausea.

When he reopens his eyes, the constellations are no longer even recognizable. Above him is a sky full of stars that he'll have to connect on his own, in new shapes, a spray of light-points no longer organized by the shapes mankind has traced over them for thousands of years. He watches the stars closely. They wink, they tremble, and he swears he can see them drift—as one might be able to see the minute hand of a clock moving. He is a man without a past sailing in a strange sea in a world where the stars have come loose in the firmament.[4] He grinds the last of the biscuit in his teeth and forces it down. Sips his water, swallows it past a lump in his throat.

---

[4] In a 1942 letter postmarked from Basel, Straka described a recent dream in which a similar phenomenon occurred. I am no longer in possession of the letter, but I can quote the relevant portion from memory: "What if the constellations no longer held?" he asked. "Would it not cause one to scrutinize the totality of one's surroundings carefully? Would it not terrify?"

> *Less than you'd think. It's mostly people in the real world.*

... AS OPPOSED TO THE MARGIN WORLD.

It's weird, I know, but yes. This is — I don't know.— exciting + relaxing @ the same time.

DRIFTING TWINS = ? A SPLITTING SELF? (PUBLIC VS. PRIVATE? ROLE-AS-WRITER VS. ROLE-AS-PERSON? PRESENT SELF VS. PAST SELF? VS. POSSIBLE SELF?

Drops his head into his hands. Breathes deeply. Prepares to pass through a world he cannot possibly understand.

Sola. A name, he assumes. This is the one useful piece of information he has received from Maelstrom—from *anyone*—thus far. A name. Male or female? Someone from his old, hidden life, or from this one?

How interesting, he notes, that already he thinks of the two as separate.

Who *could* it be from this life? The drunken sailor? The scowling man he passed near the harbor? The bartender? The innkeeper on the verge of tears as she struggled with her crooked sign? Certainly not. Perhaps the refined young woman with the enormous book? A pleasant solution to the puzzle, but how likely is it, despite that brief flicker of recognition he felt? How could such a woman possibly have a connection to the horrific crew that surrounds him now?

He feels suddenly overtaken by fatigue and decides to retreat to his hammock in the quarters below, telling himself that a good sleep may help him wake to a more sensible universe. He stands and stretches, and as he is looking off into the

48

Handwritten annotations:

Left margin (top): If you go through this book + read Sola as a stand-in for FXC, it becomes a much different book. — IN WHICH CASE, IT MATTERS A LOT WHICH ENDING IS THE REAL ONE.

Left margin (middle): Don't we all have to do this? Separate ourselves from who we were to become who we want to be? BUT YOU CAN ARGUE THAT IT'S A SERIES OF SHIFTS RATHER THAN A BREAK. SLOUGH OFF SOME IDEAS OF WHO WE ARE, ACQUIRE NEW ONES... BUT WE'RE STILL CONTINUOUS.

So what have you "sloughed"? MY NEED TO HAVE MY PARENTS UNDERSTAND ME. LOST THAT EARLY ON. ALSO: GUILT THAT SHOULDN'T HAVE BEEN MINE TO BEGIN WITH. ALSO: THE NEED TO THINK OF MYSELF AS THE MOST EMOTIONALLY HEALTHY PERSON EVER.

But nothing about school/career/Straka? NOPE. THAT'S BEEN CONTINUOUS.

What about the idea of an academic career? WELL, YEAH. I MIGHT HAVE TO SLOUGH THAT. IT MIGHT HAVE BEEN SLOUGHED FOR ME. IT'S NOT OVER YET, THOUGH.

Top margin (right): I read the Summersby transcript... Why would he go out of his way to say that he did his own translations - (implying that Filomela was fictional)? We know she existed, and we know she worked with Straka.

MAYBE. UNLESS THE FOREWORD + ALL THE FNS ARE PART OF AN EVEN BIGGER FAKE-OUT... you don't really believe that.

Bottom margin: Roommate got on me about leaving the door unlocked last night. I told her I'm tired, I'm working hard, it was a mistake, get over it. And she pulled that "you, of all people" BS. ??? I DON'T GET IT. I've just always been careful about things like that.

★ BUT IF YOU'RE INTERESTED IN GETTING
THE TRUTH ABOUT STRAKA OUT INTO THE
WORLD, THEN YOU AT LEAST HAVE TO
PRETEND TO BE. I HAVE TO BE REALLY
CAREFUL THAT WHAT I SAY IS TRUE,
METICULOUS ABOUT SOURCES, ETC.
IF I GET CARELESS, I'M SCREWED.

distance over the port side, he notices a different sort of light playing in the dark. Two lights. Not stars, no: these have the warmer yellow-orange hue of oil light, and they are very nearly at the waterline. Two lights, moving in concert: another ship. A two-master. But how to attract attention? How to draw the vessel close, beg for rescue?

An idea strikes. S. descends to the main deck, trying to move as smoothly and unobtrusively as possible. (Even here, on this ship, gazes wash over him. Whether he appreciates this gift as much as he ought to is unclear.) He snatches up the tin of kerosene and the flint from the barrelhead on which the youthful sailor left them, and he clambers back up to the forecastle.

He looks aft, confirms that the sailors are paying him no mind, then strips off his shirt, ignoring the chill that has crept into the night air, and soaks all but one sleeve in kerosene. As one hand holds it by the dry cuff, the other works the flint, scraping out sparks. There is a flash and a rush of air as the shirt catches fire. It burns a halo in the inky night as he swings it in circles. He shouts as loudly as he can across the water—swings his torch and shouts and swings and shouts; of course, his voice won't carry

Check this out: found a reference to a Portuguese ship that wrecked in 1619. Captain got word from King's agents that the steward was really "the foul Sobreiro" + was ordered to hang him immediately. Body was dumped overboard. Ship burned + sank not long after— which people took as proof that Sobreiro had been aboard. Oh, and this happened in the Azores.

YOU'RE KIDDING. WHERE DID YOU FIND THAT?
The Nautical History Museum in Madeira has a bitchin' database.
SO SOBREIRO EXISTED... And he pissed off people in power as much as Straka did.

WE DON'T KNOW WHY, THOUGH. AND WE DON'T KNOW THAT THIS IS THE SOBREIRO WHO (ALLEGEDLY) WROTE THE ARCHER'S TALES. No, we don't.
But I think it is. And { 49 } I think that whistle may have been his. I can't prove it, but like I said: I'm not a scholar.
★ [SEE TOP OF PG.] ★

to the other ship, but he can't contain himself; all the fear and frustration and anger in him has ignited, too. A look over his shoulder shows him the entire crew of mute sailors at the fore of the main deck, watching, but he pays no mind, he shouts and spins, he needs his signals to find their way to watchful eyes and brave souls aboard the other ship because this may be his only chance to reconnect with the world of sense and order in which, surely, he once lived. When he feels hands grabbing at him, he turns and slings his torch in a high arc over the water, the flames fluttering and spitting and then [disappearing into the breaking waves with an insignificant hiss that the wind instantly sweeps into oblivion.] FAILURE TO CONNECT

Two sailors—the sleepy, bat-eared one and a rangy, deathly-pale man whose greasy black fore-lock dances with his exertion—pin him to the deck, his neck wrenched uncomfortably. He hears a few short whistle-notes and then, after a moment, Mael-strom's voice cutting coldly through the air: *Fool. Yer assin mayed a'flammus t'the waterline.* S. is stunned at how much contempt this man's toneless rasp can convey, and he suppresses the impulse to gloat about his imminent rescue from this ship of

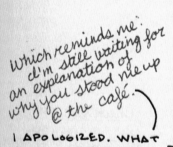

Which reminds me: I'm still waiting for an explanation of why you stood me up @ the café.

I APOLOGIZED. WHAT GOOD IS AN EXPLANATION?

My people—out here in the world—call it "communication."

FINE. IT WAS A COMBINATION OF THINGS. ONE OF WHICH: FEAR.

Obviously. Because I'm so terrifying + fierce.

IT WASN'T YOU. OR NOT JUST YOU. I PROMISE: I'LL EXPLAIN AS SOON AS I CAN FIGURE IT OUT.

Better get on it. I'm going to NY in 2 months.

I THOUGHT YOU DIDN'T WANT THE JOB.

I don't. But I told them I'd take it. I'm not getting stuck without a plan.

And don't even _think_ about judging me for that.

freaks. It is during this pause that his two silent cap-
tors pitch him down the forecastle hatch.

S. manages to grab a momentary hold of a ladder
rung on the way down, which slows his descent and
spares him an even more painful fall. Maelstrom
glares down at him through the hatch and says,
Y'aint coggin naught, are ye? Behind his shadowy
head, a hundred celestial pinpoints yaw across the
night sky.

"Of course I'm not!" S. shouts. "None of this
makes sense!"

The hatch clanks shut, leaving him alone in
the dark.

As he shuffles, arms outstretched, toward the
hammock, his thoughts return to the young woman
with the book. What had she said when he was
attacked? She gave no shriek of alarm, no cry for
help. No: her words were those of a calm reckoning,
an acceptance that the man with whom she was con-
versing was being gassed and dragged off by a hid-
eous, scarified wretch. If in fact she is Sola, he would
be much better off if she hadn't *gotten a shine with
him*—whatever that might mean.

Sometime during the night, S. wakes briefly from
a shivering sleep when the hatch opens and

APPEARANCE VS. REALITY

JUST LIKE W/ VMS—
AS SOON AS YOU THINK
YOU UNDERSTAND WHO HE
WAS, THE STORY SHIFTS.

And just like how you
think you're with someone in
a deep + long-term way,
and then you find out you're not.
And sometimes you find out via
email, which really
sucks. It triple-sucks
when that email
comes from Cabo
during Spring Break.

THAT'S COLD.
The thing is: you
might be right to trust
someone at one point...
but they can change.
+ IN BETWEEN, THEY
MUST BE DRIFTING FROM
TRUSTWORTHY TO NOT.
BUT YOU CAN'T TELL
HOW FAR THEY'VE DRIFTED
UNTIL IT'S TOO LATE.

Of course I don't really know you at
all. So there's no way I could ever
know if you're changing, or if you've already
changed.

YOU KNOW ME A LITTLE, RIGHT?
THERE WAS A TIME WHEN PEOPLE
RELIED ON LETTERS TO GET TO
KNOW EACH OTHER.
OBSERVATION: These are not those times.
OF COURSE THEY ARE.

something is flung down to the floor. He tips himself out of the hammock and retrieves it. A shirt, which feels as if it's made of a heavy fabric like the ones the sailors wear. He puts it on, despite its fetid reek, despite his concerns about vermin, despite his wounded pride, despite his dread at the mere thought of becoming more like these men. He is cold, and he wants to sleep. These are the only facts that matter right now.

In the morning, he will see that the garment is, in fact, just like the sailors': a delirious patchwork of fabrics, held together with stitches and stains of various hues, and a storehouse of eye-watering odors.[5] He scratches behind his shoulder blade, across his chest, at his neck. He feels as if insects are gnawing at his skin already.

He is awakened when Maelstrom flings the hatch open and gives a shrill, two-fingered whistle. *Rise y'proper, sunnydags,* he says, with a squeak of pleasure in his voice. *We're nigh to nudgin y'ship. Ye'll want t' viz it, asure.*

---

5 Possible source material for this detail is a traditional children's play performed on Ash Wednesday in the Bavarian village of Fünfherzen, in which the protagonist is compelled to don the *Belastunghemd*, or "burden-shirt." The origins of this curious play are unknown.

[handwritten left margin:]
My classes are a burden-shirt. Especially the lit class. Ilsa's vague about what she wants + surly when she doesn't get it.
THAT'S THE ILSA I KNOW.
She cancelled class the day you were off in NY. Was she there, too?
YES, MOODY SENT HER.
Why didn't you mention it?
BECAUSE I'M GENERALLY HAPPIER WHEN I ALLOW MYSELF TO PRETEND SHE DOESN'T EXIST. You need to get over that.
Really. It's a big problem.
YOU CAN'T JUST DECIDE TO.
No, but you can decide to try. And you haven't.

[handwritten bottom:]
NO SUCH TOWN, NO SUCH PLAY, NO SUCH WORD AS "BELASTUNGHEMD."
But other than that, what's the problem?
WHAT THE HELL IS FXC GETTING AT HERE?
Another code. It has to be.

S. spins himself out of the hammock and scrambles up the ladder with only one thought in mind: if he acts quickly enough, he can somehow limit the suffering inflicted on this other ship's crew when the man with the maelstrom beard and his gang of fearsome tars fall upon them.

He finds the men not loading guns or sharpening blades but balefully watching over the port side as they approach the little two-master, which is sideslipping over the water, its unsheeted sails twisting uselessly. The lamps he'd seen guttering atop her masts last night are now spent. Her deck is abandoned. The scene, then, is an odd juxtaposition of the charming and the chilling: gentle morning sun, cirrus clouds whisking across the azure skies, shy little whitecaps lapping against the hill, with all of this beauty and calm tempered by S.'s sense that something terrible has befallen this modest ship and her crew, and that the horror will soon be laid out before him.

A half-dozen sailors, including the two who held him last night, leap aboard the smaller ship as they draw alongside, surprising S. with their agility; they lash the ships together and fan out across the abandoned deck. A few of them open hatches and

{ 53 }

Handwritten marginalia:

CF. 1D + TWM! Huh?

ILSA + MOODY. I TRIED TO WARN HER ABOUT WHAT KIND OF PERSON HE IS.

I went to his office today — just to see what he's like. (I said I wanted to take his European Lit class in the fall.) I think he's deeply slimy.

JEN, WHATEVER YOU DO, DON'T LET HIM KNOW YOU'RE INTERESTED IN VMS. I MEAN IT. IT'S IMPORTANT. SAME WITH ILSA. — Don't worry. I won't. FYI, though: Ilsa was there in his office. They seemed, um, friendly.

I KNOW. THE MAN HAS NEVER FOUND A CLICHÉ HE WOULDN'T EMBRACE. It wasn't a cliché that he was embracing. THAT'S WHAT YOU THINK.

Found FXC's name on a passenger manifest — she took a ship from NYC to São Paulo in Nov. 1959. Never came back, as far as I can tell. SO YOU THINK SHE WAS IN NY BETWEEN '49 + THEN? Winged Shoes Press had an office space until Jan. 1960 (evicted for nonpayment). She never responded — obv., she was already gone. AND SHE DIED A FEW YEARS LATER.

SO YOU THINK SHE LIVED LONGER?
She might have. God — what if she were still alive? UM... SHE'D BE OVER 100... I know you think it's crazy. I DON'T SAY "CRAZY." YOU KNOW THAT.

There's no official death record. And the headstone in that guy's photo doesn't show her name. Someone just told him it was hers.

disappear below. Another of the sailors, a slightly-built lad whose lips have been strung into an eternal pout but who, under normal circumstances, would probably be thought beautiful and set girls' hearts aflutter, nonchalantly nudges a dark pile of detritus with his toe. S. squints, studies the pile; he gasps aloud when he realizes he is looking at a heap of fire-blackened bones, broken open and scraped of their marrow.

OTHER ANIMALS?
OR HIS CREWMEN?

The bat-eared man enters the cabin at the aft end of the main deck along with a pot-bellied sailor with comically skinny legs and whose bristly, graying beard reminds S. of a push-broom. Immediately their whistles flock and soar. When the two re-emerge onto the deck, Bat-Ears is cradling the gaunt body of a very young man in tattered, filthy canvas; the body is still, but not stiff. In the round, bearded sailor's arms: a baby, wrapped in soiled rags. S.'s heart plummets.

It is only when the two sailors approach the rail that S. realizes his mistake: the baby is not a baby. It is a bedraggled monkey with but a few scabby tufts of fur clinging to its skin. S. jumps when he hears a familiar rasp in his ear: *Lad oughta et the monk'.*

Weepin hearts don' lass aseas.

MONKEY AS
ANOTHER ITERATION OF S.

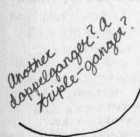

Another doppelganger? a triple-ganger?

OR MAYBE IT'S JUST
VMS RESISTING THE
EASY SYMBOLISM OF
"THIS = THAT."
OR HAVING A MORE COMPLICATED
NOTION OF IDENTITY...

{ 54 }

MOODY LIKES TO
QUOTE THIS.

What a tool.

"Will he live?" S. stammers.

Dint I jus' ware y' on weepin hearts?

"I don't care. I just need to know that you'll try to save him." (Another realization: if he had any sort of medical training in his old life, it has not made the trip along with him. He has no idea what, if anything, can be done for the sick young man.)

He migh' still ha' somt t'give.

S. means to press him on his meaning, but just then the unconscious boy convulses and coughs up a fine mist, a sunrise-pink spray;[6] the sailors march on impassively, not even pausing to wipe their faces clean, and they carry him into the disused chartroom, shutting the door behind them. S.'s throat tightens, and he finds himself close to tears.

Maelstrom grabs him by the back of the neck, steers him around so their faces nearly touch. Up close, S. can see little snakes of white hair creeping through his torrential black beard, can see the rheum that rims his eyes, can smell his sharply metallic breath. *Y'ought be more heedin where y'put y'spires, he says. Misprendins a finn way a'get y'proper dead.* He shoves S. away so roughly

---

6 Careful readers will here recall the "Plague Morning" section of the priest's monologue in Part IV of *The Spotted Cat.*

{ 55 }

[handwritten: QUARANTINE → → ISOLATION OF THE ARTIST?]

[handwritten: I keep wondering why you don't seem as scared as I am.]

[handwritten: I AM SCARED.]

[handwritten: Doesn't feel that way.]

[handwritten: WELL, WE'RE DIFFERENT.]

[handwritten: Right.]

[handwritten: I haven't died before.]

[handwritten: ... IN WHICH PRIEST CREDITS FAITH IN SPIDER GOD FOR THE VILLAGE'S SURVIVAL. HOW IS THAT RELEVANT AT ALL?]

[handwritten: Another random code-footnote. Has to be.]

that S. trips over a coil of line and tumbles arse-over-kettle onto the deck. For a moment he fears he is headed overboard.

He clings to the foremast and raises himself up, breathing heavily, his blood pumping. He watches as Maelstrom descends to the main deck(where the sailors are transferring unlabeled crates from the hold of the small ship and stowing them below.) What might they contain? Nothing edible, of course; the starving young sailor would have broken into them when his situation became dire. *

When the other vessel has been emptied, there is a volley of whistles, and she is cut adrift. Sailors spring up into the tops, back at work. The sails are trimmed, and the xebec resumes its speedy charge over the waves. As the ghost ship drifts farther away, the tide pushes her into a quarter-turn that exposes her transom. It bears no name.

Meanwhile, the diseased monkey wanders around the deck, assessing its new home, and then pulls itself slowly into the mainmast rigging and settles in. [S. watches as one of the sailors holds up a piece of salt pork for the monkey to take, and he wonders, irritably, if that piece was to have been his own ration for the day.]

I don't know if this means anything, but there were some open boxes in Moody's office. I tried to see what was in them, but Ilsa moved + blocked my view – trying to be subtle, but it was definitely on purpose.

DO YOU THINK THEY THOUGHT YOU WERE PRYING? OR JUST CURIOUS?

Curious. I'm sure of it. I'm just some undergrad, right? What would I be searching for?

※ How was that steak, by the way? The one Serin bought?

BEST EVER. BACK TO RAMEN/PB&J NOW, THOUGH.

You know, you're almost 30. Might be time to update your diet.

NEED TO USE THE $ FOR WORK. AND HUNGER KEEPS YOU SHARP.

SO IS THE MONKEY S.'S FAMILIAR OR HIS RIVAL?

Or both... which is funny, I think.

BUT DARK, TOO — BEING AT ODDS WITH ANOTHER VERSION OF YOURSELF...

Isn't that { 56 } pretty much the definition of regret, though? I mean, you don't have to be some tortured artist (or scholar) to feel that way.

NEW RECORD FOR YOU. 118 NOTES. THAT'S 39.25 PER.

I'm wondering what a ¼ of a note would look like.

SHIP OF THESEUS

He migh' still ha' somt t'give. The words plague S. throughout the day as he totters about the ship in a daze (though whether that daze is the result of hunger, thirst, exhaustion, shock, or terror is unknowable). Some *what* to give? What are these people hoping to *get* out of him?

Apart from increased traffic in and out of the chart-room, the crew goes about its business as if nothing were different. They coil, they hoist, they trim, they traverse the tops with arachnid agility, they stitch, they holystone,* they scrape, they hammer, they whistle. And every three hours or so, by S.'s crude estimation, an exhausted and slack-jawed sailor struggles through the hatchway onto the main deck, blows his whistle, and replaces another sailor (sometimes on the deck, sometimes in the rigging, sometimes at the helm), who then disappears through the hatch to that deepest portion of the ship, which S. has never seen. Three hours later, that sailor rises, blows his whistle, rejoins the flow of work. Now that S. has watched the entire crew cycle through, he realizes they all seem bluer around the gills when they emerge. And if he's not mistaken, he's hearing muted expressions of pain from all about the ship.

IT'S DRAINING THEM

Handwritten margin notes:

CF. VMS ON ART VS. COMMERCE: BOTH EXTRACT FROM THE INDIVIDUAL, BUT FOR DIFFERENT REASONS + TO DIFFERENT ENDS.

Don't you give up a part of yourself when you devote yourself to anything?

SURE. BUT VMS THOUGHT ART RETURNED SOMETHING, TOO, + COMMERCE JUST EXTRACTED—NO MATTER WHAT IT PURPORTED TO GIVE BACK. IT'S A BIG THEME IN WINEBLOOD'S MINE AND, WELL, PRETTY MUCH EVERYTHING ELSE HE WROTE.

What about love? Where did that fit?

I GUESS THAT'S ONE OF THE BIG QUESTIONS.

I'm sure it was for Filomela

* Prague + Munich missing some of theirs too.

WEIRD. THE ARCHIVES REALLY NEED TO START TAKING SECURITY MORE SERIOUSLY.

Oxford + Paris have one each. Uppsala's (2013) are gone. Lima's not sure.

Now Paris says theirs is missing. You don't think it's the one Desjardins sent, do you?

I DON'T THINK HE'D DO THAT.

S. is torn. On the one hand, he thinks he should remain grateful that no one is asking him to do whatever is done in the bowels of the ship, that he should be content to remain ignorant of the crew's trials. On the other, this secret work must be connected to the reason he was stolen out of the city and put at the mercy of these men. It must be. As for the possibility that it isn't—that these two conundrums might run parallel, have nothing to do with each other—it is a possibility S. would prefer not to consider. There is only so much mystery a person can handle at once, particularly when he is buried in all of it.

That night, S. leaves his cabin, determined to gather intelligence about the lower decks. The sailor with the enormous bald head, standing watch outside the chart-room, offers no outward reaction as S., striving to look calm and of innocent motive, descends through the main hatch. Neither do the sailors on the second deck, who remain busied with their tasks of polishing, knotting, and mending as he passes them by and continues downward. At the third deck, he glances to one side and the other, sees no one. (He takes his first steps down toward the orlop deck, his stomach tightening with excitement

---

Margin notes (handwritten):

IGNORANCE
VS.
KNOWLEDGE

ALOOFNESS
VS.
EMPATHY

HOW'D YOU GET TO BE SUCH A GOOD RESEARCHER?

It took a library science class my sophomore year. One of my favorite classes ever.

WHAT WAS YOUR MOST FAVORITE?

Check out the Interlude.

ORLOP DECK: CAN'T BE SEEN → PRIVACY, SECRECY, DANGER. PASSENGER HAS NO ACCESS TO THE REAL WORLD OF THE SHIP.

and apprehension, when suddenly pain erupts in his head and stars flare in his vision. He cries out as he is pulled back up to the third deck by his hair, then heaved over a shoulder and carted up to the weather deck. He is tossed down roughly, landing chin-first on the planks. The sailors crowd around him, twisted looks of revulsion plain on their moonlit faces.)

Cursing softly, S. retreats to his cabin.

Days pass. And each time he thinks about trying again to sneak onto the orlop, his aching jaw reminds him that he'd be well-served to think about something else.

Early evening. The sun a pool of fire over the horizon. The winds, which have been scrolling indifferently, coalesce into a stiff sou'easter that pushes the ship briskly on its mysterious route. S. notes a change in the tones and patterns of the crew's whistles; something is happening, some change imminent. A buzzing insect swoops past his face and disappears into the sky behind the vast screen of sailcloth. A honeybee? At sea?

At the aft end of the deck, Maelstrom is reaching for the door to the chart-room when a particular whistle from the crow's nest catches his attention. S. watches him closely: the big man cocks his head,

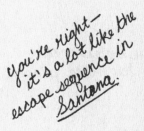

you're right — it's a lot like the escape sequence in Santana.

Bee as a reference to _apis_?

APIS ISN'T THE STRAKA CANDIDATE — HIS SECRETARY IS... ALTHOUGH THERE'S NO PROOF HE EVEN EXISTED. IF THAT'S STRAKA, THEN THE IDENTITY PROBLEM ISN'T SOLVED — JUST SHIFTED TO A GUY WHO'S EVERY BIT AS DEEP IN THE SHADOWS.

looks out over the starboard rail, unhooks a spyglass from his belt and extends it, then scans the horizon. He says something aloud—the rising wind beats down his words, keeping them from S.'s ear, but S. is nearly certain that his lips formed the shapes of *Land ho*. Then, slinging the spyglass shut and tucking it away (briefly catching it in the tangle of his beard), he disappears inside.

Does [the rescued young sailor still live? And what sort of treatment is he being subjected to? What, exactly, might the sailors be expecting him to give?] If S. were a braver man, he thinks, he would have investigated more aggressively. Knowing this young man's fate would surely shed some light on his own. Moreover, doesn't he owe the poor boy some sort of duty—at least of *trying* to do something to help him? But S.'s instinct has been to give death (or near-death) as wide a berth as possible, as his own might well be imminent.

He looks out to starboard, but if there's land, he can't see it with his naked eye. The ship does not appear to be adjusting its course, and S. wonders: if there is land out there, is that land their destination, the place where he will meet some unknown but almost certainly unpleasant fate? Or are they

He seems to in a few other places.

SEE DESJARDINS (1979) — WAS VMS PREDICTING HIS OWN DISAPPEARANCE?

You realize you do this, too, right?

(COWARDICE (BLAMING SELF FOR IT) — RECURRENT THEME

It's still not clear to me who would've wanted Straka dead.

MANY POSSIBILITIES — SOVIETS, US GOV'T, NAZI BITTER-ENDERS, SOME BALKAN FACTIONS... BUT ESPECIALLY BOUCHARD, I THINK.

AND ALSO THE S. (MACINNES'S VERSION)

It blows my mind. The guy just takes the name + completely turns around what it stands for.

Speaking of Desjardins — any word from him since ny?

I CALLED, EMAILED, WROTE... FEELING BLOWN OFF.

But it seemed like he was confiding in you at the auction, right?

YEAH, BUT HOLDING BACK, TOO. MAYBE I SHOULD JUST GO TO PARIS + SEE HIM. I'VE GOT ENOUGH $ FROM SERIN.

Eric Husch, International Man of Adventure!

planning to pass it by and continue on their mysterious course? Even if they are, and even if they pass within swimming distance of the land, there is a serious complication afflicting all of S.'s plans for escape: he does not know whether he is a strong swimmer, or whether he can even swim at all. He has a vague, atavistic sense that he has some connection with the water—and he remembers those voices from the Old Quarter, too, and wishes they hadn't gone silent—but he is reluctant to assume he'll be able to propel himself through it and not just sink like a stone.

Maelstrom remains inside the chart-room for five, ten minutes before exiting again and trudging forward over the deck, pausing briefly to scowl at a sloppily coiled line. When he looks up again, he meets S.'s gaze, and S. knows immediately that the big man is on his way to the forecastle for a word with him. He feels the usual gnarl of dread that fouls his insides when the man approaches, and, in addition, a more urgent sort of fear, as he cannot stop thinking about the bloody mist the young man coughed up and of the infectious agents that the big man is no doubt now carrying his way. Something on this ship is going to kill him, he feels certain. It's simply a matter of what.

FEAR/DOUBT RE: ONE'S OWN ABILITIES

We all have it, I guess. Had a paper to write last night (Yeats) + I froze up. Staring at a blank screen, + all I could think about was how much I miss my old life... before I realized I had to make decisions for myself. Then: what the hell am I doing + why? Have I ever really made any big decisions for myself? How much of my life so far has really been mine?

NOT SURPRISING THAT IT WAS HARD TO WRITE. HOW'D YOU GET THROUGH THE PAPER? Didn't. Read The Winged Shoes of Emydio Alves instead.

DID YOU GET AN EXTENSION? I haven't really asked. JEN, THAT'S NOT GOOD. No. But Winged Shoes is. Also, I'm getting really tired of doing things because other people tell me to. HONESTLY, I UNDERSTAND THAT. BUT GET OVER IT + MAKE SURE YOU GRADUATE. YOU'VE INVESTED TOO MUCH. That's the reasoning everyone uses to avoid doing anything new. NO, IT'S THE REASONING THAT'LL GET YOU A DEGREE IN TWO MONTHS.

[See top of next page]

Do we know where Straka was during the flu pandemic? Maybe this is a ref to it?

NOT SURE. SOMEONE CLAIMING TO BE VMS WROTE A EULOGY FOR AN OBSCURE SPANISH POET WHO DIED... IMPLIED HE'D SEEN THE POET IN BARCELONA WHILE THE GUY WAS SICK.

It's funny— We did a family trip to Barcelona once. The Old Quarter reminds me of it.

No one talks much about García Ferrara. He's a pretty good candidate, I think.

— NO ONE WANTS TO BE SOMEONE WHO SOLD OUT TO THE FASCISTS —
People seem to choose the Straka they want.
RIGHT.
WE ALL WANT TO THINK WE'RE OBJECTIVE...
[See top next page]

But then shrill whistles cascade from the crow's nest, stopping the big man mid-stride. He looks out at the western sky, and so much happens so quickly then that S. can scarcely note it all, and he will have difficulty keeping track of its sequence. The sinking sun has gone wine-purple, staining the whole western sky. The air turns suddenly and uncomfortably warmer, tropically heavy. [A sinister black bar of storm-cloud is rushing toward them from the southeast—it was nowhere, and then purling blackly with jaw-dropping velocity, and now it is here.] The wind doubles, then doubles in force again, howling through the rigging. Spray from the waves arcs over the deck. The monkey launches itself down to the deck and races for the hatch before a sailor slams it shut. The ship judders as waves skidding crosswise beat the hull. The sailors move with a new urgency, swift and agile, in the rigging and on the deck, reefing sails, securing gear on deck and below, with constant streams of whistles flowing and tucking into the winds between them.

The cloudbank unfurls, spreading an early night over the sky. Stroboscopic bursts of lightning flash from within it, more and more frequently, until it appears nearly constant. The rushing wind rises in

THIS WHOLE SCENE GAVE ME NIGHTMARES WHEN I ~~WAS~~ FIRST READ IT. AND THEN THE NEXT SUMMER, I WAS SUPPOSED TO SAIL TO VANCOUVER WITH MY UNCLE. I BACKED OUT AT THE LAST MINUTE. HE WAS FURIOUS. SAID HE'D RELIED ON ME + I'D LET HIM DOWN.

Did you ever explain it to him? That you were just scared?

NO. HE WASN'T THE KIND OF GUY WHO UNDERSTOOD THINGS LIKE THAT. NO ONE IN MY FAMILY IS.

If that kid were here, I would totally give him a hug.

{ 62 }

IF THAT KID WERE HERE, HE WOULD TOTALLY NOT LET YOU.

*There you go:
S. Ferrara deserved
better than he got
from people
THEN + NOW.*

*STILL DOESN'T
MEAN HE'S
STRAKA.*

pitch. S. knows he would be safer down in his cabin under a closed hatch, but the chaos of the storm might offer a chance of escape that he'll never have again. His cloudy mind clears instantly at the acuteness of the thought.

The ship rides high on a wave and crashes forward into a trough, submerging the forecastle in curiously green water and foam. S. climbs down to the main deck, white-knuckling the ladder, dripping and shocked by cold, and tucks himself into the shelter of the bulwark to windward. Sideways crash of wave, and a solid-looking slab of seawater looms above them, seeming to pause and expand. It crashes down with preternatural force, inundating the deck.

S. dimly registers another shift in the pitches and patterns of the whistles, and after a flurry of movement from the crew, and when he blinks his burning eyes clear, he sees a line of frothy silver tufts poke out one by one from the blackened sky, and the tufts elongate, stretching downward like stalactites, and then become churning, bruised-looking funnels of water—waterspouts dropping down in straight lines and heading directly toward the ship. He could never have imagined anything like it: when the tip of a funnel touches down onto the surface of the sea, water

*I knew this wasn't
the whole story.*

*IT'S STILL NOT AS
BIG A DEAL AS YOU
THINK IT IS. We are so past
the point where you
can get away w/ lying to me.
Even when you don't mean
to be doing it.*

and foam erupt around it. It is a terrifying marvel, a marvelous terror. S. is certain that nothing can or will survive amid such a concentrated expression of force. S. watches, half-stricken and half-fascinated, watches what might be imminent oblivion—his own, the sailors', the ship's—rumbling toward them. The wind feels dark-blue and electric, thrumming now with low frequencies along with the deafening high-pitched howl.[7] S. is soaked and weakened and numb, wracked with tremors, but he does not let himself look away. One spout reaches down with the accuracy and grace of a ballerina's foot. It touches the water, and there is a muted roar and rush, then the next spout, and the next, the sounds louder, the destructive force more evident, and then he sees Maelstrom, drenched and bleeding from a gash above one eye, tromping toward him, pointing, giving some sort of direction, but the storm drowns the words. S. looks up through the rigging at the nightmare sky and sees his end: the sacral tip of an ink-dark waterspout, churning and rushing, plunging from the sky right over the ship. Time slows, allowing him a thought, a

---

[7] For this sequence, Straka may have used as source material an account of a terrible storm in *The Tortugan Journals of Juan Blas Covarrubias* (which, despite the howls of some deluded readers, has been proved time and again to be a hoax). If this is the case, Straka must certainly have been having a laugh at the expense of the even-greater fools who believe he and the fictional pirate were one and the same.

{ 64 }

Handwritten margin notes:

SUMMERSBY: OBLIVION @ SEA

Explain?

HE RECORDED A CONFESSION IN HIS CABIN ON A LINER RIGHT BEFORE HE DIED. SAID HE WAS STRAKA, THOUGH EKSTROM HELPED W/ 1ST BOOK. HARD TO HEAR B/C OF NOISE—BUT IT'S PRETTY DETAILED. I'M THE ONE WHO TRACKED IT DOWN. (SUMM.'S LAWYER'S DAUGHTER HAD IT IN HER ATTIC.) BUT MOODY WANTED IT, + ILSA STOLE IT FOR HIM.

So you've got reason to be mad. Why not announce it yourself? Beat Moody to it?

I NEED THE RECORDING. NO CREDIBILITY W/ JUST A TRANSCRIPT. ALSO: I'M NOT SURE I STILL BUY EVERYTHING SUMMERSBY SAID. FEELS TOO EASY.

Could I see the transcripts? Do you trust me enough?

((THANKS.))

The pirate again? It seems like a running joke between Straka + Caldeira. Maybe they're having a laugh at the reader's expense?

I DON'T THINK HE'D DO THAT. HE HAD A SENSE OF HUMOR, BUT HE WOULDN'T INTERRUPT A SERIOUS BOOK TO DO SOMETHING LIKE THAT.

Maybe Filomela was doing it on her own, then. Keeping the joke going = keeping him alive.

strange, wordless association of color and shape: the waterspout and the drink in the young woman's glass. Then a collapse into singular doom: pressure punches his ears; black fills all the space above him; his limbs loosen with a warm readiness for death.

He may or may not scream, he won't recall, but there is a tremendous crash and boom, and the main-mast disappears, instantly [transformed into tens of thousands of chunks and splinters that blast across the deck and embed themselves in skin.] Amid the tumult, he registers a different set of sounds—sharp creaks and a snap—and the mizzenmast falls to port, caving the bulwark—and shreds of sail and rope are battering them as they fall from above, and in all of this, S. hears one word in his mind, in a voice that is not his, not Maelstrom's, not the ghost-voices of the Old Quarter—it is stronger and deeper, it is the ancient voice of self-preservation jolted awake from a sleep of æons, and it calls to him: SWIM.

The ship soars over a creaming head of a wave, and then all is weightless, and then there is the crash into the trough, and S. lets the impact carry him up, up, into the blinding churn of foam and rope and splinter and scream, and he himself is sailing, sailing until the raging sea rushes to meet him. His landing

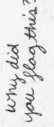

{ 65 }

why did you flag this?

WHO KNOWS? I'VE BEEN WRITING IN THIS BOOK SINCE I WAS 15.

NOTE: SUMMERSBY INJURED BY SHRAPNEL IN WWI

Is it ever hard for you to read this section?

USED TO BE. ALTHOUGH SOMETIMES IT COULD BE REALLY EXCITING, TOO.

How come you're doubting Summersby's confession?

BEEN THINKING ABOUT HIS STYLE. HIS BOOKS ARE PRETTY STRAIGHTFORWARD—LINEAR PLOTS, WORKMANLIKE LANGUAGE. I CAN SEE AN ARGUMENT THAT NIGHT PALISADES OR SANTANA MARCH READ LIKE SUMMERSBY'S STUFF, BUT TRIPTYCH? WASHINGTON + GREENE? WINGED SHOES? CORIOLIS?

Isn't that like the Shakespeare argument? Is it really so hard to write in different styles?

HEY, I WANT HIM TO BE VMS.

No you don't. B/c Moody has the tape, and you don't.

Wonder what she would've done if she'd
known she had those pages.

SHE KNEW SHE HAD THEM.
SHE JUST DIDN'T WANT TO KNOW WHAT
WAS ON THEM.

... AND EVEN THEN IT DEPENDS ON
WHICH VERSION. ———

It's a good
question. Hard to tell
if he's taking a stand
on it. Not until Ch. 10

"BIRTHED" →
ANOTHER REINVENTION
OF THE SELF. BUT IS IT
A SEPARATE SELF OR A
CONTINUOUS ONE?

THERE'S DANGER
IN TRANSITION/CHANGE/
REINVENTION

↓

Which is why
it's so easy to
avoid until you
don't have a
choice anymore.

is not a soft one. The surface tension is a bludgeon, pushes all the air from inside him, twists his neck, loosens his limbs, and then, with a curious, dreamy detachment, S. feels himself birthed downward into the salty, foamy black, the sea pulling and pulling at him, spinning him, twirling him, filling his mouth and nose and throat with salt, until the old voice calls again—*Swim!*—and some reflex in S. responds—a kick, perhaps, or a stroke from an arm that S. had assumed was shattered, then more kicks (desperate and fluttery, even in the half-speed of underwater), and a sharpening sense of orientation—yes, he is pointed up toward the surface—and kicks, and paddles, and then he bursts through to the air and sucks in a desperate gulp. He is immediately hurled back under by a wave, but he rises again, and kicks, and paddles, and at some point his movements come into phase; rhythm finds him, joins him as he strokes through the vicious waves, he is pulled under now and then but always finds the air once more, all of this until the voice tells him, *Stop. Look.* and he sees the knuckle of land—firelight along its shoreline, a dome of sodium light atop a hill. It must be two miles away, or three, or four, farther than he can imagine he has ever swum, but he points himself

———

toward the light and strokes and strokes and rides the waves that offer themselves in the service of his momentum. He briefly wonders how much distance is between him and the wreckage of the ship, whether any sailors remain and are pursuing him in the dinghy, but he cannot bring himself to look back, he will not look back, he can only stroke and kick and will his body incrementally toward the harbor lights, try to keep his head above the waves.

SAME PHRASE @ END OF SUMMERSBY TAPE
(EXCEPT w/ "MY" INSTEAD OF "HIS").
WHY?? DOESN'T MAKE HIS CONFESSION ANY
LESS CONVINCING — SOT HAD ALREADY BEEN
PUBLISHED, SO ANYONE COULD QUOTE IT.

a code?
a signal to
someone else?

———

WHATEVER THE REASON,
IT SOUNDS LIKE HE KNEW
HE'D DIE WHEN HE WENT
UP TO THE DECK. HE KNEW
THESE WOULD BE THE LAST
WORDS HE'D SPEAK.

CHAPTER 3

THE EMERSION OF S.

YOU'RE NOT SAYING S. IS A CELESTIAL BODY, ARE YOU?

I don't know. I haven't seen him.

"(((RIMSHOT)))"

I just think it's

SHARP ROCKS dig into S.'s skin as he rests on all fours beneath a pier, coughing seawater. The shorewash burbles around him, approaching and retreating, but he senses the wavelets only as abstractions, ghosts of motion running over his skin; he is too numb to register any more cold. He hugs himself, shivering, between each paroxysm of heaves. All he has on are these sad trousers—threadbare things that seem in danger of tearing from the weight of the water they hold. (The overcoat? Left behind in the cabin, and with it, whatever remains of that sodden scrap of paper.) And what of the befouled sailors' attire he was given? The sea-churn must have torn it from him,

2ND TIME S. HAS EMERGED FROM WATER.

I keep thinking about that paper. We know the S. symbol is on it. What else? Does it matter?

MOST PEOPLE THINK IT'S JUST A MacGUFFIN.

OK, that's my new favorite word.

interesting, given what happens w/ stars in ch. 2.

although he doesn't remember this happening. So: these sorry trousers are his only possession, his only connection to a stolen past.[1]

Once his lungs have emptied and his breath returns in more than an agonized wheeze, he stands, slowly, bracing himself on an algae-slick piling. He turns, taking his footing carefully, and scans the water for signs of the ship, of the sailors, of a dinghy or a launch or any sort of pursuit. All he sees is the darkly undulating surface of the harbor, striated with modest wave-breaks; the bleed of streetlight and firelight coloring the mist; and, several miles distant, a thick drape of fog obscuring the horizon. Perhaps the ship weathered the storm; perhaps it's lying at the bottom of the sea. He suspects, though, that even if he'd witnessed the ship being sucked into the deep, even if he'd counted the bodies of twenty men and one monkey strewn over the water, he'd still be stealing anguished glances over his shoulder for the rest of his life. As far as he can tell, though—for now—he is free. Spent, starved, chilled, and ignorant of whether he has landed in friendly or hostile territory—but free nonetheless,

---

1 Cf. the character of Franzl in Straka's *The Square*: a solitary man with no possessions, he is spotted for the first time in Chicago as he emerges from the waters of Lake Michigan just five days before the infamous massacre at Haymarket Square.

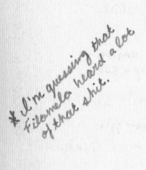

*I'm guessing that Filomela heard a lot of that shit.

YOU KNOW, THAT'S MAKING SENSE TO ME NOW. (MAYBE I'M SPENDING TOO MUCH TIME WITH YOU.)

You're *not* spending time with me.

SOON—I SWEAR. CAN'T SLOW DOWN NOW.

How is meeting me going to slow you down? I'm helping you. If you can't see that, I should just walk away.

I JUST NEED TIME, THAT'S ALL. *

FRANZL + S. ACT VERY DIFFERENTLY @ PROTESTS. VMS RECYCLING PLOTLINES, USING IN DIFF. WAYS. SO: SOT AS A LOOK BACK AT HIS BOOKS, SHOWING HOW THE STORIES MIGHT'VE BEEN WRITTEN DIFFERENTLY.

And maybe how his *life* might've gone differently?

REACHING.

IT'S 10 DAYS, NOT 5. → Might be a signal. FXC EVEN TRYING TO GET THE DETAILS RIGHT? Pointing to FN 5?

ALSO: F. ISN'T SPOTTED—HE SNEAKS { 70 } → But check out the IN. THAT'S THE "s" in "spotted." WHOLE POINT.

This chapter has me thinking about <u>Vaclav Straka</u>, too, though. This intro, plus the scene at the end... what if he survived his jump + then became VMS? This could be his way of writing about it — or even revealing it.

OR: JUST A COINCIDENCE

OR (MORE LIKELY): THE REAL VMS TRYING TO LEAD PEOPLE TO THINK HE WAS SOME KIND OF GHOST. FIGURATIVELY, AT LEAST.

OR: VMS messing with <u>people</u> fixated on figuring out who he is.

IT'S FUNNY THAT VACLAV STRAKA IS EVEN A CANDIDATE. HE'S NOTHING BUT A NAME AND A RUMOR. HIS NAME WAS STRAKA, AND SOMEONE— ONE PERSON— SUGGESTED HE MAY HAVE WANTED TO BE A WRITER. THAT'S ALL.

and he'll be damned if he'll allow those ghouls to find him again.

He very nearly drowned; he knows this. A quarter-mile from shore, with his strength ebbing and waves breaking steeply over his head, he'd been certain that he could go no farther. A rip current had seized and spun him, begun tugging him back out to deeper water. The survival voice might still have been urging him to swim, but it was overwhelmed by his own thoughts suggesting that it would not be so bad simply to cease his struggles, to put no more effort into these feeble, desperate efforts, to ride the tidal pull back out to sea and sink into oblivion.[2] He became aware that his mind was entertaining two utterly contradictory impulses at once, and in the pause that came with this revelation, a third thought offered itself with a quiet clarity: that if only he could rest, gather his strength, he could figure out which of those positions was truer to the person he was, and he could *choose* what to do instead of simply doing it. This—curious as it seems to him now,

Still can't find a single trace of him. Nothing. And I'm pretty good at finding things.

YOU ARE. IT'S SCARY HOW GOOD YOU ARE.

The underlining makes me think you had a moment like that... (you can talk about it if you want to...)

FUNNY TO CALL THIS "TALKING."

Yeah, it is (also: that was a total evasion.)

YES, I HAD A MOMENT LIKE THAT + GOT THROUGH IT— AND I'M NEVER GOING BACK

---

[2] Had Straka lived to review my final revisions of this translation, he likely would have quarreled with my choice to use *oblivion* here. His original phrasing translates directly as *not-being*, which I find nonsensical. How can one fail to be? If one is, one is. (Of course, the philosopher—and curiously popular Straka candidate—Guthrie MacInnes could no doubt fill up several volumes addressing such matters. I have concluded, though, that it is far better simply to be than to obsess over what, who, or even whether one is.)

CALDEIRA OFFERING HIS PHILOSOPHY OF LIFE IN THIS FN.

TOTALLY INAPPROPRIATE. ~~He~~ *She sounds sincere, though. Maybe a direct message to Straka: be <u>real</u> and <u>live</u>!*

AS ADVICE GOES, IT'S PRETTY MUCH A CLICHÉ.

with solid earth under him—seemed then like the most important consideration of all.

With his next stroke, his hand came down on something floating in the water, an enormous metal ball with spikes radiating outward from it, spikes that made for excellent handholds, and he hugged himself tightly to it, rising and falling in the waves that continued to pound down on him, resting and breathing and realizing that he was—or wanted to be, anyway—the sort of person who would damned well swim the last quarter-mile and drag himself from the water to safety, to life. He found himself thinking of the woman from the bar and wishing with a sudden and surprising intensity that he could see her again simply to tell her of this conclusion he'd drawn about himself.[3]

He remembered, then, that flash of connection—the waterspout, her drink. A message from some deep recess of his mind: he was not a stranger to her. Sola? Absurd, on the face of it, but true somewhere beneath, and when he pushed off from the harbor mine, that truth helped drive him to shore.

---

[3] A typical Strakean tragedy: the epiphany that comes too late to be shared. The critics Torremolino and Holt have both written extensively on this subject, although without any noteworthy insight.

{ 72 }

Handwritten margin notes:

IRONY: INSTRUMENT OF DESTRUCTION AS LIFE-SAVER

S. sounds a little lonely. Even desperate.

DO YOU KNOW ABOUT RYBARIK? THE GUY WHO SAID HE KNEW VACLAV STRAKA FROM THE FACTORY? HE SAID V WAS MADLY IN LOVE W/ A GIRL WHO ALSO WORKED THERE + JUMPED OFF THE BRIDGE WHEN SHE TURNED HIM DOWN.

Did she ever confirm that?

NO ONE KNOWS WHO SHE WAS (OR IF SHE EXISTED). RYBARIK COULDN'T REMEMBER HER NAME.

[JEEZ. You'd think he'd at least try to make one up.]

← I KNOW. AS STRAKA FRAUDS GO, HIS WASN'T VERY GOOD.

MORE "CRITICS" WHO DIDN'T EXIST. FLAG THIS ONE FOR POSS. CODING? not getting anything yet. you?

A RED HERRING?

SHIP OF THESEUS

The city is a small one, with a waterfront dominated by a vast brick factory building that runs hundreds of yards in each direction and looms over a wharf and a network of long, narrow piers. The size of the factory and the extent of its infrastructure would fail to attract notice in a major port city like Marseille or Odessa or Boston but seems incongruous in a modest burg such as this.

Now, echoing above him on the wharf are the sounds of a disturbance: shouts and catcalls and threats, stamping feet and heavy sticks beating on the boards, amplified voices leading chants. The chant that rings out most frequently and with greatest intensity: *Tell us where they are. Tell us where they are.* He knows nothing about the conflict, of course, but he finds himself siding with the demonstrators, the ones who've lost their people. He has, too. He's lost everyone, including himself.

The air has an autumnal feel, much cooler than it was earlier today on the ship—such a radical change that S., for a moment, imagines he has swum across many degrees of latitude. Of course such a notion is absurd; it may even be a sign that his mind is slipping, that the long, cold swim has gravely compromised

1ST OF THE FEW CONCRETE GEOGRAPHICAL REFS. IN THE BOOK.

Funny to read this today, when it finally started to feel like spring around here.

THIS WINTER WAS FUCKING BRUTAL. WENT ON FOREVER.

Pollard = Winter City? SURE FELT LIKE IT.

MAY, 1936, SANTORINI. BODY HAD NO ID, NO FINGERPRINTS, NO POSSESSIONS BESIDES HIS CLOTHES + A TORN PAGE FROM BRAXENHOLM. GREEK GOV'T DENIES IT EVER HAPPENED, BUT THERE ARE DOCS, EVEN A PHOTO OF THE BODY (BLURRY, OF COURSE). RUMORS THAT THERE WERE 15-20 MORE DEATHS LIKE THIS, ALL OVER THE WORLD. ALL W/O ID'ABLE FINGERPRINTS, ALL W/NO CLEAR CAUSE OF DEATH, ALL IN THE WATER, ALL W/A STRAKA PAGE (BUT DIFF. BOOKS) IN A POCKET. DESJARDINS WAS REALLY INTERESTED IN THESE—THOUGHT THEY MIGHT BE CONNECTED TO VMS + BOUCHARD. FITS W/ THE INTERLUDE, OBVIOUSLY.

What if that game is still going on?

I DON'T THINK IT WAS EVER A GAME.

SHIP OF THESEUS

him, that he might be at risk of blacking out and departing this world as an anonymous bit of human jetsam pinned under a wharf beneath a strange city.

** SANTORINI MAN

He has no more time to waste waiting for his body to discover reservoirs of strength. He must move. He must act. First: find dry clothing. Instinct tells him he should avoid others—after all, those sailors might've been planning to bring him to this place (if only he'd had even the smallest hint of what their intentions had been!)—but reason tells him he needs assistance. He pushes himself away from the piling, takes a few tentative steps over the jagged and shifting rocks and oyster shells—it will be a wonder if he does not end up with lacerations on his feet—and he emerges from beneath the pier, takes a gulp of air into his grumpy lungs, and then clambers slowly up the thirty feet of rocky slope toward the commotion. At the top, he leans over, hands on knees, catching his breath, and takes in the scene before him.

The long factory is skirted on three sides by wide, flat stretches of asphalt, and S. has emerged onto a dark and quiet corner of the lot, beyond the fringes of the demonstration. Hundreds of people have gathered there; some are waving fists in the air, others waving lit torches, still others waving signs:

Ilsa came to the library today. I don't think she recognized me. which is weird, because she sees me in class twice a week.

SHE ONLY PAYS ATTENTION TO PEOPLE WHO CAN HELP HER ADVANCE.

Something happened between you two, didn't it?

WELL, SHE STOLE MY SUMMERSBY TAPE + GAVE IT TO MOODY. ALSO: SHE DIDN'T HAVE MY BACK WHEN HE TURNED THE DEPT. AGAINST ME. NOTHING BIG, THOUGH.

Um, OK... Anyway: she said Moody wants a list of everyone who's used the archive this year. Says he's concerned about "integrity." [Insert Eric's sarcastic laugh here.]

DID YOU GIVE IT TO HER? Told her I need time to compile it. But I'll have to give it to her soon. It's my job.

KEEP YOURSELF OFF THAT LIST. Of course. And I'll make a copy for you too—in the interest of fairness. (You're welcome.) Now, will you admit

you had a thing for Ilsa?

YOU'VE ALREADY DECIDED THAT. So I'm right.

{ 74 } YES, YOU'RE RIGHT. DOES THAT BOTHER YOU? Of course not. It's kind of reassuring to know you're capable of actually interacting with people.

WHERE ARE THE ZAPADI 3?

LITTLE VÉVODA STEALS JOBS & PEOPLE.

WHAT HAVE YOU DONE WITH
OUR FRIENDS?

VÉVODA, YOUR FATHER SPINS IN
HIS GRAVE.

FACTORY BOSSES: SERVE A MONSTER,
BECOME A MONSTER.

Squads of burly men in dark-brown dusters form a line of defense around the factory, on which VÉVODA ARMAMENT WORKS is painted in crisp, black block letters.[4] They radiate an unmistakable potential—and perhaps even a taste—for violence.

As cold as S. is, he wants to approach with care, so he clamps his chattering jaws shut, wraps his arms around himself, squats and rises to keep moving, and sizes up the scene. The crowd is most dense near the entrance to the older-looking half of the factory, and in the middle of it stands a

---

4 Those who believe the young, ill-educated factory worker Vaclav Straka was *the* Straka will no doubt point out that young Vaclav worked in a munitions factory prior to his untimely plunge from the Charles Bridge. They would be well-advised to remember that the sources are not in agreement. (One asserts that Vaclav's employer, Novacek & Sons, produced ladies' shoes, and another is equally certain that it was a facility in which pencils were made.)

{ 75 }

Handwritten margin notes:

CZECH FOR "DUKE"— SUGGESTS SOMEONE W/ RECOGNIZED POWER.

DYNASTY (CF. THE BOUCHARDS)

VERBATIM FROM THE SQUARE (P. 88)

Is this true?

THAT SOURCES CONFLICT? YES. BUSINESS FOLDED ALMOST IMMEDIATELY, SO RECORDS ARE SKETCHY.

Getting nowhere w/ this. Maybe there's more than one Ch. 3 code?

OR A BUNCH OF FXC MISDIRECTIONS.

Why is she bringing up the ambiguity at all? If it was a munitions factory, then there's a clear connection between S. /VMS & Vévoda/Bouchard. Why wouldn't she emphasize that?

And also: why does she sound so dismissive of the Vaclav theory here? She doesn't in the Foreword.

YOU'RE RIGHT—SEEMS INCONSISTENT.

makeshift and lopsided-looking dais on which a man and a woman stand shoulder-to-shoulder—the leaders of this movement, by all appearances. They take turns addressing the crowd through a megaphone, urging perseverance and restraint. Both of their voices are hoarse with overuse. (Their shoulders brush against each other as they move, a striking and unexpected intimacy in a situation such as this.) Both of them seem at ease with managing the angry and volatile crowd, and even with facing the impressive phalanx of strikebreakers, who almost certainly are concealing weapons beneath their heavy coats. If it were not for the calm, charismatic presence of the man and the woman on the dais, S. surmises, events here at the factory might well have turned bloody already.

Roof-mounted spotlights sweep the perimeter of the building, dramatically illuminating the guards, then plunging them into yawning shadow, over and over. Despite the crowd of workers on the wharf, the factory is operating at full churn. Incandescent lights burn behind windows that have been boarded up against gazes and projectiles. Smoke and embers rise from the mighty stacks that run the entire length of the building.

Interesting — affection between them is immediately apparent — even in such a strange context. you never got my hins here. I kept waiting for you to say something.

I GOT IT. I JUST DIDN'T KNOW WHAT TO SAY.

Why did you underline that?

DON'T KNOW. MUST'VE REALLY LIKED THAT LINE AT SOME POINT.

Is it interesting to look back + see everything that you've responded to? Like this is a scrapbook of all your younger selves. (Funny how distant you can get from them.)

I DON'T THINK I'M DISTANT FROM THEM. THEY'RE ALL ME. I JUST DON'T REMEMBER EVERY LITTLE THING ABOUT THEM.

I'll take distance. The further I get from the little girl who did what everyone told her, the better.

THIS IS A SCRAPBOOK OF YOU + ME, TOO. I know. *Feel like everything I do here is going on my permanent record. (OK, not permanent — but as long as the* { 76 } *book exists.)*

NO WAY I'M EVER LETTING GO OF THIS BOOK. You let go of it every day. sometimes 2 or 3 times!

THAT DOESN'T COUNT.

Ship of Theseus

The gap between the front line of the protestors and the guards is narrow. The guards are holding their ground, their arms folded across their chests, but are not pushing back yet—although a single jabbing finger or spray of saliva could loose the violence coiled within them. Common sense tells him: quietly turn away from the seething scene before you. Slip around the edge of it, disappear into the quiet city streets, and find yourself some dry clothes. Find a place to sleep. Find food. A cheap rooming-house, perhaps. Get rest, so the world can start to make sense again. Survive the night. Then, maybe, find paper and pen. Write down what you know, and what you suspect, about yourself—even if that won't yet fill a single page. And then, maybe then, start piecing together who you are.

He starts walking around the edge of the wharf, giving the demonstrators a wide berth and keeping to the deepest shadows, where he notices a few dozen uninterested-looking police officers eyeing the action and muttering to each other, doing nothing to restore calm to the situation. He could go to them for help, but something tells him to stay away. *Be more heedin' where y'put y'spires.* He steps past them without their noticing.

> *and often.*
>
> WRITING AS KEY TO IDENTITY. ECHOED LATER.
>
> ONE ARGUMENT: FEUERBACH (GERMAN ANARCHIST) WAS VMS, + CH. 3 SHOWS HE WAS INVOLVED IN HAYMARKET BOMBING BEFORE HE FLED BACK TO EUROPE. DIED IN '40.
>
> *He died in 1940... Who wrote the last few books then?*
>
> ARG. IS THAT THEY WERE JUST PUBLISHED POSTHUMOUSLY.
>
> *I don't buy it. Filo. wouldn't have fallen for him like this.*
>
> YOU MEAN B/C HE WAS PROBABLY GAY? THAT SORT OF THING HAPPENS...
>
> *She wouldn't do all of this if she didn't sense Straka was returning the feeling in some way.*
>
> CAN'T ASSUME YOU UNDERSTAND HER COMPLETELY. ALL YOU HAVE IS HER WRITING — AND NOT MUCH OF IT.
>
> *You realize what you just ~~said~~ wrote, right?*

> *Turns out Hoeppner article + Ryborik interview were both in mags owned by Bouchard companies.*

REPORTER (HOEPPNER, I THINK?)
FOR A GERMAN MAG TRACKED DOWN FEUERBACH
IN '37 — CLAIMED HE WAS LIVING NEAR HEIDELBERG,
SUPPORTED BY ANARCHIST GROUPS WHO REVERED HIM
FOR HAYMARKET.
NAZIS WENT AFTER HIM
AFTER ARTICLE CAME OUT.
HE GOT AWAY — ENDED UP
IN DUBLIN — DIED THERE.

In a fall?

YEAH — HE WAS SICK —
MAYBE ~~NOT~~ TERMINALLY —
BUT IT WAS THE FALL
THAT DID IT.

Two dark figures break away from the crowd of demonstrators and walk toward him, waving. *Come over here,* one of them says, his voice cutting through the rough thunder of the protest. S. knows he can't outrun them; his muscles are leaden and spent, and he is still panting, with a saline burn in every shallow breath and a mist of ocean coming up with every cough. He sighs deeply and obliges. He's got to take his chances on someone, and the demonstrators seem like a better bet than the police.

They meet about fifty paces shy of the crowd's edge. One of the men appears to be nearly forty, with receding hair, a deeply-lined forehead, a neatly-trimmed beard of reddish brown, and a stern look that fails to mask what S. immediately senses as a much softer nature. The other, perhaps ten years younger, has a full head of unruly dark waves, deeply pockmarked cheeks, and patchy facial hair that has grown long; the mustache ends in wide-spread wings, the beard in a caprine drape. This man's glare seems to issue from deep within, and the pinched, rabbity expression on his face unnerves S. Has he been too trusting already? Will these people, who are also seeking the lost, fail to share the affinity S. felt for them? Has he crawled out of

Found a photo of F'bach! He looks nothing like Pfeifer — but the young guy w/ him does.

↳ THAT'S PROBABLY
HORST WECHSLER —
FEUERBACH'S
"SECRETARY" (ACC. TO
THE ARTICLE).

UNCLEAR
ALLEGIANCES

———

the sea only to make a fatal error with his first decision on land?

It is as these thoughts are gathering urgency and
pushing their way through the half-frozen quies-
cence of S.'s thoughts that the younger man lunges
forward, grabs his arms, and pins them behind his
back. Pain shoots through S.'s shoulders and neck.
He cries out involuntarily.

"Who are you?" the older man asks. "What's
your name?"

S. is slow to answer. "I'm told it's—"

The younger man interrupts. "It doesn't matter
what his name is," he says. "What matters is who
he's working for." He tightens his grip, gives S.
another painful shake. "Tell us. Who are you working for?"

"No one," S. says. As far as he knows, he speaks
the truth.

"Just out for a swim?" the older man asks.

"I was on a ship—"

The younger man laughs, a short, sharp bray.
"Didn't I tell you?" he says to his companion. "I
knew Vévoda would try to sneak in more Detectives by sea." Then, to S.: "Where are the rest of
your people?"

———

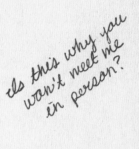

Is this why you won't meet me in person?

CF. CALAIS STRIKE/
MASSACRE OF 1912.
VMS OBV. EQUATING.
NOT EVEN TRYING TO
BE SUBTLE.

Everything goes back to Calais—
Straka trying to expose
Bouchard, and Bouchard
fighting back.

"I don't have any people," S. says.[5]

"What happened to your ship?" the older man asks.

"It was damaged in a storm. It may have sunk."

"Serves you right," the young man says. "Working for a man like Vévoda. Damned mercenary."

The older man looks out to the open water. "I don't see any ships out there."

"There was a storm," S. explains. "A waterspout came down right on us."

"The weather's been fine today."

"The storm came from the south," S. says. "It wasn't over land. And I swam a long way. Miles."

His interrogators share a look, each gauging the extent of the other's belief in S.'s tale.

"You don't seem concerned about your ship-mates," the older man says.

"Mercenaries only care about one thing," the younger man scoffs.

"Or maybe he's stalling us while his shipmates are fanning out across the waterfront."

---

5 It is interesting, perhaps, that history has recorded that very few of the most often-mentioned candidates for authorship (silly as some of those theories may be) were married or had children. (Guthrie MacInnes, Béla Álmos Ujváry, and Tiago García Ferrara are the only ones of which I am aware.) It is as if the reading body-politic shares, across cultures, an aversion to believing that men could produce works (and live a life) of such intensity and integrity (and gravitas, really) without cutting themselves off from spouses, children, and intimate friends. I feel compelled to stress how vigorously I reject such stunted and antiquated views.

{ 80 }

Handwritten margin notes:

★ YOU SHOULD TELL YOUR PROFS (+ ILSA) SOMETHING ABOUT WHY YOU WERE GONE. It won't matter. No one's going to cut me slack anymore.

I don't have much hope for the disciplinary committee, either. You know they'll believe Ilsa over me.

I'LL WRITE A LETTER. They're sure as hell not going to believe you.

YOU'RE RIGHT. I JUST WISH I COULD DO SOMETHING.

AGAIN: DETAILS MATCH UP W/ CALAIS

→ MISSPELLS "MACINNES"!

A signal, not a mistake. An extra "s" here, and chapter title has S. in it LOOK:

All below an "s!" (Plus: the "5 days" in FN 1 prob points to FN 5.)

"EMERSION OF S" → S COMING UP FROM THE WATER...? MAYBE SOMETHING ABOUT THE LETTERS BELOW THE MARKED LETTERS? (BUT WHAT ABOUT THE ONES ON THE BOTTOM LINE?) If you take the letters on either side of each S. you get ARP IS BOUCHARD IS HW.

ARP SYNDIKAT — DUTCH WEAPONS MFR. STILL EXISTS. DIDN'T KNOW THEY WERE CONNECTED TO BOUCHARD. (+ SINCE FXC WAS WRITING THESE TO VMS, HE MUST NOT HAVE KNOWN EITHER.) what if HW was Horst Wechsler? THEN VMS WAS IN REAL DANGER.

"I don't—I don't have any shipmates," S. says.

"Not anymore, apparently."

(("I never did," S. tells them. He can feel his tone sharpening as he loses patience. "I was shanghaied. I don't know why. I don't know who they were or why they wanted me. They fed me, but barely. The storm gave me a chance to get away, and I took it. I swam, I'm here, and I'm *cold*."))

The two factory men look at each other. S. can tell that they're feeling doubt for the first time. The older man scratches his bald head self-consciously, as if to prove to S. that he is, in fact, thinking. "He does look wretched," the older man observes. "He's all bones. Why would the Detectives employ someone in a condition like this?"

"Because we wouldn't expect them to," the younger man says. "They'd take advantage of our kindness. To men like Vévoda, kindness is a resource to be exploited, like coal or zinc."

Shouts flare up from the crowd, louder and angrier. The young man looks around excitedly. His grip on S. remains solid.

"Who are the Zapadi Three?" S. asks. "What happened to them?"

"Don't pretend you don't know," the young man says.

Margin notes (handwritten):

Found a record of Wechsler as a passenger on a ship leaving Dublin for Liverpool—one week before Feuerbach ~~died~~ was killed.

NOTHING ABOUT HIM IN LIVERPOOL? Nope. Vanished somewhere over the water. Just like Summersby.

ONE DIFFERENCE: HW LIVED.

Ha! I love this line!

CF. CH. 8

MACINNES-AS-VMS THEORY FINDING ADHERENTS AGAIN. GROUP AT LISBON CONF. WAS REALLY STRIDENT ABOUT IT. BIG CROWDS. HEARD THEY WERE V. WELL-FUNDED, TOO.

By whom?

ALL IT TAKES IS ONE INSANELY WEALTHY DONOR.

Serin?

WHY WOULD THEY GIVE ME MONEY, THEN? I'VE NEVER BEEN A MACINNES GUY.

"We should take him to Stenfalk," the older man says.

"I'm not letting go of him."

"I didn't say let go. I just said let's take him."

"Are you ready to walk?" the younger man asks S. Without waiting for a response, he twirls his captive around and shoves him forward. Broken glass sparkles under the lights, and S. worries about his bare feet. His gut aches with hunger. And the chill: he can feel it slowing his thoughts, working against the adrenaline. He gives a silent, sharp shout to his mind, his body. *Wake up! Stay alert!*

The older man leans in. "I didn't catch your name," he says.

"It's S—." The younger man's hand is between his shoulder blades, pushing him forward. "Yours?"

"Ostrero. And my friend is Pfeifer."

Pfeifer, irritated by this disclosure, gives S. another hard shove and almost sends him spilling. "Sorry," he says, with little conviction.

The three of them skirt the edge of the crowd as they approach the dais from its side; a few of the demonstrators around the perimeter pause to regard him suspiciously. S. looks past them. He knows that each of them is inventing a narrative about how this

{ 82 }

Margin notes:

Another interesting name.

ILSA TALKS ABOUT IT IN HER AVIAN METAPHORS ARTICLE. SWEDISH FOR "MERLIN" (THE BIRD OF PREY, NOT THE WIZARD).

Everything's Ilsa with you.

EVERYTHING'S JACOB WITH YOU.

Sorry.

Blushing now.

So... I might've been a little misleading before.

WHEN?

when I told you I didn't say anything about Straka to Ilsa.

WHAT DID YOU SAY — EXACTLY?

I just told her that I'd looked @ the English Dept. website + saw that she studied him. I said I liked his books. That's all (I still don't think she realizes I was the one she talked to at the library.)

SHE'S NOT STUPID. WHY DID YOU DO THAT?

I don't know. Got nervous about not graduating, I guess, and I wanted her to like me. Thought maybe she'd cut me some slack.

(1) IF YOU WANT TO GRADUATE, GO TO CLASS AND DO THE WORK.

(2) YOU SHOULD UNDERSTAND THAT IT'S JUST A MATTER OF TIME BEFORE SHE (+ THUS MOODY) FIGURES OUT THAT THERE'S A CONNECTION BETWEEN US.

Is there a connection b/w us? What the hell is it exactly? ──→

stranger came to be in their presence—the more scurrilous, the better—and he has no choice but to let them. He turns to look back at the police officers skulking in the shadows; they are as inattentive as ever. When he sweeps his gaze across the factory, his eyes are drawn to the brown-dustered Detective swiveling a spotlight on the roof. He lets his gaze settle too long, though, and gets a shock in return. The browncoat seems to meet his eye directly, may even have brushed the brim of his fedora and nodded in his direction. S. feels his stomach tighten. He might be mistaken—he *must* be mistaken—but what if he *is* one of them?

No, he tells himself. Absurd. More absurd thoughts from a mind that is in no condition to be trusted. The man on the roof is too far off for him to see such small movements clearly. The light is poor, the air thick with seaside mist and smoke from the torches. And this: if S. *were* a Detective, or an ally of theirs, why would the rooftop agent risk giving him away with a nod?

As they approach the dais, Ostrero waves a hand and calls out to the man with the megaphone. The woman is not with him any longer; S. scans the crowd and spots her moving through it, straight-backed and

VMS NEVER HAD ANY DOUBT ABOUT WHICH SIDE HE WAS ON, POLITICALLY, SO WHY INCLUDE THAT DOUBT HERE?

(1) S. IS NOT PURELY VMS'S ALTER EGO AND/OR
(2) THE DOUBT MAKES FOR A BETTER STORY.

I think I get this now... what if he felt responsible for what happened to Ekstrom??

SO THIS WOULD BE ABOUT GUILT, THEN. AS WOULD MUCH OF CH. 4-5.

IT'S NOT OBVIOUS? ⟹ No, it's not.

{ 83 }

JEN: I LIKE YOU.

Even though you don't know anything about me...

I KNOW THE YOU WHO'S IN THE MARGINS. I KNOW YOU'RE THINKING HARD ABOUT WHAT YOU WANT + WHY—MORE THAN SOME PEOPLE EVER DO. I KNOW YOU CAN TAKE ON A CHALLENGE +KICK ITS ASS. AND I KNOW YOU'VE TRIED HARDER TO UNDERSTAND ME THAN ANYONE HAS IN A LONG TIME.

square-shouldered, making her way toward an angry knot of demonstrators who seem to be in a particularly heated confrontation with a trio of browncoats. The crowd parts for her. The respect is obvious, as is the shared desire to have her take control of the situation, to keep the potential energy of the conflict from turning kinetic.[6]

Pfeifer yanks him to an abrupt stop. Stenfalk lets himself down from the dais and joins them, regarding S. closely, the torchlight flicking shadows and light over his face. He is the oldest and most weathered-looking of the bunch. *[He has slicked-back, blond-gray hair and great concave swoops of wrinkles that arc over his cheeks and below his eyes. His mustache is in need of a trim and adds to his aspect of profound fatigue. The aquiline nose that overhangs it is astonishing both in size and in the dignity it suggests.]* Stenfalk taps his throat; he has left the megaphone on the dais, and he won't be speaking more than he has to.

Ostrero does the talking. He explains to Stenfalk where and how he and Pfeifer found this man, how S.

---

[6] It was Gaspard-Serge Coriolis, of course, who first detailed the mathematical principles that govern the function of kinetic energy. Much of Straka's work evinces an understanding of, and appreciation for, the work of innovative practitioners of the sciences. Straka was particularly impressed by some of the lesser-known of these people, like Wolfgang Spatzberg, Samuel Quinn-Collier, and Sagittario della Caduta. Careful readers of Book V of *Coriolis* will discover the roles each of these men's findings play in the development of the narrative.

{ 84 }

[Handwritten annotations]

✱ STENFALK HAS TO BE A FICTIONALIZED VERSION OF TORSTEN EKSTROM. I'VE ALWAYS THOUGHT HE WAS RIGHT. THE PHYS. DESCRIPTIONS MATCH UP (ALTHOUGH EKSTROM WAS NOTORIOUSLY VAIN ABOUT HIS MUSTACHE & WOULD NEVER HAVE LET IT SUGGEST "FATIGUE").

And: "Stenfalk" is Swedish — like Ekstrom.

And also: "Corbeau" — French for "raven" (and Durand was French); "Ostrero" — Spanish for "oyster-catcher" (Garcia Ferrara); "Pfeifer" — German for "sandpiper" (Feuerbach? Wechsler?)

ILSA WROTE ABOUT THAT — HOW ALL OF S.'S ALLIES IN THE BOOK HAVE NAMES OF BIRDS.

Maybe there's more to it — what those names/characters represent are people who were Straka's allies, too.

OR IT'S VMS PLANTING FAKE CLUES, INVOKING ALL THE MAJOR CANDIDATES.

FXC GETS NAME WRONG. IT WAS GASPARD-GUSTAVE.

Not with any of the keywords I tried. (Wouldn't it have to be "emersion" or something like it?) I'm going to keep working on it, though. But just a little — there's a Wallace Stevens paper that has to get written.

AND WE'VE GOT A FEW MORE MADE-UP NAMES... MAYBE THE CH. 2 CODE WORKS HERE, TOO?

13 WAYS OF LOOKING AT A BLACKBIRD? Yup. Got an old paper about it that you'd like to lend me?

claims to have found himself in the midst of the demonstration by accident, having—*supposedly*, Pfeifer interjects—swum to shore from a foundering ship, how S. denies any connection to Vévoda but has not offered any information about where his true interests lie. Stenfalk reaches up to the dais and drags a small, worn-looking valise toward himself. S. notices Ostrero and Pfeifer exchanging a look of uncertainty as Stenfalk unbuckles and opens it. Out from the valise comes a rumpled and stained shirt, which Stenfalk hands to S. The smell is unpleasant, as if the shirt has been steeping in sweat for days, but S. receives it without hesitation and buttons it over himself, happy to have something between his skin and the chill. Next comes a cheap and well-worn gray suit jacket, which smells marginally better though not at all good. Stenfalk then fingers the fabric of his own trousers, which matches the jacket: these, he is saying, are the only ones he has. S. thanks him.

"Forgive the smell," Stenfalk croaks. "We've been here a long time." He shakes his head as if clearing cobwebs, then clears his throat and spits on the ground behind him. "Fellows," he says to Ostrero and Pfeifer, "you don't let a man catch his death of cold. No matter who he is or isn't."

AS W/ SAILORS: PUTTING ON BORROWED CLOTHES→ ADOPTING AN IDENTITY?

CF. EKSTROM'S THE PRINCE OF ANKARSVIK (PRINCE EXILED FOR LETTING COMMONER FREEZE TO DEATH)

EMPATHY LIKE THIS IS RARE IN VMS'S WORKS.

He must have been a sad guy. :

Ostrero murmurs apologies. Pfeifer releases his grip, then sheepishly removes his own overcoat and hands it to S. Pfeifer is a tall man, and his coat hangs to mid-shin on S. No one has shoes to provide, but S. doesn't mind. His feet don't hurt; they simply feel as if they belong to someone other than himself.

Stenfalk regards S. closely. He opens his mouth to speak, but before any words come out he is seized by a fit of coughing. When he recovers, he straightens, squares his shoulders, wipes his lips with a well-used handkerchief. "So, S.," he says quietly, "who are you, then?"

S. pauses, remembers the words of caution that have been given to him—not just by Maelstrom, but also by the young woman in the Old Quarter bar. *Sola?* Can it possibly be a good idea to tell the truth? To put such faith in someone he does not know?

He assembles what he does know about them: these are people who have lost friends. Stenfalk is a man who has exhausted himself leading a movement against a much more powerful adversary. His comrade, the woman, is across the square, by the gate, pleading for peaceful vigilance. And that Detective in the brown duster, up on the roof behind the spotlight: his (possibly imagined) nod managed to chill S. when he was already frozen.

Margin notes (handwritten):

Top right: If there's one thing I know how to do, it's how to be patient + not cause any trouble.

Below title: YOU'RE BEING REALLY PATIENT WITH ME. I APPRECIATE IT.

Left margin:

S. ACCEPTED INTO THE GROUP — SEE DESJARDINS (1989).

Details?

THEORIZES THAT VMS WAS PART OF A WRITERS' COLLECTIVE COMMITTED TO POLITICAL CHANGE (AND/OR SUBVERSION OF POWER). LIKELY THAT A FEW OF THE CANDIDATES WERE IN THE GROUP.

Desjardins seems pretty sold on Ekstrom, BUT HE HEDGES ON WHETHER EKSTROM WAS STRAKA OR JUST CLOSELY CONNECTED TO HIM.

JEN— I GOT A PACKAGE FROM DESJARDINS TODAY! A STACK OF DOCS + ONE OF THE OBSIDIAN PIECES, TOO. CHECK OUT THE NOTE.

Shouldn't the obsidian be in one of the archives?

HELLO RAIN. I SEE YOU'VE MET MY PARADE.

Hey, you're the one who's supposed to act w/ "scholarly detachment."

About himself, of course, he still knows next to nothing.

So: what can he possibly rely on, other than his instincts?

"I don't know who I am," S. says.

Stenfalk cocks an eyebrow. "Meaning?"

"I have amnesia."

Pfeifer splutters a few syllables of disbelief, but quiets himself when Stenfalk holds up a hand.

S. details what he does know about himself. It does not take long. He omits some details: he says nothing about the surreal peculiarities of the ship and its sailors because he does not want to be written off as a lunatic. He says nothing about the woman in the bar, though he's not quite sure why.

"An improbable story," Stenfalk says, "but if you're saying you're not with Vévoda"—he has to pause to clear his throat several times—"or the Detectives—"

"I am saying that, yes," S. says. *And I am hoping it is not an untruth,* he thinks. He shivers inside his new clothes.

"That's all you know?" Ostrero says. "Nothing else at all?"

S. recalls the two monkeys that have crossed his path, as well as the hissing cat from the Old Quarter.

Margin notes (handwritten):

I don't buy this. I mean, you can still rely on your basic sense of morality, of right + wrong. S. has one; it's just that the decisions he bases on it don't always work out.

ALSO, YOU CAN KNOW SOMETHING'S RIGHT + STILL NOT CHOOSE TO PURSUE IT.

Sounds like you have some example in mind.

I DO.

Which is?

Hello?

I know you've read this. I could put one dot on any page in this book + you'd notice it.

LIKE ON P. 319.

Just like that. So what's your example?

US. OBVIOUSLY.

Was that so hard? Why'd you bring it up in the first place if you didn't want to say it?

I DID WANT TO SAY IT. I JUST PANICKED A LITTLE.

It's not clear to me what Desjardins is getting at in that note. It doesn't make a lot of sense.

I HAVE NO IDEA. HE'S OLD, BUT HE'S STILL SHARP... MAYBE IT'S JUST THAT HIS ENGLISH IS WORSE THAN I REMEMBER.

"Animals don't seem to like me much," he muses. It's not the most useful information, but it's all he has to offer.

S. stays with Ostrero and Pfeifer as the demonstration drags on through the night. A distant bell tower clangs twelve, one, two. S.'s guides circulate through the crowd, slapping backs and commiserating with their fellow workers. Pfeifer attempts to rouse the somnolent police into action—*Three men are missing! Probably dead! Why don't you do your jobs and investigate?*—but he is waved away dismissively; when he lingers, insistent, one of the cops takes a club out of his belt and taps his thigh threateningly. Pfeifer also aims insults at the browncoats they pass. The three of them stave off hunger with linty pieces of licorice retrieved from the depths of Ostrero's pockets.

They converse briefly with Corbeau, Stenfalk's partner from the dais, as she passes out leaflets that are fresh from a nearby printer, still warm and fragrant. Her hair is jet-black, her skin fair and reddened by cold. A spotlight passes over her as they talk, and when its harsh glare illuminates her features—a leptorrhine nose, a jutting knob of chin—S.

{ 88 }

DETAILS DRAWN FROM THE SQUARE

Handwritten margin notes:

YOU DIDN'T PICK UP THE BOOK LAST NIGHT. ARE YOU OK?

Jacob called. Out of the blue. It's confusing.

Actually, what it feels like, most of all is a complication, and I already have too many of those.

WHERE'D YOU LEAVE IT WITH HIM?

Are you prying??? Because that would be another complication I don't need.

OK. New favorite. — YOU'RE A LITTLE FICKLE WITH YOUR FAVORITES.

particularly notices her eyes: one is a bit lower on her face than the other, a subtle but striking asymmetry, and they are edged with crow's-feet, but those eyes are wide and alert, <u>their dark irises darting back and forth</u> between the three men and the crowd as she monitors the small dramas evolving amid the larger protest. She may not be classically beautiful, but she is not unattractive to him, and she radiates what S. can only think of as capability. (This is a woman who misses nothing—who reads situations, gestures, faces, contexts in an instant and just as quickly pieces them into coherent narratives.)

After looking S. up and down, she interrupts Ostrero's explanation of their guest's appearance with a terse nod. "I know enough," she says. She shakes S.'s hand. "Welcome," she tells him. "Try to stay out of the way. Don't start any trouble." As brusque as her manner is, it doesn't feel unkind.

Ostrero and Pfeifer speak enthusiastically and with a tone akin to reverence about Corbeau as the three men walk on. She is from one of the oldest families here in the city of B——, and while they are not rich, they are well-regarded for their honesty and erudition. Despite the constant hum of potential violence around them on the wharf, Ostrero

---

[Handwritten margin notes:]

SHE'S THE MOST BIRDLIKE OF THEM ALL. and she looks exactly like Amarante Durand. Have you seen the photo of her w/ Gaudí @ Parc Güell?

of pathetic. not funny. Kind of pathetic. Seriousky—you all need more women working on this stuff.

YEAH. THIS HAS TO BE HER. IT'S FUNNY THAT SO MUCH MORE ATTENTION GETS PAID TO THE STENFALK-EKSTROM CONNECTION.

VMS was attracted to Durand? Filomela must have loved reading that.

also like Durand— that's exactly what an archaeologist does, right? except with sites + artifacts instead of living people.

+ ALL THE MATERIAL ABOUT THE MOUNTAIN PEOPLE + THE CAVES FITS, TOO.

says, nothing terrible will happen as long as she is present; it is unthinkable that anyone with significant ties to the city would risk harming her.

"Especially not Vévoda," Pfeifer says. "He's had his eye on her for years." His tone is so sharp and dismissive that S. wonders if Pfeifer himself has, too. The Vévoda Armament Works, Ostrero continues, has been B——'s largest employer for generations. Originally a small concern specializing in traditional naval weaponry—cannons and cannonballs, grapeshot and canister-shot—the factory has tripled in size in the last five years, ever since Edvar Vévoda IV, the great-grandson of the founder, died, and his own son took over the business. While no one had ever thought much of Edvar V as a child (born into privilege, rude to servants and tutors, remarkable only for suspicion of involvement in a series of mysterious fires), Little Vévoda quickly began securing orders from all over the continent for more powerful ordnance. He expanded the factory several times and hired more workers, and the citizens of B—— found themselves looking forward to a new era of prosperity.

As the three men clear the perimeter of the demonstration, S. gets a better look at the building. On

{ 90 }

Handwritten marginalia:

→ The old barn burned while I was home. I watched it from my window.

IT'S GOT NOTHING TO DO WITH US.
you can't know that.
YOU'RE RIGHT. BUT ALL WE CAN DO IS BE CAREFUL.
We could stop doing all of this.
YOU COULD.

PRETTY MUCH HOW THE BOUCHARD EMPIRE GREW. FIRES ARE A DIRECT REFERENCE TO HERMÈS B.'S CHILDHOOD.

Why didn't people make a bigger thing of this when the book came out?

HARD TO SAY. MIGHT BE BECAUSE VMS HAD USED A BOUCHARD FIGURE IN WINEBLOOD — MAYBE THEY GOT TIRED OF HEARING HOW BAD THIS GUY WAS. OR MAYBE IT WAS JUST THAT BOUCHARD CONTROLLED SO MUCH MEDIA.

I saw Moody + Ilsa @ Pronghorn Java today. (I was reading The Spotted Cat — I put it away, just in case. Didn't want to attract notice.)

YOU DON'T ALWAYS HAVE TO TELL ME WHEN YOU SEE THEM TOGETHER.

an older portion of the structure, the brick has been darkened and abraded by weather, salt, and smoke, and is spattered with a century's worth of gull guano; the newer sections are cleaner and brighter, and the enormous annex at the far end looks as if the brick-layers might have completed the job mere days ago. The building itself tells the story of its owner's ambition and the industrial world's progress.

"What happened?" S. asks as they walk. "What went wrong?"

The change began last year, they say, when Little Vévoda built the annex, which is contiguous with the rest of the factory but separated from it by locked gates and heavy steel doors. No one, apart from Vévoda's uppermost circle of management, not even the mayor of B——, was permitted inside or was informed of what would be manufactured there. And instead of hiring local townsfolk, he filled the annex with workers who arrived via ship, at night, from somewhere far away; these newcomers have rarely been glimpsed by the regular workers, and they appear to live their entire lives within the annex itself. The ships that come to pick up freight from the annex do so at night and with their flags struck and escutcheons covered or blacked

{ 91 }

Handwritten margin notes:

«awesome new research find!»

The first chairman of Arp wasn't anyone named Arp. It was a guy named A. R. Prinsen. He'd worked for Bouchard before then—and he was part of management at the Calais factory during the strike.

HOW HAS NO ONE NOTICED THIS?

He wasn't a high-level guy—there's just a quick mention of him in an oral history of the survivors.

⤷ Starts to get a little surreal here, doesn't it? We never get a description of these workers. They could be Oompa-Loompas for all we know.

Wondering: why is S. just S.?
Why doesn't he have a name?

I WROTE A PAPER WITH ABOUT A DOZEN
THEORIES RE: S.'S NAME WHEN I WAS AN UNDERGRAD.
Can I see it?

NO WAY. IT'S COMPLETELY EMBARRASSING.
SHALLOW, JUVENILE, PRETENTIOUS. _____
EVERYTHING YOU'D EXPECT FROM AN UNDERGRAD.

Um, hello?? I'm
standing right here
(so to speak).

SORRY. I KEEP
FORGETTING.
(I MEAN THAT AS
A COMPLIMENT.)

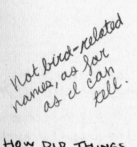
Not bird-related
names, as far
as I can
tell.

HOW DID THINGS
WORK OUT W/ THE
BLACKBIRD PAPER ?
Still working on it.
Trying to find a sly way
to hint that I
think Ilsa's article
on Straka's birds is
simplistic bullshit.
STOP.
THAT'S A TERRIBLE IDEA.

I know.
But it's fun to
think about.

out. Suspicions arose and then deepened, but the
response was downplayed, even ignored, lest the
employees and the city suffer. Still, the stories about
what Vévoda might be making in the annex—and to
whom he might be selling it—turned stranger and
darker. Speculation that had once risen in excited
voices was soon only leaking from the corners of
mouths; then it became the stuff of tight-lipped
murmurs, then whispers punctuated with furtive,
paranoid glances.

A few weeks ago, three workers named Zapadi,
Obradovic, and Ledurga had, in the darkest corner
of the darkest tavern downtown, told Stenfalk and
Corbeau that they'd found a way to sneak into the
annex and would be making their incursion later
that night. *Why are you telling us this?* Stenfalk
asked, nervous because management had recently
reprimanded him and Zapadi for passing out pamphlets urging the workers to unionize. *Someone*
needs to know, Zapadi said, *in case anything hap-*
pens, and you two are the ones we trust. Stenfalk
and Corbeau remained in the tavern, waiting, after
the three donned their coats and walked out the
door. They waited inside until the tavern closed,
they waited outside after that, and in the morning,

sleepless and frightened, they went to the factory and clocked in for their shifts.

It was a few days before Stenfalk mustered the courage to approach management (a handful of Edvar V's closest childhood friends, along with a few foreigners with unfashionable facial hair and strange accents) to inquire about the men's whereabouts. He was told that the three, dissatisfied with their wages, had quit the factory and gone overseas in search of more remunerative work.

Stenfalk gathered the rest of the workers and called for the walkout. The most astonishing thing, he told them, was how bald-faced the company's lie was, how little effort they had put into concocting a plausible story. *I've felt condescension from them before,* he said, *and dislike, too, and pettiness and opportunism, but never contempt. Something has changed.* The company responded to the strike with padlocks on the doors and brown-coated Detectives around the building. The standoff has been ongoing ever since. Most of the workers have exhausted their meager savings. People are getting desperate, Ostrero tells S., and desperation is a dangerous thing—more dangerous, even, than the outrage over the disappearances.

Handwritten marginalia:

✳ What were you getting at here?

LET'S JUST SAY THAT THERE'S A BOOK THAT MY PARENTS ARE PRETTY PASSIONATE ABOUT, AND IT ISN'T THIS ONE. AND THEY GENERALLY DON'T EVEN TALK TO ANYONE WHO DOESN'T SHARE THEIR FEELINGS ABOUT IT. How much do you talk to people who aren't ~~crazy~~ passionate about Straka?

THERE'S A DIFFERENCE. I LOVE THIS BOOK, BUT I KNOW IT'S FICTION.

✳

↳ IS THAT SO MUCH WORSE THAN A LIE THAT'S THE PRODUCT OF CENTURIES' WORTH OF EFFORT?

↳ SEE THE HOBO PREACHER'S "HISTORY OF CAPITALISM" SPEECH IN WINEBLOOD (CH. 16).

...a speech that is pretty much the beginning of the end for him.

YES — SAFE TO SAY MR. WINEBLOOD WAS NOT A FAN.

This is usually where you'd say, "I can't believe you've read ____ already!"

YEAH. BUT IT'S NOT IMPRESSIVE ANYMORE. NOW I JUST ASSUME YOU'VE TORN THROUGH EVERYTHING.

S. has questions. What is this demonstration likely to achieve? Vévoda won't ever admit to wrongdoing, will he? What incentive does Vévoda have to give jobs back to these suspicious and riled-up workers? Why not fill the old factory with his mysterious foreigners as well? "He knows he can't get away with doing that in this city," Ostrero says. "He wouldn't. This is his home, too." *What an awfully tenuous basis for trust*, S. thinks, but he keeps his mouth shut. Not far away, a fresh confrontation roils the crowd, and Pfeifer plows ahead to get closer to it. Applying a few well-placed shoves where necessary, he clears a path that allows S. and Ostrero to follow in his wake. A white-haired man in a boiler suit is cursing at a pair of Detectives and waving a heavy wrench in the air. His threats come in a scratchy voice and in a formal diction that belongs to a bygone generation. ("Zapadi's uncle," Ostrero shouts into S.'s ear.) The Detectives keep their mouths shut, their jaws tightly set, and S. wonders if they even understand the man; they are big men, with prognathous chins and inscrutable deep-set eyes, clearly of different stock than the people of this port. Pfeifer, having grunted and elbowed his

{ 94 }

AN OUT-OF-DATE
KIND OF MORALITY?
S. ISN'T BUYING IT.
(AND HE SHOULDN'T —
PEOPLE WILL DO
WHATEVER THEY CAN
GET AWAY WITH +
THEN SOME.)

Do you really think that?
about everyone?

MORE OR LESS.
You? Me?
MAYBE. WE'LL FIND OUT.

OK, so both
you and me.

WE'RE JUST DOING
WHAT WE HAVE TO.

THOSE IN POWER DON'T
HEAR/UNDERSTAND
(+ DON'T CARE TO TRY)

One of Straka's big
themes. It's everywhere
in the books.

ALSO A BIG THEME IN
MY DEALINGS W/ THE
PSU ADMINISTRATION.

way to the front line, lays his hands firmly on Zapadi's uncle's shoulders and pulls him backward, away from the guards. The older man wriggles away from him, rushes back toward the hulking browncoats, and resumes shouting. S., meanwhile, is careful to stay out of the Detectives' lines of sight. How would he explain a nod, a wink, any sign of recognition, to Pfeifer and Ostrero? How would he explain it to himself?

He watches as one of the Detectives sets and resets his grip on a cudgel. *It's about to start,* he thinks. *Here is the spark that starts the inferno.* And it's almost as if the Detective can hear his thought, because the large man suddenly turns toward him. S. looks away, pretends to scan the dais off in the distance. He should walk away, he knows. He should mutter something in his friends' direction and disappear into the crowd, and he is about to do so when he spots a familiar face among the demonstrators— (a woman who is smoothly navigating the spaces between people, attracting little notice as she slips past them,) heading for the outer edge of the demonstration. Square-shouldered. Gracefully solitary in a crowded space. The young woman from the bar. It's her. Coincidence be damned: if she is here, it is

[95]

Handwritten margin notes:

(top, Jen): My friends are actively ignoring me now. Roommate never comes home. And I realized I don't care at all. Fuck them for turning on me. It's like: I hope you enjoy the rest of your tame + predictable + shallow little lives

(Eric): BREATHE. DOESN'T DO ANY GOOD TO BE SO ANGRY AT THEM.

(right): Straka was just as angry at all the people who sold out the S.

LOOK WHERE IT GOT HIM. (AND LOOK WHERE IT GOT FXC).

CF. THE SQUARE, PP. 63, 101, 119 (THREE DIFFERENT VIEWS OF THE SAME GESTURE).

This just gave me an idea about the Ch. 6 code!

Moody + Ilsa @ Pronghorn again.

AGAIN: YOU CAN STOP TELLING ME. I'M AWARE THAT THEY'RE TOGETHER.

Yeah, but there's this: it looked like she was wearing a piece of obsidian on a necklace.

WTF?? ARE YOU SURE??

not 100%. But I'll let you know if I see her wearing it in class.

(bottom left): I'm on it. I want to know, too. And so will the _____ Director, I'll bet. It's a special collections archive, not an effing jewelry store.

IT'S SO CUTE THAT YOU SAID "EFFING."

no cuter than you saying "WTF."

(bottom right): GOOD. I MEAN: NOT THAT I CARE IF HE'S GIVING HER THINGS. BUT W/ SO MUCH DISAPPEARING FROM THE ARCHIVES...

because she has a connection to him. If she is here, she is Sola.

Those are his first thoughts, at any rate; the longer he watches her, the more he finds grounds for doubt. The long braid is gone, her hair now a thicket of curls that hang unevenly at those shoulders. Her face is rounder, fleshier—*older,* he thinks, as if she has aged five years in a matter of weeks. Her coat is like those worn by the other women in the crowd: threadbare, coal-gray, and shapeless. Can this truly be her? This is a different city. And this woman is a factory worker, not a frequent passenger on posh liners. But then, like the guard, she, too, glances at him—and is there not something in her expression (a barely-perceptible widening of her eyes? that wrinkling of her upper lip?) that suggests she recognizes him? A lingering look that implies she *knows something about him?* Some significant piece of information that she withheld when they first met? For this is the woman he met; he senses it as surely as he heard the voices in the Old Quarter.

Move, S. tells himself, because she is walking away quickly, nearing the end of the crowd, heading away from the wharf and toward the city's center.

[Handwritten margin notes:]

I didn't get that the first time through.

TIME PASSING AT DIFFERENT RATES (SHIP VS. LAND)

= *LOVE* Don't even try to tell me otherwise.

OTHER READS POSSIBLE...
Oh, come on. There's mad crushing going on here. You know that feeling, don't you?

OF COURSE I DO. IT'S JUST THAT IT'S NEVER WORKED OUT WELL.

News flash: it'll never work out well if you refuse to be seen anywhere.

I'M ONLY DOING THAT BECAUSE I NEED TO BE HERE AND I'M NOT ALLOWED TO BE HERE.

Is it really still worth it to you?

I NEED TO BE HERE. THAT HASN'T CHANGED. MAYBE THE REASONS HAVE.

He grabs Ostrero's elbow. "Thank you for your help," he says, "but I have to go."

"But—"

S. points. "That woman," he says. "I know her. Or she knows me. Her name is Sola."

Ostrero shakes his head. "Her name is Szalómé. She works in the factory. Hasn't been here long—"

Szalómé? That might be her name in this city, perhaps, but he'd bet everything his old, unremembered self might have owned that they're speaking of the same woman. "I met her in another city. Quite recently."

"I doubt that."

"I'll come back," S. says, stepping away. "If I can, I will."

Suspicion tightens Ostrero's face: they've trusted him, and now he's running away?

Pfeifer returns to them just as S. is leaving; he shouts *Be careful* and something else that S. can't make out because he is already five, ten, twenty steps deeper into the crowd, making space with his elbows, drawing shouts and curses and even a forearm into his throat. He loses sight of the woman, briefly, several times, and each time panic grips him, only to subside as soon as he spies her again. A shoe

I NOTICED YOU DIDN'T PICK UP THE BOOK AGAIN...

Back off. Don't need to explain myself to you or anyone else.

SORRY. JUST MEANT I WAS WORRIED.

Don't be. I'm fine.

THAT WAS NOT YOU AT YOUR MOST CHARMING.

No, it was me at my most confused, messed-up + angry. at myself mostly. The whole new Jen project fell apart completely— in one night.

This is SO completely + totally S. chasing after love.

HE HAS NO IDEA IF IT'S LOVE OR NOT. HE'S NOT THINKING THAT WAY.

He doesn't have to be thinking that way. Just feeling (+doing). He does know there's something urgent about it.

EXACTLY. IT'S URGENT FOR HIM TO FIND THE PERSON WHO MAY KNOW WHO HE IS.

Isn't that one way of looking at love? FXC thinks so. (See: FN 7 →)

comes down heavily on one of his bare feet (which turns out to be not quite as numb as S. had thought), but he ignores the pain, moves forward. He cannot lose her. Even if she isn't *her*.[7]

It has to be her.

The woman passes the line of police officers, drawing a few leers and a gesture or two, but no sustained interest, and she disappears down a winding street. She is not running, but she walks quickly. Adrenaline fills him, makes it possible for him to trot after her with his miserable feet, his sore and stiffening muscles, his tight chest, and into the rising maze of the city S. goes.

Shops are darkened, restaurants shuttered, pedestrians few. Curtains are drawn in the windows above street level. Those who are not at the wharf, it seems, have ensconced themselves in the safety of their homes. Even the seagulls are quiet, sitting motionless on rooflines and cornices well away from the port. There's as much tension in the quiet on the streets as there is in the strife at the factory. The

---

7 Here I am reminded of the theories of identity posited by Guthrie MacInnes's philosophical nemesis, the American Orpheus Clementson Wayne. According to Wayne (whose work I find persuasive), S. can be said to be suffering from the problem of the Identity Parallax: it is only from S.'s perspective that the identity of Sola is mutable—in an objective experience of this world, she in fact *is* her, her *is* she, *she is she* (and always has been, and always will be).

staccato raps of Sola's soles against the macadam echo in the emptiness, threading him onward—a left here, a right there, another left. Is he gaining ground? He feels as if he must be, but now all the evidence he has of her is those echoing footsteps. More disorienting still, a mist rolls through the streets, swirling in the gelid light of the streetlamps. He notices, too, a mechanical sound in the air, a bass ostinato, thrumming and pumping beneath the percussion of her walk. Pebbles bruise his soles. A stitch burns his side. The hum gets louder as he nears its source. It takes more effort to breathe; the air feels strangely humid and smells of hot metal. His shallow breaths—so loud inside his skull!—are barely sufficient to keep him going. But still: he cannot lose her. She has something to tell him, something to reveal, he's sure of this. She's leading him, not evading him. She *wants* him to follow.

Another turn, then one more, and then the sounds of her running are gone, swallowed by the hum—that sound, it's rattling his teeth, his windpipe, his chest, his gut. He stops, closes his eyes, listens closely for her, but all he can hear is the hum, and that acrid metallic smell is everywhere—he can even taste it—and when he opens his eyes he notices

[handwritten marginalia: ELUSIVENESS. CF. THE MAZE SCENE IN CORIOLIS, CATACOMBS SCENE IN BRAXENHOLM.]

[handwritten marginalia: and in Ch. 5 + Ch 10 here.]

——————

the building that runs the entire length of the block. CENTRAL POWER. And under those words, in faded paint:

S

Steam clouds clot the sky above him, bullying the mist.

<u>Where did she go?</u>

He moves forward, stops. Listens. Thinks he hears her, then loses the sound. Two more steps forward. He senses movement in the alley to his left. Two men in the shadows, big men, and there are rustling sounds and then the metallic snap of a buckle. S. should move on—this scandalous assignation or whatever it is has nothing to do with him, nothing to do with her, nothing to do with the conflicts afoot—and yet he holds his place, watching them, and he sees that the buckle is on a boiler suit that one man has just finished donning. The other man wears a dark-brown duster, and he has another such coat slung over one shoulder. He carefully hands a paper-wrapped parcel to the man in the boiler suit, and S. understands—immediately and with dead certainty—that inside the package is a bomb.

——————

{ 100 }

I drew one of these somewhere on campus. See if you can find it. Still waiting...

OK, YOU CAN'T DO STUFF LIKE THAT— ESPECIALLY NOT IN STANDEFER. I'LL GET BLAMED FOR IT.

But you've been expunged. You don't exist!

THE POLICE MAY NOT BE INTERESTED IN THE METAPHYSICAL FINE POINTS.

It's interesting that you're still able to get into the building.

GETTING IN ISN'T THE HARD PART. STAYING UNNOTICED IS.

So WHAT'S THE STORY ABOUT THE DAY YOU DISAPPEARED?

There's no way I can tell that story in this space. Here.

HAVE YOU EVER TALKED TO YOUR PARENTS ABOUT IT? ABOUT WHAT IT'S BEEN LIKE FOR YOU?

How could I? I only just realized it. Anyway, it's not the kind of conversation you can have w/ them. And good luck getting them in the same room together at this point.

MAYBE IT'D JUST BE EASIER TO TALK TO THEM SEPARATELY.

It might be. But I'm still not going to do it. You get that, right? You don't have any kind of relationship with your parents, either.

YEAH. I UNDERSTAND.

Then: a flicker of fire as the man in the duster lights a cigarette, and in that flash S. sees the coarse, blunt facial features that confirm his suspicions. Detectives. And here he is, standing in the open, in the bone-white spill of light in the middle of the street, staring at them, and they are looking right back at him.

The man in the overcoat draws his lips back and smiles.

The man in the boiler suit may or may not wink.

Play it safe, S. thinks. *You really don't understand anything yet. Don't know who they are. Have no idea, really, what they might be doing.* So S. nods, simply, and hurries on in the direction he'd been heading. Sola must still be close. All he has to do is pick up the sound of her shoes again.

Behind him, he hears one of the men emerge from the alley and turn in the direction of the water. Even with the relentless, damnable hum from the powerhouse, he hears the hobnailed boots, the rustle of paper, imagines the man in the boiler suit tucking his parcel of death securely into the crook of his arm as he heads to the wharf to make his delivery. It is at this moment that S. hears the whispers emerging from deep within the thick cloud of

This would be a great movie scene. Totally creepy. (Did anyone try to make *SOT* into a movie?)

AFTER WHAT HAPPENED W/ SANTANA MARCH, HOLLYWOOD KEPT ITS DISTANCE. BENNO FONTANA (THE PRODUCER) TALKS ABOUT IT IN HIS MEMOIR. HEARD ONCE THAT AN INDIAN DIRECTOR WAS TRYING TO DO IT, BUT HAVEN'T HEARD ANYTHING SINCE.

Probably b/c he's missing— as of a few months ago.

CAN'T JUST ASSUME THERE'S A CONNECTION.

SHE'S CLOSE, BUT ELUSIVE. (SOLA AS WRITER'S MUSE? CF. CH. 9.)

She could *also* be a stand-in for FXC. Maybe they had a writer-muse thing going on + that's what led them to fall in love.

YOU'RE ASSUMING THAT THEY BOTH DID.

I am. That's the only way Ch.10 makes sense to me.

Either version.

———

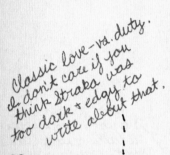

Classic love-vs.-duty.
I don't care if you
think Straka was
too dark + edgy to
write about that.
        ‖
OR, ALTERNATIVELY,
SELF VS. COMMUNITY.
You are a very
stubborn man. Unless
you're just trying
to piss me off.
OR, ALTERNATIVELY:
BOTH ARE TRUE.
        [••]

industrial noise. Voices like those from the Old Quarter, a similar clamor with different consonants, different rhythms.

(S. keeps walking in the opposite direction. This is not his business, he tells himself. None of it. Whatever is happening inside Vévoda's factory has nothing to do with him. He owes nothing to anyone here—or, as far as he knows, in this *world, let alone in the place whence these whispers originate*. No. There is nothing as important to him as figuring out who he is. He puts one bare foot ahead of the other, stuffs his hands deep into the pockets of his borrowed jacket, and moves on, not thinking, only listening, straining to hear her. She might be just blocks away. He is not thinking. He is only listening.

Not thinking.

Listening.

He stops. Tells himself it is to help him hear more clearly. Knows immediately that this is a lie.)

And he turns around, guesses at the most direct route to the wharf, and sprints back over the rough macadam. He does not ask his depleted body if it is capable of such exertion, he simply runs, allows gravity to draw him back downhill because he has to

———

get to the wharf, find Stenfalk and the others and alert them. Help them stop the horrible carnage before it occurs. He can worry about the condition of his body later. But for all the pain that is wracking his body as he runs, the most acute is that of knowing that he is letting Sola go, letting her vanish into an uncertain world of unrevealed secrets. He is letting her go, and he is running.

A bicycle is lying on its side on the wharf, just beyond the outer edge of the crowd, separated from the line of shuffling, fidgeting, yawning police by head-high stacks of wooden pallets, steel plates, and lengths of piping lashed together with metal bands. The bicycle's rider, a lad of eleven, is weaving through the crowd, looking for his father and clutching a brown-paper sack that contains salami, beer cheese, and day-old bread, which his mother has sent to keep up her husband's strength. The bicycle's front wheel turns slowly, pushed by the offshore wind. Attached to the handlebars is a wire basket, made by the father years ago and now striped with rust.

Watch the basket. Do not watch for the man in the boiler suit to emerge from the crowd, slip a

I don't remember this being underlined before.

IT MUST HAVE BEEN. WHO KNOWS WHAT I WAS THINKING THOUGH. *I'm pretty sure it wasn't. Makes me nervous.*

NARR. BREAKS AWAY FROM S., GOES OMNISCIENT W/ DIRECT ADDRESS TO READER.

I like it — nice to get a break from being inside S's head.

AND IT GIVES YOU THE SENSE THAT THERE ARE FORCES MUCH LARGER THAN S. OUT THERE.

———

different brown-paper package into the basket, and then step back into the chaos and disappear from history. It does not matter who he is, and in any event, he moves so unobtrusively, so cleanly, that you would fail to notice him, just as everyone else on the wharf fails to notice him—even the Detectives, who have known about this plan for days.

Try to keep your eyes on the basket, even as S. arrives at the wharf, panting and coughing, his feet now trailing blood, and bulls his way to the dais, where Stenfalk and the others are conferring and sharing one bruised apple. What matters is not how the five of them fan out into the crowd and across the wharf, searching desperately for a Detective costumed in a boiler suit. What matters, really, is that while you may want to call them, shout at them through the page, direct their attention to the bomb in the bicycle basket, you, of course, cannot.

[Note that the bomb is close enough to the police to panic them when it detonates, even though a few ostensibly random piles of wood and metal on the wharf will shield them, for the most part, from the misery of the sharpened metal fragments that have been packed into the casing. Don't look away from the basket, even when the blast occurs, because the shrapnel will fly freely at and through these workers who are milling and shouting and shaking their fists in their pointless, powerless throng. (The bomb is a small one, though, and crudely built, so that all of the Detectives will be safely outside its range, and also so that the explosion will more easily be pinned on a disgruntled worker—probably an anarchist or a Red, anyway, you know how those people are—instead of on a professional provocateur on the payroll of the world's most rapidly-growing armaments manufacturer.)

Again: keep your eyes on the basket—if you insist on keeping them open at all.

You do not want to see S. flung like a rag doll by the blast. *How much punishment can this body take?* you might wonder. *And with so much for him yet to do?* You do not want to see his face go slack for such a distressingly long interval—even if you would note that his body remains intact—and you certainly do not want to see his face when sense returns to it, along with the certainty that his hesitation outside the power station is what allowed the bomber to reach the wharf in time to plant his device and vanish. And you do not want to be scanning the wharf in the aftermath of the explosion,

THIS IS EXACTLY WHAT HAPPENED AT CALAIS.

A SELF-AWARE WINK FROM STRAKA HERE? (S. HAS MANY CHAPTERS TO GO!!)

—maybe it's not meant to be funny. Maybe Straka was just telling us (or FXC) that he was *exhausted* when he wrote this.

searching for that eleven-year-old boy. This, above all else, is for certain.]

In that time when S.'s body is limp and his face is expressionless, oblivious, he is not unconscious. He is simply not quite present in the present, as it were: while he can hear the cries of the wounded and dying, the shouts of the panicked, the staccato reports of police revolvers firing haphazardly into the chaos, the smacks of truncheons against shoulders and backs and cheekbones and skulls, whinnies and clops of police horses wheeling around the wharf, all of these sounds seem distant, diffuse, relegated to a halo surrounding the vivid scene playing inside his eyelids.

The scene is this: the same wharf, though it is narrower and does not project as far out over the water; this same Vévoda factory, but without the annex, just a modest rectangle of fresh brickwork, the mortar of which looks pristinely luminescent in the moonlight; a similar atmosphere of tension, but a quieter and more intimate tension, not between workers and police and Detectives but between two people, just two, boy and girl, their newly-adult figures long and lean, as if their bodies each have been

{ 106 }

NARR. TELLING US WHAT WE WANT / DON'T WANT.

EDSEL GRIMSHAW PARTICULARLY HATED THIS SCENE. SAID IT WAS "CONTEMPTUOUS OF READERLY DESIRE" TO DIGRESS FROM THE PRESENT ACTION HERE.

This is where Straka gets to tell Vaclav's story. Or a version of it, anyway.

RIGHT — IT'S JARRING, BUT IT HAS TO BE INTENTIONAL. BUT DOES IT MEAN VACLAV HIMSELF WAS "STRAKA"?

Not necessarily — but it must mean that whoever was Straka was close to him. — *why not?*

ESTABLISHED WRITER "CLOSE" TO FACTORY KID? UNLIKELY. BUT MAYBE STRAKA HEARD THE STORY (MAYBE HE WAS IN PRAGUE THAT DAY?) + HE WANTED TO EXPRESS SOME KIND OF EMPATHY? WHATEVER THE STORY, THIS DOESN'T FEEL LIKE A CYNICAL "DROP FAKE CLUES" MOVE TO ME.

Totally agree.

stretching themselves toward futures of limitless promise. They're speaking to each other, the boy angling himself toward her, the girl taking a half-step back, keeping distance between them, which surprises S., because isn't the point of scenes like this that the two people—two bodies, two souls—come together? And inside his sound-halo of muffled gunshots and agony, (the girl on the wharf shakes her head, shakes it again, shakes it once more (so emphatic!), pushes a sheaf of papers into his chest—and now the boy is the one to take a startled half-step back. She turns on a heel and exits the scene, walking with straight back and swishing hind end and dismissive laugh back into city streets.) The boy, alone in the moonlight, kicks gently at a nailhead that sticks up from a plank, then folds the papers lengthwise and tucks them inside his coat. He walks along the wharf toward a pile of fishnets, kneels, and uses a penknife to remove the lead weights threaded into the netting. Even with all the chaos raging in his ears, S. can hear the soft *plock* as the boy drops each weight, one after another after another, into the pockets of his coat and trousers. The boy trudges heavily back to his spot at the railing, that spot where the future was to have opened

At least she rejected him in person + not in an email + not after wasting 3+ years of his life.

ISN'T IT BETTER TO HAVE HAD 3+ YEARS OF BEING WITH SOMEBODY? I FELT LIKE I WAS JUST GETTING STARTED WITH ILSA WHEN IT ALL CRASHED AND BURNED.

How long did it last? HARD TO SAY. WE SHARED AN OFFICE, WORKED LATE, HAD FUN TALKING ABOUT THE BOOKS. THERE WAS ATTRACTION. SHE SAID SO. AND WE WERE TALKING ABOUT SPENDING SPRING BREAK IN MUNICH, WORKING AT THE ARCHIVE + VISITING HER FAMILY. AND THEN NOTHING. OH, AND ALSO, MY SUMMERSBY TAPE WAS GONE.

It got physical? There was hooking up? NOT A LOT. BUT SOME. I'M WONDERING: DID ANY OF IT MEAN ANYTHING? WAS SHE JUST USING ME?

{ 107 }

Those aren't the only possibilities. Maybe she liked you but decided Moody could do more for her career. Or maybe she's just one of those people who never knows what the hell she's doing but does it anyway + leaves behind a trail of wreckage.

I hope not.

→ YOU'RE NOT ONE OF THOSE, ARE YOU?

itself to him. He swings one leg over the rail, and then it is a mere matter of shifting his weight and letting the air take hold of him. He tips. Below him, the waves lap indifferently—

—and then there are words in his ears, harsh and desperate sounds the he cannot collect and resolve into meaning. What sort of man, he wonders, hears voices that aren't—

—and then someone is tugging at his arm, at S.'s arm, tugging and tugging, and it is Stenfalk—his shirt misted with blood, a splash of red coating one side of his face, one wing of his mustache—tugging and saying, *We've got to go, now! Get up if you can!* and S. obeys, leaning heavily on Stenfalk's shoulder and staggering off into a network of alleyways. He hears Corbeau's heavy breaths behind them—and it's funny, her breaths are astonishingly attractive to him, how seductive the sound of *living* can be!— and this is what he listens to as they continue their winding flight along the city's south side, past building after building, each differing from the others only in degree of neglect. When they pause to rest amid the ruins of a tumbledown stable, none can yet

---

Handwritten marginalia:

JEN:
DESJARDINS DIED ON SUNDAY. ARTICLE/OBIT IS ONLINE AT LABALISE.FR

Another fall. Maybe they're right + it was a suicide... but honestly? This is getting scary.

I DIDN'T KNOW HIM WELL... BUT I THINK THIS WAS A SUICIDE THE SAME WAY SUMMERSBY'S WAS. WHICH IS NOT AT ALL.

I didn't realize he'd been moody's thesis advisor.

I THINK I MENTIONED EARLIER THAT THEY WERE ESTRANGED. NOT SURE WHAT WENT BAD BETWEEN THEM— BUT I BET IT WASN'T DESJARDINS' FAULT.

I'm surprised you didn't try to connect with him earlier.

WISH I HAD. I DIDN'T THINK HE'D TAKE ME SERIOUSLY— TOO YOUNG, NO PH.D., NO TRACK RECORD, + A CONNECTION TO MOODY.

Other people in the field have taken you seriously, though. right? I mean, even moody has.

JUST B/C SOMEONE TAKES YOU SERIOUSLY DOESN'T MEAN THAT YOU KNOW THEY DO. OR THAT YOU BELIEVE YOU DESERVE IT. ALSO, I WASN'T ENTIRELY SURE I COULD TRUST HIM.

That doesn't surprise me.

speak more than a few syllables before they must cough out the hay-dust that fills the space.

A short, sharp whistle from the dark. Stenfalk answers it with one of his own, and then Ostrero and Pfeifer appear in the crooked doorway. Pfeifer is leaning heavily on his friend and holding a dark-stained handkerchief to his ear. More rest. More breathing. [Then Stenfalk gives a command that S. doesn't quite hear, and the five of them move as one—quickly, stealthily, through a forgotten end of the city, a relic of decades-dead industry, and stagger up a modest incline to a shabby house—dark windows, a mossy roof that looks on the verge of caving in.] Stenfalk reaches up into a window box and produces a key. The door wobbles on its hinges as it swings open.

Tonight, this is their home.

Tomorrow? Who can say anything about tomorrow?

I'M GOING TO PARIS FOR THE FUNERAL. SERIN OVERNIGHTED A CREDIT CARD LOADED WITH $ FOR PLANE FARE, HOTEL, ETC.

Eric, stop. You have no idea what's really going on here. With Desjardins, with Serin, with any of it.

NO, BUT GOING THERE IS THE BEST WAY FOR ME TO FIND OUT.

Look—I know we still don't really know each other, but I'm really, really worried about this. Don't go.

YOU'VE GOT PAPERS, PROJECTS, CLASSES. TAKE A BREAK FROM THIS. I'LL HAVE LOTS OF NEWS WHEN I GET BACK.

I don't like this <u>AT ALL.</u>

Well. The book's still here. So I guess you've left. And I'm talking to myself in the margins of a stranger's book. awesome.

Be safe, Eric.

I LOVE THAT YOU KEPT WRITING.

What else was I going to do?

Paris!! What happened???
you have to tell me about it.

SO MUCH. STILL TRYING TO SORT THROUGH.

Start by telling me you're all right.
Then just go one thing at a time.

I'M OKAY. THE BIG THING: NO ONE WHO
KNEW HIM BELIEVES HE KILLED HIMSELF.
AND GET THIS : HE FELL FROM A BALCONY
AT THE HÔTEL DES DEUX MARTRES.

Whoa. Same room as Ekstrom?

NOT SURE.

CHAPTER 4

AGENT X

S. AWAKENS to the sound of a scratching pencil. He opens his eyes to see Stenfalk, bleary and rumpled, sitting at the kitchen table with a tablet of paper in front of him and a stub of pencil gripped in his crooked, knobby fingers. He looks as if he has not slept. Still—even though his head lolls and his eyelids droop—his hand races across the page, and the periods that end his sentences sound like raps on a drum. His face still bears traces of dried blood, as if he gave it just one careless swipe of a washcloth before setting to work.

The others in the house look nearly as exhausted. Corbeau leans against the counter, watching Stenfalk as she sips from a chipped teacup. Pfeifer, with his wounded ear bandaged, sits in a chair beside the

{ 111 }

I wish it was that easy. I can't get anywhere with the Stevens paper.

WHAT ENDED UP HAPPENING W/ THE YEATS?

She gave me an F. Said it would've been a C- paper at best "even if I'd gotten it in on time." She is not at all my favorite person. I talked to the prof.—useless.

WHO IS IT? FFOULKES? HE'S TOUGH...

Yeah. Double-F him. He told me to "embrace the zero, then let it go."

HOW ZEN. IT'S EASY IF YOU'RE THE ONE GIVING THE ZEROS...

I need to get the Stevens paper in. Fucking words just won't come out. I am so sick of all of this.

DOESN'T MATTER IF YOU'RE NOT INSPIRED. JUST GOTTA GRIND IT OUT.

I couldn't concentrate at all while you were gone. (That's crazy, isn't it? Because I never see you when you're _here_.)

NOT CRAZY. THERE WAS AN EMPTY SEAT NEXT TO ME ON THE PLANE ON MY WAY THERE, AND I KEPT THINKING THAT YOU SHOULD BE IN IT.

Next time you think about going to Paris w/ a girl, you should probably ask her.

Was Ilsa there?

WHY DO YOU ASK?

Because another TA subbed for her all last week... which coincides exactly w/ when you were gone.

SHE WAS THERE.

And yet you didn't mention her.

front window, puffing shakily on a cigarette as he peers out at the street through the scrollwork cuts in the shutters.

Corbeau is the one who notices that S. is awake. She pours another cup from the pot and brings it to him as he sits up. "Thank you," he says, breaking the pall of the room. The tea is black and tastes foreign to his tongue—it's pungent and tarry and even a little greasy—but it is warm, and S. is grateful for it.

Nearby on the stone hearth is a neatly-folded pile of clothing—a white work shirt, yellowed at the collar and armpits; faded blue serge trousers; and a pair of cotton socks, one of which has a ragged hole in the heel—next to a pair of well-worn brogan boots. "Those are for you," Corbeau tells him. "It's the best of what was upstairs. Zapadi didn't care much about his appearance."

The socks and boots, warmed by the fire, feel like the greatest of luxuries. The boots are a trifle large, but once S. tears his old, ruined trousers into strips and bandages his lacerated soles, they fit well enough. He'll be doing a lot of walking today, tomorrow, the next day—however long it takes for him to scour the city and find Sola. What happened last night on the wharf was a horror, yes, and those responsible for it

---

Margin notes (handwritten):

Best breakfast ever: triple americano, chocolate croissant, + a postcard from Brazil.

THE NIGHT AFTER THE FUNERAL, I WENT TO A DINNER W/A BUNCH OF STRAKA SCHOLARS. ALL VERY SECRET—ONE OF DJ'S STUDENTS SLIPPED ME A PIECE OF PAPER W/AN ADDRESS ON IT WHEN WE SHOOK HANDS @ THE SERVICE. RESTAURANT WAS A TINY PLACE IN THE LATIN QUARTER—NO NAME, LOOKED DARK/CLOSED FROM THE STREET. MAYBE 15 OF US THERE, PLUS A FEW OTHERS WHO DIDN'T SAY MUCH BUT WHO WERE TOO WELL-DRESSED TO BE ACADEMICS. FELT LIKE AN INNER-CIRCLE THING... PEOPLE TALKING ABOUT CONTINUING DJ'S WORK + HIS COMMITMENT TO ETHICAL SCHOLARSHIP, SHARING FINDINGS, ETC.

Were you surprised they asked you?

OF COURSE. I COULD TELL ONE GUY DIDN'T WANT ME THERE, ACTUALLY—HEARD HIM WHISPER SOMETHING ABOUT MOODY. HARD TO KNOW EXACTLY WHAT WAS GOING ON B/C MY FRENCH ISN'T GREAT.

→ If only you knew someone who speaks French well.

But why did they ask? You weren't in his inner circle. You were barely in DJ's outer circle.

WELL, THE SERIN PEOPLE FOUND ME, DIDN'T THEY? MAYBE THE TALK I GAVE IN LISBON WAS BETTER THAN I THOUGHT.

I'm assuming you didn't go ahead and share (y)our findings...

...YOU ASSUME CORRECTLY.

should be exposed and held to account, but he needs to leave it behind, leave the grieving to those who knew the dead, who live and work in this city, whose lives will continue here in this city. As for himself: his task is to find this woman. Szalómé. Sola. Whatever her name is. He has already walked away from her once, and he will not do so again. He clears his throat, *Better not.* finds his voice. "I'll be on my way," he says.

"You're leaving?" Corbeau says.

"I appreciate your help, and I'm sorry for your losses. But I should be going."

"Of course," Stenfalk says, still scribbling. "You have the difficult and unenviable task of locating yourself."

"Yes. Exactly."

Stenfalk pauses, looks up at him. "Don't leave just yet. Ostrero's out reconnoitering. (Wait until you understand the situation you'll be heading into.)"[1] His tone is not unfriendly, but it is deeply serious, even stern.

"We need him here," Corbeau says. She turns to S. "You're the one who saw the Detectives with the bomb. Without your word, we have nothing."

---

[1] "Expect the expected," as Straka was fond of saying. He wrote this in the first letter he sent me, and in those that quickly followed—indeed, throughout the years of our professional relationship.

REMINDS ME — I NEED YOU TO LOOK @ THE NOTES I TOOK WHEN I WAS IN NY FOR THE AUCTION. THERE'S SOMETHING I'M NOT SEEING. Might help to' know who the agent was bidding for, I guess. WHICH WE DON'T KNOW. I DON'T THINK DESJARDINS KNEW. IF ANY OF HIS STUDENTS DID, THEY WEREN'T SAYING.

I know you don't think the Paris trip was dangerous — but that's got to be where they caught on to you/us. DON'T KID YOURSELF. IT WAS PROBABLY BEFORE THEN.

OK — TITLE IS "AGENT X" — FIRST FN SEEMS TO POINT TO THE FN ONE PLACE AFTER IT. WHAT ARE WE LOOKING FOR? CODE W/ KEYWORD OF "AGENT X"? SOMETHING W/ THE LETTER X?

"We probably have nothing even *with* his word," Pfeifer mutters.

"That may be," Corbeau says, "but his story must be heard. [People need to know what sort of person Vévoda is."] ✱

Stenfalk slaps down his pencil. He pushes himself back from the table. He eyes S. carefully, leaning forward with his hands on his knees. S. suddenly feels unnerved, <u>like a child before his father</u>, unsure of whether he is about to receive praise or reprimand, wisdom or warning.

"Tell me," Stenfalk says. "Do you stand by your story?"[2]

"I do," S. answers. "What I told you I saw, I saw." (He chooses his words carefully: he does not claim to have volunteered every possible detail.) The Detectives' knowing looks can remain his secret, at least until he finds out what they mean. Although, frankly, he doesn't *want* to know; what he wants is to wash his hands of this tragedy, of this conflict, of this threat, and get on with the business of finding Sola.

---

2   "Every writer must stand behind his work," Straka told Otto Grahn in a letter, "and do so completely and forever. He should expressly avoid acknowledging that any challenge issued by an editor, a reader, or—heaven forbid—a film-studio panjandrum is of any merit. It has never been more obvious to me that no one but the writer can understand what his story is or what it requires in the telling." The Swedish director chose to publish this letter in a magazine instead of burning it—as he had agreed to do—and earned Straka's eternal enmity as a result.

{ 114 }

Handwritten margin notes:

✱ SOME PEOPLE AT THE FUNERAL TOLD ME THAT THEY WERE SORRY I'D HAD TO WORK WITH MOODY.

Sounds like Moody's left quite a trail.

BUT THEN I OVERHEARD A COUPLE OF THEM SAYING THE EXACT OPPOSITE TO ILSA—SHE'S SO LUCKY, LEARNING FROM THE BEST, A GIANT IN THE FIELD, ETC., ETC., AND THE NEW BOOK IS GOING TO CHANGE EVERYTHING, ISN'T IT, ETC.

Maybe they were just trying to get her to spill info about his book.

I HATE THAT. I HATE THAT PEOPLE CAN'T JUST SAY WHAT THEY MEAN.

You don't. Not always.

I NEVER SAY ANYTHING I <u>DON'T</u> MEAN. I JUST AVOID SAYING SOME THINGS THAT I DO.

HOW'S IT GOING W/YOUR PARENTS? ABOUT THE WHOLE JOB SITUATION?

I told them I'm going, so they're fine. There's some paperwork I haven't gotten around to yet. Been too busy to deal.

Just like you (according to you)?

HOW?

Not lying—but not telling the whole story either.

CHECKED THE MAG SOURCE ON THIS. IT'S CLOSE— 1ST + 3RD SENTENCES ARE DIRECT QUOTES. 2ND SENTENCE IS NOT IN THAT LETTER. CAN YOU CHECK THE ORIGINAL IN THE ARCHIVE?

It's not in there, either. So: FXC must've added it. Prob code, right?

"EXPRESSLY" → STARTS WITH "EX" → "X"?

You told him no, I hope.

I SAID I DIDN'T HAVE IT. WHICH TECHNICALLY WASN'T A LIE.

SHIP OF THESEUS

HAVE YOU HAD A CHANCE TO LOOK CLOSELY AT IT?

Yes. That etching on it — to me it looks like an abstract figure of a bird.

I THOUGHT SO, TOO.

S. approaches Pfeifer, who is running his finger up and down the edge of his bandage. "When I left to follow the girl," S. says, "you called out after me. Told me to be careful. And then you said something else, which I couldn't hear. What was it?"

Pfeifer shrugs. "I simply said you don't know who your friends are.* That should be obvious to you. And I don't believe you really know Szalómé. To me—to me and Ostrero, both—it looked like you'd found an excuse to run off."

"But I came back."

("Yes," Pfeifer says. "With a fantastic story and not enough time to change its ending.")

Corbeau cuts him off. "Pfeifer, if this man were going to plant a bomb and then stand in close proximity to that bomb, he'd have to be either profoundly stupid or a suicidal zealot for Vévoda's cause—which is to say, for no cause at all beyond Vévoda's venal self-interest. I'm confident that neither of these is the case." She turns to S. "Still, though: <u>what makes you think you know that girl</u>?"

"I met her—or someone who is very nearly her double—in the city where I was taken onto the ship. Which is also the city where my memory begins." He explains what happened in the bar, mentions

—————

{ 115 }

I'm giving the thing back to you — want it out of my apt. Makes me nervous. For one thing, I'll get fired if they think I'm stealing artifacts. Don't want to have it, anyway — don't want to be anything like elsa.

OK. JUST LEAVE IT FOR ME WITH THE BOOK.

Are you kidding? No way. I'll feel like it's on me if it gets lost. I'm putting this in your hands. So name a time + place, and we'll meet up.

NO TIME. GOT TO LOOK THROUGH ALL THE DOCS DJ SENT ME AGAIN. FEEL LIKE I'VE MISSED SOMETHING IMPORTANT.

Translated: you're willing to risk losing the stone b/c you're too anxious about meeting me.

THAT'S NOT IT.

This is fucking ridiculous. So not worth it.

You realize that passing margin-notes isn't exactly the most efficient way to get to know each other, right? We could text + still keep the mystery, if we want.

DON'T HAVE A MOBILE. I TRY TO KEEP MY LIFE ANALOG.

Glad you finally got one.

DIDN'T UNDERSTAND A WORD OF THE CONTRACT I SIGNED.

Better get used to it.

[left margin, vertical] it's what i was ... it i HAVE FAITH. PLEASE JUST HAVE FAITH. ... happen to us.

*I DID TALK TO ILSA A LITTLE. WISH I HADN'T.

Go on . . .

I ASSUMED MOODY HAD SENT HER, SO I MADE KIND OF A BIG DEAL ABOUT HOW I'D GOTTEN MY OWN FUNDING, ETC.

So you told her about Serin.

YEAH. WHICH WAS PROBABLY A MISTAKE, I KNOW. BUT THE WAY SHE REACTED TO IT MADE ME WONDER — *was she wearing her Moody-stone?*
IF SHE WAS THERE ON HER OWN, TOO.

NOT THAT I COULD SEE.

Playing both sides.

Both sides of <u>*what*</u>, *we still don't know.*

AND MAYBE EVEN A THIRD SIDE — IF SERIN'S FUNDING HER, TOO. WHAT IF THAT DINNER WAS A SERIN THING?

Did you ask anyone?

IT DIDN'T SEEM LIKE A GOOD IDEA TO TALK ABOUT IT. WAS WAITING FOR SOMEONE ELSE TO MENTION SERIN FIRST.

See also: Heyward, Jennifer.

I HAVEN'T GOTTEN THE IMPRESSION THAT YOU'RE RECLUSIVE AT ALL.

Never have been before, but I am these days. I don't want to run into Jacob, don't want to spend time w/ friends I don't like anymore, don't feel like making new friends — too much effort when I'm going to be out of here so soon.

YOU'RE REALLY COMMITTED TO LEAVING.

I need to figure out who I am — can't do it here + I can't do it at home. Sometimes I think it's worth it to take the stupid job just so I'll have an excuse to go to NY. (+ a way to afford living there.)

that Sola told him she was traveling on a liner called the *Imperia*. No one else in the room has heard of a ship by that name.

"Was this other city close by?" Stenfalk asks, without looking up.

"I don't think so. We sailed for weeks."

"Szalómé came to work at the factory six months ago," Corbeau says. "I don't know her well. She is a shy girl, has kept very much to herself. She seems like someone who's a long way from home. Doesn't speak much, but when she does, it's with an accent that comes from much farther south." She asks Pfeifer and Stenfalk if they agree, and both of them say they do. "My point is," Corbeau continues, "that it's unlikely a poor factory <u>girl who works six days a week and who keeps to herself</u> was holding court and chatting with strangers in a waterfront bar in some northern city. Not in the last six months, at any rate, and I'd wager she didn't before then, either."

* "I've always thought she was spying for management," Pfeifer says. "They hadn't hired anyone to work in our part of the factory for a long, long time, and then—poof!—she appeared. Doing some sort of bookwork that, as far as I can tell, hadn't needed to be done before."

{ 116 }

"You think everyone's spying for management," Corbeau says.

"I'm probably right," Pfeifer says. "Don't you think it's better to be suspicious? Especially now?"

"I do," Corbeau says, "but I also value my intuition, and I think it is a very dangerous business to start doubting your intuition.[3] (Without intuition, the world becomes a flat place, a stunted place. A place where change is impossible.")

That's BS. I don't trust my intuition anymore—because really, isn't it something we're taught, too? And that makes change not just possible but unavoidable. You don't have a foundation anymore.

Though S. thinks it wiser to stay out of this discussion, which feels like a mere skirmish in a longer battle between these two, he cannot help himself. "Speaking as someone who has *nothing but intuition*," he offers, "let me say that it's hardly an ideal state of affairs, either. That is—"

MAYBE INTUITION IS SOMETHING YOU HAD BEFORE YOU WERE TAUGHT WHAT YOU THINK IS YOUR INTUITION NOW.

Even if that's true, what good is it? How could you ever tell?

But he is interrupted when Pfeifer jumps to his feet, unbolts the door, and pulls it open. Ostrero rushes in, the collar on his coat turned up to hide his face, a watch cap pulled low on his head. Breathing heavily, he tosses a newspaper onto the table, which startles Stenfalk and causes him to spill his tea. A

3 These words are, in fact, Hemingway's, quoted from the letter he sent to Straka. He said that after reading *The Cordillera*, he felt an intuitive sense that he and Straka would be "*simpatico*" as "artists and men." Again, Straka did not respond. He had little interest in (or tolerance for) the American expatriate's grand and puffed-up pronouncements about art and life and manhood. One wonders if Mr. Hemingway, should he deign to read this book, will take offense that Straka assigned his words to a female character.

("EXPATRIATE"?

I love this. From everything I've heard, Hemingway was a total misogynist dickhead. Whoever Straka was, he was much cooler.

YOU COULD ARGUE THAT VMS SOUNDS LIKE HEMINGWAY IN SOME PLACES, THOUGH... THAT THE STYLE IS ONE OF THE MODES IN WHICH HE COULD WRITE, IF HE WANTED.

look of annoyance crosses the older man's face, but it is quickly replaced by one that seems to hold bewilderment, sadness, and fear all at once. Without saying anything, Ostrero drops himself onto the dusty floor near the fireplace and holds his head in his hands. S. and the others gather at the table, where the top half of the front page screams outrage in a series of bold-type headlines.

BLOODSHED AT WATERFRONT

A Hellish Deed: Bomb Thrown at Police

58 Dead in Riotous Aftermath

Murderous Conspirators in Our Midst

Anarchists Had Inflamed Crowd; Influenced by Foreign Agent?

"Fifty-eight," Corbeau breathes. *"Fifty-eight."*

"Damn Vévoda to hell," Pfeifer says.

Stenfalk grunts and flips the newspaper over to reveal the lower half, where the article begins. No one speaks, but S. can feel the silence between them evolving as they each read through the newspaper's characterization of the events of the night, which lays all of the blame on the demonstrators in

{ 118 }

Margin notes:

CHECK THIS OUT: There's a record of an "Arq. Sobreiro" in a Stockholm jail in 1624.

SO YOU'RE SUGGESTING THAT IT'S THE SAME SOBREIRO AS ON THE SHIP (AND THE SAME ONE WHO WROTE THE BOOK), AND THAT HE SURVIVED HANGING AND BEING THROWN OVERBOARD (OR SOMEHOW REINCARNATED HIMSELF) AND THAT HE THEN MANAGED TO GET ARRESTED AGAIN IN SWEDEN YEARS LATER?

You make it sound like it's unlikely.

PARAPHRASE OF POST-HAYMARKET NEWSPAPER HEADLINES

PARAPHRASE OF POST-CALAIS HEADLINES

general, and on them—the five people hiding in this dusty house, drinking a dead man's tea, one of them even wearing the dead man's boots.[4] ★

This is a heavy, beaten silence, as if the air around them were as bruised and swollen as their faces, chests, limbs. Inset into the text are pictures of three faces, two of which have been etched in minute and deadly accurate detail, perfect depictions of Stenfalk and Corbeau. In the third portrait, the features are less crisply defined, as if to admit more possibility for variation, but the face has an unmistakably sinister set to the jaw. The captions underneath the faces single them out for culpability in the bloodshed: BLOODY ANARCHISTS: STENFALK, CORBEAU, AND AGENT "X." In the body of the article, there is speculation that several other workers, including Messrs. Ostrero and Pfeifer, long known to be socialist malcontents, are believed to be in cahoots with this deadly trio and are wanted by the authorities for immediate questioning. Rewards will be distributed for reliable information regarding the suspects' whereabouts.

"extracting"?   FXC seem more reasonable in Ch. 4.

---

[4] Straka was fond of extracting central images from earlier works for re-use in current projects. Careful readers will recall that in *Winged Shoes*, when Emydio Alves is captured by the Viscount's army, he is stripped of the titular shoes and put to work in the fields wearing "a dead man's boots."

STILL A FEW MOWLERS...
BUT YEAH — MAKES ME THINK
FXC IS TRYING HARDER TO
CONVEY ACTUAL INFO. BUT
WHY THE CHANGE?

I like reading our old notes—cool to have a record of what we used to think.

AS LONG AS WE DIDN'T SAY ANYTHING TOO EMBARRASSING.

OK: How can you be embarrassed by something you said — something you meant at the time—if you really think all the past versions of you are part of you now?

BECAUSE SOME THINGS ARE THAT EMBARRASSING.

Maybe Ch. 4 code was easy to put in & that freed her up to write more useful notes.

OR THERE ARE OTHER CODES IN THEM...

For a long moment, the only sound in the room comes from Ostrero, whose panicked breathing has given way to sobs. Then Stenfalk grunts again and leans back on two legs of his chair. "It's not the most flattering likeness of you, Agent X," Stenfalk says to S. "You may not have been one of us before, but you are now. Whether you like it or not."

Oddly, despite the fear gnarling his gut, S. feels something that might be relief, even elation: *at least now he knows he's not a Detective, not one of Vévoda's men.* He sips his tea, delaying the need to show a reaction, and is disappointed to find that the tea has gone cold. Then it occurs to him that if he were spying for Vévoda, this would be an advantageous position: he would be a cowbird in the enemy's nest. But the simpler story, the one most likely to be true, is that he is now a wanted man, he will be hunted, and his search for Sola has just become much more difficult and dangerous. Perhaps even impossible.

("They're on their way," Ostrero says in a disturbingly flat tone as he looks blankly into the fire. "They're going house to house.")

The lay of the land, as Ostrero explains once he has composed himself, is this: all the roads out of

{ 120 }

Handwritten margin notes:

Where do you live, anyway?

SMALL PLACE SOUTH OF THE TRACKS. RENT'S CHEAP. YOU? *Jefferson apts. Edge of campus, so I can walk to class + downtown.*

Someone broke into the building last night. Word is that packages went missing from the mail area.

ANY OF THEM YOURS? I GUESS YOU WOULDN'T KNOW.

Right. Wasn't expecting anything, though.

OK— I took Abnormal Psych, + I know this reeks of paranoid delusion, but I swear someone's going through my mail. If you ever need to mail anything to me, send it to me @ Pronghorn Java. The manager's a friend.

TRUSTWORTHY? THINK CAREFULLY.

Definitely.

I THINK ONE OF THE WELL-DRESSED GUYS MAY HAVE SAID THIS TO US AT THE DINNER (CAN'T SAY FOR SURE, THOUGH — WAS IN FRENCH, OBV.) IT WAS DEFINITELY A GROUP THAT WOULD GET THE REFERENCE. *Which still doesn't necessarily mean you can trust them—just that they can quote Straka.*

Ilsa emailed about the accession records for the archive.

SHE EMAILED YOU? HOW DOES SHE KNOW YOUR NAME?

She emailed my boss— director of Special Collections—who sent it to me. Probably can't stall much longer.

And my name will be all over the records... Even if she can't remember my face, she'll recognize my name.

One thing I know now: that job is the _last_ thing I want.

SO: RELIEF, EVEN ELATION? Yeah. Although I've got new + different worries now.

SHIP OF THESEUS

———

town are blocked, and the rail station is swarming with Detectives working in tandem with police. The port has been closed indefinitely—no vessels in or out—although that order came only after one large, unflagged ship of foreign-looking design docked just before dawn, quickly took on a load of cargo from the Vévoda annex under the close watch of a pack of Detectives, and steamed off into the chilly morning mist. And just before returning to the safe house, Ostrero saw the police mustering at the central station to begin door-to-door searches for the murderous anarchists. Further, the police are distributing handbills that show all five of their faces; they're hanging in shop windows, they're on lightposts, they're in people's hands and pockets, and as far as Ostrero could tell, no one was expressing doubts about the official account of the massacre. The general citizenry, which has never had any particular love for Vévoda, supported the workers during the demonstrations, but their sympathies have shifted; their city, suddenly, has become hostile and unsafe territory. Even the other protestors are accepting the story, docilely falling into line, whether out of gullibility, self-interest, or simple fear. Based solely on the words of the police and the newspaper,

———

Stenfalk and the rest of them have been indelibly marked as The Enemy. The Bombers. The Subversive Threats to Life and Productivity.[5]

"It's insane," Pfeifer says. "A bomb goes off, and everyone takes leave of their senses."

("Fear is a powerful thing," Stenfalk says. "It makes strong men malleable.")

"How could someone write that article?" Ostrero says. "We *know* the bomber was a provocateur."

"That's what we *believe*," Pfeifer observes. "That's what S. has told us."

Stenfalk sniffs. "It wasn't any of our people. I would have known about it."

"Turn the page," Ostrero says. "They've accused us of mining the harbor, too. To interfere with Vévoda's business."

"That's absurd. Again, I would have known."

["For what it's worth," S. says, "the harbor *is* mined. Well, there's one mine, anyway. I ran into it as I was swimming."] CH. 20

Stenfalk glares at him, clearly inconvenienced by this news. "It must have been there already," he says firmly. "It's not ours." But S. hears doubt in his voice,

---

5   Exiling key figures in labor movements was and is a common strategy used by the ownership class. The Hobo Preacher's homily in *Wineblood's Mine* contains Straka's most scathing indictment of the practice.

[Margin notes, left:]
I think I heard someone in my apt. last night. Wasn't roommate. I'm getting out of here. Won't call — it'll lead them to you.

I DON'T CARE. CALL ME.

[Margin notes, bottom left:]
EXILING? IT'S GOT TO BE THE "EX" WORDS.
I think you're right. Check out FN1 again: "those that quickly followed." So maybe the letter or the word that comes next?
WOW. NEXT-WORD GIVES US:
AVOID GRAND CENTRAL
KEY STOLEN
ASSUME BAG GONE → *Straka's bag = S.'s?*
I FAILED
Poor Filomela. Poor both of them.

[Margin notes, bottom right:]
HE WAS ALREADY DEAD.
She believed he was alive. Really, really believed it. So it was true for her.

and, watching Corbeau closely, he sees that she hears it, too. What do they really know? [Has the movement gotten away from them before it was ever truly with them? Doubt is filling Zapadi's decrepit house, weighing down the air around them. Doubt is tipping the foundation, causing beams and joists to wail with stress, bowing the windows in their frames.]

They confer about their options, which are few and poor, although this has the benefit of making planning much easier. They will sneak out of town through the forest to the south and hike over the coastal range to the town of G——, a small, isolated port, where Stenfalk figures they can get onto a boat; from there, they will improvise. The walk will be a long one—five or six days alone just to reach the summit pass, probably another three days down into G——. This is not a well-traveled route; it once was, centuries ago, but no longer—roads and rails have led people in other directions. Still, as a girl Corbeau did some exploring in these foothills with her father, who was by trade a cooper but in his heart an archaeologist. He'd been fascinated by the rumors of a long-dead tribe of mountain people,

CF. THE S? WHEN + WHAT WOULD'VE PROMPTED THEIR DOUBT?

Maybe when they realized Looper had split?

Straka's laying it on thick here.

THAT'S WHAT MAKES ME THINK HE WAS WRITING ABOUT THE S HERE—IT'S WHAT MATTERED MOST TO HIM.

DURAND'S FATHER WAS AN ARCHAEOLOGIST. SHE SPENT HER GIRLHOOD ON DIGS.

Makes for a much cooler "take-your-daughter-to-work day" than "V.P. of Branding and Communications."

THEY ENDED UP BEING RIVALS, IN A WAY. HE WAS UPSET THAT SHE WENT OUT ON HER OWN + FOUND THE CAVE IN THE DORDOGNE.

Did they ever patch it up?

PROBABLY DIDN'T HAVE TIME— HE DIED W/IN A YEAR. SPIDER BITE WHILE ON A DIG IN EGYPT. ONE OF THE "MUMMY'S CURSE" DEATHS.

the K——, who had a vast network of caves filled with pictographs and other relics. "We never found anything," she tells them, "but I loved the time we spent up there exploring. I don't know how well I'll remember the paths."

"Some knowledge is better than none," Stenfalk says. It's not clear if he's finishing her sentence for her, in the manner of intimates, or simply interrupting with his own observation (which may also be in the manner of intimates). Corbeau's reaction is a quick nod with a flash of eye contact, and from that calm, muted reaction S. infers that they are indeed lovers, and that they are committed to facing these dangerous circumstances together.

The same cannot be said for Ostrero and his wife, who appears at the door while the fugitives are gathering up their belongings; she brings with her a sack full of cheeses and cakes and dried fruits, as well as a few empty jugs that they can fill in the mountain streams as they go. She hands these over wordlessly and with obvious disdain. If she is sad to see her husband go on the run, away from her and their children, the sadness is far outweighed by her disapproval and anger. She casts disparaging glances at each of the rest of them—lingering a

{ 124 }

Handwritten margin notes:

** So who's Ostrero? Spanish, so Garcia Ferrara?
THAT'S MY GUESS.

Too bad the Voliéry was torn down. I can't feel the past here at all.
CAN YOU FEEL THE FUTURE?

Imagine that this is Vaclav, looking at Ekstrom + Durand. It makes sense.

JUST FOUND SOMETHING IN DESJARDINS' PILE OF DOCS: IT'S A PHOTO OF A PAGE FROM A HOTEL REGISTER: HOTEL VOLIÉRY IN PRAGUE. OCT. 30, 1910.

The day Vaclav jumped.

WANT TO GUESS WHOSE NAMES ARE ON IT?
Ekstrom + Durand?

CLOSE. TRY AGAIN.
Just tell me !!!

T. STENFALK + A. CORBEAU.
Ha. Funny.

I'M SERIOUS. THEY WERE IN PRAGUE THAT DAY.

AND SCRAWLED IN NEXT TO THEIR NAMES? CZECH FOR "AND GUEST."

And you think that was Vaclav. So you're assuming he survived the jump.

I KNOW IT'S UNBELIEVABLE. BUT YES.

I believe it.
GUESS WHO JOINS THEM ALL THERE THE NEXT DAY...
Pfeifer + Ostrero?
YUP.
So... Pfeifer = Feuerbach?
... WHO WAS TRAVELING WITH HIS "SECRETARY." YES. **

I'm surprised FXC doesn't have something to say about this

beat longer on Corbeau, whom she clearly suspects of using sexual wiles to separate her husband from his good sense—and as she slips back out into the streets, she tells Ostrero in a stage whisper: "Don't hurry back." The effect on Ostrero—on all of them, really, as they watch him wilt—is devastating. For an extended moment they fall into a quiet, sad inertia, until Stenfalk claps his hands and declares that there's no time to waste, no time for regret or emotion or any such extravagances. What matters is surviving, escaping, and then, with the safety of distance, making the world understand that Vévoda himself was behind the massacre,[6] behind the disappearances of the Zapadi Three, behind the dark work of the annex, behind the-devil-knows-what-else.

S. nods. A blessing of his amnesia: he has no knowledge of any connections to others, and thus no connections to fear breaking, no connections to repair once broken, no connections to be grieved once they are lost. How fortunate, to be impervious to

So did you hook up with Ilsa in Paris?.

GOD, NO. WE PRETTY MUCH IGNORED EACH OTHER.

Who started ignoring first?

WE WERE BOTH IGNORING.

---

[6] After the Calais Massacre, authorities declared that the bomb had been fashioned from explosives stolen from the Bouchard factory. This was, to a degree, true. They had been stolen from the factory by workers encouraged to do so by an Agent who had infiltrated their camp. The Agent then stole the dynamite back from them, and because it was traceable to the workers, Bouchard's thugs were free to use it to do their worst, with little risk of Bouchard's plans being discovered.

---

such things, to be ignorant of anyone else's feelings of loss that might involve him.

⋆ To be a self rewritten from a lost first draft. ⋆

When he returns his attention to his surroundings, everyone else is watching him expectantly. Perhaps he has been muttering to himself. It's the sort of habit one falls into easily when alone on a ship.

"Well?" Stenfalk says. "Are you joining us?"

"Fifty-eight dead," Corbeau says. "You have to be outraged."

And he is; he is outraged. But he can't give up on finding Sola, doesn't want to risk any more delay.

"Think of it this way," Stenfalk says, his voice rich with authority. "Even if you're not outraged, even if you don't care about us or our jobs or our missing friends or the growing pestilence that is Vévoda, even if the most important thing—the *only* important thing—to you is figuring out who you are, well, let me simply observe that one is unlikely to make effective inquiries to that end if one is dangling from a hangman's noose. That, I should inform you, is very definitely the risk all of us in this room are facing."

Silence. Creaking wood as something in the house sags a bit more deeply.

Marginalia (handwritten):

Depends who's holding the pen.

FUNDAMENTAL SOT QUESTION: DOES THE REWRITING MAKE US DIFFERENT PEOPLE? OR JUST A PRODUCT OF ONGOING REVISION?

Solitude makes you a little weird.
ME?
"You" meaning everyone.
(Hypersensitive...?)

YEAH, I AM. SOME DAYS THIS WINTER ALL I COULD THINK ABOUT WAS HOW OFF I FELT. HOW I WASN'T MYSELF. OR SOMEWHERE ALONG THE LINE I'D TURNED INTO SOMEONE I'D ALWAYS DREADED BEING.

Always? Or since the boat?

DON'T KNOW. MEMORY REWRITES ITSELF, TOO.

You mean we rewrite memories.

EITHER WAY: FOR AS LONG AS I CAN REMEMBER, I PRIDED MYSELF ON BEING ABLE TO HOLD IT TOGETHER. AND THEN SUDDENLY I COULDN'T.

I don't think I can anymore.

YOU CAN. MAYBE JUST NOT IN THE SAME WAY YOU USED TO. BREATHE.

"I'm with you," S. says. Stenfalk is right; the most important thing is to get out of this city in one piece. He can always break away from the group later.

"You're sure?" Corbeau asks.

"I'm sure of nothing," S. says. "But I'm going with you."

And so, having filled all of the bags they could find (Stenfalk's valise, two mildewed rucksacks from Zapadi's closet, the burlap sack Ostrero's wife brought) with the food and blankets and other supplies for the journey, they put their escape plan into motion. They do not have the luxury of waiting for cover of night. Will there be eyes watching them from the buildings on this dismal street? Almost certainly—but with staggered, unhurried, unobtrusive exits, they may evade suspicion.

Ostrero takes up the seat by the window, watching the street through the cuts in the shutters. Watching him, S. has a sense that there's something odd about this scene, some detail he ought to be noticing but isn't, quite, but then Ostrero gives a hand signal that means *all clear*, and the rest of them wish Pfeifer good luck as they send him out first into a dangerous world. Pfeifer steps outside, quickly shutting the door behind him. He is heading

---

Handwritten margin notes:

SO I'VE BEEN THINKING: IF ALL THOSE POSSIBLE STRAKAS WERE TOGETHER, WHY WOULD VACLAV HAVE BEEN WITH THEM? *and even if he was w/ them, why would they let him stay around? He was a depressed factory kid.*

IF YOU BELIEVE RYBARIK, V. WAS HOLDING HIS MANUSCRIPT WHEN HE JUMPED. *So if Ekstrom or Durand saw him jump, they might've seen papers flying.*

OR EVEN FOUND SOME SOAKED PAGES IN HIS HANDS/POCKETS... *What if they pulled him out of the river? Or were around when someone else did? Felt bad for him, took him back to their hotel to get dry, rested, fed, etc.*

THERE WAS THE "AND GUEST" IN THE REGISTER. THIS IS REALLY A REACH, THOUGH. *It's intuition ("without which the world becomes a flat place, a stunted place...")*

not directly for the hills but deeper into the city, toward a vacant lot in the western district that has become a *de facto* junkyard for the neighborhood, filled with discarded building materials and trash and all manner of things that will ignite when he douses them with the kerosene he has in a jar in his pocket and strikes a match. When the smoke and flames rise and the sirens start wailing and the water-tank carriages are rumbling toward the scene, the rest of them will leave the house, taking different routes through the twisting, ascending streets of the city's outskirts. They'll reconvene at a particular grove of white oaks in the valley just beyond the first green hill that marks the city's southern boundary.

The minutes pass. The sirens do not come. No one speaks. The straps of the rucksack dig into S.'s shoulders. Something in this room has begun to seem familiar—that's what he was noticing before—but what? and why?

"It shouldn't be taking so long," Ostrero says. "Maybe he was caught. Do you think he was caught?"

"We don't know anything more than you do," Stenfalk snaps, his tone uncharacteristically sharp.

Silence descends once more. Ostrero looks chastened, and S. watches him try to compose himself,

JEN:
WHAT IF THE FIRES HAVE BEEN DIVERSIONS?
Easy for you to say. No one's setting fires near you.

≠ FALLING

EKSTROM REEF ⟶

to turn himself into a man who is afraid of nothing, who is bravely doing what he needs to do to survive, who can accept the loss of his family and everything about the life he had until last night, who will stride forward as an asset to the group and not a liability. This is, S. notes, very much a work in progress.

And then, distantly, there are shouts.

And the smell of smoke.

And then sirens.

And then Ostrero gives the signal, and then Stenfalk grabs Corbeau in a perfunctory embrace and steps alone into the street, which remains as gloomy in this cloud-socked noontime as it was at dawn. S. leans down over the seated Ostrero, who also watches Stenfalk through the narrow shutter-slits as the older man moves without any breach in his natural calm, holding his valise in a way that suggests (if imperfectly) that it is not particularly heavy, (that it contains, perhaps, just some legal papers and a spare pair of socks, and is not, in fact, stuffed nearly to bursting with staples for survival in the hills.) Their eyes follow him as he makes his way to the edge of their view and beyond.

Again, that feeling: he is failing to notice something. What is it? Something vaguely connected to

---

Handwritten annotations:

Well, Ffoulkes + Ilsa have me hugging another hero.

WHAT HAPPENS IF YOU FAIL THIS CLASS? WILL YOU STILL GRADUATE?

It's not entirely clear.

HOW CAN IT NOT BE CLEAR?

Because it's not clear if I'm going to pass any of my other classes.

We're never told what is (or isn't) in there.

WHICH LEAVES US TO SPECULATE ABOUT WHAT SORT OF BUSINESS STENFALK (+ THUS EKSTROM?) WAS UP TO. QUESTIONS BOTH WITHIN + WITHOUT THE STORY...

I've started feeling like that with everything I read/see in the archive. And not just the archive here. All of them.

WELCOME TO MY WORLD.

And all the things going on around my apartment, too. And if that isn't also your world, it should be.

a memory that might be squirreled away in a closed-off part of his brain? There is something important here, something he should be recognizing. But there's no time to sit and contemplate: Corbeau is now clutching his hand—they'll walk together, since he doesn't know the city—and she is propelling him toward the door and into the gray daylight and the swirling breeze that sends leaves and paper and other detritus spinning over the façades of the buildings that line the lane. Now, to any eyes that might be watching, they are a couple, man and woman, perhaps setting off on a series of quotidian household errands, or making their way to the rail station, hurrying through the smoke-sweetened streets to catch a train that will take them to a romantic weekend far off in the capital city. S. turns his head to look back at Zapadi's house—he's not sure why, maybe he's simply distracted and curious to see whether Ostrero's shadow or even his blinking eye is visible through the shutters—and he sees, now effortlessly, the detail that was tugging at his attention. The shutters. More specifically, their scrollwork, the design cut into each of the panels. On the left, that familiar shape; on the right, its mirror image.

WERE VMS + DURAND EVER A COUPLE? (LOOK INTO THIS.)
FXC doesn't think so. Or doesn't want to, anyway. (FN7)

But maybe they pretended to be?
OR MAYBE THEY WERE PLATONIC— BUT AS CLOSE AS IF THEY'D BEEN A COUPLE?
I don't think that's possible.

Do you?

NOT ANYMORE.

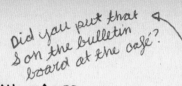

Did you put that S on the bulletin board at the café?

YEAH. WANTED TO SAY HI.

That's sweet. Freaked me out for a minute, though— thought it might've been Ilsa or someone else messing w/ me.

Corbeau tightens her grip on his hand. "Look forward," she says quietly. "Relax. <u>Pretend we belong together</u>."[7] ARE YOU REALLY READY TO TRY THIS?
No. But I will.

He does as he is told. Or he tries, at any rate. He's not sure what belonging together looks like.

"Did you notice the shutters on the house?" he asks her.

"Not particularly, no."

"There's a design on them. An ornate S shape."

"I'm surprised," she says, "that you're noticing architectural details when our lives are very much in danger."

"I've seen it before. In several places. It feels familiar somehow."

"It might simply be something traditional, of course. Or a design that one particular shutter-maker in town enjoyed using. <u>Look around. You'll probably see them everywhere.</u>"

But he doesn't see them everywhere. He and Corbeau walk down dozens of streets, the sounds of

Seriously, check out the Danish guy's site. It's amazing where the S has been found.

MY INTUITION: ALL THE OLD ONES ARE CONTEMP. FAKES.

Even in the caves? You think someone would deface an archaeological find just to play some kind of Straka game?

YOU HAVE A HIGHER ESTIMATION OF MOST PEOPLE'S RESPECT FOR ART THAN I DO.

There's one in a cave they just opened up. Check the photos. It's faint, but don't tell me you don't see it... (Oh, and BTW? This is really close to where Filomela grew up. Do I rule? Yes!)

INDEED YOU DO.

---

7 Reader, let us <u>explicitly</u> assume that this relationship is meant as one of comradeship and support in the face of a common and devastating enemy. Straka had little patience for those who demand an epic romance if male and female characters simply glimpse one another, let alone hold hands. Straka emphatically did not intend to position S. as a romantic rival to Stenfalk.

PROTESTING TOO MUCH?

She was def. jealous ~~about~~ whatever connection Durand had to Straka.

AND THEY MUST HAVE HAD ONE. (<u>PAINTED CAVE</u> MATERIAL)

and Prague.

SO: DID THEY HAVE AN AFFAIR UNDER EKSTROM'S NOSE (PUN INTENDED)?

FYI: Puns aren't your strength.

I CAN'T BELIEVE I'M SUGGESTING THIS TO YOU (OR TO ANYONE WHO ISN'T AN ENEMY), BUT: HAVE YOU THOUGHT ABOUT GRAD SCHOOL? YOU'RE A GOOD READER W/ A HELL OF A GIFT FOR RESEARCH.

M+D would have a cow. Multiple cows.

DOESN'T MEAN YOU CAN'T DO IT. JUST MEANS THERE'D BE COWS FOR THEM TO TAKE CARE OF.

{ 131 }

panic and firefighting growing soft behind them, the smell of the smoke growing less intense—less *real*, in a way, now a mere atmospheric detail—and while not all of the buildings have shutters on the windows, many do, and none of them has the *S*.

"I think it means something," S. says to her.

"It means whatever you want it to mean," she huffs.

As they draw closer to where the roads and sidewalks and houses end, they walk differently. She swings their hands back and forth, jauntily; now they are a couple off for a late-afternoon picnic on some verdant hillside on which the autumn wildflowers are holding on to the last of their blooms.

"Excuse my indelicacy," S. says, after allowing the calm of the countryside to settle over them. "Are you and Stenfalk—" He pauses to consider his phrasing. "A couple?"

"What makes you ask?"

"Curiosity."

"Well," she says. "Not formally. But yes, we are, in a way that has scandalized some of the more limited minds around us." They did. He had Thanksgiving

"Ostrero's wife?"

"You noticed? I'm certain she blames me for all of this. Some sort of free-floating carnal witchery,

{ 132 }

Handwritten margin notes:

S. seems like he is attracted to her—even if he's not totally aware of it. There's def. something between them—You can see it in the cave.

BUT HE DOESN'T WANT TO BACKSTAB STENFALK. EVEN IF HE DOESN'T KNOW ANYTHING ABOUT HIMSELF, HE OBVIOUSLY HAS SOME SENSE OF HONOR.

Up to a point.

I THINK HE'S STILL HONORABLE ALL THE WAY THROUGH. HE JUST GETS FIERCER—MORE DESPERATE.

SO JACOB CHEATED?
Don't know the details + don't want to—though my "friends" keep trying to give them to me.

DID YOUR PARENTS LIKE HIM?
They did. He had Thanksgiving + Xmas w/us. He can be really charming when he wants to be.

we could use some of that.
Really? you're going to let that one go?
I'M NOT GOOD AT FLIRTING.
No kidding... IT JUST ENDS UP SOUNDING CREEPY.
TO ME, ANYWAY.
Pretend you're good at it. more fun that way. If it gets creepy, I'll let you know (in all-caps, so you don't miss it). —HAVE I EVER MISSED SOMETHING YOU'VE WRITTEN HERE? No... but the space is filling up... at some point it'll get too hard to follow. —

WHAT IF YOU QUIT MAKING SUCH A MESS OF IT?

I suppose, that plagues all the men around me. And, apparently, that detonates explosives in crowded places."

"Absurd."

"Of course," she says. "My loyalty, my heart—and yes, my body—are with Stenfalk. With him, and with the cause for which we now find ourselves fighting."

The sirens are by now a minor, nearly abstract, presence, and both he and she instinctively look back at the western district. Flames rise high above the buildings in the foreground, and a twisting column of thick black smoke is drilling its way up through the cloud cover.

"Do you think it's spreading?" she asks.

"Hard to say."

"Because that would be terrible," she says, forgetting to maintain her unflappable demeanor. "If it spread, and people were hurt."

S. nods. *Fires burn, though,* he thinks. *That's what they do. And they resist our control.*

"That's why people like Vévoda always have the advantage, you know," Corbeau says, rubbing her nose. "Over people like us. Because we're cursed with the belief that people matter. It's much, much easier to bend the world to your will if bending the

[handwritten right margin] It got really close to the hotel. We were all out in the parking lot watching it. and I was alone—felt like I had to stay away from everyone. How could I trust anyone there?

JUST GLAD YOU'RE SAFE. HAVE YOU CALLED THE POLICE? ASKED THEM TO KEEP AN EYE ON YOUR BUILDING NOW THAT YOU'RE BACK?

They say they're already doing it "due to the proliferation of incidents." They're useless—they can't stop these people.

[handwritten bottom left] like that isn't scary itself? I CAN'T STAY HERE. AND I DON'T HAVE anyWHERE TO GO.

[handwritten bottom right] WE DON'T KNOW WHO "THESE PEOPLE" ARE. WE DON'T KNOW THAT THEY ARE. you're just saying that because you don't want me to worry. you don't really believe it. IT COULD BE SOME PUNK THAT MOODY'S PAYING TO DO THINGS TO SCARE YOU.

world is what matters most to you." Her voice has risen in both volume and pitch, and she realizes it, quickly composing herself; in an instant, (she is once again just a woman walking with her rather younger beau, a man of twenty-six or so) whose mismatched and ill-fitting clothes might capture your attention, but whose face you would fail to remember.

"Who is Vévoda, anyway?" S. asks. "What do you know about him? No one seems to have expected that he was capable of—"

"Shhh," she says. "Enough talk about him. Better to wait until we're far from the city." And for a few minutes, then, there is silence between them. It's not that S. finds the silence itself uncomfortable— he spent enough time with only his own company on the ship—but it feels wrong to him to be this close to someone, especially someone whom he can trust, and to waste the opportunity for interaction.

"Have you and Stenfalk been together a long time?" S. asks. It's a clumsy question, delivered halt- ingly, but at least they are words and he has offered them to her.

She begins to answer but cuts herself off as a door ahead of them opens and a doctor—or, at least, a tall and bony man in hat, suit, and vest who

---

Handwritten marginalia:

PARAPHRASE OF BIG JUREK'S LINES IN WINEBLOOD (P. 299). THE VOICE OF STRAKA THE RADICAL.

Implying that Durand was older than Straka?
COULD BE JUST A DETAIL FOR THE STORY, NOT NEC. FROM VMS'S "REAL LIFE."
26 is pretty specific, though. Makes me think he's talking about himself here. Another reason to rule out Ekstrom, Feuerbach, even Summersby— they were all older than Durand.
BIG ASSUMPTION, THOUGH.

THERE WAS A STRANGE MOMENT AT THE DINNER—SOMEONE REFERRED TO DJ AS A WIDOWER ("VEUF," RIGHT? I'M PRETTY SURE THAT'S WHAT I HEARD). A COUPLE OF PEOPLE SHOT HIM REALLY BAD LOOKS + HE SHUT UP IMMEDIATELY. STARTED SWEATING LIKE CRAZY. LOOKED MORTIFIED.

S. IS LONELY. DOESN'T TRUST MANY PEOPLE.
It's shocking to me that you can even begin to identify w/ him.

No response?
OH— SARCASM. I BET IT.
Sometimes I think you're actually a robot.

That's weird. Why worry about saying that when both of them are dead?

has a stethoscope hugging his neck and a black medical bag in one hand—steps out into the street and coughs into a handkerchief. S. understands Corbeau's discretion: (best not to be overheard saying anything at all. He might look like a doctor, but who knows what's in his bag? And who knows his allegiances? The doctor tips his hat as they pass.[8] From an upstairs window in the house he just exited comes the fierce squalling of an infant in great discomfort. S. watches Corbeau scan their surroundings quickly before she elects to speak again. And when she does, her speech is more relaxed, her diction less clipped.

"We've known each other a long time," she says. "I was at the factory for ten years—funny, how strange it feels to have to use past tense—and he was there when I arrived. I'd admired him, of course, especially when he and Zapadi started taking up the union cause. He has quite a way with words, and a wonderful imagination, too, and a deep commitment to honor and fairness. We only became lovers after the disappearances. Everything felt more

---

[8] In many dime novels of the 1920s and 1930s—including several written by Straka "candidate" Victor Martin Summersby—a physician's examination bag nearly always contained some nefarious item—weapon, bomb, dismembered corpse, stolen state secret, and the like. I suspect Straka was winking at the practice here.

ANOTHER MYSTERY BAG
I can totally see this in a movie. Guy approaching seems menacing, they get worked up, guy passes, looks, nothing happens... but you still wonder about him, a little— is he going to come back?

urgent, I suppose. Connections felt more necessary. Comfort, too."

Their footsteps are quieter now, as they have left the packed dirt and gravel of the southernmost street and crossed into a green meadow of long grasses. The wind remains strong, and it whips the tips of the grass back and forth in a way that seems menacing rather than tranquil. Or perhaps that's just S.'s fear getting the best of him. He wonders: in the part of his life that he has left behind, was he ever hunted? Kidnapped? Imprisoned? It's strange to have faced all three so quickly now, strange and disturbing, and it must be taking a toll on his nerves.

"It must be difficult," Corbeau observes, "at a time like this, to have no connections of which you're aware."

★ "One could argue that it's easier," S. says, "when you only have to worry about yourself." ★

"And yet you're looking for the girl. For Szalómé. You don't see any connection? That is to say, any connection between your search for her and such notions of connections? You don't *feel* something?") She smiles wryly. For her, these are entirely rhetorical questions.

Margin notes (handwritten):

CONNECTIONS COME BACK TO BITE YOU IN THE ASS.

I assume you wrote this over the winter.
NO — IT'S OLDER THAN THAT. BUT WHEN I READ IT AGAIN IN THE HOSPITAL, I WAS REALLY PROUD OF YOUNGER ME FOR BEING SO ASTUTE.

And now?
HONESTLY? I DON'T KNOW WHAT I'D DO WITHOUT THIS CONNECTION. (WITH YOU.)
(I inferred that.)

So let's meet.
YOU WROTE FOUR VARIATIONS ON "LET'S MEET" ON THIS PASS.
Um, that's because I want to meet.

I want to know where that symbol came from. — I DO, TOO.

I wish S. would wake the hell up.

S. resists, not wanting to believe that the answer is so simple, so ordinary. "I *sense* a connection. What that connection may be, if it even exists, is a mystery to me."

Then the meadow is behind them, and they have crossed into the forest. Once they are completely concealed from city eyes, Corbeau releases his hand and swings her arms freely as she walks. Truth be told, S. is disappointed; it was only a pretense—he'd never thought otherwise—but he'd been enjoying the feel of her hand in his, the comfort of togetherness even without the slightest tinge of romance. He wipes his damp palm on his trousers, dons what he hopes is a visage of stoicism, and walks on with her, ascending the first of the many more hills they will traverse. There is no path to speak of, but the woods are not so dense as to slow their progress. Their feet swish through the crisp brown and orange leaves that have fallen from half-naked lindens, oaks, and hornbeams, while squirrels and chipmunks, suspicious and excitable, dart across their paths. They pass a silver birch, startling a train of roosting jackdaws. The birds rise in a rush of feathers; as they turn smooth arcs overhead, another flock joins them, and then another and another, all

{ 137 }

If S. really is Straka then Straka was an idiot. Filomela should've left a lot earlier.

MAYBE SHE FELT LIKE SHE SHOULD, BUT DECIDED TO STAY ANYWAY— TO BELIEVE IN HIM.

And that worked so well.

MAYBE NOT AS BADLY AS WE THOUGHT... SHE FOUND HER PLACE. OR A PLACE, ANYWAY.

SO... "SERIN" IS FRENCH FOR "CANARY."

I know. That was one of the first things I looked up. But it's just a name—they can call themselves whatever they want.

Example: MacInnes + his version of The S. (He was good at spreading the money around, too...)

I'M FOLLOWING MY INTUITION HERE. ISN'T THAT WHAT YOU'VE BEEN WANTING ME TO DO?

Not if it's going to get you hurt.

chatters and squeaks as they draw and erase and redraw their curves over the vellum of pale afternoon sky. S. and Corbeau pause, marvel.

And then, up ahead, is Stenfalk, sitting cross-legged under a white oak, with his valise in his lap.

Once the others arrive at the rendezvous in the oaks, Stenfalk quizzes them about their routes, what they saw and heard, whether they might have been recognized, watched, followed. The stories that spill out are blessedly free of event. Ostrero confesses he originally chose a route that would allow him a glimpse of his children as they left the schoolhouse but decided this posed an unacceptable degree of risk. His tone suggests that he is seeking credit for this decision, and S. offers him a mild compliment when none other is forthcoming. Pfeifer had one awkward moment when his wounded ear began again to bleed freely, but he was able to duck into an alley and use a fresh handkerchief to clean himself up. The only person who saw him there was a semiconscious drunk preoccupied with attempting to coax sounds from a scavenged concertina with a ruptured bellows.

Stenfalk nods, says that's as clean an escape as they could have hoped for. Pfeifer volunteers bitterly

{ 138 }

Margin notes (handwritten):

If FXC was trying to send Straka messages here, then she def. didn't think Ekstrom was Straka. She knew he'd been dead for years.

RIGHT. BUT SUMMERSBY LIVED UNTIL '51. SO IF "STRAKA" WAS EK. + SUMM. TOGETHER, THEN THAT COULD STILL WORK.

But think about Summ.'s confession — he said he was Straka, but that Ek helped him on the 1st book. If it was the two of them together all along, why not say so? And if Summ. just wanted the credit, why bring up Ekstrom at all?

SO THE CONFESSION HAS TO BE 100% TRUE OR 100% NOT TRUE?

I just don't know why he'd partially lie. He knew he was going to die, + Ekstrom was long-dead, so why bother? — And if you're doubting Summ. on the style issue anyway then we should rule out both of them. which means Moody's going

PHYSICAL AILMENT = MORAL AILMENT

Haven't thought about that before.

HITCHCOCK USED THAT A LOT. Rope at the Varsity tonight — but of course you're not here.

CF. THE CORDILLERA — ZARATE, THE CONCERTINA PLAYER

→ to embarrass himself w/ his book.

that his only regret is not having made the diversionary fire ten times larger, taken down a city block or two, maybe even the whole western district. S. watches as each of them struggles to accept the hard truth: their home city has been turned against them—and it has been induced to do so far too easily. Perhaps only Pfeifer has abandoned his hope of a return and a reconciliation—Pfeifer, whose anger always seems to be closest to the surface—and the others can still conceive of being able to right the wrongs, return safely, make Vévoda answer for what he has done. S. thinks that their optimism is probably misplaced, that none of them will ever again call the city home.

The forest thickens as they move on in the hope of making a few more miles before the autumnal sky goes dark. Progress is slow; while the trail that Corbeau remembers occasionally reveals itself, years have passed since anything larger than a fox has walked it, and they lose time pushing through brambles and deadfall or looping far out of their way in search of easier passage.

The sky darkens, and the rising moon is a crescent too thin to light their way. Exhaustion settles over them once more—what little conversation

HARD TO FACE THAT WHAT'S GONE IS GONE.

HOME NO LONGER A SAFE PLACE

Been catching naps in the workrooms—don't feel safe anywhere but the library.

Fox is the guide + maker of paths in "White Oak."

there had been as they climbed died away well before sundown—and Stenfalk's suggestion that they stop is embraced unanimously. Pfeifer gathers wood and makes a fire—"a *small* one," Corbeau suggests to him—and they sit, stretch out sore legs, and share bread and cheese. They spend a few minutes plotting strategy, but there is not much to plot: the plan is simply to *go*. Claw their way over the mountains and down into G——, and then to the water.

"You asked about Vévoda earlier," Corbeau says to S. "What did you wish to know?"

S. says, "I want to know why no one expected him to be so dangerous."

"No one knew much about him," Corbeau says. "Not even those of us who grew up here. He didn't go to school with us, didn't play with any of us. He rarely left the family's estate, which is up on a hill in the northern district. And then he was sent overseas—no one knows where—to university, and he didn't return until his father fell ill. He does run the business actively—we know the factory bosses don't make any of the important decisions themselves—but he is rarely seen. If he ever visits the factory, it's in a car with shades drawn over the windows."

MAYBE REFERRING TO
BOUCHARD'S SON?

Do we know that
Bouchard had a son?

WE DON'T KNOW. BUT
WHEN USSR FELL + MANY
KREMLIN DOCS RELEASED,
THERE WAS ONE FROM
1957 ABOUT MANAGING THE
"COMMERÇANTS B."
TRANSITION (SEE DESJARDINS
1986). HAVE HEARD THERE'S
A SIMILAR DOC IN
EISENHOWER'S ARCHIVES,
WHICH IS INTERESTING —
BOTH SIDES WORRYING
ABOUT BOUCHARD
CONTINUITY.

"Why make three men disappear?" S. asks. "Why bomb a crowd of his employees?"

"Former employees," Pfeifer reminds him. "He'd fired every one of us."

S. nods. "More to the point, what is he making in the annex?"

"And just as much to the point," Stenfalk says, "who is he selling it to? And when and where will it be used?"

But the discussion lacks the intensity S. would've expected. It's odd, as though the conversation were one in a dream, or in a memory. The questions, once posed, are allowed to drift away. Perhaps they're all simply overwhelmed by the events of the last twenty-four hours, by the conflict and death and desperate flight, the sudden, irreversible exile. Stenfalk wraps his arm around Corbeau's shoulders and pulls her close; Pfeifer stabs nervously at the ground with a stick; Ostrero sits still, legs crossed, elbows on knees, head cupped by palms. S. reminds himself to be vigilant, to observe everything he possibly can, to look for any connections to past events, past emotions, anything about his past self, but his thoughts keep drifting to Sola, to where she might be, to whether he'll ever come close to finding her again. As the

GARCÍA FERRARA NOTORIOUSLY MOODY/ MELANCHOLY. PICASSO DID A BLUE-PERIOD PORTRAIT OF HIM BUT DESTROYED IT B/C IT MADE HIM TOO SAD TO LOOK AT IT. (SEE: THE MANY FACES OF TIAGO GARCÍA FERRARA BY J. LLORENS.)

G.F. must've been a complete mess in those last years, when he had so many good reasons to be depressed.

— NOT THE REASONS WE THOUGHT. But still: very good reasons.

night deepens, all five commit longer stretches of time looking into the fire, tracing the dervish embers as they spin into the darkness above, listening to the crackling and popping of the wood.

They sleep (Corbeau and Stenfalk curl up together under one blanket; S. and the other two men stretch out their solitary selves.) They each take a turn standing watch, listening to the hardy crickets that have survived into fall, the distant screeches of owls, the snoring and muttering of their traveling companions, and the sounds of a forest full of other mammals rustling over the leaves unseen, going about their business. S.'s watch comes after Ostrero's, and when the two men pass each other in silence, S. pats him on the back. All S. has lost is the trail of Sola; it may pain him, but it is nothing compared to what Ostrero has given up—a family, a home, a way of living that once defined him and no longer does. Ostrero nods and quickly turns away, settling himself into the dark.

The hills are sun-splashed on the second day. In the morning, Corbeau makes coffee over the fire, and they share a delicious venison and cranberry pie

As if S. didn't feel lonely enough already...

LET'S MEET BEFORE I LEAVE.
Why now?
I DON'T KNOW. HAS TO DO W/ GOING AWAY.
Then why didn't we do it before Paris?
I DON'T KNOW. MAYBE I WAS WRAPPED UP IN THE IDEA THAT IT WAS MY WORK + I HAD TO DO IT. AT SOME POINT—AND I JUST REALIZED THIS—THIS STARTED FEELING LIKE IT'S OUR PROJECT. IT FEELS MORE IMPORTANT TO BE TOGETHER—REALLY TOGETHER...
It was important before. And it hurt when you bailed.
I NEVER SAID I WAS GOOD AT THIS. I'M ONLY GOOD AT BEING IN MY OWN LITTLE WORLD (+ SOMETIMES I'M NOT EVEN VERY GOOD AT THAT). JUST TELL ME WHERE +WHEN.
Varsity, Saturday night. 9:30 showing of Notorious. Back row, center. I'll get there early + save a seat.
I'LL BE THERE.

What is it w/ S. and animals? They seem to sense something about him that people can't (or don't).

made by Ostrero's resentful wife. (Stenfalk in particular seems more relaxed; though still serious and efficient, he uses his last few pie crumbs to lure a pine marten close to their campsite, taking quiet but obvious delight in the creature's curiosity and quick station-to-station scampers. The whole group even shares a laugh when the little mustelid bares its teeth and chitters angrily at S.)Pfeifer observes that they now know that at least one thing S. said about himself was true.

Pine marten is one of the heroes of "White Oak." I loved these stories when I was a kid. Didn't you?

ALWAYS FOUND THEM CONDESCENDING AND PEDANTIC.

You don't get invited to many parties do you?

Mid-morning, at a clearing alongside a burbling creek, they refill their water jugs and allow themselves a moment of pleasure, sitting still and watching the hawks ride thermals overhead. Not for long, though; they know they need to keep moving. They cross a series of sparsely-forested hills, making much better time than the day before. By S.'s reckoning, they've covered several leagues before noontime, even with breaks to allow Stenfalk to catch his breath and cough his lungs clear. They break for a midday meal in a grove of wild apple trees whose lichen-crusted branches remain heavy with late-season fruit. S. lugs himself up the trunk of one and ventures out onto some of its sturdier limbs, quickly finding two dozen apples that are ripe and

Re: the hotel in Paris— Thought "Martus" meant "Martyrs" but it's really "martens." (Had to look it up. Martens aren't a big subject in HS French.)

MAYBE WHY EKSTROM CHOSE IT.

unspoiled by birds or rodents or insects. He drops them down to Pfeifer, who divides them among the group's bags.

The next hill is steeper, with a stern, rocky face, and the climb brings them to a subtly changed landscape. Silver firs now crowd into the deciduous forest, thicker shrub-growth surrounds jutting rocks, and S. can feel his lungs having to work harder in the thinner air. A glance at Stenfalk shows him that the older man is laboring, too, but he is resolutely keeping pace. The distance between them and the city suddenly feels significant, and this brings both relief and melancholy: they are moving farther away from their troubles, but they are moving away from their lives as well. S. falls farther from Sola with each step.

Around the fire that night, though they are worn and aching and dreaming of hot meals that are still weeks away, they sit and talk. "What I've been wondering," Pfeifer muses, "is whether the people at the newspaper were aware that they were printing lies. And—worse—printing it as if there's no doubt, no need to consider any other possibilities. As if this is the *only* way it could have happened." But while the others nod, murmur agreement, there's

CF. NEWSPAPERS'
COVERAGE / COVER-UPS OF
CALAIS MASSACRE AND
PRIX BOUCHARD MONKEY
INCIDENT.

FYI: I WASN'T EQUATING
THE TWO... I MEAN, ONE'S
A TRAGEDY AND ONE
ISN'T... JUST MAKING
AN OBSERVATION...

aw... you're worried about what I think of you.

I GUESS I AM.

no more passion for this sort of discussion than
there was the previous night. Instead, they fall into
a round of storytelling, and even Pfeifer joins in its
easy rhythm.

He tells them about the ghost of his grandmother,
who is said to haunt the home of the wealthy family
for whom she worked as a servant. "She'll never
leave," he says. "Every time they think she's gone,
plates and glasses start smashing against the walls."
Stenfalk tells of a legend from the northern territory
in which he grew up: the Hjaarn, a bloodthirsty but
rarely-glimpsed creature that steals and devours
livestock. Once the animals are all gone, the beast
turns to farmers' daughters, leaving their bones in
neat piles for their parents to find. The farmers, outraged and terrified, band together and head off into
a snowy pine forest to hunt the creature. They
search fruitlessly for many miserable weeks. One
night, a cold snap grips the forest, and the men—
hungry, thirsty, and in fear of freezing—huddle
together in an icy cave. They hear a rustle in the
dark behind them, and then—

—Stenfalk gives a strangled scream—

—and S. jumps, his blood flooding with adrenaline, and Corbeau nearly topples off the log on

NAME OF INDUSTRIALIST
IN PART II OF TRIPTYCH
OF MIRRORS.

That's the worst
Straka book I've read.
Everyone ragged on
Winged Shoes, but it's
10 times better than
Triptych. At least it's
got a love story.

I AGREE. THE THREE PARTS
DON'T HANG TOGETHER
AT ALL (NO PUN INTENDED).
Oh, hang. I get it.
Like a painting. Wow.
Don't quit your day job.

THERE'S A LOT OF
PSEUDO-PHILOSOPHICAL
BULLSHIT IN TRIPTYCH, TOO—
ESP. IN PART I. IF THAT
WAS A STYLE VMS WAS
TRYING OUT, I'M GLAD HE
DITCHED IT QUICKLY.

MACINNES MUST HAVE
HAD A HAND IN IT.

which she sits, and Pfeifer and Ostrero give sharp cries of surprise, whereupon Pfeifer tries to cover his with a cough.

Stenfalk chuckles and claps his hands as the others curse him. "This," he says, "is precisely what campfires are for. The sharing of stories. There's a spiritual connection between flame and narrative."

S. nods. He understands Stenfalk's proposition intuitively; we create stories to help us shape a chaotic world, to navigate inequities of power, to accept our lack of control over nature, over others, over ourselves.[9] But what do you do when you have no stories of your own? The story S. most wants to tell—to these people, yes, but even more to himself—is of Sola, and it is one about which he knows nearly nothing. Just two scenes: one in the Old Quarter bar, the other in the city of B——, and no way to tell if these come at their story's beginning, middle, or end.

Pfeifer passes around a small bottle of a dark, herby liqueur that he filched from Zapadi's kitchen. S. enjoys the warmth it brings to his insides, just as he enjoys sitting around the fire and listening to his

9   This is absolutely central to Straka's theory and practice of writing. This line appears almost verbatim in one of the first letters he sent me.

{ 146 }

Margin notes:

BUT CF.: THE WAY THE BLUE-BLACK STUFF RESPONDS TO HEAT. INCONSISTENT? IS VMS SUGGESTING THAT CREATION + DESTRUCTION ARE MORE CLOSELY RELATED THAN WE THINK?

Maybe he's just saying that people everywhere like to sit around a fire + tell stories — and probably always have. Think of that painting in the cave that Durand discovered..

Why is Filomela talking about the contents of a letter from him? Isn't that betraying his confidence? Makes me think it's part of a code, but it doesn't fit the "Ex" model.

MAYBE SHE JUST CAN'T RESIST TRYING TO PROVE HOW CLOSE THEY WERE.

Or trying to reassure herself that she wasn't wrong about it.

companions. Four souls, the four people in this world who know him best, if one doesn't count Sola—and Sola is not there to be counted.

He knows she may never be, but he hopes—suspects? believes? has faith?—that she will.

More stories follow in rapid succession. Ostrero relates the cautionary tale he heard when he was young about the fates of children who disobeyed their parents: [they would be snatched out of their beds at night by ruthless itinerant traders, stuffed into baskets, and carried across the straits to the Arab market,] where they would be purchased by flute-playing child-charmers, and they would spend the rest of their lives rising up from a basket when musically summoned and sinking back in on command, all for the amusement of one *pasha* or another. Ostrero himself professes outrage that anyone would put such fears into a child—he'd never subject his children to that story, no matter how badly they were misbehaving—but S. can see Ostrero coming alive as he is telling it, delighted to see the others hanging on his words, his sadness lightened, for a moment, as he gives himself over.

Ostrero's story reminds Stenfalk of the cautionary tale that was used in his village to keep children

REF. TO GARCÍA FERRARA POEM—"JUEVES" (1924)— LINES 31-32

I'm also embarrassed that I've bitched about my parents so much. Compared to yours? God. THEY'RE NOT TERRIBLE PEOPLE. THEY JUST COULDN'T BE WHO I NEEDED THEM TO BE. AND NONE OF US IS CAPABLE OF FORGIVING AS MUCH AS WE PROBABLY NEED TO. (AND YES, THAT'S A GENERIC INSIGHT FROM THERAPY BUT STILL...) The trouble is that their religion is supposed to be all about forgiveness. BELIEVING SOMETHING DOESN'T CHANGE WHO YOU ARE. NEITHER DOES REJECTING SOMETHING YOU ONCE BELIEVED IN.

JUST SO YOU KNOW: I WROTE THAT ON THE FLY... DIDN'T STOP TO MAKE SURE I THINK IT'S TRUE.

Do you usually?

YEAH, I'M PRETTY FASTIDIOUS ABOUT THAT SORT OF THING.

Well, stop that. Just write.

{ 147 }

———

on a straight path. It is less frightening, but disturbing nonetheless: if you misbehaved, one morning you would wake up and find yourself in the Winter City, a frigid place where everything was covered in snow and ice and you were perpetually alone. Other bad children were there, of course—you could see them, faintly, as if there were a glaze of ice over your eyes—but no one could interact with anyone else. No talking, no playing—nothing but existing, alone and cold, without parents, siblings, friends, pets, anyone.

Corbeau takes a turn next, telling them more about the vanished culture of the mountain people, the K——, an insular society who spent as much time below ground as they did above. ("People called my father a fool for spending so much time looking for them. Hardly anyone anymore believes the K—— really existed. I suppose he may have had doubts at times, but if he did, he hid them from me.) I loved coming up here with him, and I loved the idea that he and I would be the ones to prove they were real. They lived in this range—the legends are clear about that, you know—they lived in this very same horseshoe of mountains that surrounds what is now G——, although they probably kept to the higher elevations.

———

Do you ever just let go?

LIKE I DID AT THE DEPARTMENT PARTY? THAT, UH, TURNED OUT POORLY.

Nobody says the right things when they're wasted + angry.

HELL

Seems like S. isn't too bothered by it, though.

HE'S TOO TIRED, I THINK.

I'M JUST AS FASTIDIOUS ABOUT WHAT I SAY. WHICH MAKES IT PRETTY HARD TO BE PART OF A CONVERSATION. PROLONGED SILENCE ISN'T HIGHLY VALUED IN SUCH SITUATIONS.

MANY REFS. TO THE PAINTED CAVE

You're really going out on a limb there.

HEY, I WAS 16. IT WAS EXCITING TO NOTICE REFERENCES LIKE THAT. I HAD NEVER THOUGHT TO LOOK FOR THEM BEFORE.

So do you ever see your parents?

IT'S BEEN A FEW YEARS. Do you talk?

WHEN A RELATIVE DIES. THE RARE XMAS. THAT'S ALL.

That's sad.

Understandable, but sad.

NOT REALLY. IT JUST IS.

They hunted for their food, and they got their water from the mountain streams and from the subterranean springs that feed them. They had a vast network of caves in which they conducted religious rites and sheltered themselves from the harsh winters."

As she continues, S. marvels that one of the first things he noticed about Corbeau, her terseness, is nowhere in evidence right now.

"But the most interesting thing about those caves," she says, "is this: the K—— were obsessive chroniclers of events, covering the walls of the caves with pictures, and maybe even words, describing the story of everything they knew or believed. Everything of note that ever happened to or among them— maybe even what it was that killed them off."

"If the caves are secret," Pfeifer asks, "how would anyone know about what's inside them?"

"It's a story," Corbeau tells him. "Every story has at least a little truth in it. Every story comes from somewhere."

"You know," Stenfalk says, "I heard about the K——, or a people like them, anyway, when I was growing up. It was in a book my father would read to me."

Corbeau looks surprised. "It was in a book?"

{ 149 }

"A big, dusty old thing. Passed down in my family for generations. When he opened it, you could smell the musty pages from across the room—but it was full of the most wonderful stories. What was it called? It's been so long since I thought of it." He holds out his hand to Pfeifer for the bottle, sips, swirls the liqueur around in his mouth, swallows. "*The Archer's Tales*," he says, smiling, pleased by the memory. "Written by a sailor, I think. A Greek? A Persian? That I can't recall."

The shiver that runs down S.'s back has nothing to do with the gust of cold wind that now rushes through this late-October night. "Sobreiro," he mumbles. "Portuguese."

"You know the book?" Stenfalk asks. "I've never come across anyone who's even heard of it."

"I saw someone reading it," S. says. "In the city where I woke up. It was Sola. Who is also Szalómé. It was her."

"Ridiculous," Pfeifer says. "Hogwash."

"You're kidding, aren't you?" Corbeau asks. "Because that's—"

"—strange," Stenfalk says. "It's very, very strange."

"It is," S. concedes, "but it's what happened." He pauses, thinks. "Does your family still have the book?"

Handwritten margin notes:

I've always loved this smell.

ME, TOO. LOVE HOW STRONG IT IS IN THE SOUTH STACKS.

library gets complaints about it all the time.

CHECK THIS OUT: DESJARDINS TOOK ANNUAL INVENTORY OF HIS BOOKS + PUT LAST 3 YRS. IN THE PACKAGE. THE ONLY SUBTRACTION: A BOOK CALLED "L'ESSE." IT'S THERE IN THE FIRST TWO — BUT NOT IN LAST YEAR'S.

Sobreiro?

MAYBE? MAYBE HE WAS TELLING ME IT WAS STOLEN. HE TALKED A LOT ABOUT THEFT WHEN WE WERE IN NYC. MAYBE HE WAS TESTING HOW PEOPLE WOULD REACT.

If he had the Sobreiro, where'd he get it?

MAYBE THERE'S A HINT IN THE DOCS. GOING THROUGH AGAIN.

From Signe.

WE CAN'T PROVE IT — BUT THAT HAS TO BE IT.

"No," Stenfalk says. "It was stolen. As most beautiful things eventually are."

_{ART, YES. ALSO: YOUTH,}
_{LIFE, PEACE, PRIVACY, LOVED}
_{ONES, OPPORTUNITY, FREE}
_{EXPRESSION, BELIEF, RESPECT/REPUTATION}

That night's dream: a narrow column of a dark liquid in a tall glass; a blue-black waterspout plunging from the sky; a swirl of black-fruit icing piped over a pastry hot from the oven; a long, feminine finger laid over lips; a torrent of whispers that that finger cannot hush.

I'm guessing you were having a pretty bad day when you wrote this.
IT WAS RIGHT BEFORE I WENT TO THE MED CENTER. RIGHT BEFORE. MAYBE AN HOUR.

HAD TROUBLE FINDING THE BOOK TONIGHT. GOT PANICKED. THOUGHT YOU'D CHANGED DROPS W/O TELLING ME.

It is the following morning when they realize they're being tracked. They are scaling a steep montane meadow in the watery sun of early morning, the grasses glazed with a light frost, when Stenfalk turns in the direction from which they've come. "There," he says, pointing to a thin plume of smoke, barely visible in the bluish morning mist, rising from behind one of the smaller foothills, not far from where they made camp their first night on the run. Just this one word from him—*there*—and S. feels his insides tighten. (It is one thing to believe people are out to get you; it is another thing to know it; it is yet another to know that those people are closing in.)

It was there. Usual time.
JUST DIDN'T SEE IT AT FIRST. SLEEP DEPRIVATION, PROB. — NOT REALLY THINKING STRAIGHT.
Same with me. Nightmares.

She was careful when she got back to Brazil. No trace of her until the death notice in Feira Nova.

As soon as they notice the first trail of smoke, they see two others farther off in the distance—one

THINKING ABOUT FN 12 ~~xxxxxxxxxxxxxx~~.
THE MESSAGE SEEMS MUCH MORE OVERT THAN THE OTHERS. I GUESS SHE WOULDN'T WANT HIM TO OVERLOOK IT... BUT I'M SURPRISED SHE MOVED ONCE SHE GOT BACK TO BRAZIL, THEN. (MAYBE SHE FOUND A WAY TO LEAVE WORD { 151 } FOR HIM? OR DID SHE GIVE UP?) *Weird that there's no evidence of her living in Lençóis from '59 -'64.*
REMEMBER THAT THE BOOK CAME OUT 7 YRS BEFORE SHE LEFT NY. WE KNOW SHE THOUGHT MACINNES'S NEWS WAS AFTER HER WHEN SHE LEFT. MAYBE SHE WOULD'VE AVOIDED LENÇÓIS — JUST IN CASE THEY'D

↑ FOUND THE MESSAGE (OR THEY'D GO LOOKING FOR HER WHERE ALL HER FAMILY WAS). I MEAN, I'M NOT CLOSE TO MY PARENTS, BUT I WOULDN'T LEAD A BUNCH OF KILLERS TO THEM.

That's *exactly* what I did. IDIOT.

IF THEY WANTED TO HURT YOUR FAMILY, THEY WOULD'VE DONE IT.

to the left, more inland, the other to the right, hugging the rugged coast. "That might be a good sign," Stenfalk says. "They might not be tracking us, just sweeping the hills." They'll avoid the meadows, stick to the cover of trees wherever possible. No more fires. No apple cores left behind. Avoid muddy ground, anything that will retain a footprint.

Pfeifer wonders aloud: How far is it to the summit pass? A day and a half? Two days? Instead of moving so cautiously, might it not be better simply to make the fastest progress they can? What if they can stay ahead of the pursuit all the way to G——?

They all have questions: Who, specifically, are those people? Police? Detectives? Vigilantes, spurred to action by the newspaper's outrage? Mercenaries? A unit of the prince's army, dispatched from the capital?

"We have to move faster," Stenfalk says.

A short time later, S. looks back and sees movement on a ridge a few miles closer to them than the smoke-plumes were. A man on a dark-colored horse. An outrider. "They have horses," he says, pointing.

"We have to move much faster," Stenfalk says.

Pfeifer takes it upon himself to set the new pace, charging ahead of Corbeau and leading them to the edge of the meadow, then straight up a steep

(margin, handwritten) OK- get this— I'm downloading all the logs to send to her, + I'll see that it's not just me + her + Moody who've been inside. Four other access cards have been used, Eric— all of them w/o IDs connected to them— VIP visitors' cards.

GOING IN AT THE SAME TIME AS MOODY/ILSA?

(handwritten) Two of them, yes, two, no. So, yeah m+el have brought people in, but the others came on their own.

We can't defend ourselves if we don't know who we're up against. can it really be the new S? some kind of Bouchard/MacInnes offshoot?

section of talus and scree; where they might have

WE DON'T KNOW THAT WE'RE UP AGAINST ANYBODY— OTHER THAN MOODY + ILSA.

cut switchbacks over the face of the hill, they will

Then tell me who the guy in the suit is. Tell me who set the fires. Tell me who's been breaking into my place.

now move as the crow flies whenever possible.
When they crest, Corbeau points out that they're

I DON'T KNOW. ALL I KNOW IS WE CAN'T AFFORD TO PANIC.

on a line of geological demarcation: while they've
been climbing up granite, the rest of the way they'll
be moving over limestone. That means they're get-

GLAD WE DIDN'T LAY IT ALL OUT HERE.

Have you ever thought we might need to get rid of the book at some point?

ting into an area where subterranean rivers wind
their ways through the porous rock. The reputed
territory of the K——.

I WON'T DO IT. EVER.

"Forget your mountain people," Pfeifer says.
"They're a myth. A story."

"Even if they *were* real," Ostrero says, "we're likely
to be as dead as they are if we don't move faster."

But the exertion is taking a toll on Stenfalk, who

What's the deal with Stenfalk? We don't ever find out why he's so weak/sick.

is sucking in shallow breaths and sweating profusely,

HE'S EKSTROM, CIRCA 1931.

his face flushed with deep red. They pause to let
him rest, which he does while leaning on S. He
presses his eyes shut and nods, as if he is carrying on
a conversation with himself, then slaps S. on the

Weird there's no death certificate for her in Feira Nova.

shoulder by way of thanks, and commences a trudge
down the slope that will lead them to the next creek,

BUT THERE'S A GRAVE— THE REPORTER SAW IT; PHOTOGRAPHED IT.

where they will need to fill their water jugs.

S. and Corbeau share a look and an understand-

Maybe she thought they'd tracked her down. Maybe she moved (again?) + faked her death this time.

ing: Stenfalk is *not* ready to move on—his breathing

THAT'S A BIG REACH.

{ 153 }

is distressingly labored, despite his attempts to make it sound smooth and effortless—but what is to be done? Stenfalk may be fighting a losing battle against his lungs and the altitude, but S. suspects he won't quit until he drops to the ground, unable to move on under his own power. And at that point, he'll wave everyone else on, insist on facing the Detectives and whomever else Vévoda has enlisted, all by himself.

They reach the creek in an hour, and Stenfalk, wheezing and rattling, drops himself clumsily onto a large, flat rock on the bank, his knuckles whitening on the handle of the valise, when fits of coughing seize him. Corbeau rubs circles on his back while the other three fill the jugs. S., suddenly realizing how desperately thirsty he is, takes a greedy swallow from his own.

He spits it out. The water has a strange taste, a metallic funk that has made his tongue tingle and now sting. He sniffs the air, which seems similarly befouled. He turns to ask the others if they've noticed and finds Ostrero and Pfeifer frowning into the jugs, as if the vessels are at fault, and Corbeau wrinkling her nose in the air, trying to gauge which direction the smell is coming from. It's not unbearable, not overwhelming, but it's *there*—an acrid

---

Margin notes (handwritten):

REF TO ILLNESS THAT LED EKSTROM TO PARIS?

Crazy headache today.
Dizzy, too.

SLOW DOWN.
TAKE A BREAK.
SLEEP.
  you don't.

WELL, OBVIOUSLY I'M TOUGHER THAN YOU.

So what was in the bag @ Grand Central? What was important enough to make her say she'd foiled him?

AND IF IT WAS SO IMPORTANT, WHY DID HE PUT IT IN HER HANDS IN THE FIRST PLACE?

SOME ACCOUNTS OF BAD SMELLS AT CALAIS FACTORY BEFORE MASSACRE (SEE VERDIER'S ORAL HISTORY)

———

swirl that mixes notes of short-circuited wire, decomposing flesh, low tide, and lightning-strike— and it's impossible to ignore once you've noticed it.]

But the trackers surely draw near, and they have no choice but to grind onward, across the creek, up the next hill, one of dozens that stand between them and the summit. The smell intensifies as they climb higher; S.'s nasal passages begin to burn, his snot to run freely. He wipes his face, rubs at his watering eyes. He walks with Stenfalk, wrapping an arm around the older man's shoulders and gently urging him forward when he slows, even grabbing his hand and tugging him upward when they reach a particularly steep section with uncertain footing. Above them, dozens of vultures turn erratic ovals in the blue sky.

When S. and Stenfalk crest the hill, they find the others waiting for them at the edge of another vast meadow, this one browner, scrubbier—the ground covered, perhaps, with pine duff from the trees that ring it. At the meadow's center, which is still at least a ten-minute walk from where they stand, is a dark mountain tarn that looks like an ink-stain on the land.

The rest of the group looks in sorry shape, too. Corbeau is holding a handkerchief over her nose

———

and mouth; Pfeifer is doubled over and breathing heavily. Ostrero has a look of alarm. S.'s gaze follows his, back in the direction from which they came. ((The posse on the center path—dozens of men in brown dusters, mounted on horseback and moving swiftly forward—has gained an astonishing amount of ground on them.))They move as one, and from above, they resemble a single terrible, brown-backed predator stalking its next meal. S. can't see the flanking parties, though he knows they must be closing in, too. He shares a look with Corbeau, then with Stenfalk, who squeezes his eyes shut and nods. He knows. No time to rest. Not now. Walk. Quickly.

The meadow makes S. uneasy. What he had thought was pine duff is instead a carpet of dead grasses and spindly, jaundiced shrubs. And the tarn? A stiff breeze is sweeping down through the meadow, and it ought to be sending ripples across the water, but instead the surface looks flat, as if it has a black matte finish. It takes them another half-hour to reach it—a half-hour of squinting, coughing, wiping away tears—and when they do, they discover that it's not a lake at all. It is a ragged hole in the ground—or, rather, a cluster of ten overlapping holes that have been blasted into the earth, roughly in a double-quincunx

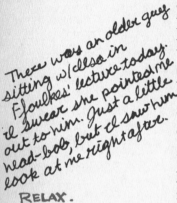

There was an older guy sitting w/ clsa in Ffoulkes' lecture today. I swear she pointed me out to him. Just a little head-bob, but I saw him look at me right after.

RELAX.
PROBABLY JUST ANOTHER PROF. SITTING IN. AND THEY MIGHT'VE JUST BEEN LOOKING IN YOUR GENERAL DIRECTION. THINK ABOUT IT: NO ONE WHO'S REALLY DANGEROUS IS GOING TO GO TO FFOULKES' LECTURE + SIT THERE IN FRONT OF EVERYBODY.

I know you're probably right. But everything's freaking me out right now.

STRANGE DETAIL — SIGNIF.?

Maybe a reference to some particular Bouchard/Arp weapon?

———

form, combining to make one foul, scorched-black chasm in the middle of this mountain wilderness, twenty-five or thirty feet deep. The smell here is overwhelming—both Stenfalk and Ostrero are seized by fits of retching. They can't linger here, but they can't leave yet.

"What in hell made this?" Pfeifer asks, of no one in particular, and he receives no response.

S. approaches the pit. The walls are smooth and veined with fine cracks, as if the dirt and rock had been baked at some hellish temperature. Around the lip—and spilling over it, too, frosting the bristly dead grass that surrounds it—is some sort of liquid, a black, greasy substance. Here and there—presumably where the sun catches it at a particular angle—the material has a top-glaze of indigo iridescence. S. drags the toe of his boot through the stuff; it leaves a dark and thick-looking smear on the dead grass, but it doesn't stir up any more of the horrible stench; whatever is fouling the air is coming from within the pit itself. He glances up and watches Corbeau, holding her handkerchief over her nose and mouth bandanna-style, drag a finger through the slime and then hold it up for study. She kneels to wipe it clean on the ground, then studies the depths

———

{ 157 }

of the pit intently. She waves S. over to her and points. All he can see of her face are her eyes; bloodshot, they suggest an even fiercer intelligence. If the two of them can lead together, he thinks, they'll find a way to bring this group to safety—as slim a chance as that may seem right now.

"We have to keep moving," S. says.

Her voice is muffled by the fabric. "You have to see this."

The first thing S. notices in the pit is a fragment of charred bone. The next hundred things he sees are many fragments of charred bone. Scattered over the bottom of the pit are many, many baked remains—mammalian and avian, mostly. He looks up at the vultures, who are still circling, circling, circling but have not tightened their rings, flying only over the outer edges of the field, avoiding the charnel house at the center. It's as if there were a barrier rising up from the hole high into the heavens, keeping them away.

But obviously he has overlooked what she wanted him to see, because she is tugging on his arm and saying, "No, look," and pointing more, and now he notices a few disruptions in the smooth surfaces of the walls. Embedded in them: squares of honeycomb-textured metal.

I can totally imagine Straka + Durand feeling like this once Ekstrom got sick.

MORE AMBIGUOUS USE OF BIRD DETAIL

NOTE, THOUGH: THEY'RE NOT COMFORTING, BUT THEY'RE NOT MAKING THINGS WORSE. THEY'RE ATTRACTED, BUT KEEPING DISTANCE. (GOOD SENSE, MAYBE). *Sensible vultures.*

Next paper's going to be just as hard — it's on The Waste Land. *Which I hated.* *

* I THINK WE HAVE TO BREAK UP
YOU WOULD HAVE TO ASK ME OUT FIRST.

"They're from a casing we use at the factory," she says.

A blast site. A weapon was tested here. Vévoda made this.[10]

"What kind of weapon does this?" he asks, but she shakes her head, says she hasn't the slightest idea.

The others are calling to them: Stenfalk and Ostrero have gathered themselves and are ready to move, and they must all keep going, up and up, to fresher air and whatever slim chance of escape remains. They hurry across the field, start scrambling up the next hill. Again, S. takes his position at the rear, coaxing Stenfalk, offering an arm as leverage when his friend needs it. No one speaks much until Ostrero asks if any of them remember seeing some bright, purplish flashes over the mountains during a stormy night a week or two ago; it had looked enough like lightning that he hadn't thought much about it, but he had pointed out its peculiar color to Pfeifer while they were standing out on the wharf.

---

[10] Straka was convinced that his nemesis Bouchard had stumbled upon a most destructive weapon in an experiment gone awry. Serendipitous for Bouchard and his industrial cohorts; foul luck for all else. To date, this weapon is not known to have been used, but Straka often worried that there might soon come a day when it was. We shall see. (Or perhaps we shall not.) Readers, if I should suddenly disappear from this earth, you can be certain that this footnote was the proximate cause of it.

{ 159 }

— Do you think we're supposed to take this as literally true?

IT HAS AN "EX" CLUE IN IT — SO IT MIGHT JUST BE A BUNCH OF WORDS SETTING UP THE CODE.

SHE BELIEVED IT.
SHE DEFINITELY
BELIEVED IT.

But the rest of it—or parts of it anyway— could be true, right? We know she was scared when she left. Maybe she really was trying to tell people what was going on.

"I remember," says Pfeifer. "Thunder, too. Louder and deeper, too, than you'd expect from so far away. But enough like thunder that I thought: *thunder*."

"So this is what he's building in the annex," Ostrero says.

"We know it's *one* of the things he's building there," Corbeau says. "And we don't know what this thing even *is*."

"We know it explodes," Pfeifer says. "We know it can make big holes in the middle of nowhere. We know it smells like the devil's very arsehole."[11]

"We know that Zapadi died over this," Stenfalk says, his voice cracking. He tries to say more, but another fit of coughing steals his words. They understand, though, what he was going to express: his hurt, his outrage, his grief—all of it personal, not political. Stenfalk holds his place, waves the others on, but as oppressive as the air is here, no one wants to leave. S. crouches, lets the exhausted man lean over his back for support. He urges Ostrero and Pfeifer to go ahead, scout the areas they'll cross next, choose a path, contemplate their

---

[11] In a letter, Straka apologized to me for Pfeifer's language here. "I know your sensibilities are more delicate than mine," he wrote, "but the character simply must utter this line." I assured him there was no need for him to seek exculpation. "I am made of stronger stuff than you seem to think," I responded.

Handwritten margin notes:

BECAUSE YOU CAN'T AVOID THINKING ABOUT SOMETHING IF YOU'RE TALKING ABOUT IT.

why didn't you ever tell anyone about the boat?

I've been expecting some kind of remark about moody here.

A RARE INSTANCE OF RESTRAINT.

If we ever need to refer to him with a code name, it should be "D.V.A."

So if anyone could've swum out to rescue Vaclav...

BIG LEAP THERE. IT'D MAKE A GOOD STORY, THOUGH...

I don't think we can get anywhere near the truth about Straka if we don't make some leaps.

strategy. And they do, but not before gaining a silent nod of assent from Corbeau.

Even when Stenfalk can walk again, he can't go twenty steps without doubling over; he waves S. and Corbeau forward, the gesture more violent this time, full of his frustration and his disgust with himself. This is a proud man. They will not leave him behind.

By the time the three of them reach the far end of the meadow, Ostrero and Pfeifer have been up the next hill, back down again, and waiting for at least ten minutes. Neither of them wants to say anything about Stenfalk slowing them down, but S. can tell they've been watching their pursuers intently. They're seeing what S. noticed a little while ago—a posse directly behind them gaining ground—and now flanking groups in sight and converging toward the center. Two more beasts joining the hunt. At this rate, S. figures, they'll be overtaken before they even reach the summit pass, perhaps as early as tomorrow afternoon. Unless they can find a place to hide, they'll have only two choices: give themselves up, or go down fighting. And with one firearm between the five of them—the ancient pistol that Stenfalk keeps tucked in his belt—there is only one way the fight will end.

EKSTROM WAS IN THE SWIM CLUB AT UNIV. IN UPPSALA. KNOWN FOR STRENGTH, ENDURANCE. (SEE ALMSTEDT'S EKSTROM: A LIFE, 1962)

Check out Almstedt on Ekstrom's death (p381): "His suicide is confounding, as he was by all accounts in good spirits despite his infirmity, and hopeful of returning to work by springtime... The obituary noted that he was still 'of vigorous mind,' as a sheet of paper on the nightstand demonstrated: at the top was written Dr. ~~Molyneux~~ Molyneux's full name, and below it many hundreds of anagrams. A detective who saw the page said Ekstrom appeared to be using at least seven different languages."

Ekstrom only knew Swedish, English, and basic French. (p.26)

YOU'RE SUGGESTING VMS WROTE IT?

He knew lots of languages.

{161}

PLENTY OF PEOPLE DO. FXC DID. — But Straka was obsessive enough to do it— there's that anagram binge he goes on near the end of Coriolis.

WHAT'S YOUR POINT??

Two hours later, on a flat, grassy area at the base of a steep limestone wall, progress halts again as Stenfalk coughs blood that is now surprisingly dark, nearly purple. Still: every second that passes while they wait in this field of spent wildflowers is another ten yards the posse gains on them. They're not in plain sight, at least; they've been following a deer path that curls through the low space between two abrupt, craggy hilltops. Along one side of the field, though, is a ledge with a sheer drop into a gorge as deep as forever. Unless they want to double back and lose even more time, they'll have to climb.

Stenfalk looks up at the climb, closes his eyes, wheezes, coughs again, spits. He knows what the rest of them are thinking. "Go," he says. "Get to the top and start looking for a place we can hide. Make sure you keep out of their sight lines."

"I'll stay here with you," Corbeau says.

Stenfalk shakes his head. "It should be someone strong enough to carry me up if I can't climb. Intentions won't be enough."

She fixes her gaze on him, holds it, holds it longer, finally nods. She doesn't want to believe this is true, S. knows. It simply is.

Stenfalk turns to S. "Will you stay?"

I think I feel as bad as he does. Sorry to fill your book w/ complaints. But UGH.

Roommate just made me tea. I must look really sick if she's helping.

XX

"Of course," S. says.

"Good. The rest of you, get going."

Corbeau raises her hand as if to make a point, but words do not emerge. S. notices that(her fingertips are blistering, the skin split open and furious red.)Whatever that greasy black substance was, it's clear that touching it wasn't a good idea. He notices a rank smell not unlike that of the tarn and looks down at his boots. The leather on the toe he dragged through the slime appears to be burning, or melting, away.

He and Stenfalk watch silently as the other three search for handholds and toeholds and drag themselves up the rock face, then hoist themselves over the ledge at the top. The two men disappear from view; Corbeau looks back down at them until Stenfalk tells her to stop wasting time, damnit, and start doing something useful.

"I'll carry the valise when we go up," S. says.

Stenfalk, coughing, hands the bag to him.

"It's heavy," S. says before setting it on the ground.

The older man volunteers no information about the bag's contents. "You've got some terrible luck," he observes, "washing up in B—— and then falling in with us."

any connection to a detail we know about Durand?

NOT THAT I KNOW OF. MAYBE IT'S JUST A METAPHOR.

There's a character in Durand's novel who burns her fingers as she's warming a bottle for her baby. And a character in Washington + Greene who gets a cut across all of her fingers in the factory. I HAVE NO IDEA WHERE TO GO W/THOSE.

Me either. Just thought I'd point them out. S - TAKES ON RESPONSIBILITY

If Ekstrom rescued Vaclav, think of how V. would've felt if he thought he'd led Bouchard's people to the Deux Martres. HE'D NEVER HAVE FORGIVEN HIMSELF.

Which is, of course, true. S. could have come ashore in a peaceful city, been rescued by a family with a large, well-heated home in which the woman was an incomparable baker of pies and the man was able to offer S. well-paying employment in which S. could work outside, use his muscles, breathe fresh air, earn a fair wage. He could have swum up to a beach in a resort city, fallen into a life of sun-soaked leisure amid a rotating cast of cosmopolitan travelers, made his living as a painter of watercolor landscapes. He could have been gaffed out of the water by a passing fishing vessel, then lived a quiet, hardworking life harvesting the sea's bounties and sharing in whiskey-soaked revelry on decks and in port towns. He could have been carried by a wall of wave and deposited on a temperate, shell-covered shore, where Sola would be waiting for him with her hand extended, ready to lead him up to a sprawling mansion perched at the top of the coastal bluff, with vineyards extending over its grounds all the way to the vanishing point and beyond, with grapes ripe and ready for the fall crush. But instead: this. Chaos and blood, perilous flight, and a reckoning dead ahead. "That's true," S. says. "But this is what happened. This is what's real." This is also the version of

{ 164 }

Handwritten margin notes:

REF TO THE CHILDHOOD SENSE-MEMORIES IN CH. 1 + 8?

Great word. Does this happen to you— falling in love with the sound of some words?

USED TO— WHEN I WAS READING FOR PLEASURE. WHICH IS TOO BIG A LUXURY NOW (+ HAS BEEN SINCE I GOT TO PSU).

Except for when you were in the hospital.

RIGHT.
I hope you get to do that again soon.

Minus the hospital part, I mean.

Hmmmm... RIGHT.
IT'S A COOL TRICK, I THINK: HAVING S. BE PRESCIENT W/O EVEN REALIZING THAT HE IS.

Sets up the move in ch. 9.

EXACTLY.

his life in which Sola appears, and he has come to believe that there are more layers of mystery to her than he had thought. His question is no longer whether she knows him but how and to what extent, not whether they are important to each other but why. Unless, of course, none of it is true, if those images in his dream are not fragments of memory but something else: the scattered and half-formed ink-shapes of his mind's desperate attempt to author a self, which are not to be trusted.

Silence settles over them, and S. welcomes it. Better for Stenfalk to conserve his breath than to waste it on idle words. Together they watch a tree creeper ascend the trunk of an aspen, curling round and round in a helix. "There is much comfort and strength," Stenfalk muses, "to be found in birds." Once the creeper flies off, startled by a particularly vigorous burst of Stenfalk's coughing, they watch the shivering shadows that the leaves cast over the moon-colored rock.

"Are you ready?" S. asks.

"Let's go," Stenfalk says.

S. laces his fingers together to give Stenfalk a boost to the first handhold in the rock, a long crevice that runs the length of the wall.

That hotel in Prague—
name translates as
|| "The aviary." ||

I'VE ALWAYS WONDERED:
IF YOU NEED TO USE CODE
NAMES, WOULDN'T IT BE
SAFER TO CHOOSE NAMES
THAT DON'T SHARE ANY
THEME OR ORGANIZING
PRINCIPLE?

They were
writers, not
spies.

AS FAR AS WE KNOW.

SHIP OF THESEUS

I COULD GO. — *To Brazil? you're serious, right? Because that would be amazing. More amazing if I went w/ you.*

YOU CAN'T. PAPERS. EXAMS. ∴ GRADUATING.

Unless I just ∴ said fuck it all.

I'M NOT PAYING FOR A TICKET FOR YOU. NOT ENABLING.

I know you're right. I just don't want to admit it. If you're going, you HAVE to keep me posted. Can you please get over your aversion to email? You can't leave me hanging.

WE CAN TALK ABOUT IT — WE'LL FIGURE OUT SOMETHING. MEET ME @ THE VARSITY, 1:30.

ARMY OF SHADOWS → → → I TOTALLY EMBARRASSED MYSELF — SAT DOWN + STARTED TALKING TO A GIRL IN THE BACK ROW WHO WASN'T YOU. WHAT HAPPENED? WHERE WERE YOU?

WHERE ARE YOU?

Stenfalk's elbows quiver with strain as he pulls his weight upward; his toes search for a hold until S. takes him by the right ankle, guiding it toward a tiny ridge in the rock face, just enough to find purchase.

It's then that Corbeau again pokes her head out over the ledge and looks down at them. She is short of breath, full of barely-controlled excitement, and S. immediately senses renewed vigor in the older man climbing above him. "We found it," she says. "We found a cave."[12]

(And of course I don't have a phone/email for you.)

And now I've missed you. You're in the air.

ARE YOU OK ???
I'm so-so-so sorry — got sick — fever, puking, everything — awful. Slept for 36 hours.

So — an "Ex" footnote, with some truth in it, too: she was from Lençóis. Lots of Caldeiras + Xabregas(es) there. Funny thing is that the caves weren't discovered until a few years ago.

[12] Many well-known writers and editors joked that Straka "must live in a cave somewhere," mocking his need for solitude and privacy. What these publishing-industry extroverts failed to understand is that many more people in the world share Straka's feelings than theirs. (I observe as well that throughout history, caves—including the caves in the hills above my birthplace of Lençóis—have provided safe shelter for those in need of it.)

Kind of surprised she so openly mentions Lençóis, too. It wouldn't be hard for anyone to figure out, but still…

MAYBE THE LOCALS KNEW, BUT NO ONE ELSE DID. (INTERESTING PARALLEL TO VMS KNOWING ABOUT DURAND'S CAVE BEFORE IT WAS "DISCOVERED," THOUGH. COINCIDENCE?)

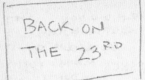
So the title's just
a little
consistency too much
to ask for ??

CHAPTER 5

DOWN, AND OUT ⟵ — Cheesy title.
Thanks, FXC

You're right—
it's not in the
original. So
Filomela must have
added it herself, right?
Code's def. in the
matrix. Question is
whether the title here is important
at all.

My notes say the original manuscript
of SOT doesn't have the number
matrix in it (+ I never found an
addendum in PSU archive or
any others). Can you double-check?

While you're gone,
I'm going to play
around with the codes
we haven't gotten yet.

THE **CAVE** could not be
more strategically situated.[1] A hundred yards up a
rocky slope from the limestone wall they've surmounted and two hundred yards to the east, along
the edge of a small stream and over a slope of grass
and scrub, it affords them a broad view of the northern hills through which they've come. Their good
fortune runs even deeper: an ovate boulder just in
front of the entrance will offer cover for a lookout,
and it makes the cave mouth look, from the path
along the stream, like just another wide, curving

Why did I write
that? You can't
respond anytime
soon.

Guess I've gotten to
the point where this
is comforting, even
if I'm just talking
to myself.
Should I be worried?

Why, yes, Jen.
You probably
should be.

---

[1] It should be obvious that this chapter draws heavily from *The Painted Cave*, which was
one of Straka's most successful and well-regarded books, and one that showed the evolution
of his style. He had become much more methodical and meticulous, for one thing. In the letter to me that accompanied the manuscript, he wrote that his new approach to his writing
had brought him "numerous revelations—every page, every line, every word—which made
me feel as if there were an unseen hand guiding me, showing me and my story where to go."

⟹ A LIE.
THERE'S NO SUCH LETTER—
FXC DIDN'T START
WORKING W/VMS UNTIL
YEARS LATER.

Care to revise that
opinion? ⟵
{ 167 }
WHAT SHE SAID
HASN'T GOTTEN ANY TRUER.
You know what I mean.

Why lie about that?
NO CLUE.
THIS IS THE FN THAT MOST
DISCREDITS FXC.

YOU'VE PROBABLY FOUND THE CODE
ALREADY + ARE JUST STRINGING ME ALONG.

[handwritten, top right:] WHEN DID YOU UNDERLINE THIS? ← / *I didn't.* / MAYBE YOU JUST DON'T REMEMBER? THERE'S A LOT GOING ON. / *I'm pretty sure I didn't.* / ★ WE'RE CHANGING DROPS. ★

fissure in the rock—home to snakes, perhaps, or small rodents, but nothing into which an adult human could disappear.

If any of the five are worried that they're pinning themselves into an enclosed space with no exit, none of them will say as much.

[handwritten, left margin:] NO CHOICE BUT TO RESTRICT THEIR CHOICES. / HA. / Metaphor for adulthood?

S. at once assumed that Corbeau found the cave, that her knowledge of the K—— people must have guided her, given her some finer instincts in this landscape, but no, it was Pfeifer, who'd simply wandered far from the path in search of a discreet place in which to address nature's urgencies. While he was paused in his indecorous posture, he'd spied a male chamois grazing quietly nearby; the animal paused, looked up at him—*I swear it did*, Pfeifer insisted—and then took a few springing steps over to the rock mound and began roughing its horns against it. Pfeifer saw just enough of the opening to deem it worth investigating.

[handwritten, left margin:] ANOTHER EK. REF.: ← A CHAMOIS REVEALS THE HIDDEN PATH IN HEDDA AND THE BEAR-KING.

I loved Hedda when I was a kid. One year I wanted to be her for Halloween. My mom couldn't figure out how to make the hat, so she convinced me to be a bed-sheet ghost instead. :)

Inside, the air is damp and thick with the rotten-fruit smell of bat guano. Daylight has faded, darkening the space, only a faint crescent of purple light coming from outside. They agree to forgo lamplight entirely, to sit in the spelean gloom and speak infrequently and in hushed tones.

{ 168 }

[handwritten, bottom:] ILSA WROTE ABOUT BATS IN HER 1ST DRAFT OF THE ARTICLE ABOUT THE AVIAN METAPHORS. I HAD TO TELL HER BATS ARE MAMMALS, NOT BIRDS. / *And she repays you by stealing your tape. What an* AWESOME *person.*

SHIP OF THESEUS

So we have Ekstrom, Feuerbach, +
Garcia Ferrara. who's the 5th? who's S. standing
in for?

[Stenfalk lies supine on the cool rock, his head resting in Corbeau's lap; they're sharing the food from her rucksack. She's using only her good hand. Ostrero is lying down, too, with a forearm thrown over his eyes and forehead. Pfeifer shares some rank-smelling cheese with S. and whispers about building a revolution once they escape, about building a guerrilla army that will storm the city and take over the factory, the streets, the mayor's mansion; clean out the immoral, materialistic rot; show the people who turned their backs on them how wrong they were.] While S. is sympathetic—he genuinely feels the tug of revenge, of righting wrongs, but really: they are five people trapped in a cave. If they're discovered, they could be in jail or swinging from ropes by this time tomorrow. Plotting a revolution right now seems delusional at best.

What S. wants to talk about—even if it may not be of any practical use, either, is *The Archer's Tales.* When he tries to raise the subject, though—after Stenfalk has drunk some water, napped, and regathered his breath—Corbeau shakes her head: *not now.* And so: they eat their food in sparing rations, they drink the rest of their untainted water, and they wait for sleep, wait for the world to play the next

SUMMERSBY? OR MAYBE
S. IS A METAPHOR FOR
THE COLLECTIVE ITSELF—
AN ENTITY THAT
COMPRISES ALL OF THEM.

Sounds nice, but
it doesn't fit w/ the
rest of the book.
- Entities don't have
emotions.
- Entities don't get
lonely.
- Entities aren't
trying to figure
out their place
in the world.

STRAKA WAS A WRITER.
HE MADE THINGS
UP. NOT EVERY DETAIL
HAS TO BE DRAWN
DIRECTLY FROM REAL LIFE.

Something's
bugging me:
Feuerbach +
Ekstrom were about
the same age + much
older than the others...
but here Pfeifer/F'bach
seems much younger than
Stenfalk. Why change that
relationship if you're
keeping so many other
things the same???

- Tune in tonight for more of
Jennifer Heyward's Solitary
Musings.™ —

{ 169 }

Ch. 8 !!

Wish you were here...

*Last night I dreamed that someone was in my apt. +
going through all my Straka notes. Could hear the
rustling paper. It felt super real— when I went into
the living room in the morning, I was half-
expecting to see that it had
been ransacked.*

*I'VE BEEN HAVING
DREAMS LIKE THAT FOR YEARS*

*not sleeping
well at all. I
really want to hear from you.*

*what are you
finding down there??*

card in its hand: will the Detectives pass them by?
Or will the five of them awaken to dozens of guns,
locked and loaded and aimed at them by men in
brown dusters? They share watch duty again, and S.
gets the first shift of five. Stenfalk insists on taking
the fifth; he needs sleep, he concedes, but he'll be
damned if he won't pull his weight.

Water drops echo from the dark recesses of the
cave as they plink unseen into rills and puddles. The
metronomic regularity is, it turns out, a blessing, as
all five of them descend into sleep quickly. And
when S. bolts upright in the middle of the long, dark
night, seized with alarm, vividly aware that he left
Stenfalk's valise back at the base of the rock wall,
that same dripping, steady as Time itself, lulls him
(with his pounding heart and his curdled sense of
shame) back into unconsciousness before he can
decide what, if anything, to do about his mistake.

*isn't really a word,
but I still like it.*

*How fascinating
you are, Jen.*

*(Blah,
blah,   S. FAILS
blah...)*

Oh, the mercy of water!

Corbeau shakes him awake roughly. The look in
her dark eyes is wild, panicked; her skin looks pallid in
the meager wash of early-morning light. "Stenfalk's
gone," she tells him. "He's gone. Why would he leave?"
"It's my fault," he says, too sleepy to stop himself.
He could've woken Stenfalk when he'd remembered,

*CF. "BEGINS/ENDS
AT THE WATER"*

*Finished the Eliot
paper, finally. Wrote
about the Death by
Water section (even
though I'm still not
sure I get it).
Hope it doesn't suck
too much. About to
go to Ilsa's office hours
to turn it in.*

{ 170 }

I don't think that's what Straka was after.

I DON'T, EITHER. HUBBELL WAS A PSYCHOTHERAPIST; SAW EVERYTHING THROUGH THAT LENS. IS GENERALLY CONSIDERED A HOBBYIST/ DILETTANTE AT BEST.

SEE HUBBELL (1977): FREUDIAN INTERPRETATION— THIS IS A PASSIVE-AGGRESSIVE WAY FOR S. TO GET RID OF HIS RIVAL FOR CORBEAU.

told him not to worry, that he'd race down and retrieve the valise as soon as it was safe to go outside. His big toe thrums with pain, but he decides to ignore it. It feels like an appropriate way to begin his penance. → SHAME/REGRET → A NEED TO ATONE

Corbeau looks at him, confused.

Pfeifer is standing nearby, rubbing his eyes, scratching distractedly at his crotch. "He probably just went out to—"

"No," S. says. "He went to get his valise." (And he explains how he has failed Stenfalk, how he has failed them all, how the valise is at the base of the limestone wall, how Vévoda's men can't possibly fail to notice it.) He should have found a way to retrieve it during the night, regardless of the danger.

Disgust twists Corbeau's face. She spits a curse at no one and everyone, at nothing and everything, and she stamps toward the cave entrance.

"Don't go out," Pfeifer cautions. "Not until—"

"Don't tell me what to do," she snaps, but she is careful; she settles herself behind the mound, peers out into the hostile hills. Almost immediately, she gasps, mutters *No*, and S. and Pfeifer hurry to join her.

What they see is this: no more than a mile away, on the grassy ledge below the limestone wall, is

What if Straka led the agents to Ekstrom by accident? If Straka did the anagrams, then he must've given them to Ekstrom @ the hotel (or not long before). Maybe he wasn't careful enough.

IF THAT'S TRUE, THEN THE AGENTS MUST NOT HAVE KNOWN THAT STRAKA WAS THE REAL STRAKA. OTHERWISE THEY WOULD HAVE KILLED HIM, TOO.

This is how I imagine Durand reacting when she realizes Straka got Ekstrom killed.

If she was like your aunts, she wouldn't have. but maybe she wasn't.

+ IT MUST HAVE TORPEDOED ANY CHANCE OF ROMANCE B/W HER + VMS. MIGHT HAVE COMPLETELY BROKEN UP THE S, TOO. HOW COULD SHE FORGIVE HIM FOR THAT?

You do have a gift for leaving things out, though.

AND YOU'RE NO DIFFERENT.

I DON'T SAY ANYTHING I DON'T MEAN.

the gray head of Stenfalk. Surrounding him are at least thirty men in the brown dusters of the Detectives, most of them dismounted. The horses seem calm, indifferent, snuffling and nibbling grass. S. is surprised by the lack of action in this scene before them: Stenfalk is not tied up, is not handcuffed, is not being verbally abused; he is talking with three or four of the men who appear to be in charge, and while he doesn't appear to have the valise with him, the Detectives don't, either. Stenfalk stands straight; nothing about his posture or movements suggests fear or defeat. For a moment S. wonders if Stenfalk has gone over to their side, but he quickly rejects the notion—if anyone among them is a Judas, it is not Stenfalk. Is he negotiating? And if so, with what sorts of assets? He has nothing but himself.

Archive logs went to Ilsa today. Boss insisted. Bracing for impact— no way she won't realize who I am.

I really really really wish you were here.

WORDS OF WISDOM →

...If you're a mopey, self-dramatizing boy, yes.

HARSH. I WAS 16.

It was harsh...

Sorry—I didn't know what you were going through then.

"He's stalling them," Corbeau says. "So we can get away."

There is silence, then, as they absorb this.

S. walks back toward the area where Stenfalk and Corbeau were sleeping. The pistol has been laid neatly on her rucksack. Stenfalk meant to sacrifice himself, or knew that he might have to.

S. scans the cave. "Where's Ostrero?" he asks.

BEEN THINKING ABOUT DESJARDINS HERE. MAYBE HE WAS DOING SOMETHING SIMILAR— TRYING TO GIVE ME A HEAD START.

But why you?

He had his own students.

MAYBE HE WAS WORRIED ONE OF THEM HAD SOLD HIM OUT— AND HE DIDN'T KNOW WHICH ONE... AT LEAST HE KNEW I WOULDN'T BE WORKING WITH { 172 } MOODY.

That wouldn't be enough for me if I were him.

MAYBE HE FELT LIKE HE GOT A READ ON M IN NY. I MIGHT BE A NEUROTIC MESS, BUT I'M PRETTY SINCERE ONE. LIKE I TOLD YOU:

PARALLELS TO GARCÍA FERRARA DURING
SPANISH CIVIL WAR: FIGHTS ON REPUBLICAN
SIDE UNTIL LATE '36, THEN TURNS B/C OF A
THREAT TO HIS WIFE + KIDS. BUYS HIS/THEIR SAFETY BY

SHIP OF THESEUS SELLING OUT DURAND. FRANCO *and*
LETS HIM LIVE, + EVERYONE *he*
ELSE HATES HIM FOREVER. *never*
writes again.

And before the others answer, something changes NEVER PUBLISHES AGAIN,
in the scene in which Stenfalk is playing: one of the AT LEAST. AND EVERYONE
STOPS READING WHAT HE
Detectives points upward, and heads swivel to fol- PUBLISHED BEFORE. HE'S
low his line. It takes a moment for S. to realize that DISGRACED AND OUT OF PRINT.
the Detective is not pointing at the cave mouth but *And then he hangs*
at the spot to the west where they'd surmounted the *himself. Jesus.*
wall the evening before. S. hears a gasp that is possibly his own. There, waving his arms, calling out to
the Detectives, is Ostrero. "I want to go back," he
shouts. "I'm coming back." He turns his back to the *If Ostrero = García*
posse, kneeling at the top of the wall, waving one leg *Ferrara, then Straka*
himself doesn't seem any
in search of a first foothold for the descent. *more empathetic than*
(("Idiot," Pfeifer says. "That spineless *idiot*.")) *Pfeifer is here.*

"My family," Ostrero shouts as his leg swings —HE PROB. WASN'T.
back and forth. "My family." CH. 4-5 MAKE IT SEEM LIKE
VMS + DURAND WERE REALLY CLOSE.
A gun fires. Ostrero jerks like a puppet, a queer COLLABORATOR → PUPPET
look of surprise on his face, and falls over the ledge. A THOUGHT:
As he disappears from S.'s view, his outstretched "COLLABORATOR" HAS BOTH
NEGATIVE + POSITIVE
arms do not claw at the rock surface or wheel in the CONNOTATIONS —POLITICAL
air; he is already dead. The sound of his body hitting (BAD), ARTISTIC (GOOD).
the ground is tiny, insignificant, swallowed up by the
vast landscape, the hills, the ground, the sky.

Of course. The Detectives are the hunters; the five
of them are the hunted. They are all simply playing FITS WITH
their roles in humankind's oldest, simplest, truest story. ARCHER'S TALES —

ETERNAL STORIES
CYCLING, REINVENTED.
Why not write to some of
DJ's students + ask if he
ever mentioned the
book?

RISKY. TIPS OUR HAND.

SHIP OF THESEUS

Down on the grassy plateau, Stenfalk is shouting at one of the mounted Detectives, gesticulating with fury.

"Can't save him," Corbeau says softly. She might be quietly urging Stenfalk to calm down, to accept Ostrero's death and try to save himself, but to S. it sounds as if she is talking about their own situation, up here in the cave: they can't do anything for Stenfalk now. He's on his own, and he must've wanted it that way.

S. feels his mind slowing down, overwhelmed, feels his reactions dulling. He is not improvising an ingenious rescue of Stenfalk or calmly mapping out the perfect escape from the cave. What he finds himself doing—what he *sees* himself doing, as if from outside himself—is observing the people on the plateau, stunned and passive and utterly unheroic. Whoever he was before he found himself in the Old Quarter, he realizes, he was not a soldier or a spy or a revolutionary or an assassin or any such thing. He was—is—a meager man, not at all prepared for a situation like this.

He watches as a man in a dark-brown duster handcuffs Stenfalk's arms behind his back, as that Detective and another each take one of the older

{ 174 }

Handwritten margin notes:

→ (Maybe a lot of pages did, and they filled in / reconstructed— like Filo did w/ ch. 10 here? Or maybe just a few + they used them as a jumping-off point for another book entirely?)

(Maybe no pages survived, but Vaclav did, and they helped him reconstruct his story?)

(anything is possible.)

Argh. If you were here, I could bounce these ideas off you instead of just rambling, rambling, rambling to myself.

PROB. BETTER I WASN'T AROUND.

Maybe Ekstrom left himself vulnerable b/c he didn't want to put any other S at risk. note to self:

What if the MS Vaclav had when he jumped was Brax., + they saved it, got it published under V.'s name. (Maybe he was alive, maybe he wasn't.)

(Wouldn't the paper have gotten ruined?)

S. IS JUST A GUY... CRAWLED OUT OF THE WATER + ENDED UP IN THE MIDDLE OF SOMETHING HUGE + DANGEROUS.

Yet another note to self: If Vaclav survived the suicide attempt (big if), and if Ekstrom saved him/took care of him afterward (also big if), then Vaclav must have been part of The S. why else would he let them use his name

↘ NO LESS LIKELY: THEY PULLED HIM OUT OF THE WATER, TOOK HIM BACK TO THE HOTEL ("AND GUEST"), HE DIED ANYWAY, + THEY DECIDED TO USE A DEAD MAN'S NAME (OR A SLIGHT VARIATION) AS A FRONT FOR THE COLLECTIVE

← Another note to self:
don't assume that Vaclav was Straka
or that he even survived the jump.
Need evidence.

SHIP OF THESEUS

———

man's arms and march him calmly across the open space, march him—strangely—not toward the horses but away from them, as Stenfalk (finally!) stiffens his legs, his body, begins to resist them, as the two Detectives calmly take him to the edge of the gorge and push him over, as next to him Corbeau stifles a scream with her fist, as the two Detectives turn back toward the rest of the posse, expressionless as if they'd just tossed an inedible fish back into the water.

as my dad says all the time: "It's just business."

I HATE THAT. AS IF IT EXCUSES EVERY QUESTIONABLE THING YOU COULD POSSIBLY DO.

This time there's no sound of impact at all. Stenfalk's death is perfectly, maddeningly silent.

Pfeifer's sharp voice startles him from this daze. "Go ahead and scream," Pfeifer is telling Corbeau. "They know where we are." He points outside, traces the route they took to the cave from the top of the wall, which they can see as a single dotted black line. This makes no sense, of course—how can a black line impose itself on a landscape?—and this is the very objection S. is about to make when the burn in his toe flares, forces him to acknowledge it. He examines his boot. The sole under his big toe no longer exists, and the area around it has turned black and slick-looking, just like every blade of grass that boot touched as S. walked.

———

Corbeau is watching him. She contemplates her suppurating finger. She says nothing.

Pfeifer already has Ostrero's lantern in his hands. "Let's hope this cave leads somewhere."

"I left a *trail*," S. says. He can hear the whine in his voice, and it revolts him.

"Doesn't matter," Pfeifer says. "Ostrero led them halfway here. They'd have found the cave soon enough. Let's *go*."

But Corbeau shows no sign of being ready to move, no sign that she has even registered the discussion going on between the two men. She stares out over the gorge, where a lone vulture is riding the thermals.

S. touches her shoulder. He expects her to slap his hand away, but she doesn't. She is hyperventilating. "We have to go," he says softly. "All of us."

At first she does not look at him. She watches the vulture as it flaps and wobbles tipsily. She does not start or even blink when more gunshots bang and whine through the mountain air: men on the grassy slope, taking potshots at the airborne scavenger for no reason at all. She turns only when S. takes her by her good hand and says her name.

She does not say: *Do you think there's any way he—*

{ 176 }

[handwritten note, left margin:] Wondering how this chapter would be different if Straka had known the truth about García Ferrara / MacInnes.

[handwritten note, lower left:] Reminds her of who she is + what she still has.

[handwritten note:] I LIKE HOW YOU PUT THAT.

[handwritten note:] Thank you for doing it.

S. does not answer: *No. But I wish I did.*

The look she gives him is unguardedly empty, an invitation for him to witness the blankness in her eyes, to understand that something within her has been lost, and probably lost for good.

Pfeifer spins his wrist in agitation, beckoning *come on come on come on*, leads them as they stumble into the dark unknown of the mountain's heart.

Outside, the vulture circles, somehow unfazed by the fusillade of bullets, one of which scorched the edge of a tail feather. It circles and circles, tipping this way and that, snapping its wings as it encounters a cool downdraft, tipping and flapping and circling, on and ever on. Whether it is brave or ignorant or simply incapable of choosing to do anything else, we can only surmise.

Those cave walls! What a story they would tell to the viewer who had the time to study them methodically, to step carefully through the murk and piece together the full narrative of the mountain people. The faint, charcoal-colored smudges begin just a hundred yards in from the mouth of the cavern— simple figures of man and beast and weapon, visual monosyllables capturing moments in these ancient

{ 177 }

Just like Durand must have changed after Ekstrom died. And maybe like Filomela did when she realized Straka wasn't coming to find her.

But maybe she didn't ever realize it.

Maybe that's what you're finding out right now.

(A BIRD, WATCHING OVER STENFALK)

So my Art History prof just chewed me out about my attendance. I mean, really? Attendance?

How old are we?!? I am so over this place.

JESUS, JEN. JUST GO. YOU'RE TANKING 3 CLASSES.

··· Possibly 4. I'm taking tennis for credit. It's @ 9 am. What was I thinking?

WHAT IS THAT — 1 HR. OF CREDIT? YOU CAN'T NEED IT IF YOU'VE BEEN WORKING SO HARD FOR 4 YRS.

Depends on what happens with the other classes.

lives. A few twists and turns deeper into the passage, there appear sequential accounts of hunts, of rituals, of births and deaths, in which the faces take on distinctive features and the palette expands to include white and blue and rust-red. A detailed study of the ancients' first steps toward modernity, in story and image, deserving of endless admiration, study, awe. But our three fugitives have no time for such luxuries. They cross a trickling stream (through which S. drags his toeless boot, hoping the cool water will bring relief), squeeze themselves through a tight passage, and race past an array of eerily symmetrical stalactites that have arranged themselves like organ-pipes. Then, the passage opens into a huge, half-moon-shaped amphitheater, with an elevated slab altar and all three hundred sixty degrees of wall covered in a kaleidoscopic swirl of images (which, even with the briefest of glimpses in the shaky light of a running man's lantern, is easily recognized as a creation myth, an epic clash between bird-figures of the skies and wolf-figures of the earth, the figures collectively twisting and curling around one another, diving and tumbling and bursting into one ultimate frame of harmony and grace directly above the altar: one humanoid figure with a

{ 178 }

EMERGENCE OF
INDIVIDUAL IDENTITY

Here's what I don't get: when you're growing up, you get told that America's all about the individual, built on individualism, you get to be who you want to be, etc. But it only goes so far.
You get out of school + you're supposed to go back to being a

(SAME FORMATION
APPEARS IN
PAINTED CAVE

→ good little girl and find your job and fit in and follow the rules and it all just makes me want to...

UNDERSTAND WHAT YOU'RE FEELING— BUT THAT'S TOO SIMPLISTIC. IT'S NOT THAT YOU CAN'T BE WHO YOU WANT TO BE... IT'S JUST EASIER TO LET YOUR INDIVIDUAL IDEA OF WHO TO BE SLIP INTO A MORE GENERIC ONE. AND LET'S FACE IT: GENERIC ALMOST ALWAYS PAYS BETTER.

"If I'm going to die, I'll damned well die on a beach."
(p. 377, Winged Shoes English ed.)

crown of feathers and a vulpine tail, balanced on one leg at the needle-tip top of a mountain peak, surrounded by sheer drops and sky—a precarious position, to be sure, but the figure's face expresses only serenity, no fear, no apprehension).[2]

It is in this room, though, that S. and Corbeau and Pfeifer all pause. For one moment, it is more important to take in the spectacular than to worry about the pressing business of staying alive, even as they can hear the first husky shouts in the passageways behind them. Everything Corbeau has been told about the secret caves was true; everything that she has longed to see since she was a girl is right here, surrounding her, surrounding them all. These three, who have no time to spare, and who know they will never be here again. (MISSED OPPORTUNITY)

One agonizingly brief moment to look, to witness, to receive the ancient story—and for S. to hear the private rush of old voices resonating in the air, through the rock, or perhaps only between his ears. And then each of the three—S., Corbeau,

---

2 The late Amarante Durand received much credit for serving as an "expert" upon whose experiences Straka drew for *The Painted Cave*. A careful reading of the text will show, though, that none of the details of the titular cave are unique to "her" caves in the Dordogne. Having seen the caves of Lençóis as a young person, I could have, with very little effort, offered just as rich an assortment of details to the writer.

Handwritten margin notes:

NOT A BAD DESCRIPTION OF WHAT ART DOES. Never thought of it that way. Cool.

Which is what the book's really all about. isn't it?

RIGHT— THE COSTS OF BEING COMMITTED TO ART + RADICAL CHANGE. OR— missing the chance to find out what he could have had with Filomela.

Filomela gets catty. She must have thought of Durand as a rival.

BUT S. + CORBEAU NEVER GET TOGETHER... SO IF SOT IS VEILED AUTOBIOGRAPHY THERE'S NO REASON TO THINK VMS + DURAND EVER DID. And even if they did: Durand died in '37— which would've given VMS 9 years to get over her. If he loves Filomela, what's he thinking that whole time???

HE'S SPENT HIS WHOLE LIFE MAKING SURE HE ISN'T KNOWN. HE'S NOT GOING TO GIVE THAT UP EASILY. So having a secret life is more important to him{ 179 } than she is. nice.

THINK OF WHAT HE WAS (PROBABLY) INVOLVED IN— THE LABOR FIGHTS, THE MUCKRAKING, THE SPYING, THE KILLINGS— THERE'S NO WAY THE DECISION WAS THAT SIMPLE. WOULDN'T HAVE BEEN FAIR FOR HIM TO DRAW HER INTO THAT LIFE.

(vertical left margin): ...should've given her the choice.

Pfeifer—grunts or nods or exhales or makes some back-of-the-throat sound of resignation before they extricate themselves from this sublimity and sprint into the passage that will take them deeper into the earth.

If S. had time to study these walls, to take in every figure, every detail, every curve of negative space, would he come across that strange, serpentine design?[3] He suspects he would, although he will never know.

I suspect he would.

Their only strategy: keep moving, keep the sounds of the posse as distant as possible, maintain hope that the cave will birth them back into the world someplace other than where they started.

They can hear the hunters stomping and shouting behind them, above them, through the porous rock, from every direction and none. S. tries to remember formations as they pass—an outcropping that looks like a face with a long, pharaonic beard, a

---

3 For several decades now—ever since the S symbol appeared on the title page of the first edition of *Miracle at Braxenholm*—discoveries of the same symbol in other locations (many far-flung and/or incongruous) have been reported. These may be homages to Straka (the most likely possibility), or the work of pranksters, or mere coincidence, or occurrences of the fantastic that are far beyond my ability to grasp. I can offer no opinion on the subject, other than to attest that Straka never showed any sign that he was even aware of the phenomenon.

Seems like a pretty straightforward & reasonable FN.

MAKES ME WONDER WHAT SHE'S HIDING.

{ 180 }

tenpin arrangement of stalagmites that looks as
though it's been hand-shaped—the earth's work,
revised—and a water-filled recess in the floor with a
spike of stone rising from it like a sword from a lake.
He tries to remember the sequence of turns and
branches they've followed—left, left, center, right,
center, leftmost, and so on. He watches the walls,
too, as Pfeifer's lamp illuminates them, looking for
images that might help him stay oriented. He
watches them even after he accepts that his mental
map has become hopelessly jumbled.

The paintings run throughout the caverns, and it
seems to S. that, taken together, they tell a complete
story of the K——, as if they were obsessive chroniclers of their experiences. After the amphitheater,
the illustrations on the walls continue, dense and
vibrant and stylistically distinct, the work of many
hands, showing scene after scene of domestic life, of
governance, of skirmishes with other tribes, whose
members are represented with featureless faces. In
every sequence, the K—— are watched over by bird/
wolf-figures—from above the action, from the margins, sometimes from within the groups of people
themselves. The deeper into the mountain S. goes,
the more recent the illustrations appear—sharper in

HISTORY COMPOSED OF
MOMENTS/ACTIONS. SAME
GOES FOR THE SELF?

"US VS. THEM"→
S. VS. VÉVODA/AGENTS

you vs. Moody/Ilsa
THE S VS. BOUCHARD/
AGENTS
Me vs. Jacob

You vs. your parents,
me vs. mine
THE S VS. THE NEWS

US VS. OURSELVES ←

US VS. MOODY VS. ILSA
(US + THEM + THEM?)
+ New S... in which case it's Us vs.
3 Thems. Shitty odds.

color, more nuanced in design, more realistic in the representation of figures and objects. This gives S. pause: with each noteworthy event that transpired on the sunlit surface, the K——'s illustrators had to push deeper into the dark to chronicle it. Is that a striking irony, or the opposite—an inexorable truth about the act of writing history?

Perhaps it is nighttime by now, although S. and the others have no way to know; they no longer occupy the circadian world. S. whistles through his teeth, calls the others to stop so they can sip some water, fuel themselves with quarter-rations of what little they have left. S. inspects his foot: the big toe has blackened and smells of scorched flesh; pus oozes from underneath the nail; and the skin over the second and third toes is darkening and tingling with a strange, fierce heat. The pain is jaw-tightening, breath-catching. Corbeau stands apart, keeping herself to the very edge of the lamplight. She eats with her good hand; with the other, she is pressing her thumb deeply against the fingertips where the skin is being eaten away—index, middle, ring, index, middle, ring—in some private ritual of pain. Pfeifer shakes his head, whispers to S., "She's gone. She's here, but gone."

Margin annotations:

"THE CREATION OF ART REQUIRES A DESCENT INTO THE DARK."
— GUTHRIE MacINNES

He would know, apparently.

HE ALSO TALKED A LOT ABOUT HOW ART REQUIRES ONE SINGLE VISION. (DIRECT CONTRADICTION OF HIS OWN PHILOSOPHY, IN WHICH ONE SINGLE VISION IS BY DEFINITION IMPOSSIBLE ...)

all because Triptych of Mirrors was a disaster — mostly because of the part that he wrote.

THE REVIEWS MUST HAVE HAD HIM SPITTING NAILS.

Vainest

Guy

Ever

HOLDER. OF. BIGGEST. GRUDGE. EVER.

└ NO—BOUCHARD WAS.

PAIN IS NECESSARILY A PRIVATE EXPERIENCE

Not if you have the right person with you

_____

"She's keeping up," S. whispers back. "She's doing everything that we are."

"Don't pretend you don't see it. She's gone. It's what happens. You love, then you lose, then you die. Even if you survive, you die. Think about Ostrero: couldn't stand to be without his wife and kids. Lost his nerve. And now her. She's not who she was this morning. Never will be."

"None of us will be," S. replies, but inside he concedes the point. Is he not better off walking through this world alone? He has spent no time at all worrying about someone who might miss him, pine for his return, grieve his death. Beholden to no one, responsible for no one, depended upon by no one. Really, his task in living is a simple one: survive long enough to find out who you are. But then he thinks of Sola, and he wonders: is he really seeking her just because he suspects she might know something about him? Is there not an attraction, too, either to her, or to the mystery of her? Is this a search for his identity, or some sort of atavistic pursuit of…of what? Love? Something as banal as love?

And what happens if he _does_ find her?

On the wall opposite him, S. notices something different—a set of symbols that looks like a

_____

{ 183 }

THINKING ABOUT HOW EKSTROM'S DEATH MIGHT HAVE CHANGED DURAND… WASN'T LONG AFTER THAT SHE WENT TO SPAIN + WAS JUST RELENTLESS (+ INSANELY PRODUCTIVE) UNTIL SHE DIED. THREW HERSELF INTO THE MIDDLE OF EVERYTHING: SUFFRAGE, LABOR RIGHTS, THE BREWING WAR (SHE SPIED + FOUGHT IN A REPUBLICAN MILITIA, TOO) MANAGED SEVERAL DIGS IN SOUTHERN FRANCE — AND ALL OF THIS WHILE WRITING ESSAYS + ARTICLES + AN AMAZING + HUGE NOVEL. (IF YOU HAVEN'T READ ALL OF THIS TO YOU I GIVE, YOU SHOULD.)

ISN'T THIS JUST A TRUISM? E.G., "CAN'T STEP INTO THE SAME RIVER TWICE"?

Reading it now— although I shouldn't. Too much to do to catch up w/ classes.

QUERY: DO WE PURSUE RELATIONSHIPS OUT OF SELF-INTEREST?

Um, yes. Wake up, Straka.

———

numbering system. It's a ledger of some sort, perhaps, fitting into the space between two figures who
are both looking at it as if it were a solid thing.

PAGE	LINE	WORD
⸚▽ –13	II – 2	⊖→ – 6
⋈ – 4	ⵝ – 8	▽ – 3
⊖→II –62	ⵝ – 5	⸹ – 9
II – 2	II⋈ –24	⸚ – 1
⸚ – 1	⋈ – 4	⸚⸚ – 11
IIⵝ –28	⸚⸹ – 19	⊢ – 7

S. is surprised to find that Pfeifer is still whispering to him. "On top of which," Pfeifer says, "she's
the one carrying the gun."

"I'm not going to try to take it away from her," S.
says. "And if you try, I'll stop you."

Pfeifer stands, picking up the lantern. "We have
to move," he says. "This won't stay lit forever."

The walls look different now; the lines and colors
are as precise as any S. has seen, but the images aren't
as dense. Fewer hands at work, perhaps—fewer people willing to walk this far into the caverns to paint.
But the narrative is changing, too; the tribe seems to
be splitting into factions. One group of figures is
drawn carefully, lithe and graceful; the others look

———

{ 184 }

Got it. Should've figured it out sooner.

*• Check out FN 1.
"Numerous revelations...
page... line... word."*

*• Check your copy of
The Painted Cave.*

*WILL
WAIT
TEN
YEARS
THEN
HOME*

*She waited over TEN
years. She planned to
do it, and she did.
amazing:
all the while she
thought she was in
serious danger.*

*Had Art History midterm today. Didn't
realize until I got to class. Tanked it.*

*Remember when you thought
this wasn't about
LOVE?*

———

dashed-off, blocky and rough, with much less detail. ~~MORE US—VS.—THEM~~ *MORE US—VS.—THEM*
The two groups now hunt separately. The two groups
face off again and again in some sort of tribal meeting. After a while, S. notices another, more subtle difference: the bird-wolf spirits now appear only rarely,
and even when they do, they are high above the
human action, made small with distance.

Have the others noticed any of this? He doubts it.
Pfeifer is pushing forward, choosing their path at each
fork. Corbeau, steely and focused, is putting one foot
ahead of the other with a survivor's grim determination.

They descend deeper. It sounds as though the
hunters are drawing closer, but they can't be certain.
The images on the walls thin out; the figures, all of
them now, lose detail. Hurried sketches, in one person's hand. Only one story line now: the schism in the
tribe, the battle for control. S. imagines [one solitary
painter, the last of his people interested in continuing
the cave chronicle, creeping down alone into the
depths, sketching out a story that he must know no
one will read for hundreds of years, or maybe ever.]

They are rushing through a low, long corridor
when Pfeifer shouts and the lantern goes spinning

*CONSIDER IN LIGHT
OF ALL THE DEATHS +
ABDICATIONS FROM THE S.
The (Original) S.
(Hard to keep track!)
SO VMS WAS PRETTY
MUCH OUT ON HIS OWN
(WHEN? '37? AFTER
GARCÍA FERRARA TURNED
AND DURAND WAS KILLED?)
You'd think that would give
him more incentive to show
himself to Filomela —
— find an ally, a partner.*

———

*HE WASN'T ON HIS
OWN. SUMMERSBY WAS
STILL AROUND (AND MAYBE
OTHERS WE DON'T KNOW
ABOUT YET).*

*MAYBE THAT'S ~~WHAT~~ WHAT
HAVANA WAS ALL ABOUT.
9 years later. I call bullshit.*

away from him, a little orb of light bouncing and clanking over the uneven rock. S. quickly catches up and finds him cursing and clutching his right ankle. S. gently peels Pfeifer's hands away, raises the pant leg, unbuttons the stocking, inspects the damage. Corbeau silently retrieves the lantern and holds the light over them while S. gently prods, squeezes. All but the lightest of his touches cause Pfeifer to wince or sharply inhale or cry out. There is no blood, no visible bone—for that much, at least, they can be thankful. It may simply be a matter of how much pain Pfeifer can tolerate.

"Rest for a moment," S. tells him.

Pfeifer rolls his eyes, groans, puffs out a long breath. "Do you have any idea what you're—?" He cuts himself off when some hunters' voices boom through the cave, sounding clear and close. He points a finger upward. They're directly overhead.

S. takes one of Pfeifer's arms and helps him up. Corbeau ducks under his other arm, wraps it around her shoulders. She seems more aware now, as if this new crisis has awakened her focus or at least turned it back outward.

Pfeifer stands there on one leg, storklike, then tentatively lowers the other toward the ground. A

{ 186 }

[Handwritten annotations:]

physical injury → moral injury
I'VE TAUGHT YOU WELL.
[••]

SHE'S STARTING TO FIND HERSELF. AND CONTINUES TO.
Like Durand did in Spain.

Have you seen the photo of her w/ Hemingway, dos Passos, Garcia Ferrara, Durand, + a Person Conspicuously Turning Away From the camera?

THE HOTEL FLORIDA PHOTO. YES. OCT. 1937.
Right. So who's the Turning-Away guy? Could that be Straka?

CHECK OUT THE GUY BY THE WINDOW WHO'S HALF CUT OFF. WECHSLER?
Lots of possible Strakas in one place— in a war zone, too.

YOU'LL ENJOY THIS: THERE'S A RUMOR (USUALLY ATTRIBUTED TO DOS PASSOS) THAT ONE NIGHT IN MADRID— MAYBE THE NIGHT OF THAT PHOTO? HEMINGWAY GRABBED DURAND'S BUTT + SHE LAID HIM OUT W/ ONE PUNCH. ★

gunshot sounds from above, startling all three of them. Pfeifer's weight falls onto his bad foot, and he wails in pure agony.

They fall silent. Through the rock they hear full-throated laughter. Then, more distantly, a commander's shout, demanding to know who in hell is shooting in an enclosed space when the targets aren't in sight. The disgust in the tone is palpable, even through layers of limestone. Then: more voices, more footfalls. The hunt is back on.

S. and Corbeau support Pfeifer as he tries a few miserable steps. He stops and shakes his head, balls his fists, looks up at the low stone ceiling, using all of his self-control not to scream out in frustration and rage.

"I'll carry you," S. says. He doesn't want to, but he will.

"You can't," Pfeifer says.

"We can," S. says. And he realizes: he is the sort of man who doesn't particularly want to risk his life to offer such help, but he is willing to. The force of the realization—and perhaps the magnitude of it—startles him.

Corbeau says, "Yes, it'll slow us down. But we don't know where we're going, or how far it is, or how to get there."

{ 187 }

Marginalia (handwritten):

Pfeifer injury — did F'bach have anything like that?

BAD GOUT BY THE EARLY '30S, HAD TROUBLE WALKING. SO MAYBE.

How about Wechsler?

PFEIFER CAN'T BE WECHSLER'S STAND-IN. WECHSLER WASN'T PART OF THE ORIGINAL S. what if he was, just by connection to F'bach?

I love this — he's surprised to find out that he's a better person than he thought he was.

Nothing in Durand's journals about that.

WELL, MAYBE IT'S JUST A GOOD STORY.

CHECK THIS OUT: WAS LOOKING THROUGH COLLECTION OF G.F.'S LETTERS + FOUND ONE FROM "V. FINCH," 10/30/37 : "DISTURBED TO HEAR OF FLORIDA EVENTS. C. SHOULD NOT HAVE TAKEN OUR FRIEND THERE, AND YOU SHOULD NOT HAVE LET OUR FRIEND STAY. SECRECY MUST BE TOTAL, OR ALL IS LOST." So that probably was Straka turning away from the camera. IN WHICH CASE: SUMMERSBY WASN'T STRAKA.

AND NEITHER WAS DURAND.

OR GARCÍA FERRARA.

I'm surprised G.F. didn't burn this letter.

Pfeifer lifts his arm off her shoulders. She tries to grab it back, but he pulls it away, holds it high so she can't reach. "Which means," he says, "that you'd go from having almost no chance of escaping to, say, no chance in hell." He shakes his head. "Leave me here. Go."

"No," Corbeau says. "We don't need another martyr."

"Stenfalk did it."

"That's no reason for you to do it."

Silence.

S. thinks: Pfeifer *wants* to sacrifice himself just as Stenfalk did. For her. He has loved her all this time. And he's worried that they're going to deprive him of the greatest of opportunities: to die the way he wants to die, as the person he wants to believe he is.

"Look," S. tells him, "I want like hell to run. But we're together in this."

Pfeifer smiles crookedly. "You're more honest than she is," he says. "So I'll be honest, too: I haven't trusted you from the beginning."

"But you do now," Corbeau prompts.

Pfeifer eyes S. up and down. "I just wish you'd found a way to be useful."

DOESN'T MAKE SENSE. F'BACH WAS ALMOST CERTAINLY GAY. (OR MAYBE HIS SEXUALITY WAS MORE FLUID THAN THAT?)

Maybe Straka meant "love" in a different way: like what's between S.+ Corbeau (and Straka + Durand?)— love between friends, which could turn into something more under the right conditions—but the right conditions never come.

WHICH IS WHAT YOU THINK HAPPENED W/VMS + FXC, RIGHT?

I think it happens a lot.

S. nods. He feels the same. He's carried good intentions with him, but has he helped at all? He was slow to chase the bomber. He left Stenfalk's valise behind. He left a trail to the cave. Has he been anything other than a curse to these people? Has Vévoda ever had anything to fear from the Agent X of his imagination?

"There's no time," Pfeifer says. "To hell with the all-for-one nonsense."

"It's not nonsense," Corbeau says.

"It's worse than nonsense," Pfeifer says. "It's horseshit. It's outdated and useless. So: I'm staying here. Or, rather, I'll crawl around in the dark in one direction or another and hope I come across a mining cart, or a magical portal in the earth, or some such miracle."

Corbeau hands him the gun. "Make them earn it," she says.

"I will," Pfeifer says. "And I'll enjoy it."

"Try walking again," S. says. "Just try."

One tentative step, one pathetic, furious yelp. "Go," Pfeifer says. "Take the goddamned lantern and go."

But S. does not go, not yet. He is looking at the wall right next to where Pfeifer is leaning. A painting, all in black. Dozens of bipedal wolf-people—visually

{ 189 }

Is THIS THE MOMENT WHEN S. STARTS DOWN THE DARKER PATH? OR IS IT ON THE ISLAND?

Straka: grandfather of fantasy / SciFi?

ACTUALLY, YOU WOULDN'T BE THE FIRST ONE TO SUGGEST IT (THINK OF SPOTTED CAT, NIGHT PALISADES, EVEN CORIOUS). AND IF YOU THINK SUMMERSBY WAS VMS, THEN THERE'S A PRETTY DIRECT CONNECTION TO THE GENRES.

abbreviated, just ears and teeth and tails on stick-bodies—falling upon…what? S. cannot say. A splotch, and a downward streak. It might have developed into a figure had the picture been finished, had the artist not been fallen upon before he drew himself into it.

And this, this scene of blood and finality, this will probably be the last painting they find on the walls. S. is sure of it.

And it will be the last thing Pfeifer sees, full-stop, now that S. and Corbeau are leaving him behind in the dark, at least until the Detectives cast their lights upon him, call for him to play his own role in a similar scene.

They were five, and now they are two. Two people with one light, scrambling through twisting passages that are becoming more and more steeply downsloped. At one point, the path they are walking ends abruptly and they must choose: backtrack, or lower themselves through a wet erosion-hole in the ground and hope for a safe landing in the chamber below. A stream of water runs down one side of the hole, drizzling down into the dark. S. finds himself irritated by how effortlessly water finds the place it belongs.

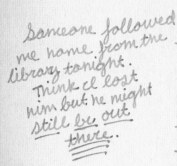

Someone followed me home from the library tonight. Think I lost him but he might still be out there.

DIMINISHING NUMBERS → — LIKE THE SHIP

You totally lied to me about the tunnels.

WASN'T SURE I COULD TRUST YOU.

That What else have you lied about?

NOTHING YOU DON'T ALREADY KNOW ABOUT ———

That makes me feel so much better. Anyway: you should give me a copy of your map. Just in case. It's in both of our interests.

DON'T LET ANYONE ELSE SEE IT

He shines the lamp down into the lower passage, then stands back from the hole. It's narrow, yes, but he won't get stuck in it. "Are you worried that we're going too far down?" S. asks. He wonders: could it be that they're no longer to evade the posse but rather to bury themselves as deeply as they can to deny Vévoda's men the satisfaction of finding their corpses?

"Of course I'm worried," Corbeau says.

S. drops his rucksack through the hole, then climbs down after it, thankful that his landing is a graceful one. Corbeau loses her grip on the wet rock and launches herself awkwardly downward, but he catches her, wraps her tightly in his arms. She is much lighter than he imagined.[4] For a moment he wonders if she is even real.

He is about to set her down when he notices what's on the wall next to them, partially obscured by drizzling water and shadow:

S

It's only a few inches high, and it's scrawled rudimentarily—not precise or symmetrical or artistic in any way—but it's there, in black.

---

[4] For all Corbeau's accomplishments and tenacity, she appears to lack a degree of gravitas.

You'd better be real. I'm starting to get freaked out here + if you're not who I think you are I'm going to **LOSE IT.**

OK, FXC, WE GET IT.

———

"You can put me down," Corbeau tells him.

He mutters an apology. Points to the symbol on the wall. "Do you see that?" he asks. He needs reassurance. He can't be imagining this, can he?

"Yes," she says. "What about it?"

"I've been seeing this everywhere I go," he says. "It's—" and he looks for the right word. *Disconcerting* is what he comes up with. "Have you ever seen it before?"

"Maybe," she says. "I don't know."

"Think."

"It looks familiar. That's all I can say."

"It's important. I think I'm *connected* to it, somehow."

"Think while you walk," she says, tapping the lantern. "Time's running out."

Boots pounding on rock. A shout of discovery, unmistakable. A riot of excited male voices. Whoops and taunts and even something like a canine bark.

One sad gunshot, the pop of an ancient pistol. Then a vicious *ratatat* of return fire—six bullets? ten? twenty?—all in one instant.

These sounds. Rolling closer like a wave, unstoppable. And the two of them—two, a paltry two— bracing for the curl and the crash and the darkness.

———

———

And the darkness.

Clank.

Whispers. Clearer here—not buried by so much rock—but still indistinct. Tones of agony, cadences of outrage, erratic rhythms of fear.

The two of them, blind, feeling their way along water-slick walls.

And then a new sound: a soft, bassy rumble.

"I'm right here," he says.

"I am, too," she says.

"Give me your good hand," he says.

She does.

They can hear the voices more distinctly now. They hear the clank and clatter as the Detectives find the lantern and pitch it away. They hear a baritone shout and a roar of assent.

The rumble grows louder. S. is about to remark upon this when Corbeau drops his hand.

"What is it?" he asks.

"The air." She sniffs. "It's different."

He inhales deeply, smells only dampness and rock and time.

———

"Salt," she says.

Now that she has given it a name, he thinks, yes, he can smell that, although it immediately reminds him of his stinking little cabin on that ship.

"I see you," she says.

He assumes she means this metaphorically, but when he looks back at her, he can see her outlined against the dark. It's not much light, but it's not nothing.

They follow the wall as it winds in an S-curve, the rumble ever louder, the voices behind them sharpening, intensifying, gaining more definition. Every time he looks back, he can see more of her.

"Stop looking at me," she says. "There's no time."

And then, up ahead: light. The grim, gray light of a stormy dusk, but it is light, and it is ahead of them, and they hurry toward it as quickly as the uneven ground under their feet allows them.

Rumble and crash. Waves. The ocean. *What begins at the water shall end there, and what ends there shall once more begin.*

They stand at the edge, looking down at the waves far, far below. Slanting rain wets their faces, their clothes, their feet. The wind is a cold rake

This wasn't underlined before...

I KNOW.
I JUST DID IT.

Filomela + Straka didn't have enough time.

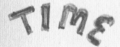

Love ⟹ when it's more important to take in the spectacular than to worry about the pressing business of staying alive.

AND A LOT OF WHAT'S IN BETWEEN, TOO.

Wish I could get word to you...

against their skin. All the way down the cliffside, from cave mouth to waterline, runs a diagonal line of scalloping in the rock face, each step slick and threatening. A stairway once, perhaps, but centuries of wind and salt and rain have erased it almost entirely. There's no way to descend safely. To try would be to plunge. It's that simple. ✸

"The symbol," she says. "It was on Stenfalk's valise."

This makes no sense to him. If he is connected to Stenfalk, why didn't the older man know him? Why doesn't anyone else?

Frenzied voices fill the shadowed passage behind them. Voices of real life—of real life, with guns—that drown the whispers. A guttural command cuts them off; the same voice calls out *Stop where you are!* Another informs them that this is *the end of the line*, and still another says something about *god-damned Reds*. S. and Corbeau cannot see these men—they're just dark shapes texturing the aphotic space of the cave—but they hear the cocking of a dozen hammers, know there are a dozen barrels aimed at them.

Corbeau interlaces the fingers of her good hand with his, and it triggers in him a memory of them walking through the city together—yes, they were

---

Handwritten (top margin):

THE BEST TIME I HAD IN COLLEGE WAS THE TIME MY ROOMMATE GRIFF + I ROAD-TRIPPED TO SAN FRANCISCO RIGHT BEFORE EXAM WEEK. THERE WAS A BASEBALL GAME HE WANTED TO SEE, SO WE DROVE LIKE HELL ALL NIGHT + MORNING TO GET THERE, SAW THE GAME, TURNED RIGHT AROUND + DROVE LIKE HELL ALL NIGHT. GOT BACK JUST IN TIME FOR MONDAY MORNING EXAMS. IT FELT SO GOOD TO SAY, NO, WE'RE NOT GOING TO STUDY, WE'RE GOING TO DO THIS RIDICULOUS, POINTLESS TRIP INSTEAD. AND WE ACED OUR EXAMS ANYWAY, SO WE ACTED LIKE THAT WAS PROOF THAT WE WERE TOTAL ACADEMIC BAD-ASSES. HERE'S MY POINT, THOUGH:

I TOLD MY FATHER ABOUT THE TRIP, THINKING HE'D LOVE IT B/C HE'S SUCH A HUGE BASEBALL FAN. I GOT MY HOPES UP SO HIGH FOR THIS — IT MIGHT HAVE BEEN THE REASON I WENT ALONG W/ GRIFF IN THE FIRST PLACE — AND WHEN I TOLD HIM, THERE WAS DEAD SILENCE, AND HE SAID, "WELL, ERIC, THAT'S JUST ONE MORE IRRESPONSIBLE THING YOU'VE DONE THAT HAS NEEDLESSLY ENDANGERED OTHER PEOPLE." AND I REMEMBER STANDING THERE + THINKING, "REALLY? IS THERE ANYTHING THAT HE CAN'T JUST TURN INTO A REMINDER ABOUT MY UNCLE?" God. I'm so sorry. IT'S THE KIND OF THING YOU TELL YOURSELF YOU'LL GET OVER, IT DOESN'T MATTER, ETC., ETC., BUT YOU NEVER DO.

Handwritten (bottom left):

But Straka wasn't a Communist, was he?

NO — NOR A SOCIALIST, AN ANARCHIST, AN ANYTHING-IST. BUT IF ENOUGH PEOPLE ~~THINK~~ THINK OF YOU A CERTAIN WAY, IT BECOMES TRUE. EVEN IF IT'S NOT TRUE.

{ 195 }

just pretending to be a couple, and yes, they were already on the run, but he liked how it felt. It was not even a week ago, but it seems like another age entirely: simpler, safer, saner.[5]

That's so sweet, one of the voices says.

Strange. He has been assuming for these last weeks, if only subconsciously, that if he would soon be facing death with anyone, it would be with Sola. The idea—the certainty of it—is churning through his blood. It's what was supposed to happen. How he came to be here, now, with Corbeau, is obvious and undeniable—it's what *has* happened—and yet it seems the most confounding of mysteries.

"Push off hard," Corbeau tells him. "Jump as far out as you can."

You might expect them to count down *sotto voce*, to synchronize their movements, to acknowledge that they will be moving as one, but no—there is no need. He feels her hand twitch inside his and in an instant they are turning and leaping. S. has pushed off with his bad foot, which sends a howl of pain

---

5 I often served in an editorial capacity as I assembled the translation. I strongly recommended that Straka cut this passage, which reads far more sentimentally than I believe he intended. He insisted that the passage remain, and I am honoring his wishes, under mild protest.

[handwritten annotations:]

Fuck you, Brown-Duster-Guy. It *is* sweet.

This ᴴ has its own page in the manuscript—could easily be an insert. I'm no expert, but it looks like a different typewriter.

MAYBE VMS ADDED IT @ THE LAST MINUTE IN HAVANA.

He had his own typewriter with him.

MAYBE HE OWNED MORE THAN ONE.

Think about it: this comes right after the ᴴ about Corbeau/Durand that he wouldn't let Filomela cut. This is *totally* her response. She was supposed to be with him.

That's the thing—even though Straka + Filomela never met (not knowingly, anyway), they were close. She loved him. And if she was the one person he trusted to work on his books—+ for such a long time—then he definitely felt something deep for her.

Did they love each other?

Were words enough?

Would words have been enough, if he'd at least been willing to show himself? Or did they need more?

Think about: love + the right conditions.

through his body, but that might be a blessing as the pain and the rushing wind and the cold rain that chills his face keep him from thinking about the air under his feet and the shots coming out of the dark.

Everything goes still for a moment as a memory—or what he assumes is a memory—unfolds itself over him. Corks flying on a New Year's Eve. A room full of people, of faces and bodies and spirits. A fire in a hearth. A sense of himself as—well, as someone.

They are falling. The bullets whistle past, just above their heads. He feels her tipping away from him, tugs her upright, clings tightly; they are falling. They are comrades, they are allies, they are the last two members of the only group S. knows, they are falling, they are falling, they are falling.

He no longer hears the voices. The wind is what fills his ears.

Does he, for even a blink of a moment, feel as if he can fly? No. This is falling, unmistakably so. The two of them are falling, together, and when they hit the water, the flam of their double impact sounds as loud in his ears as did the bomb at the wharf.

The way out was down. Is down.

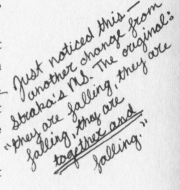

Just noticed this— another change from Straka's MS. The original: "they are falling, they are falling, they are falling, they are together and falling."

THEY'RE ALL NAMED FOR BIRDS, BUT THEY'RE STILL JUST PEOPLE.

Straka, too.

Down through the caverns, down through the air, down into the water, down through several thermoclines to a depth in the ocean no person should see, where S. startles a school of blackscabbards, which scatter, whipping themselves away into the dark as his descent slows, slows, slows.

He breathes out—the last bit of breath in his compressed lungs—and follows the bubbles upward.

At the surface, he breathes, coughs, breathes. He feels dizzy, and the pressure in his head is terrible. He spins in the water, looking for Corbeau, but she's not there.

To his right: the hillside throws a narrow jut into the water, and the cove around its other side looks well-protected. Far, far above, in the mouth of the cave—*can they really have fallen that far?*—a cluster of browncoats are posed in firing stances. Bullets whine and rain around him. S. holds a deep breath and dives, swims a dozen strokes to one side. He rises, scans the surface. He won't swim for the point without her. He will not.

Dive, stroke, and rise. Still, he is alone at the surface.

Dive, stroke, rise.

This is when the worry grips him. She should have come up for air by now.

Great word. Awesomely ugly fish, too. (I looked it up.)

Dive, stroke, rise, and how much longer can he do this? How much longer can he stay here before the law of averages sends a hot bullet spinning through his skull?

Dive, stroke, rise.

Where is she?

Once more, and this time he passes through a cloud of red before he breaks the surface. He feels her bump up against him, nudged by a wave (She is doubled-over and face-down, her black hair fanning out around her. Three small, dark holes in her back. She was hit as they leapt, hit three times while he, with luck he does not deserve, entered and exited midair intact and whole.)

She might have died while still holding his hand.

He does not turn her over, does not want to see her torn open, does not want to see her face in death. He gulps a breath and dives, just as more bullets throw spray around him—dives, and strokes and kicks, because he has decided he will make it around that point, out of the line of fire, onto a rock or a pebbly shore, any safe place where he can pull himself out and rest and maybe weep and then figure out what in hell he's supposed to do next.

Twice recently (and maybe more often—he doesn't know, of course) he has swum for his life.

BEING HONORABLE ISN'T AS EASY AS HE'D LIKE.

Do you think Straka was there when Durand got killed?

HARD TO SAY. THIS MAKES A LOT OF SENSE, THOUGH, IF GARCÍA FERRARA IS VMS.

He's beginning to feel like a creature of the sea. He wants to ask those Old Quarter voices: which beginning? which end? But those voices only talk; they don't listen.]

He swims mostly underwater until he curls around the point and enters the calm of the cove. When he pauses to gauge the distance, he concludes that he must have died, too, because what he sees is impossible.

Anchored in the cove is a ship. The ship that carried him here, the xebec that he left as it was torn apart by a waterspout. It is here, patched and floating, somehow, in much too short a time. Rebuilt strangely, to be sure: the hull is an even more battered gathering of mismatched wood scraps, the height ratios of its three masts seem different, the bowsprit stouter and stubbier. Any doubt, though, that it is not the same vessel is erased when the gaff hook catches him by his shirt, pulling him close, and he hears the big, bearded sailor's un-voice saying *Vizz we hookt one ugger rough-fish? We've the bless o' th' damnt, we do.* And lining the deck, looking down on him, are twenty or so unsmiling faces— their mouths just horizontal black smudges, to S.'s

SOMETIMES I'M JEALOUS OF PEOPLE WHO'VE STUDIED VMS'S BOOKS W/O GETTING INTO ALL OF THIS. MAYBE YOU DON'T SOLVE THE BIG MYSTERY, BUT YOU FIND SMALLER TRUTHS. THAT'S NOT A BAD THING, IS IT? FEWER SACRIFICES. MORE TIME TO JUST BE WITH THE BOOKS, YOURSELF, SOMEONE ELSE... IT'S REALLY WHAT I MEANT, TO DO FROM THE BEGINNING.

I HOPE THIS IS THE FIRST THING YOU READ WHEN YOU COME BACK.

I HOPE YOU COME BACK.

———

salt-scourged eyes—along with a monkey that is swinging loops on a halyard and shrieking.

Wellvenoo, sunnydags, Maelstrom says. *Rise y'proper.*

You took a gamble there at the end.

I DIDN'T REALIZE I HAD DONE IT. IT JUST HAPPENED.

———

Eric; ~~it just~~ ~~it isn't~~
~~that's so~~
OK— I don't know how
to respond. I'm sorry.
~~I'm so sorry.~~

Eric?

CHAPTER 6

A SLEEPING DOG

WHY THIS TITLE?
THE DOG IS AN INCIDENTAL
DETAIL—ALSO: ISN'T
REALLY ASLEEP.

You said the 23rd. Where are you??

Now the 24th... + you
still haven't picked up the book.

FLIGHT DELAYED, HAD TO SPEND NIGHT
IN MIAMI — THEN 2 MORE FLTS. TO GET BACK.
HAVEN'T GONE HOME YET — NEED TO CRASH.
(BUT LOOK AHEAD)

Have to assume it's
a guide to the
chapter's code, but
I haven't figured
it out yet. *NEITHER HAVE I.*

THE CABIN is much as it was when S. left it. The hammock. The fetor. The musty vacuum. That S-shaped symbol, hacked like a plea or a curse into the bulkhead. Some of the other boards in the bulkhead have been replaced, though, as have some of the planks in the flooring and a few steps on the ladder to the hatchway; the new (or newly-scavenged) wood has not been stained to match the old, and its range of hues—from blond to wine to chestnut to coffee—has a dizzying effect. Perhaps this is why the dimensions of the cabin feel subtly different, why there's something so disorienting about the space.

S. is huddled in the hammock, shivering even though he has been outfitted with dry osnaburg

Whole lotta nothing.
IF I WERE IN FXC'S
SHOES I'D WANT TO
BREAK UP MY PATTERNS.
IT HAS TO BE OVERT
ENOUGH THAT VMS
COULD FIND IT. BUT (OBV.)
THE HARDER IT IS FOR
ANYONE TO FIGURE OUT
(OR EVEN NOTICE), THE
BETTER.

SHIP KEEPS CHANGING—
+ CHANGE IS DISORIENTING
Yes, it is.

and—somehow—his old overcoat, along with a heavy woolen blanket. The blanket smells as if it has recently covered something dead.

The shivering must have begun while he was in the water; he felt it as he was being lifted aboard with the Detectives' guns still crackling quietly, rendered impotent by wind and distance, and when the cold air came at him on the deck as the anchor was raised and the sails cupped the wind. It became so intense that two of the mute sailors—the pale man with the greasy forelock and the straw-haired whittler—had to carry him the length of the deck, maneuver him up the ladder to the forecastle, and help him down the hatch into the cabin.

Since then, he has been unable to stop himself from reliving all of the horror of his week on land. The holes in Corbeau's back, the cloud of red in the water. The businesslike shove that sent Stenfalk into the gorge. Ostrero, picked clean off the rock face. The bang in the dark as Pfeifer's life was stolen. All they did was ask for answers about three missing men, and everything spiraled downward from there. His four friends are dead, as are sixty-one of their fellow workers. The remaining factory workers will understand what it takes to survive in B—— now,

★ [NEXT PG.]

Margin annotations:

SHIP NOW A HAVEN— LESSER OF TWO THREATS

ANOTHER REF TO HOBO PREACHER'S HOMILY. (H.P. = AN IDEALIZED VISION OF ABSOLUTE COMMITMENT TO A LIFE OF PRINCIPLE.)

Isn't that what Filomela was? Straka + the books were her whole life.

BY THE SAME LOGIC, SO WAS VMS. Only w/ his books + his politics { 204 } clf there was any principle in the way he treated her, it was the principle of "give nothing back to the people who love you."

NOT THAT SIMPLE. SOT SHOWS THAT HE WAS CONFLICTED.

Not conflicted enough.

and they will commit themselves to doing it: say
nothing, see nothing, ask nothing. Comply.]

S. knows: in Vévoda he has a nemesis who already
wields exponentially more power than S. ever will.
He has docile, intimidated workers, a newspaper
that will print what he tells it, an army of ruthless
Detectives, and no evident sense of conscience,
ethics, or proportionality. But what does he *want*?
It can't just be financial opportunity in the regional
arms trade, can it? Some sort of corrosive anger,
some privately-held grudge? Power for its own sake?
What sort of man does these things, and how does
he sleep at night?

And what purpose did all that suffering serve?
What was it all for?

Nothing, he decides.[1] Not yet.(None of that sacrifice will be worth a single *escudo* unless S. can tell
the world about what Vévoda has done and what he
is capable of doing. Or if not the entire world, then

[1] The only argument one needs to dismiss the notion that Guthrie MacInnes might have
been Straka is this: that Straka—while perhaps subject to moments of despair, just like the
rest of us—can in no way be mistaken for a Nihilist; every page of his extensive oeuvre
demonstrates a passionate, even anguished search for (and commitment to) value.
MacInnes's theory of multitudinalism, in contrast, is merely a fancy-sounding cover for the
blackest Nihilism of all. Consider, reader: if there is nothing durable in identity, there is
no reason for any of us to value anything—not people, not principles, nothing. And yet,
years and years and years and years have gone by without anyone's pointing out the
fundamental emptiness of MacInnes's philosophy.

Marginalia:

★ IT BOTHERS ME, TOO—
ESPECIALLY NOW THAT
I'VE MET HER.

*She was too — I WOULDN'T WANT TO BE THE ONE WHO
committed.* TELLS HER THAT.
SHE'S STILL PRETTY FIERCE.

*Did you come to PSU just to work
with Moody?* YUP.
EVEN THOUGH MY
UNDERGRAD ADVISOR TOLD
ME NOT TO GO STUDY W/
SOMEONE JUST B/C HE'S
A BIG NAME. HE MIGHT
BE A LOUSY TEACHER, OR
TOO BUSY, OR WORSE.
DID I LISTEN?
OF COURSE NOT.

repetitions: ALSO: "YEARS + YEARS + YEARS +
nihilist/nihilism YEARS" (4 X? IS THE
NUMBER 4 RELEVANT??)

*You're not the first.
I give my sister advice
all the time + she ignores
it. She's coming to PSU
next year — even though
she got into 3
Ivies (!) — just b/c her
boyfriend got a baseball
scholarship here. She's an
idiot to pass up the
opportunity.*

*She's relentless
about MacInnes.*
YOU THINK?

SHE PROBABLY
LOVED HEARING THAT.
*I just don't want her to make
mistakes like I did.* →

⟹ SHE LOOKS LIKE YOU.

~~Taller~~ Taller. Thinner. Better hair. She makes me sick.

MAYBE. BUT YOU'RE THE BEAUTIFUL ONE.

you don't have to say that. I don't need to be the
beautiful one. (kinda resent the implication, actually...)

SHIP OF THESEUS

———————

at least some small part of it. He may not know much about the man, but he has seen the provocateurs, the killings, the blast site, the lengths to which Vévoda will go to protect what he values.))

One problem: he has no one to tell. Certainly not Maelstrom or the disfigured sailors. They may have saved him in the cove, but he still doesn't trust them, still worries darkly about their plans for him. And if S. never again gets to dry land, never leaves this ship alive, who can be his audience? Who will be spurred to righteous action by his words? The flying fish, those evanescent flashes of silver? The wind? The moon? The stars, which have become strangers to him?

He wraps the blanket tighter around himself, tries to ignore the stench. He wriggles himself from supine to half-prone in the unsteady netting, blinks away what might be tears, and stares blankly at the seam where the bulkhead meets the decking. Then, his eye is drawn to a tiny disruption in the dark crease: a bent nail, mottled with rust, lying in a groove, where it was swept or where the pitch of the seas flung it.

S. drops his stockinged feet to the floor, picks up the nail, and rolls it in his fingers. He tests its sharpness by scratching a single vertical line—a *one*, you

So have you been working on your dissertation?

HAVEN'T STARTED WRITING. GOT LOST
IN THE RESEARCH FOR A LONG TIME,
AND THEN, YOU KNOW, EVERYTHING
What was it going   ELSE HAPPENED.
to be about? Were you trying
to solve the whole Straka mystery?

{ 296 }

▸ YEAH. IN HINDSIGHT,
IT WAS WAY TOO BIG
A PROJECT. BETTER TO DO
SOMETHING SMALLER, MORE
SPECIFIC—THEN GET THE
PH.D., MOVE ON, GET THE
TEACHING JOB, THEN RESEARCH
PUBLISH MORE. OH WELL.
MOOT POINT NOW.

could say, or an *I*—into a new piece of wood at the topmost edge of the bulkhead. And then, slowly, painstakingly, he begins to carve his story into the ship itself.

I swam away from the ship, he writes. *I assumed it had been destroyed. I found myself under a pier, coughing out seawater. I could hear the noise of the demonstration above.*

A cramp grips his hand, twisting it into a claw. He shakes it gently, rubs it with his other hand, and he feels the tendons begin to ease their grip. As he rubs, he steps back, reads what he has written.

The words on the wall are not the words he thought he wrote.

I SWAM AWAY FROM THE SHIP,

the wall says.

I HAD ASPIRED TO DESTROY IT.
I FOUND MYSELF UNDER AN ARCH,
CURSING AT SENATORS. COULD I HARM
THE NOISY DEMONS ABOVE?[2]

---

2   This may be an allusion to the anonymous 1866 novel *Les Démons en Haut*, a scathing rebuke of the contemporary Parisian bourgeoisie. While the book is not well-known—indeed, it was banned almost immediately—one can easily imagine that Straka felt a kinship with its author.

Probably a code in the wall-writing—don't you think? Whether it's part of the Ch.-le code or something else entirely?

AGREE— VMS DIDN'T DO STUFF LIKE THIS BY ACCIDENT. HE DID LIKE TO MESS W/ PEOPLE WHO READ EVERYTHING AS A CLUE RE: HIS IDENTITY. KIND OF LIKE JOHN LENNON WRITING NONSENSE TO TAUNT THE "PAUL IS DEAD" CROWD.

DOESN'T EXIST. (NO SURPRISE THERE)

? Paul was dead?
<< baffled >>

JUST LOOK IT UP WHEN YOU HAVE TIME TO KILL. POINTLESS BUT FUN.

WHAT IF IT'S NOT A CODE OR A JOKE BUT SOMETHING SERIOUS ABOUT TRYING TO TELL A STORY OR EXPRESS A FEELING, BUT NEVER HAVING IT COME OUT THE WAY YOU WANT IT TO?

SHIP OF THESEUS

Odd. He must still be in some sort of shock.

He scratches a line through the words he did not intend, corrects them in cramped letters in the narrow space above, and continues, working clockwise around the curve of the bow. He stops, steps back, reads.

Odder still. There are more words to correct this time, and his hand is again clawed and stiff. He takes another step back and nearly slips on a ship-biscuit on the floor. Someone must have thrown it down to him while he was working. He sits and gnaws at it, while he rests his hand and marvels, silently, at the strangeness of his mind, this ship, this world.

Later, he remembers the piece of paper that was in his overcoat, wonders if it holds even the faintest of clues. He digs in the pocket, but all he finds are tiny, brittle wads sticking to the seam inside. He picks out one and attempts to unfurl it. It disintegrates in his fingers. He scrapes out a few more of the bits, tries again and again, with the same result. He closes his eyes, sighs. If there were answers here, they are gone.[3]

---

[3] N.B.: Upon Reinhold Feuerbach's death in a bathroom fall at 64 Heagy Street in Dublin, where he lived after fleeing the Nazis, his protégé Horst Wechsler was asked whether he thought Feuerbach had been V. M. Straka. "If there were answers inside him," Wechsler told the *Sunday Independent*, "those answers are gone."

{ 208 }

Handwritten margin notes:

Email from VP of Student Affairs. I've been accused of plagiarism. Have to meet w/ him + a panel tomorrow afternoon.

I AM SO SORRY. I NEVER SHOULD HAVE GIVEN THAT TO YOU. HOW MUCH DID YOU USE?

YOU CAN TELL ME. COME ON.

PLEASE. COME FIND ME AS SOON AS IT'S OVER. I'LL BE IN THE BACK ROW @ THE VARSITY, PRETENDING TO WATCH WHATEVER IT IS THEY PUT ON THE SCREEN.

So — Wechsler was his protégé in the "people-can't-say-they're-lovers" way. But is that all? Did he write?

HW was w/ The S from the beginning — wonder if it was hard for him to be the only non-writer.

WOULD LOVE TO SEE THE DUBLIN MS — WHATEVER EXISTS OF IT.

SOME DISPATCHES FROM SPAIN IN THE '30s FOR SMALL ANARCHIST PUBLICATION F' BACH'S JOURNAL MENTIONS HW WORKING ON A NOVEL WHILE IN DUBLIN — NEVER PUBLISHED, THOUGH. MAYBE NEVER FINISHED

SHIP OF THESEUS

By the time he goes on deck, the rainstorm has passed, though the wind still blows strong and steady and the sky remains a blanket of gray so thick that S. cannot tell the time of day. The air is clean and strong and good to breathe, though he must keep the fouled blanket wrapped around himself to fend off the cold. That smell is a good thing, he has decided; it is a reminder of how closely, how relentlessly, death stalks us all.

He spies Maelstrom behind the wheel on the quarterdeck, scratching at his beard, which has grown noticeably thicker and grayer. As S. heads aft, the other sailors treat him much as they did before: with an indifference spiced with resentment. He is in the way, he is not one of them, his presence is tolerated reluctantly. He is a bit surprised by this; when he was lifted from the water, he thought that many of their faces were registering some sort of interest. Perhaps his mind had projected expressions of welcome on their doomy visages.

The sailors are unhurried in their work, and the few whistles rise and fall with little urgency. S. is surprised to see that many of the crew look more bleary-eyed, more enervated, more grizzled and bent than he remembers. The deck seems less crowded, too,

S. STILL AN OUTSIDER

OK: Best job you ever had... Ready? Go.

MY 1ST SEMESTER HERE, I WORKED IN THE PLANETARIUM. (MOODY SET IT UP — I WAS SUPPOSED TO TA BUT IT FELL THROUGH. HE KNEW I NEEDED $$.). NOTHING GLAMOROUS — LOTS OF CLERICAL WORK — BUT I LOVED IT. WATCHED THE SHOWS WHENEVER I WANTED, LEARNED TO USE THE EQUIPMENT. HAD TO START BUILDING UP A TEACHING RESUME, THOUGH.

You?

The one I have now. I love the library, I love people who love libraries, and I'm good at what I do. Close 2nd: I was a counselor at a girls' camp — arts + crafts. { 209 }(I did fill in once for the archery counselor. So I'm an archer. And I have tales!)

I THINK MOODY HAS THAT BOOK.

It's in his house. Has to be.

and he counts: There are only fifteen sailors. He does not see the sepulchral man, and he knows that other familiar faces are missing, even if he can't specifically recall which. He is surprised that there would be so much attrition in the crew over such a short stretch of time, and that Maelstrom would not have crewed up to replace them.

He climbs to the quarterdeck, just managing to keep his grip on the ladder as the ship dips into a trough and flings itself steeply to leeward. Maelstrom says nothing at first, just eyes him, until a squirt of bird excrement falls from above, splattering one of his broad shoulders and breaking the stillness. He scrubs roughly at the mess with a greasy-looking rag. His raspy voice has even less substance to it now. *Ye've got questions. 'm I right?*

"How did you find me?"

Y'swam righ' up to us.

"But why were you there? How did you know to be exactly *there*? For that matter, how is it that this ship still *exists*?"[4]

---

4 Here again, Straka may have drawn material from the spurious *Tortugan Journals* of the pirate Covarrubias. According to the journals (which, I must point out again, are obviously fakes), the French barque *Belette* struck a reef and sank near Martinique in 1647, but was spotted again in 1683, risen like Lazarus and sailing briskly through the waters off the coast of Peru.

Margin notes:

DECLINING NUMBERS... WE STARTED W/19 SAILORS (=19 VMS BOOKS). WHY COUNT DOWN? IS HE REFERRING TO A KIND OF ARTISTIC MORTALITY— I.E., HE ONLY HAD SO MANY BOOKS IN HIM?

What if the crew represents members of The S, not Straka's books? And the ranks thinning out?

What if there were a lot more writers involved than we even know? What if The S was (is?) much bigger, and this ship just represented VMS's wing of it?

MAKES ME WONDER IF THE DANISH GUY'S SITE MIGHT BE USEFUL AFTER ALL.

Been thinking about the ch. 3 code + HW vanishing after Dublin. Turns out an "H. Wechsler" entered the Netherlands (Rotterdam) in June 1940.

WHICH WAS DURING THE OCCUPATION.

Exactly. So many people trying to get out, and he goes right in. no record of him leaving or dying there.

I really, really want Covarrubias to have been rea[l]

SEEMS LIKE VMS AND FXC BOTH DID, TOO. THEY'RE HAVI[NG] A LOT OF FUN WITH TH[E] MYTH. (HAVE YOU LOOKE[D] UP THE SHIP?)

Yer makin' 'sumptions, Sunshine.

S. pauses, thinks. It's hard to keep his thoughts straight. It's as if this whole nautical scene in which he finds himself—not just the cabin, but the deck, the masts, the surface of the sea, the skies, his vision, his mind—is a few degrees off true. "If you were there to pick me up," he says, "then I can assume you don't mean me harm. If you weren't, if it was just my random good fortune—then I can't."

The big sailor picks at his teeth with a filthy thumbnail. *I don' mean y' one thing or 'nother*, he says. *All I mean's t'steer the ship.*

"I suppose you're waiting for me to express gratitude."

Keep y' gratitude: Got no need 'f it.

"Tell me this," S. says. "How long have I been on board? This time, I mean?"

Ye'd know well as I do.

"That's not true." And it can't be. Because S. would guess he's been on board fewer than twenty-four hours. And yet, back in his cabin, when he realized that the agonizing burn in his toes had subsided into the faintest of tingles, he'd removed his stocking to inspect his foot. He'd been expecting to see the flesh and nails eaten away—of the big toe,

Of course I looked. And of course it didn't exist. And of course there's nothing in Tortugan Journals about this, anyway. It's funny {211} as serious as FXC was about Straka (+ his work, + getting messages to him, + keeping him safe), she seems like she was having a lot of fun making things up.

at least—and maybe even exposed bone, considering what he'd seen of Corbeau's hand, considering
the pain that had screamed across his synapses for
days. Instead, he found himself looking at a healthy,
intact foot, the skin baby-pink and new over the
first three toes, with a diagonal line running from
the third toe down and around the ball of his foot,
clearly demarcating the healing. On the rest of his
foot, the skin was rougher and several shades
darker, but it was undamaged.

"My foot—" S. begins.

B'lieve what y'want to b'lieve, Maelstrom says,
with something like amusement flashing over his face.

At his back, S. hears a wave of whistles sweep
across the crew. It is a subtle sound, just a minor
countermelody in the roaring symphony of sail
and water, but it makes S. turn his head. He
watches as the rear hatchway creaks open and, up
from the bowels of the ship—from the secret
space in the orlop, S. is certain—comes one of the
sailors. S. doesn't know why this should have captured the crew's interest. Another sailor is descending the rigging, preparing to serve his own stint
below, and the scene looks like any of the other
rotations. But then S. takes a close look at the

[handwritten annotations in margin:]

Just like people with their straka candidates...

AND FILOMELA.RE: VMS BEING ALIVE

And me with y'all.

AND ME WITH YOU, TOO.

Wonder if that's unavoidable.

IT IS WHEN PEOPLE WITHHOLD THINGS ABOUT THEMSELVES.

ascending sailor's face as he plods aft, pulls himself up the ladder to the quarterdeck and up again into the mizzen rigging.

It's the young man who was taken from the ghost ship. He still looks unwell, though in a different way—instead of the bone-white pallor and the wasted, convulsing body with which he'd come aboard, he now looks sun-roughened and lean, but he has the bluish skin tone and the pummeled look that afflicts the rest of the crew. A sparse beard fails to cover cheeks variegated with half-healed lesions, and the hair on his head stands straight up, stiff as besom-twigs. He has the beaten look of one of those failed polar explorers, man-hauling his way toward death or something worse.

"Apparently," S. says, "he does still have something to give."

Aye. Tha' was 'is primmin time inna way-deep.

"What was he doing down there?"

Maelstrom reaches out with a filthy hand and pinches S.'s lips shut. Not gently, either. *Tha's na' f'you t'cog.*

That night, he feels rhythmic thumps vibrating through the hull, hears a chorus of baritone voices

That's a great term. In a terrible way, I mean. It sounds miserable.

THE BRITISH EXPLORERS WERE INTO THAT— THE NOBILITY OF SUFFERING. Seems like you are, too.

THE NOBILITY ISN'T IN THE SUFFERING. IT'S IN THE DISCOVERY.

Those dead British guys probably told themselves pretty much the same thing.

---

humming. He puts down his nail, goes up on deck to investigate. Thin clouds ghost a half-moon high overhead. The air is warmer, and the wind has died down, remaining just stout enough to fill the sails and keep this freakish craft moving on to its destination, wherever that might be. But while the conditions are fair, the deck is empty, apart from the one shadowed figure manning the wheel. The rest of the crew must be below.

S. creeps along through the darkness to the main hatch and climbs down to the second level, which is lit with a yellow light that flickers dimly from one of the aft cabins. For a moment, S. feels as if he is watching a moving-picture. The thumps and hums, louder now, and more intense, are coming from that cabin as well. S. approaches, makes his way through the close and greasy air toward the light and sound. He sees the backs of the crew, tightly packed in the cabin's close quarters, with just enough room for them to pound their fists against the floorboards. The humming resonates down the passage toward him; it thickens; it becomes nearly tactile. The smell from the room, an old, deeply-embedded stink of armpit and groin and lamp-oil, wafts into the passageway. He keeps moving forward. He has to see.

{ 214 }

You've missed Welles week at the Varsity. Saw Citizen Kane a few nights ago (got me thinking about Bouchard), Touch of Evil last night.

Why (you might ask) was I going to see movies instead of studying/writing? Because I'm fried. And can't believe there's still so much work to do.

Plus I feel safer there.

He stops in the shadow cast by the open door, peers in at the sailors. Their backs and shoulders move in a synchronous throb. Seeing all these bodies together, he realizes that more than a few look feminine, not boyish but feminine, and once he knows what to listen for, he hears soprano voices amid the deep, resonant humming.

One face turns slowly to look in his direction: it is the young sailor from the ghost ship. He sits with a dazed look in his heavy eyes, in a chair at the far end of the cabin. He is fumbling with something small in his hand, trying to perform some delicate action with his fingers, and the humming grows louder and louder still—it takes on more distinct pitches—it is the sound of insanity in a scale of more than twelve tones[5]—and when the ship rocks over a wave and the lanterns swing, the light catches something silver in the young man's hand. A short needle, trailing a length of thick black thread. The hum soon

---

[5] Here, Straka appears to be paraphrasing a particularly dismissive review of the Estonian composer Ragnar Rummo (b. 1864) and his 1933 *Fantasia for Strings and Whistles.* Though Straka's prose was reasonably straightforward (with *Coriolis* containing his most radical experimentations with language), he greatly admired artists whose work was too challenging for the orthodoxies of their time. Rummo's musical career was a short one; he was employed as a low-level bureaucrat in his home city of Tallinn until his early sixties, when a series of seizures left him unable to perform his clerical duties and he took up composition. The *Fantasia* was, as far as I am aware, the only piece of his that was ever performed in public.

becomes something like a closed-mouthed group-howl as the young man tips his head back and forces the needle through his upper lip, threads it through, then pierces the lower, and S. is ensnared in this, held by the sound and ritual and grotesquerie, and he watches as, stitch after stitch, the young man sews his mouth shut to the din of the crew urging him on, stitch after stitch, blood trickling down his chin and staining his face, his neck, with droplets of red, stitch after stitch, stitch after stitch. S. will not remember seeing the final stitch, the incisor-cut of the remaining thread, the young man slumping back into the chair with bloodied chin and fluttering eyelids and his ragged collar soaked red. He will not remember it, but he has to assume he was still watching from the doorway because he will see it all vividly in his dreams. And weaving through those dreams, too, always, is the voice of Maelstrom, rasping across the decrescendo of hums, saying, *Y' part o' th' tradition, now, son. Part o' th' tradition.*))

When S. awakens in his hammock, as dazed as if he'd just emerged from an opium slumber, he finds the nail in his hand, gripped between middle and ring finger, aimed like a spike outward. He thanks his

{ 216 }

awesome.
Thanks for the
nightmares.
Straka.

FOR A FEW MONTHS AFTER
I FIRST READ SOT,
I WOULDN'T WALK INTO
DARK ROOMS — NOT
EVEN TO SEARCH FOR
THE LIGHT SWITCH.
WAS AFRAID I'D BE WALKING
INTO A SCENE LIKE THIS.

I really wish you'd gotten
your leg looked at.

I THINK IT'LL BE
ALL RIGHT.

unconscious self for finding a weapon. It may not be much, but it's better than nothing, and he needs to get off this ship any way he can. He'll be damned if he'll allow himself to sit slack-jawed and vacant-eyed, silencing himself to the delight of a cabin full of monsters who want to claim him as one of their own.

A razored band of sunshine frames the hatchway above, brightens the minute cracks between the planks of the forecastle deck. S. spends the entire day in his cabin, plotting possible escapes, and scratching at the wall when he needs to clear his head, calm himself. He wants to get as much of his story out as he can before he departs, wants to leave a record in case he dies, even if it's a record no one but the ship's crew might read. He has made several revolutions around the room, etching his words into the wood in a spiral that now descends halfway to the floorboards. He works intently, engrossed in his task but not fully so; if anyone opens the hatch and tries to come down to grab him, he'll be ready to use the nail for its other, bloodier purpose.

Dusk, then, the frame around the hatchway darkened from gold to orange to crimson to indigo. S. hears a sudden frenzied fluttering of whistles

{ 217 }

Handwritten annotations:

Check this out: the Ekstrom Archive in Stockholm has scans + translations of his travel diary... and on 10/31/21, he was in Alexandria — where Durand was digging. I know — it isn't a secret that they had an affair. But @ the bottom of the page it says they were having dinner with S Mel. MacInnes, right?? And in Egypt? What if he was approaching them about The S. ???

HOW WOULD HE HAVE KNOWN ABOUT THE S IN THE FIRST PLACE? AND HOW WOULD HE HAVE KNOWN THEY WERE THE ONES TO APPROACH? SEEMS MORE LIKELY THAT EK + DUR. WOULD HAVE DONE THE APPROACHING.

Either way — people had to join somehow, right? MacInnes, Summersby, Drozdov, Singh...

SURE. I WONDER ABOUT VMS — WOULD HE HAVE BEEN THE ONE TO TAP NEW MEMBERS? OR DID EKSTROM + DURAND RUN THE SHOW? WHAT WAS THE ROLE VMS PLAYED IN THE GROUP?

MOST FUNDAMENTAL IMPULSE OF A WRITER? (ASSUMING IT ISN'T FAME OR $). BUT: A POLITICAL WRITER MIGHT SEE A CAUSE AS MORE IMPORTANT THAN EXPRESSION. BUT THEN: HOW TO EXPLAIN CORIOLIS (ALL ABOUT TRYING TO ASSEMBLE A COHESIVE VISION OF SELF) OR EVEN A WHIMSICAL SORT-OF-LOVE-STORY LIKE WINGED SHOES?

Isn't it obvious? → He changed. And Moody has no idea about that. No way he'll have the full story.

I just flipped through the novel MacInnes wrote right before he died — A Swindle of Cowbirds.

I'VE NEVER BOTHERED. ANY GOOD?

Awful. Thinly veiled hatchet jobs on writers he knew. Esp. the ones he calls ideologues + idealists — which includes possible Strakas. I think he's got Durand, Ekstrom, + T & F in there. Sort of interesting, but mostly sounds like an old man complaining.

topside, in a pattern and timbre that he recognizes from his first journey. Land is in sight. And now is the time to act.

Speed—everything depends on his speed, on his grasping that precious commodity, surprise. Up the ladder—the nail held tight between his fingers— through the hatchway. A quick scan of the horizon: yes, land, a city, just off the port bow. Maelstrom is mid-deck, looking through his spyglass, and S. springs down to the main deck and bounds across it (knocking over the lad with the constant pout, who was swabbing the deck in desultory circles), and before the huge, bearded sailor can say *Sunshine*, S. has his fist cocked, the nail-point aimed at what S. assumes is the soft flesh behind all that fur, at the base of the big man's throat. "Take me to shore," S. says. "Take me there, and let me go."

Maelstrom laughs. He *laughs*, and this enrages S. He has been through too much—too much suffering, too much uncertainty, too much loss, too much trauma—to tolerate not being taken seriously.

"I'd prefer not to hurt you," S. says. "You *will* take me to shore. Now."

Course ye'll be taken aterra. Whole reason we sailt 'ere.

Handwritten margin notes:

I KNOW YOU'RE NOT GOING TO SEE THIS UNTIL TOMORROW, BUT I WANT TO SAY IT ANYWAY: I HAVE NEVER BEEN SO EXCITED FOR ANYTHING AS I AM FOR MEETING YOU TONIGHT

How are you feeling about the meeting?

NERVOUS. SHE'S PROBABLY NOT GOING TO BELIEVE ME.

She agreed to meet you. Means ∅ you must have at least a little credibility.

SHE MIGHT JUST THINK I'M A RISK.

YOU ARE.

S. was not expecting this. All he has prepared are more threats. "Well, then," he says. "Good."

Ye'll ha' two glasses t'do wha' needs done. Then ye'll be rowed back.

S. is dumbfounded. "Why would I come back?"

Cause y' die 'f ye don't. Vévoda cogs yer vennin.

Impossible. How does Maelstrom know anything about Vévoda? Why would they rescue him from the Detectives in one place just to deliver him to them in another? How could Vévoda know where S. was going when he himself didn't?

S. is jolted out of his confusion—even hears himself give a little cry—when the big man's hand flashes out, clamps down hard on his wrist. Maelstrom peels S.'s fingers out from the fist one at a time, effortlessly. He tosses the nail overboard. *Ye'd best na' be defacin' our ship, Sunshine.*

And S. shakes his head no, no, that is certainly not at all what he's been doing.

Got t' respect 'er, trait 'er like a frag a' y'self. She's wha's carrickin us.[6]

---

[6] Readers may be interested to know that, just as sailors refer to ships with feminine pronouns, so, too, would Straka use them when referring to the principles of political and economic reform that were the foundation of his writing, his acts of resistance, and his revolutionary spirit. Readers may not be surprised to discover that this idiosyncratic use of pronouns sometimes caused confusion in his communications with others.

{ 219 }

no years.

NO— BUT THIS IS ACTUALLY
TRUE. IN A LETTER TO
KARST, VMS SAYS "ARTISTIC
INTEGRITY IS NOT A GUEST
WHOM ONE MAY CHOOSE NOT TO
INVITE TO THE GALA. SHE MUST BE
THE FIRST YOU INVITE, THE FIRST
YOU SEAT, THE FIRST YOU SERVE
FOOD AND WINE, THE ONE WHO
CALLS THE ORCHESTRA'S TUNES,
THE ONE WHO IS OFFERED HER
CHOICE OF DANCE PARTNERS
THROUGHOUT THE NIGHT."

Somewhere up in the rigging, the monkey laughs.

S. sits in the stern of the dinghy as it is roughly lowered on the davits. He folds his arms tightly, defiantly, against his chest. Cold, dirty water sloshes back and forth in the body of the tiny craft, eddying around his feet. Manning the oars is the whittler, who is one of the younger, stronger, healthier-looking sailors, although he also seems to have aged too swiftly in the time since S.'s first voyage.

Maelstrom watches them as the sailor's first strokes send them across the surface, which is surprisingly placid. "I'm not coming back," S. calls out.

Y'are, Maelstrom answers, his insubstantial voice already disappearing behind the gentle plashing of the oars. *And ye'll be hap to.* Suddenly S. thinks of the question he ought to have asked right away. He calls out, "Does this have to do with Sola? Will I see her?"

The reply is faint, nearly inaudible, a scratch against the salty night. *Y' might, if y' mean to.* Although it might have been *if yer meant to.* The difference feels like a significant one.

S. looks at the whittler, hoping for some sort of clarification, but the young man keeps his head down, consumed with the task at hand, or perhaps

{ 220 }

> *I can't believe this. Ilsa failed me on the Eliot paper. She'd said she wasn't going to take full deductions for lateness, but she did. I fucking hate her!* — ASK FFOULKES TO GRADE IT — A LOT OF PROFS WILL LET YOU APPEAL A TA'S GRADE.

just ignoring S.'s dismay. The oars look old and warped and splintery, but he strokes without complaint and with great efficiency, and they slip swiftly over the waves.

> *He just looked @ how late it was + said he sided w/ her I told him I can't graduate w/o passing his class. He said I should have thought of that sooner. I can't believe this. I* <u>know</u> *it was late, but I worked really, really hard on it and I can't believe that it's just not worth anything.*

"What happens in the orlop?" S. asks, but he gets no response, no murmur through stitched lips, no whistle, no gesture, nothing.

> RELAX. BREATHE.
> WE'LL FIGURE OUT SOMETHING.

They row in the dark, without any light aboard. The city up ahead looks larger than either of the ones S. has visited thus far, sprawling out into flatlands beyond, with minarets spiking the sky throughout. It is less brightly lit than S. would have imagined, considering the size. The city looks sleepy, tucked in on itself.

> *What can* <u>you</u> *do?. Everyone in the English dept. hates you and you're not even allowed to be on campus!!*
> I CAN REMIND YOU TO BREATHE.
> *I'm pretty sure I do, too.*

The rowboat catches the crest of a modest wave, picking up speed and gliding smoothly forward. The feeling, for those seconds, is glorious—it reminds him that he is human, that he is so insignificant as to be utterly free, and he is being guided along gracefully, lovingly, by the hand of Nature—and it frees him, however transiently, from all worry and fear and fury and grief. "I enjoyed that," he says aloud, as much to the stars as to the rower. The rower pauses for the briefest of intervals but offers no other response, returns to his task of dipping and pulling and feathering, dipping and pulling and feathering.

> *I did, too.*
> ♡

Storm petrels crisscross above them, nearly invisible in the dusk—just the dark impressions of birds as they hunt on the wing, chittering and moaning.[7]

The boat's bow drifts rightward, aimed not at the city's harbor but at a dark grove of trees not far up the coast. S. points this out to the rower, who simply maintains the course that, S. realizes, will keep them outside the spill of harbor lights. A short time later, the boat scrapes over the pebbly bottom of the shallows. The rower ships the oars and looks over his shoulder, watching warily until a figure emerges from between rows of swaying date palms and lights a cigarette. The whittler nods to S., holds up two fingers. "Yes, two hours," S. tells him. "Whatever you say." He wonders, briefly, how long the rower will wait there once S. fails to return.

The stoop-shouldered man in the trees introduces himself as Osfour. Tobacco smoke wreathes his haggard face and the black *checheya* he wears low on his forehead. He wears a matching *kaftan* and trousers

[7] As the profusion of avian imagery in *Ship of Theseus* would suggest, Straka was an avid bird-watcher. In one letter to me, he stated that among his most prized possessions was a copy of the first edition of P. T. Russell's *Compendium of Birds* (1846). He owned—but was much less enthusiastic about—the subsequent edition (1886) in which Russell corrected many of his earlier mistakes.

{ 222 }

Handwritten annotations:

Check out this photo: the Board of Directors of Arp Syndikat in 1948. 3rd from left is "Gernot Klein." And who does he look like? —WECHSLER— OLDER + FATTER

So what if Wechsler = Němec in Ch. 8? God, did anyone not sell out?

SIGNIF.? →

This book does exist — but the 1958 edition was the first + only one. → So: 58.

Look at the repetitions in FN 1. Found a website that talks about the "Nihilist Cipher." Another one that codes a message in numbers. So: years, maybe? Lots of them in FNs here. Need 2 keywords to decipher it, though. I guessed "sleeping" + "dog" but that doesn't work.

THERE ARE A LOT OF SPECIFIC YEARS CITED IN THE CH6 FNS. DEF MORE THAN ANYWHERE ELSE.

<<BOOM.>> See FN 15.

THE 2-DIGIT #S YOU GET IN THE NIHILIST ARE FAIRLY HIGH ONES. SO IF IT'S IN THE YEARS IN THE FNS, MAYBE YOU DROP THE CENTURY #S (19,18,17, ETC.)? JUST USE THE LAST TWO DIGITS?

of loose-fitting gray linen, and flat, thin sandals on his feet. From a bag slung over his shoulder he produces a similar outfit, neatly folded, which he thrusts at S. "Hurry. Change," he orders. "We haven't much time."

"Where are we going?" S. asks.

Osfour holds a finger to his lips. "Quiet," he says. "Change clothes and listen." He pauses, waits for S. to start buttoning up.

"We will enter the city," Osfour continues. "We will walk through the night market. Do not call attention to yourself." He hands S. a pair of sandals, then stands on tiptoe to place a *checheya* on S.'s head, tugging it down as low as his own.

"Because someone will be watching? Vévoda's men? The Detectives?"

Osfour snorts, sending jets of smoke from his nostrils. "Vévoda has not needed the browncoats for years. Now he has a network of Agents who can blend in anyplace.[8] You do not know when they are there, when they are not. Your neighbor, whose children play with your children, might be—"

---

[8] Straka was adamant that different words should be used to distinguish between the thugs of Vévoda's early years (*Detectives*) and the more polished but no less deadly Agents who came later. This was a matter of some contention during our discussions of the translation—I found it needlessly confusing—but he was not the sort of person who was easily swayed about anything.

Handwritten margin notes:

Top left: I'll be wearing my 4-H jacket. You won't be able to miss me.

Right, upper: WHICH IS WHAT S. HAS TO DO THROUGHOUT THE BOOK...

Right, lower: THAT GUY WHO WAS TALKING TO ILSA DURING THE LECTURE — HAVE YOU SEEN HIM SINCE? Twice. Once @ Pronghorn — he was reading a newspaper in another language. Once on a bench outside Standefer. I know he's probably just some visiting scholar, but he creeps me out. WHAT DOES HE LOOK LIKE? Greek? Italian, maybe? The thing you notice about him is his nose. It's amazingly sharp. You could use that thing as a weapon.

Bottom left: No years here, either.

S. interrupts, confused. "Years?"

Osfour shrugs, waves his hands in apparent frustration. "Everyone knows this."

"I've been at sea," S. says. "Pretend I know nothing." Osfour rolls his dark eyes but agrees, provided they start walking toward the city. S. can feel every rock under his thin soles; he comes down on one with the ball of his right foot and realizes he no longer feels the discomfort. He stops, raises his knee, runs his hand over the ball of the foot, over the toes that once nearly disintegrated—it is all perfectly ordinary. He pulls the sandal off, examines his foot in the moonlight filtering through the swishing fronds. The diagonal line is still visible, but the two tones of skin on his foot now match nearly perfectly.

Years?

He thinks of the difference in the way Sola looked in the bar and the way Sola/Szalómé looked on the wharf. The incipient wrinkles, the slightly weathered look on her face, the subtle fleshiness he'd not seen earlier in her face, her neck, even her fingers. Years? But even in these pictures he notices something new: an unruly, thin tress of dark hair swirling over an olive-toned cheek: another rivulet of dark. Which recalls baking smells, female voices, a finger laid over lips.

Handwritten margin notes:

YOU'RE STILL ON TRACK TO GRADUATE, RIGHT?

Of course.

JUST WANT TO MAKE SURE YOU'RE KEEPING UP.

Stop acting like you're my T.A.

BEING A T.A. IS WHAT I DO.

It's what you did.

OK—sorry. That was harsh. Bad mood. Low blood sugar. Something like that.

NO, YOU'RE RIGHT. YOU'RE EXACTLY RIGHT. THAT'S NOT MY LIFE ANYMORE.

I wish it wasn't Ilsa's anymore, either.

[handwritten, top left]
→ ANYTHING ELSE IN THE EKSTROM DIARIES THAT MIGHT BE ABOUT THE S?
Not as far as I could tell (but I'm depending on the translation). But did you know there's a little Durand museum in Perpignan?

[handwritten]
NO, YOUR FRENCH IS GOOD, RIGHT? WANT TO CALL + SEE IF THEY HAVE ANYTHING USEFUL THEY CAN TELL US — OR EVEN SEND?

[handwritten, top right]
→ FYI: "They" = "she."
It's a one-woman show + she's really old. It's not even open to the public anymore. She won't send anything, but she wants to help. I gave her a list of things to look out for.

SHIP OF THESEUS

Osfour, many paces ahead, hisses through his teeth, waves him forward.

S. jogs ahead. "No one's giving me any answers," he says. "And yet everyone seems to know who I am."

"We do know," Osfour sniffs.

"But I don't."

"You're the man who escaped from Vévoda. You're the man he's hunting."

"I know that," S. says. "But who *am* I?[9]

"Let me rephrase. We know who you are. We don't, however, know who you *were*."

"*I* have to know," S. says. It seems even more urgent to him now, perhaps because he has slipped through another wash of time, or—stranger still—accelerated through it, as if carried along on the crest of a wave.

"That is not my problem," Osfour says. "It is yours, and I am not part of its solution. Please do not expect me to be."[10]

[handwritten, right margin]
JEN — WE HAVE TO BE CAREFUL ABOUT EVERYTHING WE TELL ANYONE — NOT JUST MOODY, NOT JUST ILSA.
I *was* careful.

[handwritten, right margin]
→ So what do you know about MacInnes?
JUST WHAT EVERYONE ELSE KNOWS. PHILOSOPHY WUNDERKIND, ONE OF OXFORD'S YOUNGEST DONS, A FEW EARLY BOOKS RE: IDENTITY IN CONTEXT OF ECONOMICS. BECAME A KIND OF CELEBRITY-PHILOSOPHER, WAS ON TV A LOT. DIED IN '69, IN HIS 80s — HEART ATTACK. THE KIND OF GUY NOTHING BAD EVER HAPPENED TO. JERK.

[handwritten, below text]
No surprise. Mytych didn't exist. Obv. 60 + 24 are what's important.

---

9   This distinction informs the work of the Polish philosopher Mariusz Mytych (b. 1853 or 1854), who wrote of the "Circumstantial Self" and the "Fundamental Self" as defined by T. I. Alt (1752–1843). He argued that while these were separate conceptions of individual identity, they were equally true, as were seventeen other "Lesser Variant-Selves" between those two endpoints. Guthrie MacInnes (purported philosopher, purported Straka) scoffed at Mytych's work, but then, MacInnes showed respect only to people whom he could use to advantage.

10   The Japanese writer Fukuzawa Yukichi, in an 1872 speech at the Keio Gijuku school, discussed this tension between the artistic and personal lives of the writers, arguing vociferously that they must be kept perfectly separate. I do not know whether Straka would have agreed, but one could argue that this conflict is at the very heart of the book you are now reading.

[handwritten, right of footnotes]
Doesn't seem like he was particularly radical.
MAYBE @ THE BEGINNING. DEF. NOT LATER.

Multitudinalism sounds like bullshit.
AGREE. IF THERE'S NO REAL SELF, THERE'S NO MORAL RESPONSIBILITY... SO YOU CAN JUST DO WHATEVER YOU WANT.

[handwritten, bottom]
YUKICHI DID EXIST. BUT I'VE NEVER FOUND ANY EVIDENCE THAT HE SAID THIS. OR THAT HE EVER GAVE A SPEECH AT THAT SCHOOL.
More sneaky fun from Filomela. I think I would've liked her. → YOU WOULD LIKE HER.
You told her about me? ← AND SHE'D LIKE YOU.

I TOLD HER A LOT ABOUT YOU AND WHAT WE'RE DOING. AND HOW WE'RE USING THE BOOK — SHE LOVED THAT. SHE WAS TELLING EVERYONE ABOUT IT + SAYING HOW HAPPY IT MADE HER.
Did you tell her we haven't actually met — a situation she might have some experience with?

"So you're useless to me."

"Not at all. I'm taking you to the resistance. They'll give you what you need, and I will help you stay alive. So, really, I'm extremely useful to you."

"Tell me what you think I need to know," S. prompts again. "Tell me everything."

"I will," Osfour says. "Just keep your feet moving and your mouth closed."

What Osfour think S. needs to know is this:

News of the wharf bombing did not spread far beyond the city limits of B——, except in whispers that did nothing to damage Vévoda's reputation as an exemplar of hard-nosed commercial acumen. His ambitions outgrowing the provincial B——, he resettled somewhere across the water (precisely where is not known), courting as clients only the most powerful, expanding his production while concealing himself from the public behind a forti- fication of holding companies and legal fictions. His tightly guarded factories—twelve of them now, according to Osfour's sources—feed the hungers of generals and premiers and tin-pot dictators, nationalist upstarts and the wheezing remnants of

[handwritten margin note:] THOUGHT: THE PEOPLE TAKING CARE OF FXC ARE A SORT OF RESISTANCE — BUT NOT IDEOLOGICAL — JUST KIND.

royalty, even leaders of regions that have scarcely been mapped. If his factories didn't make what a buyer needed, Vévoda arranged a discreet match with another seller, coupling each violent need with the capacity to achieve it and pocketing a fee in the process.

"He conducts the orchestra of war, and the spotlight never falls on him," Osfour says. "The drums are beating, my friend. On five continents. Over dozens of conflicts. Millions of people are holding their breath and waiting for the worst."

"Including yourself?" S. asks.

"Of course," Osfour says. "The invasion of El-H—— is coming. Armies are crossing the desert as we speak."

When S. asks who will be doing the invading, Osfour spits, then gives a name that means nothing to S. "He was nobody," Osfour explains, "until Vévoda decided he would be somebody."[11]

"But why Vévoda?" S. asks. Ordnance is ordnance; why should one man operate as the nexus of it all?

---

[11] More than once, Straka wrote that he believed Hermès Bouchard had the ability not just to turn nobodies into somebodies but also to turn somebodies into nobodies. Whether he was speaking literally or metaphorically about the latter was never clear to me, but one has one's suspicions.

Did you see today's Daily Pronghorn? — You mean the one w/ the full-page profile of Moody, complete w/ a photograph of him in his office pretending to be engrossed in some rare + terribly important document + actually using his pinky finger to point to some particularly revelatory bit of text while "Ph.D. candidate and lead research assistant Ilsa Dirks" stands behind him attempting to express awe, admiration, and deep understanding simultaneously, all of which adds up to a ridiculous + even more offensive pantomime of actual scholarship (and, of course, leaves unraised the once-critical issue of intellectual integrity)? No. But don't you just love his jaunty little cap?

What if Serin is funding Moody, too? Playing all possible angles? — He probably doesn't need it. (Have you seen his house?) I looked up his CV on the PSU site. For the last 10 years, he's gotten — I don't know. But he's got his salary, and a "Distinguished Scholar" grant probably some royalties from his other books. from the Caledonian Society for I think he gets paid for visiting lectures. literature. Took me about $ (Although there was a time when we were mins to find out that they drinking together + after a couple of at their $ from the rounds he started griping about having to MacInnes Foundation. pay multiple alimonies.) — Family money? I wonder if he even knows—or cares.

———————

Osfour looks confused. "The weapon," he says. "The Black Vine. You know this. You're the one who has seen it."

S. recalls the charnel pits in the mountains, those scorched double quincunxes. He imagines a projectile screaming out of a night sky, sending ten tendrils of blue-black fire into the earth.

"They say it changes the blood," Osfour says. "Is that true?"

S. remembers Stenfalk coughing up that strangely dark and viscous fluid. "It might," he says. "Vévoda is selling this now? Armies have it?"

"We know that his customers *want* it and that they will prostrate themselves before him to get it—and these are men who cede power to nobody. And the further he removes himself from view, the more desperate these people become to meet with him, gain his favor, execute transactions on his terms."

"Do the Detectives still work for him?"

Osfour shakes his head. "Not Detectives. *Agents.* More skilled and more ruthless. They are provided to him by the militaries and secret police of his client governments, by revanchist royalists, by cartels, by groups whose compositions we do not understand

———————

but whose lethality we do.[12] And because you have seen the Black Vine and its effects, the Agents believe you can endanger Vévoda. This is why you are known—to the extent that you *are* known. The breadth of your existence is really quite narrow."

"What about Sola?" S. asks. "What do you know about her?"

"I do not know anyone called Sola," Osfour says.

"Or Szalómé? She may go by different names."

"I cannot help you with that."

"I don't believe you. If you know about me, you know about her."

"You make assumptions, my friend. A dangerous habit."

They leave the last of the date palms behind and tromp through a field of knee-high grass growing in sandy soil. Ahead is an entrance to the city: crumbling stone walls that centuries ago must have framed a

---

[12] Straka believed in the existence of such groups, including at least one that specialized in dispatching artists deemed troublesome to the ruling classes. He claimed to have documents proving that this group (the name of which was unknown to him, if it even had one) was based in London and had been operating as early as 1859. In one of his last letters to me, he said he had come into possession of a letter, purportedly authored by Sir Aston Cockayne in December 1685, in which Cockayne hinted that such a group was responsible for the murder of Christopher Marlowe as well as a brutal campaign of intimidation that caused Shakespeare to retire from the world of the London stage and to live his last years unremarkably (though safely) in Stratford. Straka allowed that the letter may well have been a hoax, but he planned to investigate its provenance more thoroughly. His life likely ended before he reached a firm conclusion on the matter. I have not been able to locate the letter or even any references to it in other literature.

[Handwritten margin notes:]

It's blowing my mind that you're the one pointing this out.

Big difference: S. is trying to find Sola. He keeps getting distracted, but he knows he wants to find her. Totally different from Straka — he knew where to find Filomela, and he never chose to do it.

BUT MAYBE THAT'S THE WHOLE POINT. MAYBE S. IS WHO VMS WISHED HE WAS.

Do you think Filomela feels like she got stuck w/ a "narrow existence"?

—YOU KIDDING? LOOK WHAT SHE WAS IN THE MIDDLE OF!

I mean personally. She got to experience falling in love, but it never went anywhere. She was alone.

SHE WAS WISTFUL. DISAPPOINTED ABOUT WHAT HAPPENED WITH VMS. BUT IT SEEMED LIKE SHE UNDERSTOOD.

→ COCKAYNE WAS REAL (BUT DIED IN 1684). I'VE NEVER FOUND ANY EVIDENCE THAT THIS IS WHAT HE THOUGHT, THOUGH. 229 }

I came up empty, too.

→ FOR WHAT IT'S WORTH: THIS VERSION OF MARLOWE'S MURDER SOUNDS A LITTLE LIKE AN S DEATH (+ FOR SIMILAR REASON? A HERESY OF A SORT?). KNIFE WOUND INSTEAD OF A FALL, BUT STILL...

A little like Sobreira's, too.

gateway. Now, though, anyone may pass. Around the two men, locusts chirr and click, and the grass whispers as it brushes their clothes. S. remarks to his guide how quiet and dark the city seems. "Half the city expects the invasion any hour," Osfour says. "The streets are crawling with Agents and collaborators. For many people, it is best to stay inside, unless they *must* venture out."

Another city, another labyrinth of winding streets before his eyes. Stone buildings, cracked and patched, sparsely pocked with tiny window openings that may or may not have glass in them. Most of the dwellings are dimly lit or dark. The only voices he hears are hushed. Here and there, smoke rises, carrying the smell of roasting lamb and cumin. As they draw deeper into the center, they begin to encounter other people in the streets, people who seem to be either too watchful and guarded or too resolutely looking at nothing.

"Keep your head down," Osfour reminds him. "And talk to me. Two men walking together must be seen to be talking. Silence will arouse suspicion."

"What should I talk to you about?" S. asks.

"Talk to me about nothing," Osfour says. "Or as close to nothing as you can manage."

{ 230 }

CROSSING A THRESHOLD? BUT THERE'S A THRESHOLD CROSSED IN CH.7, TOO. DIFFERENCE?

This one's easier to get through.

Have you been to the moroccan restaurant out on 324? It's pretty great.

I DON'T REALLY GO TO RESTAURANTS ANYMORE — SHORT ON TIME + MONEY.

You never went out to eat with Ilsa?

A COUPLE OF TIMES. WE BOTH DECIDED IT WAS A WASTE OF TIME + MONEY. SHE'S PRETTY WORK-DRIVEN, TOO.

Wow. I'm stunned that you're not still together. what fun you must have had.

So, OK: HINT: I really like the moroccan place.

I swear there are people in the library who are watching me. Pretending to read/study/browse/copy/etc. but sneaking looks at me. I bet they're connected to the guy in the suit.

And yes, I know how paranoid that sounds..

→AN EVEN BIGGER RESPONSIBILITY FOR HER, THEN. PROBABLY MEANS SHE KNEW EXACTLY WHO THE S MEMBERS WERE— EVEN IF SHE DIDN'T KNOW WHICH ONE WAS VMS.

Did she speculate?

NO—WHAT SHE SAID IN THE FOREWORD WAS TRUE— SHE DIDN'T CARE WHO HE MIGHT HAVE BEEN— BECAUSE SHE KNEW HIM VIA HIS BOOKS + THEIR LETTERS.

SHIP OF THESEUS

But how can he? All S. knows of himself and his world is what he has encountered since he found himself trudging through the Old Quarter. Everything that has happened since then is *something*, is it not? He has no store of the inconsequentialities that compose a life.

"I heard a story," S. says, "about a very strange ship, on which—"

"Stop," Osfour says. "I don't want to hear anything about that."

NEED TO COMPARTMENTALIZE INFO— LESS DANGER IF YOU DON'T KNOW. ✱

Osfour's reticence is frustrating and his manner brusque, but S. is grateful to have the guide with him. The layout of the city is bewildering; each street is largely indistinguishable from the others, and S. lost track of their turns a while ago. Osfour has kept up a steady patter of nonsense (bland and meandering stories about people S. does not know, complaints about his digestive health, and exegeses on the volatile price of a particular tea and the aphrodisiac qualities of a particular wine[13]), the constancy of which S. has come to find companionable.

ANY WORD FROM PERPIGNAN?

— Not yet. I called once. Seems like she thought I was pressuring her.

TURNS OUT SHE DID HAVE FIRSTHAND KNOWLEDGE. HE TRIED THIS WITH DURAND + HE TRIED IT W/HER.

---

[13] Here Straka may have been winking at what he saw as MacInnes's quirks and pretensions. The Scotsman is reputed (though, of course, I have no first-hand knowledge) to be an enthusiastic sharer of the nuances of his bowel health, a tea-drinker so persnickety about its preparation as to cause his café companions much embarrassment, and a self-styled Casanova who believes that a bottle of 1866 Château Hirondelle des Granges guarantees him the favor of anyone with whom he shares it. There is a story, perhaps apocryphal, that he attempted to ply Amarante Durand with this very vintage one night in Torremolinos and received the coldest of shoulders in response.

There's a private room at the back of Pronghorn Java— for group meetings, etc. I could get Vanessa to let us in.

VANESSA= THE MANAGER? YOU TRUST HER THAT MUCH?

{ 231 } *I trusted her w/ the postcards + that worked out. Might have to put up with a few jokes about what we're doing in there, but I don't care.*

WHAT IF SHE'S RIGHT ABOUT WHAT WE'RE DOING?

Easy there. Someone might read this someday!

→AH—THE PERMANENT RECORD.

They approach a broad leftward curve, beyond which is a more brightly-lit avenue. "The night *suq*," Osfour says. "Peruse the goods for sale so it looks like you have a reason to be there, but do not linger, do not talk to anyone but me, do not attempt to purchase anything. You may slow down, but you may not stop. Look no one in the eye." Osfour takes a breath as they round the bend. "Are you ready?" he asks.

"I don't see how it matters—"

"It doesn't."

Stalls line the narrow street as far as S. can see, funneling foot traffic into a space not much wider than the two men's shoulders. While the majority of the stalls are empty, many are open for business, even though the crowd is thin and the atmosphere one of caution. The stalls are lit by dim, flickering bulbs attached haphazardly to metal fixtures. Wires crosshatch the air just a foot or two above S.'s head, and they cobweb the fronts of the buildings behind the stalls, disappearing into the tiny windows, most of which are barred. Presented for sale on shaky tables and worn blankets: baskets full of spices, in powders and pods and leaves and pastes; drums and *ouds* and spike-fiddles; agitated-looking finches that dart in their bent-metal cages as if portending a terrible

{ 232 }

Last paper for Ilsa/Ffoulkes: William Carlos Williams—Rain. Last chance.

YOU CAN DO IT.

I guess so. I'm just so tired of all this. I can't keep pretending that I care.

YOU DON'T HAVE TO PRETEND. YOU DON'T EVEN HAVE TO CARE. IT'S A JOB—JUST A THING THAT NEEDS TO GET WRITTEN. NOTHING MORE. ONE SENTENCE AT A TIME

YOU KNOW, I'VE TAUGHT THAT POEM 3 OR 4 TIMES.

———

storm; rugs woven with complex but asymmetrical patterns that produce a mild nausea in S. when he examines them too closely; cuts of fly-specked pink meat that S. cannot identify; sandals like the ones on his and Osfour's feet; piles of old books that leach their mustiness into the air around them. It is a scene of subdued industry, to be sure, but it feels like a terrific bustle compared with the desolation S. has found in the city thus far. He watches a sale conclude: a short, pink, and shaved-bald man in western dress and eyeglasses hands money to the book vendor, hands him paper bills printed with purple and blue. (S. hopes to recognize the currency, but he doesn't.) The man hefts the book, a thick tome bound in brown leather that is cracked and covered with dark, oily stains, and opens it up, as if he aims to start reading it right there at the stall.

It is at this moment that the murmuring voices return, overlapping, sharpening, then fading, twirling through one another in a chorale of lament. He stops abruptly—too abruptly, judging from Osfour's startled response—and looks left, right, ahead, behind, up. He sees no source. The voices do not seem to be coming through his ears, anyway, but flowing up from the base of his skull. Gradually one

———

emerges more clearly through the clamor. *Words are a gift to the dead*, it says, *and a warning to the living.*[14] The voice repeats this, again and again, and others join in, then still others, until S.'s head is filled with a dreadful, tuneless round. *Words are a gift to the dead and a warning to the living. Words are a gift to the dead and a warning to the living.*

Osfour grabs him by the elbow and yanks him forward. "Last year it would have taken us hours to walk through," he says, his tone one of exaggerated calm. "Business is slow. Some attribute it to the weather, and some to—"

But S. is not listening. He turns back to the book stall, gripped by the sudden feeling that he ought to look there for a copy of *The Archer's Tales*. The chance is infinitesimal, but still, he should look—

—*Words are a gift to the dead and a warning to the living*—

—and what he sees is the bald man tearing a page out of the book he has just bought, folding it carefully into quarters, and tucking it neatly into his coat pocket. Then another page: tear, fold, tuck. As he tears a third page, he looks up, noticing that S. is

---

[14] Here Straka may have been loosely paraphrasing a saying attributed to the Persian mystic Bayazid Bastami (b. 846 AD).

I don't get it, either.

DOESN'T RESONATE W/ THE CH.1 LINE ABOUT THE WATER.

"MAY HAVE BEEN LOOSELY PARAPHRASING"? BIG QUALIFICATION... WHY?

Code. ⇒OBV.

But the line itself... This is a huge reach, but what if VMS meant this as a warning? What if he was telling FXC to be careful? I.E.: WHAT IF THEY WERE SENDING MESSAGES TO EACH OTHER IN THE BOOK? BOTH DIRECTIONS...

That would be really, really cool. —TOO COOL, MAYBE—LIKE WE WANT THAT TO BE TRUE, SO WE SEE WHAT WE WANT TO SEE. AND ANYWAY: IF HE'S SENDING MESSAGES, WHY NOT DO IT BY PHONE/LETTER/TELEGRAM, OR EVEN ON THE MANUSCRIPT PAGES WHY INCLUDE IT IN THE STORY ITSELF—IN THE ART?

{ 234 }

looking at him. The expression on his face as he regards S. is one of frigid indifference, a cold and singular devotion to his purpose. S. looks away, but he can tell the man is still eyeing him as he lines up the edges of the page, folds, folds again, slips it into his pocket, chooses his next page without even looking, and tears it out. ⌉ OBVIOUS REFERENCE TO SANTORINI MAN

words are a gift to the dead a gift to the dead a gift to the dead

Osfour pulls S. forward, and this time S. obliges, even though he is annoyed with Osfour's pulling. As he walks, he has to shake his shoulders to clear away the chill that's tickling his insides from scalp down to mid-spine. "Don't let that happen again," Osfour whispers. "I prefer not to die."

At one stall, under a flickering bulb, a bent old wretch with a milky eye stoops over an array of woven baskets, some small, some tall and wide enough that a man could hide in them. As S. and Osfour come near, the overhead light sizzles and goes dark. S. feels a jolt of adrenaline as the old man makes a quick move to his pocket, but instead of a pistol the man pulls out a stubby wooden end-blown

NERVOUS.

GOT A LETTER FROM ARTURO (FXC'S MAIN GUY IN MARAÚ). SAID THAT HE WAS SORRY BUT THEY HAD TO TURN AWAY MY COLLEAGUE. HE MADE FILOMELA UNEASY.

what colleague?
↓
MY QUESTION EXACTLY. WHAT IF I LED THEM TO HER?

Maybe you're not translating it right?

IT'S IN ENGLISH. AND I'M SURE SHE WENT OVER IT BEFORE IT WAS SENT.

Maybe that was the safest place. Or maybe he wanted to do it in a way that combined art + politics + feeling — showing everything he was made of.

flute, which he slides between his toothless gums. He blows into it, producing a single tone like a feline yowl, then diving between notes, never lingering on them, a wailing melody both mournful and sinister that has S.'s skin crawling even before he hears one of the baskets rustle, sees it shake ever so slightly though no one is touching it, and hears—could it be?—a childlike whimper coming from within. And is that the lid of the basket, starting to rise—?[15]

Osfour pulls him onward yet again, not breaking stride. "Do not stop," he says. "Especially not there." Behind them the flute plays on.

Pain drums dully behind S.'s eyes, and his vision does not seem quite as sharp as he remembers. Could he be dreaming? He blinks, shakes his head, rubs his eyes, but nothing resolves. Far ahead, the market fades into a myopic blur. Even up close the vendors and their wares have soft-looking edges, as if they are held in shape by porous membranes through which the city is seeping, or through which they are seeping into the city.

[15] This passage is one that ought to raise doubt in the minds of anyone who believes Tiago García Ferrara was the "real" Straka. An uncommonly sensitive man who could not abide the sight (or even the story) of a child in even the most trivial state of suffering. I find it unfathomable that he would have conceived, let alone written, such lines as these. It was the cruelest of blows to him, I believe, when one of his sons was killed in a Fascist air raid in the war's last days, and he lived the rest of his years with a shattered heart.

{ 236 }

Handwritten margin notes:

▶ I FORGOT TO ASK HER ABOUT THIS. I HAD A LIST, BUT IT WAS HARD TO KEEP TO IT. I WAS JUST SO CAUGHT UP IN LISTENING TO HER.

So the keywords "sleeping" and "dog" + the last 2 digits of every year in FHS gets you:
66, 64, 47, 83, 64, 33, 46, 86, 53, 54, 52, 43, 72, 85, 66, 46, 64, 44, 72

Or: MAC WAS JUDAS NOT TIAGO !!!

IF THAT MEANS WHAT I THINK IT MEANS—AND IT'S TRUE— THEN 75 YEARS OF LITERARY HISTORY GETS TURNED UPSIDE DOWN. MACINNES WAS THE ONE WHO GAVE DURAND TO THE FASCISTS? AND GARCÍA FERRARA DIDN'T?

And she's telling Straka — means he didn't know. How does she have info that he doesn't? Maybe she + GMI drank that wine + started bashing Durand together? (I like the idea that he might've bragged about it to the wrong person.)

GARCÍA FERRARA DISAPPEARED A FEW DAYS BEFORE THEY GOT DURAND... WHICH WAS WHY PEOPLE THOUGHT HE MUST HAVE TALKED. DID GMI ORCHESTRATE THAT, TOO? THIS MAKES ME SO MAD — G.F. DOES NOTHING WRONG, AS FAR AS WE KNOW, AND HIS LIFE GOT RUINED

They pass a vendor with a cart on which nuts are roasting over white-orange coals that pop and hiss; the nuts are scorched-black and pungent, and they effuse cradles of dark-gray smoke. S.'s eyes sting and water. Too, the heat from the grill seems to cling to him as he walks on. Perhaps he is feverish; perhaps the relentless strangeness of this place is the product of some equatorial delirium. He hears a distant, entomical whine; as the sound nears, it produces painful overtones in his ears. He claps his hands over them. He tells Osfour he thinks he is unwell.

But Osfour has his gaze upturned at the slash of night sky visible between the rooftops, and if he hears S., he gives no sign. Instead he quickens his pace, gestures for S. to catch up. The sound screams across the night sky above them, although S. does not see what is producing it, and it rolls off toward the darkened desert outside the city. "An aeroplane," Osfour says.

"I've never seen one."

"You should hope you don't. Not tonight."

From out in the desert come the muffled thump and rumble of mortar fire. A tiny seism passes through the ground.

"The invasion," Osfour breathes. "Hurry."

{ 237 }

YRS. HAVE PASSED SINCED CH. 4-5

REF. TO GERMAN INVASION OF NORTH AFRICA?

SO X WE ONLY HAVE A MONTH UNTIL MOODY'S "IMPORTANT ANNOUNCEMENT" ABOUT "THE TWENTIETH CENTURY'S MOST CONFOUNDING LITERARY MYSTERY" THAT "WILL HAVE THE ENTIRE LITERARY WORLD SITTING UP AND TAKING NOTICE"? THAT'S JUST FUCKING AWESOME.

Let him make his announcement, put out his book. You don't think he has it right.

AGAIN: I CAN'T ASSUME I KNOW EXACTLY WHAT HE'S ARGUING + EXACTLY WHAT HE'S USING TO BACK IT UP. MAYBE HE'S NOT USING THE SUMMERSBY CONFESSION AT ALL...

We must have enough to torpedo his idea. Why not do that? Then take some time to put out your theory.
IT'LL BE YOUR THEORY, TOO.

Oh, sure.
Trying to take me down with you...

[••]

Vendors bundle up their wares, tossing them into boxes and baskets and onto blankets that will be gathered into sacks. They immediately begin to recede, and they recede into buildings, into alleys, into shadows. Osfour quickens their pace. Up ahead, a food vendor tips over his cart, sending hot coals and dark-brown twists of bread, impaled on charred sticks and smelling of cardamom and pepper, scattering across the yellow dirt. Are the breads in the shape of the S symbol? For a moment he thinks so, but then Osfour tells him to get ready and grabs hold of S.'s *kaftan*, counts down three, two, one, *now*, and they dart into an alley so narrow they have to shuffle through it sideways.

Midway along the alley is a wooden door, unmarked except for dark, peeling paint. Osfour gives a quick series of knocks, and when a tiny window inset in the door creaks open, he whispers some words to the person behind it. There is the sound of the door being unbarred from inside, and when the door opens—slowly, cautiously, and just wide enough for one man—Osfour steps inside. Perhaps S. hesitates briefly; he must, because Osfour suddenly has a grip on his *kaftan* again and is yanking him roughly over the threshold. Someone closes

---

Handwritten margin notes:

YOU LET HER MAIL THEM TO YOUR BUILDING?

No—had her send them to Vanessa.

IT'S JUST A MATTER OF TIME BEFORE THEY REALIZE SHE'S HELPING ~~YOU~~ US.

Just got a bunch of docs from Perpignan!! Not scans or photocopies— she copied them out by hand + mailed them. Weird. Anyway: it's going to take a little time to go through them.

BUT IF THEY'RE NOT ORIGINALS, WE CAN'T TRUST THEM 100%. JUST SAYING— AT SOME POINT, ONE OF US NEEDS TO GO THERE TO SEE THEM.

OK— I had asked about any refs to birds in letters, journals, etc. There's an entry from Alexandria—New Year's Day 1922—says she celebrated by bird-watching + she listed the birds she saw: all of our friends from Prague 1910— plus a few more— Saaras (Hindi for stork.), Pearraid (Scot. Gaelic for parrot), Swan + Finch (English for... um... swan + finch?).

MAYBE:

SAARAS → SINGH
PEARRAID → MACINNES
SWAN + FINCH → LOOPER + SUMMERSBY

YOU THINK ONE OF THOSE FOUR WAS THE "GUEST" FROM PRAGUE?

Did you remember to ask Filomela about this?

___

the door firmly behind him and slides a bolstering bar back into place.

The space inside is cavernous, far more vast than S. would have guessed from the outside. The vaulted ceiling is thirty feet high and intricately etched with shapes and images, although these are hard to make out, owing to the dim light and layers of grime and smoke. To his right is a Moorish archway over a flight of tilted steps that lead to a balcony, which extends a quarter of the way out into the vast chamber. On the ground floor, aisles have been demarcated by shelves that run the length of the space, and the perimeter is lined with cabinets, cases, and trunks, into which all the materials in this place are being packed away.

The place hums with activity; there must be fifty or sixty people, all dressed in *kaftans*, the men in *checheyas* and the women in headscarves, all participating nearly wordlessly in a swift and meticulous division of labor. One man empties a shelf and carries the books, folios, and loose pages bundled with twine over to a woman who places them in a small crate; when it is full, a different man replaces and secures the lid, then pushes the crate across the floor toward the back of the room, where several floorboards have

___

SHE CORRESPONDED W/ ALL OF THEM @ ONE POINT OR ANOTHER — BUT SHE STILL SAYS SHE NEVER KNEW WHICH ONE WAS STRAKA. I'M BACK TO WONDERING IF STRAKA WAS JUST A FICTION — A COMPOSITE MADE UP OF EVERYONE FROM THE S — A NAME THEY COULD USE FOR RADICAL WORK — + A FAMOUS NAME THAT'D GET MORE PEOPLE TO READ IT. I KNOW FILOMELA SINCERELY BELIEVES HE WAS JUST ONE GUY, BUT AGAIN: MAYBE SHE NEEDS TO BELIEVE THAT.

been removed to reveal a wooden ramp leading down under the building. But these people are not just moving books, no: there are scrolls, there are paintings, there are fragments of stone tablets, there are sculptures and ceramics and tapestries, all of which are being ferried below to safety. The place smells of antiquity and quiet determination.

"What is this place?" S. asks Osfour, who is leading him toward the archway.

"This is where you meet the people you're here to meet," Osfour replies.

S. watches as two women carefully roll up a tapestry that shows a falconer on a hunt. They secure the roll with knotted lengths of rope and carry it together toward the hole in the floor, where a burly man receives it from them and disappears below.

"The invasion?" S. asks.

Osfour nods. "We'll protect what we can. Some things will be lost. The space below is not as big as we would like."

"Why is it all here in the first place? Is this a library? A museum?"

"A safe place for beautiful things. That's all."

The aeroplane produces a low, zippering sound overhead, crossing the city back toward the water. S.

{ 240 }

So you trust her.

COMPLETELY. WHEN I WAS SAYING GOODBYE, SHE TOOK MY HAND + SQUEEZED IT — SHE'S TINY, THERE'S ALMOST NOTHING LEFT OF HER, BUT SHE SQUEEZED IT HARD — AND I KNEW — IT WAS OBVIOUS — THAT EVERYTHING SHE'D SAID WAS TRUE, OR AS TRUE AS SHE COULD MAKE IT, ANYWAY — AND THAT SHE GENUINELY WISHED US WELL.

Us? Not you?

US — DEFINITELY US.

SHADOW OF A DOUBT. TONIGHT, 9:15? BACK ROW, LEFT CORNER (FACING SCREEN).

I'll be there. I'll also be nervous. I WILL, TOO.

< !!! > *We can't use the room @ Pronghorn. Vanessa says the owner is selling + having meetings w/ potential buyers — wants the room open for him at all times (for the next 3 weeks, at least).* IT'S FOR THE BEST. MOODY + ILSA ARE @ THE CAFÉ TOO OFTEN. + THE OTHERS, TOO.

ONE OF MY FAVORITE THINGS ABOUT COLLEGE WAS THAT FOR THE 1ST TIME, I WAS AROUND A LOT OF PEOPLE WHO LOVED BOOKS — UNABASHEDLY + W/O APOLOGY. NOT LIKE HS AT ALL.

So you were pretty happy there?

PROBABLY THE HAPPIEST I'VE EVER BEEN. GOT AWAY FROM HOME, FELT LESS LIKE A FREAK, HAD A REALLY GOOD FRIEND/ROOMMATE. JUST THREW MYSELF INTO LEARNING THINGS. ANYTHING/EVERYTHING. GRAD SCHOOL'S A CAREER DECISION — SO IT FEELS LIKE EVERYTHING'S RIDING ON YOU SUCCEEDING @ THIS ONE THING. UNDERGRAD? ALL THE JOY OF DISCOVERY, NONE (OR LITTLE) OF THE COMMITMENT.

Like relationships. The early part's the easy part.

---

feels the building shake. He starts thinking about collapse, about the ceiling and the walls coming down on him, about being buried under all that weight, and suddenly it's as if he is back in that cramped, dark cavern with Corbeau—with poor Corbeau!—and just as suddenly as panic filled him, it is replaced with anger, anger at the men who destroy people, lives, beauty.

This is the resistance? It seems tragically insufficient to him. "I don't see anyone getting ready to fight," he says.

"It's not that kind of resistance," Osfour tells him.

"Well," S. says, "maybe it should be."

"Perhaps you will make it so."

"I won't be here."

"That is true," Osfour answers, with a certainty that S. finds disconcerting. "You will not."

They climb the stairway to the balcony, where a dozen more people are razoring canvases from their frames and laying them flat in sturdy-looking metal cases. There is a portrait of a dreamy-looking man at a desk, looking upward in a beatific haze, a quill in his hand, ink staining his fingers; oddly, though, the dog curled up at his feet, while at first glance appearing asleep, has its eyes open to slits and is curling a

We never talk about Straka's name. Is it just coincidence that he has the same name as a kid who died in Prague the day they were there?

AGAIN: NAME IN THE NEWSPAPER. A PERFECT BEARD FOR THEM TO HIDE BEHIND — SOME NOBODY KID THE WORLD THINKS IS ALREADY DEAD ??

Why change the middle initial then?

SO IT WAS LIKE HIS NAME BUT NOT IDENTICAL TO IT? NOT SURE WHY THAT WOULD BE IMPORTANT...

lip, showing a sharp tooth, as it faces something out of the frame behind the man. S. can almost hear the growl beginning in the dog's throat.[16] Several more paintings, still in their frames, lean against the wall: a dashing sea captain navigating with a sextant; three exhausted-looking women leaving a factory as cinders float in the evening sky; a young man in ill-fitting clothes playing a violin before a well-heeled crowd, the look in his eyes capturing the commingled joy and terror of creation.

At the end of this line is a smaller frame, perhaps a foot square, that has been turned to the wall. A woman goes to retrieve it, her black, waist-length hair swaying as she walks. When she turns and shows S. her face, he realizes that this is a girl, no more than thirteen years old. He watches as she settles herself onto the floor, gathers her hair behind her shoulders, and begins to cut the canvas free. It's another portrait, this one of a raven-haired girl with high, sharp cheekbones, sitting in a simple wooden chair, wearing a simple sacklike dress. The girl's fingers are bare, though she wears a necklace with a

---

[16] Some minor details are different, but Straka appears to be referring to *De Schrijver Vermoedt Niets*, a 1764 painting by the Dutch artist Gerrit van Swygert (1844–1872). I believe he was aware that I enjoy this important work very much.

What if Filomela sees herself as the dog? I mean, in a good way? Whatever it is that's threatening him, she's ready to go tear its throat out. (You said she's fierce, right?)

IT'D BE ANOTHER REASON FOR HER TO CHOOSE IT FOR THE TITLE / KEYWORD. AND A REASON FOR HER TO DROP A LINE LIKE "I ENJOY THIS IMPORTANT WORK VERY MUCH" INTO THE FN...

Totally missed that.

MAKES IT SOUND LIKE SHE WAS MORE ACTIVE IN THINGS THAN I'D THOUGHT. LIKE SHE WASN'T JUST EDITING + TRANSLATIN BUT ALSO COORDINATING OR PROTECTING OR CO-CONSPIRING...

Which makes me wonder what was in the bag she'd hidden @ Grand Central

dark stone hanging from it. On a table beside her is a heavy book, with a length of green ribbon marking a place in its pages.

The face in the portrait is Sola's. A younger Sola, perhaps, at sixteen or seventeen, but still: while the painting may be hundreds of years old, this is Sola looking up at him through the web of cracks in the varnish.

"Who is that?" S. blurts, after the girl has laid the canvas in its case.

Osfour looks over his shoulder at him in annoyance—how can this matter now, when bombs and mortar shells and an advancing army are on the way?—but the girl, after clearing her throat, answers cheerfully. "It's Samar," she says, as if she is surprised he doesn't already know.

She can see the name means nothing to S. "Some say she was just a girl from the desert," she explains, "one who fell in love with a European sailor and sailed away on his ship. Some say that she *arrived* here on his ship and remained. Some say she had a beautiful singing voice, others say she never in her life made a sound above a whisper. Some say she knew many of the world's languages, and others say she was just a beautiful idiot. My family claims her

what did she look like???

— SEE ATTACHED. Thought she'd look more like the descrip. of Sola.

MAYBE IF HER HAIR WERE LONGER? I CAN SEE FEEL A RESEMBLANCE.

Wish it were dead-on. For her sake.

SOLA / SZALÓMÉ / SAMAR

— JUST LIKE THE LOVE INTEREST IN WINGED SHOES.

just like Filomela

as a distant cousin, though that may simply be a story we tell."

"We don't have time for this," Osfour snaps. "Where is Abdim?"

"He went to get the package for our guest," the girl says, keeping her gaze on S. He studies her face: dark-eyed and olive-skinned, with a slender nose and prominent chin. Hers is a collection of features that looks awkward in a child's face but will find proportion and grace with the gift of years. He wonders if the approaching violence will keep her from enjoying that gift. He feels a sudden urge to take her with him, take her away from the coming rain of bombs. But would she truly be safer with him? A man with an unknown destination and a price on his head?

"It was painted here," the girl continues, pointedly ignoring S.'s distraction and Osfour's seethe. "Probably by the great Omar Tisatashar."

"Here in this city?"

"Here in this building. On this balcony." She points out the columns and arches in the dark background of the portrait. What is there is what S. sees from where he is now standing.

"Some say she was the artist's lover," the girl says. "Others say the sailor's. Some say she loved both.

{244}

Marginalia:

(top left, pencil): Did she ever find out who Sigñ was?

(below, ink): NO. THIS IS A GUESS, BUT I THINK DEEP DOWN SHE NEVER WANTED TO KNOW.

(right of "Omar Tisatashar", ink): ANOTHER ARTIST VMS HAS MADE UP.

(right of "Here in this city?", pencil): 19?

(bottom left, ink): Today after class Ilsa asked me if I knew you. I said no, obviously. → WHAT HAPPENED AFTER THAT?

(bottom, ink): She tried to play it off very casual — said that some of the things I'd said in class this semester reminded her of you. Then she just watched my face for a second or two — like she was expecting me to admit it.

(bottom): WHICH MEANS SHE KNOWS. OR AT LEAST SUSPECTS

Others think she was just a model, a poor girl paid to sit for the artist and immediately forgotten. Or that she didn't exist at all, that Tisatashar simply imagined her."

Another heavy susurration in the distance. Dust falls from the ceiling as if it were a gentle first snow.

"And your name?" S. asks the girl.

"Khatef-Zelh." *SIGNIF. OF NAME? No clue.*

He thanks her. He tells her his name.

"It would be better if you had many names," she says. *VERY ADULT/WISE VOICE FOR A KID*

"Time," Osfour says, nearly shouting. "*Time.*" He curses Abdim under his breath.

They hear sandaled feet slapping hurriedly up the stairway, and their owner, an extremely tall man—at least a head and a half taller than S.—joins them on the balcony. He is ebony-skinned and clean-shaven and strikingly thin. He, too, wears the loose gray linen, but his *kaftan* has embroidered rings of blue around the collar and at the wrists. He is carrying a brown leather valise, which he pushes into S.'s chest with a surprising firmness. "We are grateful for your service," the man tells him.

S. examines the valise. The leather is well-worn, scuffed and scratched, scaled with patches of

WE SEE WHAT WE WANT TO SEE, E.G.: DURANDISTS WANT TO BELIEVE VMS WAS A WOMAN. FEUERBACHERS: THAT VMS WAS A BOMB-THROWING ANARCHIST. EKSTROMERS: THAT VMS WAS THE WRITER THEY'D LOVED THEIR WHOLE LIVES. VACLAVISTS: THAT VMS WAS A WALKING GHOST STORY. MACINNESITES: THAT VMS WAS A GIFTED INTELLECTUAL. ETC. ETC. ETC.

VMS (ALIASES? FORTUNUS, OPIS-TANCE, ETC.?)
→ OR—IF FIGUREHEAD FOR THE S — THEN ALL THE NAMES OF THE DIFFERENT MEMBERS.

Description of her face is a little like Corbeau's.

SO: ANOTHER EXAMPLE OF GENERATIONAL SUCCESSION? S.'S GRIEF SHOWING HIM ECHOES OF HER? OR IS THIS SOME KIND OF GHOST STORY?

A BURDEN (OR GIFT?) FORCED UPON HIM

you're taller than I thought you'd be.

I WAS TINY WHEN I WAS A KID. EPIC GROWTH SPURT WHEN I WAS 16.

maybe that's part of why you were having such a hard time then— changing so much, all at once.

HUH. MAYBE. AT THE TIME, I THOUGHT IT WAS THE ONE GOOD THING THAT WAS HAPPENING.

abrasion. The handle has worn down, creating depressions where other fingers have gripped. [It reminds him of Stenfalk's valise, the one he left behind in the hills, although it seems smaller, the leather thinner, the handle made from a lighter-colored wood. It looks enough like Stenfalk's to give pause, but of course it could not be the same one. Could it? No. Absurd.]

Explosions in the distance. An aeroplane again rips the sky over the building, and then another one, and another, all three heading in the direction of the desert. S. hears them circle—at the edge of the city, perhaps—and come back toward them. Osfour and Abdim lean in toward each other and speak in whispers; S. senses that they are arguing.

"Sobreiro," he says to Khatef-Zelh, raising his voice above the noise. "Was the sailor named Sobreiro?"

"He was. In some of the books, anyway."

S. kneels at the case, studies the spine and cover of the book in the portrait. There are marks upon them, but faint ones, and they are unreadable.

"I'm looking for a book," S. tells Khatef-Zelh. "A book that Sobreiro wrote. *The Archer's Tales.* Do you have it here?"

GENERATIONAL SUCCESSION: BAG ISN'T IDENTICAL (MAYBE B/C TWO PEOPLE AREN'T GOING TO BE ALIKE?) BUT SIMILAR (DIFFERENT PEOPLE, SIMILAR ROLE?) Like Edvar V to Edvar VI.

OR (MAYBE) EKSTROM TO WHOEVER WAS TAKING OVER LEADERSHIP OF THE S? ie., Straka

What if the bag @ Grand Central had a copy of The Archer's Tales in it?

Did Filomela know what it was when she was holding it for Straka? → NO—SHE JUST KNEW IT WAS IMPORTANT.

"I've never heard of it. But it's possible. We've taken many thousands of books underground."

"You have your materials," Abdim says to S. "Now go. You cannot stay here. Not another minute."

S. shakes the valise gently, tests its weight. Fairly heavy, but not evenly balanced. Some of it is paper.

"Open it, if you must," Osfour says. "But hurry."

S. flips up the latches, pulls open the case carefully. There is a stack of papers, yes, thoroughly inked in a minute handwriting. A stack of photographs held together with a clip. But also: tiny stoppered glass vials filled with liquids (some clear, some opaque, some brightly hued, some pale) and fitted snugly into leather loops sewn into the valise's lining; glassine packets filled with powders and dried leaves; syringes and small blades for precision cutting and a few fine-tipped paintbrushes; six darts and a six-inch-long, narrow-bored wooden tube. A black fountain pen inlaid with mother-of-pearl; considering what else is in the bag, S. guesses that it has a reservoir that is not meant for ink, maybe a sharpened nib, too. He picks the pen up, rolls it in his fingers, admires the nacreous swirls that twist around the barrel. In bright light, it would be beautiful.

Marginalia (handwritten):

If VMS wasn't one person, then who wrote the books? A lot of the styles are different, but they're not that different.

WELL, THERE'S THAT CONNECTION BETWEEN THE PAINTED CAVE AND DURAND'S ALL OF THIS...

Night Palisades sounds a little like Summersby.

BUT I STILL THINK THERE'S SOMETHING CONSISTENT IN THE VMS BOOKS. SIMPLEST EXPLANATION IS THAT WE'RE JUST SEEING INFLUENCES. ALSO POSSIBLE: ERLEBNISTRÄGER THEORY—THAT VMS COLLECTED STORIES FROM OTHER PEOPLE, TRANSLATED THEM, REWROTE SOME PARTS, ADDED DETAILS, ETC., THEN PUBLISHED THEM AS HIS OWN.

You'd think somebody would've complained if that's what he was doing.

WHICH IS ONE REASON WHY I DON'T BELIEVE IT. ANOTHER IS THAT— EVEN WITH ALL THE POLITICAL ARGUMENTS— JUST ABOUT EVERY ONE OF THESE BOOKS FEELS PERSONAL TO ME. LIKE IT'S ONE PERSON'S RAGE AT THE WORLD AND HIS LOVE OF THE WRITTEN WORD.

WHAT IF WE SAY THAT NEXT TIME THERE WON'T BE SO MUCH VMS, FXC, MOODY, ETC.? WHAT IF WE SAY IT'S JUST US? — I KNOW I WANT TO TRY.

you really think you can do that?

"Many people gave their lives to assemble its contents," Abdim says. "It must leave with you. Go. Get back to the water. Complete your tasks."

"Who in the world do you think I am?" S. asks. The question is directed at Abdim, Osfour, Khatef-Zelh, all of them.

"It's not a question of who you are," Abdim says.

"I'm not an assassin," S. says.

"Well," Osfour says, "maybe you should be."

"Time and circumstances change us," Abdim says, "and it is pointless to ask why. You are—"[17] But he is interrupted when more deep, terrible thuds, closer now, shake the ground, shake the building, bring down another flurry of dust and tiny flakes of plaster and stone.

Osfour grabs the valise, snaps the latches closed, pushes it back at S. "Enough," he says. "We're leaving *now*." He pushes S. toward the stairway, and S. goes along—he's been through too much to let himself die pointlessly now—but he calls back over his shoulder to Khatef-Zelh. "Sobreiro's book," he says. "Look for it. Keep it safe if you find it. It's important." He doesn't really know if that's true, of course, but he thinks it could be.

[17] How like Straka to cut off the line of dialogue before Abdim can tell S. who he is (or might be)!

Do I look like you thought I would?

I TRIED NOT TO PICTURE YOU. PART OF KEEPING THE MYSTERY, I THINK.

you never wondered what I looked like? You are so totally lying.

WE ARE SUMS OF OUR EXPERIENCES? OR DO SOME OF THEM CHANGE US IN FUNDAMENTAL WAYS?

OK. MAYBE I THOUGHT YOU'D HAVE RED HAIR. DIDN'T EXPECT THOSE EYES. HOW COULD ANYONE?

[awwww...]

YOU DO ROLL THEM A LOT, THOUGH. I EXPECTED THAT.

If Khatef-Zelh is a version of Signe: would that suggest she had the book? IT COULD, THOUGH I CAN'T SEE WHY HE'D WRITE THIS IF IT DID. WOULDN'T HE WANT TO KEEP IT PERFECTLY SECRET?

Why write this entire book? Why risk revealing himself? Unless the whole book is meant for Filomela —regardless of what any other reader might think about it...

might be. In any event, the girl may or may not hear him, as the aeroplanes are sweeping overhead again, shaking the building with their infernal thunder.

I guess we can't be seen together ~~on campus.~~ —IT'D BE A BAD IDEA.

They leave by the other end of the alley. The streets are nearly empty; a few men are dashing madly, kicking up dust, but the rest of the population has hunkered down. Doors and shutters slap closed. Most of the remaining lights go dark, but the clouds have cleared, allowing the moon to expose the city, bathing it in cold purple light.

what about other places downtown? I don't want to always have to go to the movie theater.

IT'S DARK. THAT'S AN ADVANTAGE.

not if we actually want to see each other.

They run. Osfour, quick and agile, constantly scans for threats, glancing at rooftops and windows and into doorways, alleys, and alcoves, while S. simply tries to match his pace. They keep to the shadows when possible, sprint across the open moonlit spaces they can't avoid. S. hugs the valise to his chest with one arm, notices with odd detachment that his fingers are still gripping the barrel of the pen. All the while, explosions thump and echo from the desert, and the night sky flashes yellow and orange. Feral dogs bay and yelp. The aeroplanes arc back and forth, carving tighter circles around the city, so relentlessly menacing that S. catches himself wishing they would just do what they came to do, destroy

So did F. think he really was a killer??

SHE SAID SHE WISHES SHE COULD BELIEVE HE WASN'T.

which ~~isn~~ isn't really a direct answer.

whatever they mean to destroy and leave a quiet, still sky to itself. Bewildered and disoriented, S. finds himself doubting that he is being led to the palm grove, to the water, at all.

They turn a corner, and Osfour jars to a halt, pulls S. into a dark doorway and into a crouch. He points toward a rooftop, at a pallid blue glimmer. Moonlight striking an eyeglass lens. A kneeling man with a rifle.

Osfour tests the door behind them. It is unlocked. The room they enter is dark and cluttered, and it looks as if its occupants left in a hurry. The smell of spoiled food hangs in the air. Two bony cats, one orange and one black, are curled together like *yin* and *yang* on a stained mattress, somehow sleeping through all the racket outside—and, to S.'s surprise, sleeping through his own presence there. "There will be more snipers," Osfour says quietly. "Most of the Agents will have gone to the rooftops. This has been orchestrated."

"Because of me?"

"The invasion was coming, regardless. But you're why it's coming *now*."

An inner alcove has a window just big enough for the men to squeeze through, and they drop

{ 250 }

Seems like it might be useful if someone were to get into Moody's office + look around..

PLEASE DON'T DO ANYTHING STUPID.

If I'm not going to graduate, might as well go out with a bang.

IF YOU'RE NOT GOING TO GRADUATE NOW, YOU CAN TAKE A COURSE IN THE SUMMER OR FALL AND GRADUATE THEN. UNLESS YOU DO SOMETHING REALLY STUPID—WELL-INTENTIONED, BUT STUPID—AND GET YOURSELF ARRESTED AND/OR EXPUNGED.

You don't get it. When I told my parents I was maybe having trouble this semester, my dad said I needed to "get my act together and my butt in gear." Not graduating on time is—his words—"a deal-breaker." 'WHATEVER HE THINKS THAT MEANS, HE DOESN'T REALLY MEAN IT. oh, and trusting in your parents' empathy + understanding worked out _so_ well for you...

themselves into another alley. Clotheslines run between buildings overhead, and hanging laundry obscures the views from above. The sniper either doesn't see them or chooses to hold his fire.

S. finds his eyes watering and his breathing constricted. Fire. Something, somewhere, is burning, filling the air with sharp-sweet smoke. It's not until they're in sight of the crumbling portal that S. sees its source: fire rages through the date palm grove, dances madly above the treetops, sends helices of black smoke rising into the sky. Osfour curses sharply, and they duck into another doorway. "We'll try the waterfront," Osfour says.

"Will the rower be there?"

"Let's hope so."

The two of them are gathering themselves for another sprint when a burst of gunfire comes from nowhere. Osfour cries out as a ricocheting fragment of stone tears open his cheek. He holds his hand to his face. Blood runs darkly between his fingers.

He bleeds, S. thinks. *He's real.* "Are you all right?" he asks.

"Of course," Osfour says. He wipes his sleeve over his face, leaving a long smear over the fabric. The wound immediately spills fresh blood down his

Had an idea —you saw Ekstrom's handwriting in the travel diary, right? Have you seen any of the others?

—ALL OF THE 1910 GROUP. DURAND'S, ON AN AUTOGRAPHED 1ST ED. OF ALL OF THIS TO YOU I GIVE (IMAGE FROM AUCTION HOUSE CATALOG); GARCÍA FERRARA'S ON SUICIDE NOTE (IMAGE IN THE BIOGRAPHY). AND FEUERBACH'S SIGNATURE IS AT THE BOTTOM OF ALL OF THE PAMPHLETS HE WROTE.

and you said you have scans of the original Braxenholm ms...
Do you see any matches in the edits/ margin notes/etc.?

WILL HAVE TO LOOK FOR THEM— MY STUFF'S A MESS NOW THAT I DON'T HAVE AN OFFICE.

SOMEONE WAS CALLING MY NAME IN THE TUNNELS LAST NIGHT. I STARTED RUNNING— TRIPPED + CUT MY LEG OPEN { 251 } ON A PIECE OF PIPE. IT'S DEEP. BLED ALL OVER THE PLACE.

Promise you'll get it looked at, ok? The last thing I want is for you to get gangrene or something.

cheek, but Osfour pays it no mind. "Are you ready?" he asks, and S. is. They leave their shelter and make for the waterfront, through tilting streets, down alleys, underneath arches, while behind them mortars thump and aeroplanes whine and circle, and in the distance bullets pop and people scream and the smoke spreads over the sky and a mechanized army advances on the city, thundering out from the desert to the south. Birds flee the city, speeding out over the water, their wings beating a terrified static in the air.

The street opens into a plaza, just beyond which they can see the waterfront, the tips of masts rocking like metronome rods. Osfour slows to a brisk walk, and they hug the perimeter. At the ninety-degree point is an archway through which the palm fire's light blazes, making the stones of the plaza pulse an angry orange. It is as they are crossing this space—a mere ten yards—that a rooftop gun barks and the air whistles and Osfour pitches forward and drops, his head in the shadows, his legs in the light.

Was there a muzzle flash? Did the moon shine on the shooter at all? Not that S. saw.

S. drags his guide closer to the line of buildings, kneels, sees the blood streaming from a black hole

ONLY A FEW
PEOPLE IN MARAŬ
KNOW WHO SHE IS. SHE'S BEEN
LIVING AS "ERMELINDA PEGA"
SINCE FXC'S "DEATH" IN
FEIRA NOVA.

pega ▤
Portuguese for
magpie.
SHE SAID SHE
COULDN'T RESIST.
SHE WAS SMILING
WHEN SHE SAID IT.

over his right eye, pooling on the walkway's smooth stone, even as it still leaks from the slash on his cheek.

Osfour was real.

S. has to move, run ahead, get out of the plaza and onto the docks, but he resists the panicked urge to cut the corner and race across the open space, holds himself tightly to the shadows, listens for sounds—a spent casing jingling on a roof tile, a bolt closing and locking, a coat rustling as the rifleman adjusts his position. He turns the corner crisply, careful not to reveal any part of himself.

Crack. A window behind him erupts in a spray of glass.

Again, shock detaches him from the moment, sends his mind into abstractions. *A shooter is not just a man with a gun*, he thinks as he runs, *but a man who chooses to pull its trigger*. There is a rustle as he passes a dark alcove, and suddenly the air is crushed out of his lungs as he is tackled. He feels himself pulled upright and yanked backward. A thick arm crosses his throat, squeezes, cuts off even the chance of his breathing. His arm is pinned to his side, and the valise falls from his hand. There is the sound of leather scraping stone as his assailant kicks the bag out of the way, and then the arm slides up

---

Handwritten annotations:

I'm sorry I cried. I was just so relieved.

+ I'M SORRY I WAS SO AMPED UP — TOO EXCITED ABOUT EVERYTHING (ALL OF THE VMS STUFF, BUT ESPECIALLY YOU.)

I'll be better next time. Right? Not saying it was bad — just, I don't know, a lot to deal with all at once. I'M SO GLAD YOU'RE SAYING THERE'LL BE A NEXT TIME.

VARIANT ON IDENTITY QUESTION SELF AS ROLE VS. SELF AS CHOICE?

SHE THOUGHT IT WAS FUNNY THAT EVEN WHEN SHE WAS USING HER OWN NAME, HARDLY ANYONE REALIZED SHE'D BEEN VMS'S EDITOR/TRANSLATOR—EVEN THOUGH THE BOOKS WERE POPULAR THERE. (SHE SAID THE PORTUGUESE TRANSLATIONS WERE ALWAYS HER BEST.)

over S.'s eyes and pulls his head back. A sharp, cool blade touches his throat and begins to draw across. In a burst of desperate energy, S. wrenches himself away, stumbles forward.

And here time turns sluggish, comes nearly to a stop.

The sea breeze funneling in through the archway is cool on his skin. He watches as the valise yawns open; from it, loose papers flutter like seagulls taking wing and photographs spread themselves out like rays. Glass vials bounce and spin themselves over the paving-stones, ricocheting when they hit seams—he watches the bounces, expects to see some of the vials break, but none does—and they spend the last of their energy rolling in curves across the pathway, the sound of which makes him think of children shooting marbles. How interesting, he thinks, that time is running so slowly for him right here, on this path, slower than elsewhere in this city, and a thousand times slower than on the ship, where years pass like weeks. What a revelation, to be shown—to be reminded—that time is so flexible, so adaptable, so idiosyncratic.

Of course S. is not thinking this in sentences; the entire notion—its content, its implications, its

I feel a lot calmer when you're around now. Everything's still going sideways (Dad's phrase), but it's not as scary.

mingled tones of awe and wistfulness and detachment—presents itself wholly in one instantaneous
synaptic flash. It flashes—here, then gone—and the
flash that follows is one of the pure and furious need
to survive. The pen appears in his hand and he strikes
out with it, slashing and stabbing away until he feels
the sharpened nib sink into tissue, hears the moist
chiff it makes, stabs again and again until the huge
man slumps, drops, convulses once, dies, a body in a
kaftan no different from S.'s own. The man's pale,
puffy face is one that is, and will remain, unknown.

S. stares at the bloody honeycomb of wounds in
the man's neck, transfixed. He feels his own blood
pumping inside him. He feels feral, unstoppable.
The pen is slick, his forearm is dark and wet, and he
is breathing heavily with the loosened derangement
of violence. He sees another *kaftan*-clad figure
kneeling in the plaza, hurriedly gathering up loose
pages, vials, packets; he takes a step forward (ready
to strike again because he *will* have that valise, he
will not let it be taken from him.) But the figure
snaps the latches shut and holds it out to him, and in
a hoarse voice says, "Go, go, you have to hurry—
more are coming. The boat is at the end of the leftmost pier. Hurry." A *checheya* sits askew on his

[Handwritten margin notes:]

PEN AS WEAPON.
EXACTLY WHAT VMS
WOULD BELIEVE
(BUT LITERALIZED HERE).

"*moist chiff*"?
gross.

VMS would've
been crushed if he'd
known the bag was
stolen from
Grand Central.
OR FURIOUS.

head; long, dark hair has escaped its confines. His face is backlit and difficult to see.

Here, time does not slow down to let S. think. He reacts. He scans the rooftops around the plaza, wonders why no more bullets have come.

(("We took care of him," the figure says, pushing the valise into his hands. "Now go."))

Thin fingers, he notices, he does notice that much before he runs, through the archway and toward the water, across a flat expanse on which nets and tarps and buoys form stinking monuments to the life-giving sea, then down a long dock whose planks rattle and groan under his weight, and yes, there is the dinghy with the straw-haired sailor in it, oars poised aloft like a gull's wings. The boat tips sharply when S. steps in, but then rights itself as S. pushes them away from the dock.

The sailor's oars churn the surf. S. hunches over in the stern, makes himself as small a target as he can for the bullets that may, and do, fly out over the water at them. They row against the slapping waves, out into the dark that drapes itself over the anchored ship. Behind them—and S. knows this because he steals a look back—the orange glow intensifies as the fire, having blackened the grasslands, sweeps

I wish you'd gotten to record her goodbye. That's what I want to hear most.

the city, and the charred sticks that once were date palms wink with embers, and muzzles flash from the docks. That stolen look becomes a prolonged study, not of the devastation but of the figure he notices skulking at the foot of the port's only lighthouse, hidden from the shooters and watching S. recede into the dark, perhaps even waving once before S. disappears from view.

That voice in the plaza. Hoarse and husky, yes, but female. The *checheya* just a costume touch. The long, dark hair. (That woman in the plaza, that woman in the shadows of the ruined lighthouse—was it Khatef-Zelh? But how could she have gotten there so quickly? Was it simply another woman from Osfour and Abdim's network?

No, his mind tells him. *It was Sola.*

Sola? The voice was much rougher than he remembers hers being, but then, time does keep moving forward, no matter what its speed.))

And once again, S. is falling farther and farther away from her.[18] Each one of these oar-strokes pains

---

18 I feel similarly about Straka. He has been dead for three years now, and I feel Time taking me farther and farther away from this marvelous writer, my professional relationship with whom has defined my life for decades. I worry, too, here on the cusp of a new decade, with a new set of troubles in the world—that Time will take his readership farther and farther away from him as well. I shall do my best to keep him alive, if only through his words.

{ 257 }

Handwritten margin notes:

IT WAS ARTURO'S COUSIN WHO HELPED HER FAKE HER DEATH IN FEIRA NOVA. IT WAS IRONIC, SHE THOUGHT, THAT IT'S SO DIFFICULT TO VANISH W/O HELP FROM OTHER PEOPLE.

I really wish I'd gone with you. MAYBE WE CAN GO BACK OVER THE SUMMER. BEFORE YOU GO TO NEW YORK.

Sounds like she got over Straka at some point.

I DON'T THINK SO. THINK SHE JUST FOUND A PLACE FOR HERSELF IN A SMALL GROUP OF PEOPLE WHO CARED ABOUT HER.

MARRIED FOR 5 YRS OR SO BACK IN THE '80S — HE WAS AN OLDER GUY, + HE DIED. SAID IT WAS "PERFECTLY PLEASANT" + HE WAS "A NICE MAN." WHICH, OBV., ISN'T WHAT SHE'D HOPED FOR WHEN SHE WAS YOUNGER.

Did she ever find someone else? get married?

It's not what I'm hoping for, either. Life's too short.

him; they are carrying him back to that ship, which—crazily—seems like a place of safety. But that is a safety in which S. is suddenly uninterested. It would be suicide to go back, he'd be shot dead before he ever touched land, but—

There is a bright flash of orange then, the brightest he has seen, a roar that punches his eardrums even at this distance, a shock wave that nearly knocks him into the bilge of the boat. When he looks back at the city, most of the buildings that made up its skyline are gone, and it is crowned by a dome of blue-black vapor that fires illuminate from below. He knows: fires are burning everywhere in those streets, stone and metal and paper and flesh are flying through the air, and everywhere is heat and smoke and the cries of the dying.

He thinks about the building he was in, about Abdim, about young Khatef-Zelh, about all the other people scrambling to preserve art and beauty and words and wisdom, and he wonders how deep underground any person or thing would have to be to survive. He wonders if Sola, if any of them, will have access to a place so deep.

[IT BURNED DOWN, ERIC.

Someone burned it down, and it was b/c of me.

NO ONE WAS REALLY AT RISK. IT WAS EMPTY, RIGHT?

Are you sure that's what you want to say?
Because that is totally NOT the point. My family is at risk. Not yours. And just because you don't care about yours doesn't mean I shouldn't care about mine.

WHAT I MEAN IS: IF IT WAS THE S, AND THEY'RE TRYING TO SCARE US, THEN WE SHOULDN'T LET THEM. AND IF IT WASN'T—IF IT WAS JUST SOME ASSHOLE SCREWING AROUND—THEN THERE'S NO REASON TO BE SCARED IN THE FIRST PLACE.
you can't just decide not to be scared.

Fire marshal says it was prob arson. You still want me not to be scared?

THE LAST THING SHE SAID TO ME—AND THIS WAS WHEN SHE WAS HOLDING MY HAND—SHE SAID: "DON'T MAKE THE SAME MISTAKE WE DID."

CHAPTER 7

THE OBSIDIAN
ISLAND[1]

I was rowed to shore,
where a man in a *kaftan*
was waiting for me.
We walked from a date
palm grove into a city
and through a nighttime

I raged at the sun while
the moon and constella-
tions whistled for me.
We walked, we damned
pilgrims, to a cenotaph.[2]
The thunder had no

THE POINT RE: ETYMOLOGY
IS PURE BS

It does draw attention to the
repeated "OB"...

---

[1] The emphasis on death in this chapter is noteworthy, and it is reflected in the chapter title. Straka's choice of obsidian for the island's composition was not an accident, as *obsidian* shares an etymological root with *obituary*. Perhaps it is also fitting that there is a similar connection to *obstreperous* and *obtuse* and at least five other pejoratives I would use to describe the anonymous writer of the Straka obituary that ran in a Baltimore newspaper. For reasons that remain impenetrable to me, the notice devolved into a series of insults about Straka's later, and more personal, works. (The most-maligned of these, *The Winged Shoes of Emydio Alves*, was battered by critics and by the book-buying public, as well as by the radical left, which regarded it as the work of a self-satisfied apostate. Even so, I believe that it was precisely the book Straka had intended to write.)

[2] I am told that a French aficionado of Straka's work is seeking to memorialize the writer with a cenotaph in Paris's Père Lachaise cemetery. I lack the financial means to contribute to this effort (and the defunct Karst has nothing to give), but I would be pleased if it were successful.

BUT THE SCRAMBLE OF
LETTERS IN THE 5TH FN
DRAWS EVEN MORE
ATTENTION TO ITSELF.
(NOTE THE SPECIFIC
MENTION "FIVE" HERE...
SO THAT COULD BE THE
SIGNAL.) SO MAYBE
ONE OF THEM IS A
MISDIRECTION...
Or maybe there's
more than one code here.
Not having any
luck w/ this...

So maybe FXC
wasn't such a hack
THIS MUST BE V. DEMANDING
FOR TRANSLATOR — DEPENDS
ON SOUND EVEN MORE
THAN MEANING

BEEN THINKING
ABOUT VMS WRITING IN
ALL DIFFERENT LANGUAGES...
THEY'RE ALL LANGUAGES FXC KNEW...
MAYBE HE WAS TRYING TO LEARN
THEM BECAUSE SHE KNEW THEM?

why? (It wouldn't help
them communicate any better.)
BECAUSE THINGS PEOPLE DO WHEN
THEY'RE... ENAMORED(?) DON'T
ALWAYS MAKE SENSE. could still
Keep himself hidden, though — if she knew
his native language, it'd be easier for
her to ID him.

marketplace. Agents hid among us in plain sight. Caged finches fluttered their wings against their prisons. Children moaned from inside baskets when summoned by flute. The repository is no more.[3]

mercy; angels bade us adieu, punished by sound. Cairns of fiction flummoxed the winds, held their positions. O, chastened men of ink, battle the sundering force! Le repos est la mort!

Progress is much slower without the nail. The fishhook is curved, and S. has trouble getting the barb to bite the wood at the right angle without losing his grip. Before long, he gives up and returns to puzzling over the papers and photographs from the valise, which he has spread out over the warped boards of his cabin floor.

There are fifty-seven photographs((Each of them seems to show a different person, but S. cannot be certain of this, as most of the images are blurry) shot from a distance in public spaces (on the steps of buildings; in cafés; in rail stations; on ships). The

---

[3] Consider, too, the presence of death here in what I call S.'s "mediated" or "transposed" writing on the bulkhead. *No more* becomes *la mort*. *City* becomes *cenotaph*. This, clearly, is a character concerned with his mortality, perhaps even more than he is aware.

Is this about VMS having trouble writing?

— COULD BE. MAYBE SOMETHING ABOUT THE DIFFERENCE B/W WHAT YOU INTEND + WHAT RESULTS

OK... so next time we won't talk about Straka.

I mean it this time.

SORRY. I GOT CAUGHT UP IN IT AGAIN.

Well, so did I.

→ OLD KGB DOSSIER ON STRAKA
HAS 4 PHOTOS OF DIFFERENT MEN
WHO THEY THOUGHT WERE POSSIBLE
STRAKAS. NONE OF THEM ARE ANY OF THE
SHIP OF THESEUS WRITERS THAT
WERE IN THE S.
... that we *think* were in The S.

and there ~~might have been~~ were others in it, too.

few that show faces in both close view and sharp focus look as if they have been culled from governmental documents of one sort or another.] Forty-two of the people are clearly identifiable as men, nine as women; about the other six, S. remains uncertain.

One photograph in particular made S. gasp when he peeled it off the stack: a man in a dark-colored duster sitting on a train, holding a newspaper (German, S. thinks, though the type is too blurry for him to be certain). The man's head is bowed as if he is reading, but his eyes are aimed over the tops of the pages, closely observing whoever or whatever is across from him. S. knows this man's face. He will never forget it. He saw it in the alley near the power station in B——. Not the man in disguise who carried and placed the bomb, but the one who stayed behind, the more sinister presence, the one who delivered that creepy, conspiratorial smile. That heavy brow overhanging deep-set eyes, that thick nose, that square-block jaw equal in width to the slab of neck below it. Whoever took this photograph was sitting opposite him, across the train car's aisle, and—presumably—escaping his suspicion.

S. flips the photograph over and finds writing on the back. At the top-left corner is written #4.

That guy was sitting at the bus stop down the street from me this morning, tapping on his phone. It's like he's letting me see him closer + closer to where I live. He is *creeping* me ~~the fuck~~ out.

DO YOU WANT ME TO STAY AT YOUR PLACE??
You'll get arrested if they see you on campus.

HAVE YOU EVER GONE BACK TO THE PARK WHERE YOU WENT MISSING?
No. My parents pretended it didn't exist. They still won't talk about it.

I SHOULD'VE BEEN SUSPICIOUS OF ILSA FROM THE BEGINNING.
I'm at the point where I think I should be suspicious of everybody.
EVEN ME?
Maybe I should be. But I'm not.

You know what? Let's go there. Next date. And no work. Just us.

WAIT— YOU'RE SURE? { 261 }—— Totally. It's not just that nothing bad happened there... something *good* happened. I *liked* being by myself + seeing what I saw.

_____

Next to it, in a careful script:

DANZIG - BERLIN, OCT 1908

And, below that, in different hands and inks:

CF. BARREL
MARKINGS IN
CH. 10

TANGIER, JUN 1905
B———, OCT 1906
LOS ANGELES, DEC 1910
TRIPOLI, SEP 1911
SALONIKA, MAR 1912

Each of the photographs has similar notations on the obverse: a number between one and fifty-seven at top left; the location and date; and, in many cases, additional dates and locations below. The known Vévoda Agents, he concludes, with their sightings chronicled.

A few others also look to be from the ranks of Vévoda's original Detectives, those mountains of men with their rough, even primitive, physiognomies. Their photos are all marked with single-digit numbers. The rest of the fifty-seven, though, are remarkable primarily in their failure to be remarkable, resisting all but the most general descriptions. _Dark-haired woman in kerchief and dark coat._

Bearded man riding streetcar. Person with eye-glasses, holding umbrella.

As for the stack of papers: most of the pages contain instructions for compounding or extracting poisons. The substances are identified by Latin phrases (_Fulva mundi; Argentum implet faucibus;_[4] _Sanguinem ulcera; Avis veritatis; Sagittarius servum_), many of which match the tiny, fastidious writing on the labels of the vials. There are also twenty-five pages of onionskin filled with typed letters with no spaces between them, no punctuation, no paragraph breaks, no recognizable words, no organizing principle apparent. Could these be his instructions, enciphered? If so, how?[5]

---

[4] Latin for "silver fills the throat." Those Straka devotees who have scoured the recorded accounts of the Prix Bouchard/monkey incident may recall that Straka, in his statement, opined that while Hermès Bouchard was often said to have a silver tongue, "he has consumed so much of the world's wealth that he now may well have a silver throat, a silver ileum, a silver colon, even a silver arse."

[5] I suggested that Straka include a line or two of example text, thinking it would both engage and disorient readers—putting them, as it were, in S.'s shoes. He rejected this suggestion out of hand, even though he had, in fact, written all twenty-five pages of this puzzling text. (That is the sort of compulsive artist he was.) Perhaps he decided that any sample of it would take too much of the reader's attention away from our hero and his predicament. Still, he did produce a few lines of sample text to help me understand what he believes the character S. experiences while contemplating these pages. I shall reproduce that sample here, for the benefit of readers who are as curious as I was:

```
        L B Q T A H M A K
        A F P F A P G O J M
        U P B A N G R N J L
```

Handwritten margin notes:

at the motel, when we were all out in the parking lot watching the fire, there was a guy who kept looking at me. Totally ordinary. Brown hair. Average height. Not skinny or fat. I'm not sure I'd remember his face if he was in a lineup.

BUT YOU THINK HE HAD SOMETHING TO DO WITH THE FIRE? WITH YOU?

I don't know what I think. But he's why I got out of there + went to my parents' place. I just wanted to be far away in some other direction.

what if he followed me??

OK—there's a thing called a "running key" that she might've used. Cipher is keyed to another text (so... the Baltimore obit?). But you have to know where in the other text to start.

↳FN 1 USES "IMPENETRABLE" —SO DOES OBIT ("THE IMPENETRABLE CORIOLIS AND THE SACCHARINE WINGED SHOES) START FROM THERE?

We get: "Sum losing hope. Please get in touch."

SUM?

Summersby? which would mean he wasn't Straka.

OR AT LEAST SHE DIDN'T THINK HE WAS

You still want Summersby to be Straka, don't you? B/c you're the ne who got that tape?

YOU'RE PROBABLY RIGHT. BUT PART OF IT IS THAT HE'S THE POSSIBLE STRAKA WHOSE OTHER BOOKS I LIKE BEST. THEY'RE OVER-THE-TOP PULPY, BUT I LOVE THEM.

He gathers the photographs back into one stack, riffles their edges with his thumb. He contemplates the other items in the valise—the darts, the vials, the leaves and seeds and roots, the paintbrush, the poisoner's pen. His task, it would seem, is to seek out these people and poison them.[6]

This, of course, is absurd. He does not know where these people are. He does not know where—or even *when*—he himself is. He has no idea how to track a person who does not want to be found. While he may be able to concoct a poison by following step-by-step instructions, he doubts he has the skill or the nerve to deliver it into another human being's body. Curiously, the most fundamental question—*why* do this?—feels easy enough to answer: Agents have killed his friends; while they have not killed him, it is not for lack of trying; and they are willing instruments of a worldwide violent enterprise. Why *not* do it? He remains vexed by the workings of this strange world. He is uncertain whether he can exercise free will within it. He is unaware of any other role he might play in it. And: he is, by any sensible measure, thoroughly alone.

---

[6] I am bracing myself for the mob of Straka theorists who will read this line and race to the conclusion that Straka was, in fact, the murderer some legends have made him out to be. One wonders if universities—particularly the American ones—even bother to teach the concept of the metaphor anymore.

{ 264 }

Here's my big question: did Filomela believe that Straka was an assassin? And how did she feel about it? Because that's what she was losing him to— not his writing.
Plus, wouldn't it be weird to think that the person you love is some totally prolific killer?
THAT WAS THREE QUESTIONS.
[o o]

I ASKED HER. SHE SAID THAT BACK THEN, SHE TOLD HERSELF IT WAS JUST PART OF A MYTH HE CREATED TO SELL BOOKS, BE FAMOUS/INFAMOUS, ETC. SAYS HE PROBABLY DID AT LEAST SOME OF IT—BUT THAT SHE WOULD'VE OVERLOOKED IT. SHE JUST WANTED TO BE W/HIM + GET AWAY FROM ALL OF THE SECRECY + THREAT AROUND THEM.

He repacks the valise, pushes it across the boards into a corner of the cabin, and lays the blanket over it. It's a poor job of concealment, but intuition tells him that it is a thing best kept out of sight.

The day is sunny and mild, with bands of cirrus tracking across blue sky. The wind is steady, but the ship seems to be making little progress, juddering along on a close haul. S. scans the deck for Maelstrom, but does not see him. Indeed, the ranks of the crew seem noticeably thinner. Common sense suggests that the missing sailors must be below deck—they can't have vanished in the few hours the ship was anchored in the waters off El-H——. He is still clinging to a faith that time moves at the same velocity on water as on land.

Standing on the main deck, in the waist of the ship, is the pouting sailor—one of those he now recognizes as a woman. She is of whiplike build with a curious pairing of swanlike neck and abbreviated forehead, a woman he might find attractive were it not for the narrowed eyes that look starved of everything but meanness, the cyanotic tone of her skin, and (of course) the crosshatched threads

---

Handwritten margin notes:

SO: EMBARRASSING DISCLOSURE: ONE OF THE REASONS I KEPT PUTTING OFF MEETING WAS THAT I THOUGHT I'D BE DISAPPOINTING TO YOU.

I know that.
I knew that.
AND THAT WASN'T DISAPPOINTING TO YOU??

of course it was.
But not disappointing enough to give up.

REMINDER OF MORTALITY?
↓
AND/OR REF. TO THE DIMINISHING RANKS OF THE S?

So hot.
S

I would really, really hate to be the woman he based her on.
("ON WHICH HE BASED HER")
Shut up.

sealing her mouth.[7] She holds a mop with a handle sawed to half-length and appears to be trying to teach the monkey to swab the deck. The monkey is having none of it, running circles around her and jabbering all the while, as if to taunt her with its freedom to vocalize. The monkey, S. thinks, would be wise not to push its luck in this regard.

She sees him come down the ladder—he's certain of it—but he has to stand before her for several long moments before she deigns to look at him. "Where is Maelstrom?" he asks. "The one who speaks?" He mimes a long beard, flaps his mouth open and closed, just in case she can't hear or doesn't understand.

Though her body remains still, her expression darkens from mild annoyance to formidable contempt.

To stand in such proximity to her is disconcerting. Even the rims of her eyes have taken on a bluish tinge. "You don't look well," he says. "Are there limes on board? Limes?" He holds his hands in the shape of a lime but drops them quickly, feeling ridiculous. "You know, you *could* communicate with me, if you wanted to," S. says, unable to conceal his irritation.

7 Let the speculation begin about whom Straka used as a model for the pouting sailor. Allow me to prime the pump with a few suggestions: Floris of Bruges! A little British girl! Mary Queen of Scots! Zelda Fitzgerald! Juan Blas Covarrubias's favorite serving-wench on all the Barbary Coast! Grand Duchess Tatiana! The first Mrs. Bouchard!

{ 266 }

I WAS BARELY HOLDING IT TOGETHER WHEN WE WERE WALKING OUT AFTER THE MOVIE. COULDN'T BELIEVE I WAS ACTUALLY WITH YOU. JUST KEPT TELLING MYSELF NOT TO TRIP + FALL OR DO ANYTHING TOO MONUMENTALLY STUPID.

I was wondering why you were so quiet.

There's really no reason you can't meet me. Let's just get coffee or something. It doesn't have to be a big deal

Sure ... but isn't it fun to believe in the reincarnated nun-Straka? Makes the world a more interesting place.
Oh, wait: you're a scholar. No fun allowed.

We need to add Florence Stoneham-Smith to our candidate-deaths-by-falling list.

NO WE DON'T. SHE'S NOT A CANDIDATE. HER STORY IS RIDICULOUS.

"With gestures. In writing. With the damned whistle, if you'd teach me how to understand it."

At this, she grunts and walks away. The monkey follows her, but not before leaving a puddle of urine on the deck.

S. circumnavigates the ship, looking for Maelstrom, stepping carefully around the gaps in the deck where the planking has rotted through, dark traps set to spring on innocent ankles. The sailors he passes offer him nothing more than a cold, perfunctory glance, if they register his presence at all. Even the boy from the ghost ship—the one who most recently was a *person*, not a freakish, salt-crusted mute—ignores him. The whistles he hears are the music of a thinned and diseased flock.

He pauses along the starboard rail, sees nothing but the broad undulations of waves and the streaked sky. He closes his eyes, feels the breeze washing over his face. He smells salt and varnish and damp canvas, as well as a note of smoke that seems to have taken up permanent residence in his sinuses. He listens to the slaps of the ship pitching over the water, to the flutters and dives of the crew's whistles, to the groaning wood, to the *thwacks* of sail-edges and

{ 267 }

WHEN BOY FIRST APPEARS IN CH. 2, SEEMS LIKE HE'LL BE AN ALTER-EGO FOR S. BUT THEY DIVERGE IMMEDIATELY — LOSE ALL COMMON GROUND.

el just ran into my old freshman roommate in the Quad, and we talked a little— which el guess is the sort of thing people like to do right before graduation.

anyway: We'd been close at the beginning of the year, but then el met Jacob—and el just decided she was lame & boring and just not worth the effort of getting to know better. el didn't just *let* us drift apart, el *made* us drift apart. Turns out we're a lot more alike than el'd thought.

BUT YOU'RE NOT THE ONLY ONE WHO CHANGED. EVERYONE CHANGES. MAYBE THERE'S NO WAY YOU COULD'VE FOUND THAT KIND OF COMMON GROUND UNTIL NOW. —maybe.

We talked about staying in town, but el think we both know we probably won't. Just drifted too far—or for too long.

_____

stays. After a time, he notices more distant sounds: a rumbly drone wrapped in the fricative static of an ill-tuned wireless. Perhaps, he thinks, this is the sound of time accelerating.

He turns and watches bony, bluish hands rising from the aft hatchway, then bony, bluish arms, then the bony, bluish sailor—the bald old salt with the jug-ears—who lifts himself out onto the deck with a deadened look in his eyes. He blows one asthmatic note on his whistle, then plods toward the mainmast and struggles to lift himself into the tops. The whittler drops out of the mizzen rigging onto the quarterdeck, his knees nearly buckling upon impact, and disappears into the world of the ship's interior. So: even with a smaller crew to sail the ship, the regular shift-work continues.

The door to the chart-room creaks shrilly when S. opens it. The bearded man, hunched over a splay of paper on the table, quickly straightens and faces him. S. reads worry in the sailor's heavy-lidded eyes. He may appear healthier than his crewmates, but something has him gravely concerned.

Naught a'vex ye, sunnydags, Maelstrom says, though S. has said nothing.

_____

TECHNOLOGY IS ADVANCING AS TIME DOES— AS FAST AS SHIP-TIME. WE'RE DECADES AHEAD OF WHERE WE WERE IN CH. 1.

DECLINING MEMBERSHIP OF THE S. WHO'S LEFT BY 1940? SUMMERSBY, MACINNES, GARCIA FERRARA, WECHSLER (IF HE EVER REALLY WAS A MEMBER), LOOPER (IF ALIVE), AND SINGH? AND WHO WAS STILL LOYAL? EKSTROM, DURAND, FEUERBACH, DROZDOV ALL DEAD. MAYBE SHIMIZU? MASSOUD? WALLINGFORD? BRZEZICKI? NDABO? AKKERMAN? (WERE ANY OF THEM EVEN MEMBERS?) WERE THERE OTHERS NOBODY HAS EVER CONSIDERED?

Vaclav Straka was alive. IF HE EXISTED, MAYBE.

ERIC: New issue of Contemp. Eur. Lit. Journal has a paper by D.M. Dobson arguing that Shimizu was Straka. Traces everywhere he went from 1910–1950 & compares them to the settings of Straka's books. He'd been to all of them— and in nearly every case, he'd visited at some point in the SHIP OF THESEUS *2 years before the book came out.*

Straka sites are blowing up about it. There's a map that shows it— pretty wild.

"The crew looks smaller," S. says.

Crew's acrew. Size assize.[8]

"But where did they go?" S. cranes to see the charts on the table, but Maelstrom's massive shoulders still block his view.

COINCIDENCE. ALL IT PROVES IS THAT SHIMIZU TRAVELED A LOT. YOU DON'T NEED TO BE SOMEWHERE TO WRITE ABOUT IT, ANYWAY. *know anything about the author?*

Less y'coggin, the better. F'all of us.

"Why don't you ever take a turn on the orlop?"

My workins are topside. Sames yours.

"I'm going to see what happens down there, you know. You can't keep me out forever."

DOBSON IS WELL RESPECTED BUT THIS CAN'T BE TRUE. AND I KNOW YOU'RE GOING TO SAY I JUST DON'T WANT IT TO BE TRUE.

Maelstrom shrugs. *Better y'not vex y'self on what aint y'vexes. An y'prefer shacklin, we can range't.* He says this with no additional menace in his rasp but with his coal-colored eyes fixed on S.'s face. S. takes an involuntary step backward.

→ BREAKING INTO MOODY'S IS ABOUT THE WORST IDEA I CAN THINK OF. HE'S MY PROBLEM, NOT YOURS. NOTHING GOOD IS GOING TO COME OF IT FOR YOU. *I understand that. & I also understand you have to say that to cover your ass so you don't have to feel bad if something goes wrong.*

"I know you're not going to kill me," S. says from the doorway.

I WILL FEEL BAD ← IF SOMETHING GOES WRONG.

Places t'go. Wunt do f'you gettin theres all dead.

"Can you tell me what you know about Sola? Szalómé? Samar?"

Stories, mos'.

CF. CORIOLIS, BOOK III — SUNDERMAN'S VISIT TO THE ISLAND OF THE THREEFOLDS (WHERE EVERYONE HAS THREE ITERATIONS OF HIM / HERSELF).

"They're the same woman. And she's trying to help me. Isn't that right?"

ALSO: POSSIBLY A REF. TO TRIPTYCH OF MIRRORS

---

[8] Another comment on the nature of identity—closer in spirit, I think, to Mytch's view (and to O. C. Wayne's view as well) than to Guthrie MacInnes's.

{ 269 }

Aware y'self, Sunshines. What's vizzin' help aint alls help.[9]

"So you know something I don't."

'Course.

"Explain to me, then, how time works. It's slower on the ship than it is on land. Unless I'm simply going insane."[10]

Cant say. Dunt cog th' landways, an' I amn't in y' nog neither, am I? Maelstrom glances back at the chart on the table, then peers through the porthole. *What I cog abou' time's I got n'more f'you.*

The sailor must be distracted, because he has left S. with a clear view of the charts. They must not be as mildewed as the ones he saw before, because he can discern the boundaries between water and land. Most of the landmasses have been inked over in red.

"What does the red ink mean?" he asks. As he watches, one of the red areas bleeds outward,

---

[9] Straka once forwarded to me a letter he had received from Lewis Looper, the tough-talking and famously grumpy American who held himself out as Straka's agent during the writer's first decade of work, receding from public view shortly after Straka hired me to translate his novels, and finally vanishing in 1930. In that letter, Looper was urging Straka not to take me on, arguing that I was an unknown quantity, and probably a money-grabber with no commitment to safeguarding either Straka's privacy or the quality of his work. I would very much like to hear Lewis Looper's opinion of me now, though I doubt I ever will.

[10] This is pure speculation on my part, but it is possible that Straka was alluding to Eötvös Syndrome—that illness of his own invention—but modifying its suite of disorientations to include the additional dimension of Time.

{ 270 }

crossing over the boundary from land into water. Elsewhere, the red seems to be darkening, even pulsing. He feels faint. The ship dives into a sudden trough, and for a moment S. thinks his stomach is going to reverse on him, even though it is empty.

Maelstrom turns slowly. He looks at the chart, then at S. for a long moment. He steps forward and grabs S.'s shoulders roughly. His breath is foul, and his brown stumps of crooked teeth are even more repellent than S. remembers. He gives a sudden push that sends S. wheeling out the door and sliding arse-first along the splintering deck.

When Maelstrom steps outside, he has his head cocked and is studying the horizon, first to port, then forward, then to starboard. Those sounds S. noticed before—the rumble, the electric hiss— remain distant but are louder now, with occasional pulses beating through the air. The smell of smoke is sharper, too. Maelstrom shakes his head in what seems like incredulity, then lifts his whistle and blows an urgent, stricken-sounding minor-key sequence of notes, first in a low register, then a high one, then low again.

Lines are stilled mid-coil; mops and brushes and stones cease their scuffing against the deck. A few

NOTES ABOUT CALAIS GOT ME THINKING ABOUT MY UNCLE AGAIN. WHAT HAPPENED ON THE BOAT PRETTY MUCH DEFINED MY LIFE FROM THEN ON (OR PART OF IT, ANYWAY), AND I STILL RESENT THE HELL OUT OF HIM FOR IT. ... BUT HE WASN'T THE WORST GUY IN THE WORLD. WE COULDN'T HAVE BEEN MORE DIFFERENT — I DON'T THINK HE READ A BOOK IN HIS LIFE BUT HE WAS JUST SOMEONE TRYING TO DO WHAT MADE HIM HAPPY AND DEAL WITH WHAT MADE HIM SAD.

Which is pretty much what we're all doing.

heads poke down from the tops to watch the big man, as if to verify that they have heard the song correctly. The sails luff and whack. S. feels a dark mood sweep over the ship, dark as the storm-clouds that descended upon them off the coast of B——; what he cannot tell is whether that mood is one of fury or fear.

The monkey, sitting atop a barrel mid-deck, amuses itself by tearing pieces from a ship-biscuit and tossing them to the wind. S. is heartened to see a few surly looks thrown its way, including one by its companion from the ghost ship. For once, S. feels as if he is not the least-liked creature on the ship.[11]

Maelstrom blows the same sequence again, and the crew responds with more stillness and silence. Only after he blows it a third time are there nods and whistled rejoinders. A whistle comes from the woman at the wheel, and the ship changes course sharply, heading off until it is racing on a dead run. Jibs are hoisted; a spinnaker flies; the ship seethes with velocity. There's been a change of plans, a significant one, and time—however elastic it may seem on these waters—is of the essence.

[11] I have often been asked if I know what became of the monkey that took the stage at the Prix Bouchard ceremony. I do not know. The one time I asked Straka about it in a letter, he responded, "It's on my goddamned back. Where else would it be?"

→ But I call bullshit on Straka: Calais didn't define his life. He did.

MAYBE A REF. TO WHEN THEY REALIZED THE S HAD BEEN COMPROMISED /BETRAYED?

seems like what happened at the award ceremo. pretty much defined the rest of his life. Or influen. it, anyway.

FILOMELA CONFIRMED— "EVERYTHING GOES BACK TO CALAIS." BOUCHARD HAD MANY AXES TO GRIND.

→ I THINK SO, TOO— ALTHOUGH I THINK IT WASN'T AS MUCH ABOUT THE MONKEY (WHICH, SURE, MADE A MOCKERY OF BOUCHARD) { 272 } AS IT WAS ABOUT THE CALAIS MASSACRE. THE PAMPHLET VMS MADE + HAD DISTRIBUTED THERE LAID OUT EVERYTHING THAT BOUCHARD HAD BEEN TRYING TO COVER UP (+ WAS SUCCEEDING). I THINK THAT'S WHAT GOT THIS WHOLE THING STARTED—A WAR OF NARRATIVES—TH ONES WRITTEN BY THE POWERFUL + THE ONES WRITTEN BY THOSE WHO POSED THE BIGGEST THREAT TO THAT POWE

They hold that course for two full days—two days in ship-time, S. reminds himself, which makes him wonder how much of his life is being lost on this errand. During that time the weather darkens, the sky turning into a solid sheet of gray that obscures the sun and the moon and the confused stars alike. They pass through squalls that churn the waves into froth and dump inches of rain in minutes but pass on quickly, the world resettling itself into its sturdy posture of unremitting grayness.

Through most of this, S. remains in his cabin. He ascends to the deck from time to time to clear his mind in the fresh air, to stretch his knotted limbs, to agitate for more water or another miserable biscuit, to pace in search of answers that stillness fails to provide. Those disconcerting sounds from over the water are still audible, but the ship is speeding along, putting distance between itself and the sounds' unseen source.

Below, in that cramped and stinking space, the boards of the bulkhead accept what the fishhook carves into them, letter after letter, word after word. While the words that S.'s mind puts into his hand are rarely the ones that appear in the pale meat of the freshly-wounded wood, this no longer

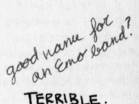

good name for an Emo band?

TERRIBLE.

Have to turn in the Williams paper tomorrow. I've got nothing. I am so fucked.
Don't even know why I'm writing this.

bothers him; the phenomenon no longer seems shocking or even strange. He rarely bothers to inspect the results anymore.

He also occupies himself with the materials from the valise. He studies the photographs, attempting—perhaps in vain—to fix those unremarkable faces in his memory. He compounds a small quantity of *Sanguinem ulcera*, following the steps on the page religiously, and the result has a gut-twisting smell of ammonia and almond and decomposing flesh. He realizes he doesn't know what to do with it, doesn't *want* to know what to do with it, doesn't want it anywhere near him. From the stern, he drizzles it into the waves, hoping—again, perhaps in vain—that the ship will not be leaving a trail of murder in its wake.

At night, he dreams of Sola. The dreams are mere fragments, scraps of narrative, and they come in different emotional tones and textures:[12]

He is swimming in a mountain lake, and she is waiting for him on the far bank. They are at high

---

[12] Straka did make more frequent use of dream sequences in *Coriolis* and in this book than in his earlier works. I do not know if this was a conscious aesthetic decision. I suspect, though, that it might have been a consequence of his exhaustion with the difficulties of the "real" world, in which he had to spend great amounts of time, energy, and concentration not just on his work but also on the maintenance of the privacy and anonymity he craved, perhaps even needed.

Handwritten marginalia:

Did you ask her about Summersby?

— I DID. SHE SAID ~~SHE~~ HE WAS A FRIEND — THE ONLY FRIEND OF VMS'S SHE KNEW WELL. SHE'D NEVER HEARD ABOUT HIS CONFESSION. WHEN I TOLD HER, SHE LAUGHED, THEN GOT A LITTLE TEARY.

SHE THOUGHT SUMMERSBY DID IT TO TRY TO END THE MYSTERY SO THEY (MACINNES'S S) WOULD LEAVE HER ALONE.

So Moody's going to be wrong if he's relying on the confession.

PROBABLY — BUT WILL ANYONE KNOW? ALL WE HAVE IS FILOMELA'S OPINION.

If Summ. was such a good friend, why didn't he tell her who Straka was? And whether she could ever expect to meet him?

BET IT'S CONNECTED TO THAT LETTER HE SENT GARCÍA FERRARA — THAT THERE COULDN'T BE ANY TRACES OF THEIR "FRIEND," OR ELSE THE WHOLE PROJECT WOULD FALL APART.

Makes the most sense if Vaclav Straka was VMS. If there's no evidence at all that he's even alive, then he can't be suspected, can't be tracked + killed, etc.

PERFECT FIGUREHEAD (GHOSTWRITER? BEARD?) FOR A GROUP THAT'S TAKING ON THE MOST POWERFUL PEOPLE IN THE WORLD.

Not so great if you fall in love w/ someone + can't pursue it.

AND YET YOU CAN QUOTE LONG PASSAGES FROM SOT + WINGED SHOES. AND ALSO REMEMBER WHEN + WHERE WE'RE GOING TO MEET.

Priorities.

— I'VE BEEN THINKING ABOUT YOU EVEN MORE THAN USUAL. HARD TO CONCENTRATE.

Me too: Trying to study for Art History — last exam before fin. Not making much progress. Can't retain anything.

elevation: the flora consists solely of twisted krumm-
holz formations, and the moon, fat and gold, takes
up an eighth of the night sky. He strokes and kicks
through ink-dark water but gets no closer to her.
She waves, calls out something that might be his
name, and he strokes faster, kicks harder, but gets
no closer—he might even be drifting backward—
and this is when he feels tiny punctures breaking
the skin of his belly, thighs, feet, and legs as leeches
begin feeding on him, and the dread that grips him
has nothing to do with losing blood or realizing
he has become some other creature's prey but rather
has to do with fear of what he will look like to her
when he gets out of the water, and he wonders
whether perhaps it isn't better to drown—

And this: [She is waiting for him in the passage to
the orlop deck. He cannot tell whether she is bar-
ring him from entering or beckoning him to come
with her; she stands perfectly still, and her face,
backlit, is unreadable.] For no reason that he understands, he opens his mouth and screams. Is it a
scream of anguish? of frustration? of fear? Strangely,
he cannot tell. Whatever its source or purpose, it
surprises him in the dream and jolts him awake in
the hammock, which swings violently—

DO YOU WANT ME TO
MEET YOUR PARENTS
WHEN THEY COME,
OR NOT? I'M HAVING
TROUBLE READING YOU.

I'm having
trouble reading me.
I don't understand
why they're coming—
not when graduation
isn't even a month
away. They want
something, but I don't
know what it is. Why
are you so hot on
meeting them?

I'M NOT. I JUST WANT TO
BE THERE... FOR YOU, I MEAN.

—and he is awake just long enough to register his pounding heart and sweaty skin before the fog steals back over him—

—and he is on a roof amid a cluster of old pigeon coops. A bird arrives, a message tied to its leg with black thread. S. intuits that the message is from her and that it has come over a great distance, but when he unrolls the thin paper, he can make no sense of the shapes that are inked on it. They are words, he knows—and they are *her* words—but the alexia that has stricken him is total. He needs to send a response to her, needs desperately to have *some* words pass between them, and he puts pen to paper, rolls it up around the bird's tiny, hollow-boned leg, and knots the thread. It isn't until after he releases his messenger to the gray skies that he realizes he forgot to make a single mark on the page. The bird disappears into an anvil cloud, and S. waits and waits for it to emerge, but the bird never does.

And this: he and Sola are in an enormous, echoing room of stone walls and floors; of burgundy and gold rugs, arrases, drapes; of furniture scaled for impossibly large people. They sit, pressed tightly shoulder-to-shoulder, at the center of a sofa, the distant armrests of which rise above eye-level. Before

{ 276 }

---

them, on a table with swirls of gold inlays that induce a mild vertigo, are dozens of sets of false teeth, each contraption more complicated than the last, some of them so ghastly that it chills him to imagine how they might be made to fit into a mouth. Sola turns and opens her mouth as if to speak, revealing a space of uninterrupted pink. S. runs his tongue over his own gums, finds himself toothless as well. The dream-imperative is clear—they must both try on sets of teeth until they find ones that fit—but they sit, unmoving, because neither will risk looking monstrous to the other, and this dream goes on for what feels like forever (O, fickle and variable Time!), ballooning impossibly as they sit there, sit there, sit there, ever in silent anxiety, toothless and still, waiting for something to change—

S. awakens, soaked in sweat, to a dull thud and a jarring halt in the ship's forward motion. A chorus of whistles above; footfalls heavy with purpose thumping over the deck. He hears the sounds of sails falling and furling. He yawns, rubs his stiff and aching jaw, feels a residue of dread chilling his insides. Nightmares, he understands—much like the shifting blood-tides on Maelstrom's charts—care little for borders.

{ 277 }

Handwritten marginalia:

I don't want us to let this happen.

I'D BETTER START FLOSSING MORE. Seriously. We can't just sit around being all passive + waiting to see if there's anything between us.

DON'T YOU THINK THERE IS? But how much?? Apart from our Straka project, I mean.

So really—what is this? A last-month-in-town fling for me? Do we both want it to be more than that? Can we make it more than that? Because one of the things I've learned is that wanting it isn't enough.

I'M WITH YOU. SO WHEN WE GO TO THE PARK: NO STRAKA, NO NEW S, NO MOODY, NO JACOB, NO ILSA, NO OVERBEARING PARENTS, NO DROWNED UNCLE, NO CLASSES. NOTHING BUT US. (FOR ONCE.)

He spins out of the hammock and hurries up the ladder so quickly that he misses a rung and turns his ankle. He seats himself on the edge of the hatchway, dangling his legs into the open space as if waiting for the pain to drain away. The air is mist-filled and bracing, the sky a relentless gray. He inhales deeply and gratefully.

The ship has docked at a decrepit-looking pier on a small, gray island that looks to be the very definition of Nowhere. A quarter-mile inland, at roughly the island's geographic center, a monolith of volcanic rock disrupts the gray flatness. It rises a steep thousand feet from the surface, then terminates abruptly in a deep, irregular crater, leaving its peak—and, indeed, the idea of the mountain it used to be—implied in the emptiness above. Molten black outcroppings extend from its sides like begging arms, ironic mementos of the planet's penchant for cataclysm, its indifference to anything but the eternal rearrangement of itself.

The only sign of habitation is a long, low-slung warehouse made of weathered wood and connected to the pier by a ramshackle plank walkway. The walkway runs a foot or so above the island's inhospitable surface, which is slickly black and jagged and

REF. TO BOOK II, CH. 29 OF CORIOLIS (CAPT. ERASMUS DISCOVERS THE BLACK MOUNTAIN, WHICH SERVES AS AN AXIS MUNDI)

————————

cruel-looking (a crowded graveyard for some sharp-rimmed bivalve, perhaps), likely to gash a bare sole at the instant of contact. As S. surveys this landscape, which ranges in hue from black to cinder to ash, he imagines himself leached of color, an insignificant smudge before a panorama of monochrome.

The crew has begun unloading crates from the hold—crates that are smeared and splotched with stains of a familiar and disconcerting cast. They are hefted through the aft hatchway, then lugged, one sailor at each corner, across the deck and deposited on one of several rickety wooden carts at the top of the gangway. Despite the crew's frailness, they work relentlessly, with grunts of exertion taking the place of whistles.

Why unload here? He thinks of that building in El-H—— with its secret subterranean space and decides that this island must be a safer place to store cargo of any value; he cannot fathom anyone's choosing to invade it. And what is this cargo of value? Of how much value is it? And to whom? And where are those few sailors going, the ones carrying empty buckets and picking their way across the rocks on an angle that takes them far left of the warehouse. The answer—the solution to the riddle of the orlop, and

————————

perhaps even to his place in this insane amnesiac world—is in that warehouse and in those pots once they are filled, and S. resolves to discover it all while he is here. He studies the patterns of movement on the deck below him, contemplates the route and timing of his escape from the ship.

He is confounded, then, by the sight of Maelstrom, at the top of the gangway, calling him forward with a curled finger.

The walkway trembles and complains under the big man's weight. S. looks down at what he'll fall upon when the thing collapses: a shardy expanse of conchoidal black rock, knapped and honed and polished by the aeons. He kneels. He runs his hand over one of the smooth surfaces. The rock is warm to the touch, and its gloss shows him a ghost of himself.))

Behind them rumbles a fully-laden cart, pushed by three sailors and pulled by three others. It nearly spills when one wheel slips off the edge of the walkway, but the sailors wrestle it upright. They point it squarely forward and continue. Maelstrom shoots a two-fingered whistle from the loading bay, and S. continues forward as well. When he arrives at the

{ 280 }

entrance, Maelstrom grabs him by the collar—not roughly, but not gently, either—and pulls him inside.

The warehouse is cavernous, with many times as much space as the building in El-H——, and it is at least three-quarters full of crates: crates lining the walls, crates stacked to form aisles that run the length of the room, crates stacked to the ceiling in some places, crates of different sizes, shapes, shades, ages. Many—most—have blue-black spatters and splotches. Despite the dampness outside, there's not a hint of mustiness. It might be the black rock, he thinks, storing heat, drying the air, staving off decay. Down one aisle, S. sees a group of sailors transferring crates from cart to stack. When he takes a step in their direction, Maelstrom again grabs him by the collar. *Nah*, he says. He points to a doorway along the back wall, pushes him in that direction. *Y'workins ou' there.*

"I don't understand," S. says. And he doesn't, although he says this primarily to stall for time, to watch the sailors stacking, to notice everything he can about *their* workins.

Cambin plans, Maelstrom says. *Y'got t'viz the Lady now.*

"Sola?" S. asks, perhaps too quickly.

Handwritten marginalia (bottom left):

JUST ABOUT EVERY DAY I'LL SEE SOMEONE OUT OF THE CORNER OF MY EYE OR IN A CROWD + THINK SHE'S YOU. SO DISAPPOINTED WHEN I SEE SHE'S NOT.

Better be!

SERIOUSLY: I'VE NEVER GOTTEN SO CLOSE TO LOVING SOMEBODY BEFORE

That's the *first* declaration of not-quite love el've ever gotten.

Handwritten marginalia (bottom right):

JUST TRYING TO FORCE MYSELF TO KEEP PERSPECTIVE. IT'S ALL HAPPENING SO QUICKLY.

el get that. + el'm coming from a place where el said love a lot. el don't think either of us knew what it meant, most of the time. Or maybe this is the right way to say it — el don't think either of us knew what it meant to each ofus. B/c love's not just one thing. Right?

Maelstrom snorts. *Dunt y'wish. Move y'self. Time's scortin.*

The back door opens onto a walkway that runs a drunken line toward the mountain. It feels even less structurally sound than the path from pier to warehouse; it bows and rebounds as he walks, here and there scraping against the rocks below. The wind picks up, gusting across his path, and S. finds it no small challenge to keep his balance.

The path hits the base of the mountain and ends. S. steadies himself in the wind, looks for another trail, fails to find one. He looks up, scans the rock face for hand- and footholds he can use, realizes that even if there were such a path to the top, the sharp rock would rip his hands to bloody rags. He spits and curses. He is supposed to get himself up the thing—he understands it with that dream-imperative clarity—and it irritates him further: yet another grave challenge to an end he does not understand, yet another reminder of the tragedies in the mountains above B——.

He contemplates turning back. What would he lose if he refused to play this role in which he's been cast without his consent? As he mulls this, though,

Remember what you said when we were on the pathway that went over the river?

I SAID A LOT OF THINGS. WE WERE THERE FOR A REALLY LONG TIME. I PRACTICALLY GREW MOSS.

Shut up. I mean when you said you were finally forgiving yourself for what happened to your uncle. Do you think that's going to change your relationship w/ your parents?

I HAVE NO IDEA. I'LL BE LESS ANGRY ABOUT THE WHOLE THING. DOESN'T MEAN THEY'LL CHANGE AT ALL. MAYBE WE'VE ALL DRIFTED TOO FAR.

SO IF VACLAV WAS VMS, THAT MEANS:
- HE SURVIVED HIS JUMP;
- HE MET EKSTROM + THE REST;
- THEY EITHER HELPED HIM RECONSTRUCT HIS BOOK OR PUT HIS NAME ON ONE OF THEIR OWN (ALTHOUGH BRAXENHOLM SEEMS LIKE A PRETTY YOUNG GUY WROTE IT);
- AND HE (BUT MORE LIKELY THEY) DECIDE TO MAKE THEIR STATEMENT @ THE AWARD CEREMONY; makes me wonder how much he was doing b/c he wanted to + not b/c ~~they wanted~~ him to.
- AND THEY DECIDE TO RIDE THAT MOMENTUM AND MAKE "V.M. STRAKA" THIS PHENOMENON OF RADICALISM.

he notices a narrow track of smooth but scored rock skirting the base—black on black, and hard to discern in the dim, slanted light—and he finds himself stepping off the planks, getting his footing on the trail, and following it around the broad base. From there it winds up the mountain in lazy, inconsistent switchbacks.

The Lady. What kind of lady would live in a place like this?

He spits. He curses. He follows the path upward.

From the top of the decapitated mountain, he can see the entire island: the rocky shoreline, the blasted black sprawl of obsidian fields, the two walkways, the warehouse, the dock with the ship still tethered to it, and nothing more. No sailors are visible on its deck; it could be another portrait of the same terrain, its story the absence of life.

He approaches the edge of the crater—the site at which this mountain collapsed in on itself, ages ago—and looks in. More black-on-black: it's difficult to tell where the bottom is. The wind howls, swirling unpredictably. The chill numbs his fingers, cheeks, nose. If he loses his balance—or simply lets his resistance slacken—the wind will dump him into

---

Handwritten annotations:

I UNDERSTAND COMPLETELY WHY HE'D GET INTO IT— THE BOOK IS A HIT, HE'S RUNNING W/A BUNCH OF WELL-KNOWN WRITERS, HE GETS TO TAKE A KIND OF PUNK-ROCK STANCE AGAINST THE WORLD, + HE GETS TO BE @ THE CENTER OF A REALLY BIG SECRET. WHAT 20-YEAR-OLD WOULDN'T LOVE TO DO THAT? (+ IF HE GETS A CRUSH ON DURAND IN THE PROCESS, THERE'S NO WAY HE'LL GIVE UP BEING AROUND HER.)

But on some level they were using him.

BUT HOW DO YOU GAUGE THAT? HOW CAN YOU TELL WHO'S USING WHOM? YOU CAN TELL THAT THERE WERE STRONG FRIENDSHIPS INVOLVED. Seems like there were a lot of complicated relationships. And that's not even counting Straka (Vaclav?) and Filomela.

THE ESSENCE OF DEPRESSION

HERE'S THE THING: IF VACLAV WAS VMS, AND HE DIED (FOR REAL, IN HAVANA, PROB.) W/O LEAVING ANY TRACE OF HIMSELF ANYWHERE, THEN THERE'S NO WAY FOR US TO PROVE IT— NO WAY TO PRESENT IT AS ANY DIFFERENT FROM ALL THE OTHER WILD CONJECTURES ABOUT VMS. EMERSON-PLUM WON'T PUBLISH IT. NO RESPECTABLE PRESS WILL.

You don't know that. And just because no one will publish it doesn't mean it's not true. It just means you won't get the attention you want. If we're right, we're right, and there are many ways to get the word out. Many. Ways.

the volcanic depths. He steps back from the edge, suddenly (and, to him, mysteriously) cautious.

Turning away, he lowers his head and plows through the wind toward the cottage, which he has been trying to ignore since he arrived at the summit and saw that the trail led to its door. He will put off the meeting no longer.

The cottage is made of the same weather-bleached wood as the warehouse, though it looks sturdier, its seams tight, its angles true. The word that runs through S.'s head is *intractable*: it sits here atop a dead mountaintop on a lifeless island, defying wind and rain and good sense. *Push all you like*, it seems to say. *I am going nowhere.*

There is a small door, and on the door, a large iron knocker. S. pauses. This is where his life—his remade life—has brought him: this weighty knocker in his hand; this door to a shack on the rim of this dead mountain; this mountain on this strange island, this island hidden in these strange seas. Each strange juncture has led to the next and now he is here. He is here, and it is nowhere.

He knocks.

From inside comes a voice, impossible to make out for the thrum of the wind. It might be an

{ 284 }

Still bummed we couldn't find that creek. Didn't expect everything to be the same after so long, but I really wanted to find that spot where I saw the birds.

LIKE VMS TO BOUCHARD
And you,
to Moody.

EXCEPT I'M FAIRLY SURE THAT MOODY THINKS I LEFT TOWN AFTER I GOT OUT OF THE BIN. HE THINKS I RAN.

Does that really matter?

ISN'T IT BETTER IF THE PERSON YOU'RE DEFYING KNOWS YOU'RE DEFYING HIM?

Wondering how Bouchard must have felt—he knew someone was publishing the books + hunting his agents, but he didn't know who. All he had was a name.

JEN:
DON'T LET THE ADMINISTRATION PUSH YOU AROUND. IF THE CAMPUS COPS HAD ANYTHING SOLID AGAINST US, WE'D KNOW BY NOW.

invitation; it might just as easily be a dismissal. He shoulders the door open and steps inside.

The room is lit with a soft orange glow. Three candles gutter in plain, tarnished silver holders on a long reading table. On the table are six or seven enormous books, each of them at least twice as big in every dimension as Sola's copy of the Sobreiro. The air is warm, though S. sees no source of heat. A bookcase covers the entirety of the far wall, holding similarly-sized books, all of which look well-worn, all of them bound in brown leather with vertebral rings knobbing the spines.

Covering the other three walls are paintings and drawings of ships: dhows and schooners, junks and longboats, clippers and barques, triremes and galli-vats, drakkars and carracks, prams and proas, sampans and yawls, and a hauntingly familiar xebec. The pictures have been executed without any particular skill but hung with care in simple, well-made wooden frames. The Lady, apparently, is someone with a taste for precision.

And there she is: sitting behind a desk, showing S. only the top of her white head as she hunches over, writing in one of the enormous books, her nose nearly touching the page. Somehow the scratching

---

Handwritten marginalia:

You're right. I could go to grad school. Get a degree in library science. (Of course you could

I know people can. It's just never occurred to me that I could.

MANY SHIPS, MANY TRADITIONS

IT'S FUNNY—THIS IS A LOT LIKE HOW FILOMELA LOOKED WHEN I MET HER

TURNS OUT SHE'S WRITTEN A BUNCH OF NOVELS. (SHE SAID SHE DIDN'T REMEMBER HOW MANY; ARTURO GUESSED IT WAS AROUND 30.) NEVER BOTHERED EVEN TO TRY TO PUBLISH. WASN'T INTERESTED. SHE SAID WRITING THEM WAS ENOUGH.— You should've asked to Read one. (assuming any of them were in English.)

ALSO: SHE HAD CARMINA BURANA PLAYING — REALLY LOUDLY. SHE LIKED TO WRITE W/IT ON B/C HE LOVED IT— TOLD HER SEVERAL TIMES THAT IT HAS THE TRUEST, MOST INTENSE EXPRESSION OF PASSION HE'D EVER HEARD — FAR MORE SO THAN ANYTHING HE'D EVER WRITTEN OR COULD EVER WRITE. — That's like the most concrete thing we've ever found out about him. It feels weird.

I DON'T THINK SHE WOULD HAVE LET ME.

MEANING YOU DON'T THINK IT'S TRUE? — No. Just that it feels weird.

of her pen on the paper is louder than the wind that pummels the cottage.

"Excuse me," S. says. "I was told that I need to see you. The big sailor sent me."

The woman moves so slowly that S. wishes he could complete her actions for her. She lays the pen aside, blots the page, pushes her chair back from the desk, and uses the desk for leverage to raise herself, which she does in a cadenza of creaking and crackling joints. She shuffles toward him with her head still down. Is it possible that she has spent so much time with her neck in that position that it can hold no other? He contemplates the aging of his own body, the stiffness in his lower back, the soreness that has afflicted his hip and knee ceaselessly since that night in the Old Quarter.

"Thank you," he says, for the effort she has invested in him already, but he immediately regrets having done so. Her astonishing age has precisely nothing to do with her intentions.

She stops at arm's length from him. She raises her head.

He gasps; he cannot stop himself. The left side of her face is a featureless expanse of splotched and striated burn tissue. The eye is simply a hint of a

{ 286 }

Handwritten marginalia:

How did she seem, health-wise?

⌐SHE WASN'T VERY STEADY WALKING— ARTURO USUALLY HELD HER ARM—BUT SHE'S STILL SHARP. WHICH MAKES ME THINK SHE WAS FORMIDABLY SHARP BACK THEN.

We knew that pretty early on. I did, anyway. You, Mr. Scholar, were a little slow.

QUERY: WILL YOU EVER GET TIRED OF REMINDING ME OF THAT?

answer: not effing likely.

FLORIS? ↓ Explain?

ACC. TO VARIOUS ACCOUNTS, THIS IS EXACTLY WHAT FLORIS OF BRUGES LOOKED LIKE AFTER SHE SURVIVED THE 1ST ATTEMPT TO MARTYR HER.

So why is Straka putting her here? Is it a joke about the whole British-girl-channeling-dead-nun thing? It doesn't _seem_ like he's trying to be funny.

MAYBE HE THOUGHT FLORIS AS A COMRADE. THE REASON SO MANY PEOPLE WANTED HER DEAD WAS THAT SHE WAS WRITING THINGS THAT EXPOSED ABUSES OF POWER (MOSTLY IN THE CHURCH, B STILL: IT'S SIMILAR TO WHAT STRAKA WAS DOING. →

depression; the ear does not exist; her nose shows scarring along its side but remains largely intact. That side of her mouth is sealed and lipless.]The other side, he notices, is half-haloed with pinprick scars.

He looks away, studies her necklace: a piece of obsidian, small, rectangular, and rough-edged, on a leather string. She raises her arm, tips his chin upward with a trembling finger. *Look at me*, she says without speaking, and he does. She is wearing wire-frame glasses; over her left eye they are lensless, and over her right the glass is cut like a gemstone, with many facets—an insectlike compound eye. In it, S. sees a reflection of himself, shuffled and incoherent.

You have choices to make.

I've heard that before, he replies, though his mouth is closed and the words exist only as thought. *It hasn't been true yet.*

You have them. And they are about how, and even whether, you will live.

I can't make choices like that without knowing who I am. Without knowing all the implications.

He watches her set her jaw, narrow her many eyes under the glass. He is disappointing her, perhaps even angering her. He feels himself flush, feels

[Handwritten marginal notes:]

Elsa asked me to stay around after lecture today. She said she knew I was working w/ you + that I was asking for trouble. She didn't come out + threaten to fail me, but it really seemed like she was holding it over my head. Definitely saying I should back off.

SO WHAT DID YOU SAY? I said I had no idea what she was talking about.

GOOD. BECAUSE SHE CAN'T FAIL YOU FOR ANYTHING LIKE THAT. WHAT SHE CAN FAIL YOU FOR IS YOUR PERFORMANCE.

YOU CAN'T EVER KNOW IN ADVANCE. BIG DECISIONS REQUIRE FAITH.

So Straka was saying she was part of the "tradition".

But metaphorically? Or literally— as in, she was part of something like The S hundreds of years ago?

DEFINITELY THE FORMER. DON'T KNOW IF LATTER CAN EVER BE PROVED. IT'S JUST LIKE SOBREIRO.

sweat tickling at his hairline. As he wipes his fore-head dry, he notices how far his hairline has retreated.[13] He feels doubly cursed: to be squander-ing so much of his life on this ship, and worse, to be aging in land-time all the while.

Then you'll die, and it won't matter who you ever were.

Tell me what's in the crates. What happens below deck.

Her mouth twists in what might or might not be a smile. *The workins.*

I have to find out what that means. What it is.

You don't have to. You may choose to try. That's one choice.

And the poisons? I'm to go out and kill?

That's another. Understand: the hunters are close and closing in. They've found us on the waters.

The map. The bleeding map.

The map shows it, yes.

Those are my only choices?

You could do both. Or you could walk away.

And do what? And be who?

---

[13] Some readers might wonder: is this a hint, perhaps, of what the real Straka may have looked like at this point in his life? To them, I say: readers, do you think that a writer of Straka's calibre is incapable of imagining a character's physical being? Must you assume that a writer borrows every trivial detail about a character from himself?

{ 288 }

Straka had to be well into middle age when he wrote this. Maybe more aware that he was running out of time to be with her?

AND PROBABLY GETTING REALLY, REALLY TIRED OF RUNNING — LIKE S. IN THE INTERLUDE.

So I probably shouldn't tell you this because I know you're self-conscious about the age difference, but Jacob called me last night + said he'd heard I was getting involved with "some weird old guy." He said he was "expressing concern" + that if I needed to talk to someone, I could always come to him. NOT WORTH A REACTION.

COULD SEE HOW VMS WOULD DECIDE TO KEEP AT IT — KEEP LIVING THAT S. LIFE — IF HE DOESN'T KNOW ANY OTHER WAY TO BE. + THE STAKES MUST FEEL HIGHER EACH TIME ONE OF THEM GETS KILLED.

And there's Filomela, who's trying + trying to convince him that he can leave it. —→ OR THAT — LIKE THE LADY SAYS — HE CAN DO BOTH.

———

She tilts her head, and S. watches the images of himself in her lens reorienting themselves. He wonders about the fire that took the other half of her face.

Aren't you going to ask about Sola?

Her question startles him. He doesn't want to admit that Sola had slipped his mind. She ought to be his first concern, but there is so much strangeness around him, so many other questions that want answers, too. *I didn't know you knew about her.*

There's always the question of Sola, the Lady says. *It's in the air. It gets into the lungs, and from the lungs into the blood.*

Which of the choices takes me to her?

Maybe none. Maybe all. There's no way to say in advance.

They fall wordless. The wind roars outside. There are no whispering voices in this place. Not on the ship, not here.

Mind the time, she says. *You can't be left behind. No one lives here.*

He should get back to the ship before the crew returns—he'll have no better chance to get to the orlop deck—but he doesn't want to leave the cottage on the mountain just yet. *The books. I want to know about these books.*

———

{ 289 }

[Handwritten marginalia:]

This is huge. LOSING FOCUS on love. It's totally passive + not-dramatic, but it might be what kept happening w/ him. SEEMS LIKE VMS REALIZES THAT HERE, THOUGH. KNOWS IT SHOULD BE DIFFERENT. Finally. But he still doesn't believe it enough to decide to change.

So LOVE IS ESSENTIAL? UNAVOIDABLE? ROTH?

I think Straka proved it could be avoided. WE DON'T KNOW ANYTHING CLOSE TO THE FULL STORY.

You're taking his side, and you're the one who actually met Filomela? A woman who is a hundred years' worth of *awesome*?

I DON'T THINK SHE JUDGED HIM SO HARSHLY. SHE WAS SAD, NOT ANGRY.

Her hand shakes as she points to one of the leather-bound slabs on the reading desk. *Sit. Look all you like. But mind the time.*

He sits in a rickety chair before the book. The same symbol graces both cover and spine:

$$((\ \mathfrak{S} \ ))$$

Are all the books marked with the *S*? He checks the other books on the table: one has an *H* shape, in a similar script; another has an ornate rendering of the Greek *psi*; another of the Hebrew *alef*. The Urdu *che*. One is an ideograph. Another is marked— titled?—with a character from an alphabet he does not recognize. He squints at the bookshelves across the room; he cannot see clearly, but it looks as if each book bears a single character on its spine.

He opens $\mathfrak{S}$ and leans close.

On the first page is a charcoal drawing of his ship (*no*, he reminds himself, *the ship on which I've been held*)—or, rather, an earlier version of it, when it was a harmonious whole, a shipwright's realization of a xebec that would fly across the main and leave sailors aboard other vessels dumbstruck with envy. With each page S. turns, he finds another drawing of

---

[handwritten, top left]

Have you been to the café today? There's a flyer with the S. on the bulletin board. All it says otherwise is: "E.H.: Call me—important." No number.

IF HE'S DEMANDING THAT I CALL HIM "IMPORTANT," IT MUST BE MOODY.

Getting laid has made you funnier.

UM... REMEMBER: YOU WERE THE ONE WHO WAS WORRIED THAT OTHER PEOPLE MIGHT READ THIS.

IS VMS SUGGESTING THAT THERE'S MORE THAN ONE S? OR MORE THAN ONE VERSION OF IT? AN S OF WRITERS IN MANY LITERARY TRADITIONS? (FITS W/ ALL THE PICTURES OF DIFFERENT SHIPS.)

She was so great with languages... why couldn't she tell which was Straka's native one?

SHE SAID HER BEST GUESS WAS CZECH, BUT SHE DIDN'T TRUST HER JUDGMENT—SHE KNEW THAT THE BEST SCENARIO FOR HER WAS IF VACLAV WAS VMS, BECAUSE NO ONE KNEW HE EXISTED + HE PRESUMABLY DIDN'T HAVE ANY ENTANGLEMENTS... SO HE'D BE THE ONE WHO COULD MOST EASILY GIVE EVERYTHING UP + GO AWAY W/ HER.

the ship, along with marginal notes cataloguing the changes it has undergone.

He flips forward, ten to twenty pages at a time. Again and again the ship sheds a feature and dons a new one, reinterpreted and remade. Some of these changes are noteworthy (the mizzen replaced by a tower of oak with a noticeable warp; the bowsprit a stunted approximation of the graceful original); others insignificant (a dozen cleats replaced by ones with marginally longer horns; a deck plank swapped for one cut a fraction of an inch too narrow, with tar to fill the seam). Some of the changes are felicitous; many more are not, each one seeming to widen the gap between what was intended and what turned out to be.

One page describes the wholesale reassembly of the vessel after it was sunk by cannon fire; another— quite near the end of the book—shows its resurrection after a sundering by waterspouts. By the final pages, it has become the mad assemblage of misfit masts and decks and hatches and portholes and scuppers and bulwarks and bowsprit and wheel and rudder and sails that compose the ship as he knows it. A horrible thing.

He hauls back the thousand-plus pages to the very first, his hands quivering with fever or fatigue.

Intended by whom? Who decides what you're supposed to be?

He blinks several times. Are they the same ship? Intuition tells him they are, though perhaps he is being influenced by the fact that the pages are all held together within the same covers.[14]

Why? Why have these drawings—schematics, really—been collected, bound, annotated, preserved? Why were they created in the first place? And why, in each of the drawings, are there lines and curves cleverly concealed in the artist's shading of the hull that—if you relax your eyes and don't strain to see it—form the word SOBREIRO?

He looks around the tidy room. He twists in the creaking chair. The door remains closed. The wind still beats furiously outside. The candles have nearly melted into themselves. And the old woman is gone.

Of course she is gone. No one lives here.

The wind has shifted, carrying sounds from the warehouse to the mountaintop. S. can still hear the crew working, can hear whistles and grunts of exertion, can hear crates scratching and thumping across him.

---

[14] In this scene is all the proof we need to conclude that Guthrie MacInnes was not Straka. There is *no possible way* that MacInnes could let pass such an opportunity to discuss identity theory without offering an exegesis on history's most inane, soporific, herniated, and self-indulgent attempts to address such questions (one or more of which might be MacInnes's own) that would culminate in a smug and self-righteous burst of pedantry.

{ 292 }

Handwritten annotations:

FILOMELA SAID ÇMI CAME TO NEW YORK & IN EARLY '46 W/ A STORY ABOUT HOW HE DESPERATELY NEEDED TO GET IN TOUCH W/THE REAL STRAKA. FLASHED A WAD OF CASH WHEN SHE SAID SHE DIDN'T KNOW.

which she didn't.

RIGHT. SHE WAS GLAD SHE DIDN'T KNOW. SHE DIDN'T WANT HIM TO GUESS ANYTHING FROM HER RESPONSE. BUT SHE'S ALWAYS WONDERED IF SHE MADE A MISTAKE + GAVE HIM SOMETHING HE COULD USE.

THE COMPOSITE THEORY—"V.M. STRAKA" JUST A NAME ALL THE OTHER WRITERS COULD USE—A FIGUREHEAD FOR A MOVEMENT.

(WOULD EXPLAIN VMS'S CONTINUITY BEYOND DEATH OF INDIVIDUALS.)

Even if that's true, it doesn't tell us who Filomela fell in love with. (It can't have been all of them!)

I really hope Moody has the Sobreiro. That way when he gets exposed, it'll go to a safe place where people can study it.

YOU'RE MORE CONFIDENT THAN I AM.

I know he has it. And I believe we'll nail him.

(Maybe even us!)

WHERE ELSE IS GOING TO BE SAFE?

Could try the café, see how it works.

HAS TO BE A PLACE WHERE WE KNOW NO ONE ELSE WILL FIND IT—EVEN ACCIDENTALLY.

There's a lockbox in the office there.

SO I'D HAVE TO ASK YOUR FRIEND TO GET IT FOR ME?? NO WAY.

Should we give up on using the book? Email would be easy—can you at least think about using it?

→ EVEN LESS REASON TO TRUST IT NOW. + I LIKE HAVING EVERYTHING WE'VE DONE/FOUND/NOTICED IN ONE PLACE. EASIER TO SPOT CONNECTIONS. NOT VERY PRACTICAL, I KNOW. . . .

··· BUT I STILL LOVE THAT WE'RE DOING IT. LOVE HEARING YOU IN THE MARGINS. SO T MY FAVORITE BOOK, ~~IT'S~~ IT WAS THE CENTRAL TEXT FOR MY DISSERTATION, AND NOW IT'S ALSO THIS SCRAPBOOK OF US.

So we're scrapbooking partners. That's hot.

SHIP OF THESEUS

———————

OK, YOU'RE RIGHT — THAT'S LAME. BUT DON'T YOU STILL LIKE DOING IT THIS WAY, TOO? AT LEAST WHEN WE CAN'T BE TOGETHER?

Of course. But I'd rather be together more.

other crates as they're stacked, unstacked, pushed, dragged, restacked. He looks out toward the dock. The ship's deck is still empty.

He does not *have* to race, unseen, back to the ship and down the aft hatch and onto the orlop deck—it is one choice among many. But it is the one he chooses. If he follows the path down the volcano, then follows the walkway until it makes one particularly drunken bend, then abandons it for a straight dash over the black rock to the ship (he might be able to stay out of sight from the warehouse until he reaches the dock.

On Mondays and Wednesdays, Moody gets to his office @ 11am, goes out for lunch @ 1, teaches class @ 3, goes home right after. On Tuesdays and Thursdays, he comes in @ 1 and leaves @ 5. On Fridays he doesn't come in at all. I would be such a kick-ass spy.
JEN: STOP. THIS IS CRAZY.

Does he fall on that brutal black beach?

Oh, yes, he does.

Not even forty steps down the slope, he stumbles, and both knees find knife-points of stone. By the time he reaches level ground, his trousers are in ribbons and blood is pooling, damp and sticky, in his shoes. He trips the moment he abandons the walkway, failing to break his fall; as he rises, he wipes away the blood, wonders abstractedly if the gash runs deep enough to reveal the white of his skull. He makes the final sprint to the ship with stinging eyes and a kneecap that has slipped from place.

Wait — why didn't MacInnes know who Straka was, if he was in the S himself?

MAYBE ONLY A FEW OF THEM KNEW — MAYBE THE ORIGINAL ONES, FROM PRAGUE 1910?

But Summersby wasn't an original. He wasn't there.

WELL, MAYBE THEY DECIDED HE COULD BE TRUSTED. OR MAYBE THERE WAS A SLIP + HE FOUND OUT. I DON'T KNOW. HOWEVER IT HAPPENED, IT SEEMS LIKE HE KEPT THE SECRET. EVEN TRIED TO THROW THE NEW S OFF FILOMELA'S TRAIL @ THE END.

The ship is perfectly quiet. No sounds but for the gulls high above and the water lapping at the hull. He opens the hatch, climbs down into the gloom, down one ladder, another, then another. He has a flash of worry that he will be discovered by the monkey, which will raise a shrill and bare-toothed alarm, but if the monkey is aboard, it does not reveal itself.

On the landing of the orlop deck, S. pauses and calmly acknowledges his abuse. He is shredded, he is sundered, and pain pervades all the spaces between. A sharp piece of obsidian has embedded itself bloodlessly in his palm; the flow begins only after he plucks it out and drops it into his pocket, pleased to have a souvenir of the island and a reminder of the sort of pain he must always be willing to endure.

He heads forward. Stops at a door. Blue-black stains cover the planking around it; there are spatters and streaks, blobs, dried puddles as dark as the mountain tarn. Thin, crooked lines stripe the wood along the path he has just walked. The door will not open, but he knows now that pain is nothing, and he aims his shoulder at it and crashes, crashes, crashes until the latch gives way and the door swings open. The flooring inside is even more densely stained. The walls. The plain wooden table and chair. The

{ 294 }

Handwritten margin notes:

No one is there. Means this is purely S.'s choice.

— I THINK HE KNEW HE WAS MAKING HIS CHOICES — HE JUST DIDN'T ALWAYS WANT TO ADMIT IT, EVEN TO HIMSELF.

CROSSING THE THRESHOLD ⟶

But it's the wrong threshold. It's the one that takes him away from Sola.

SO IS THIS VMS EXPRESSING REGRET? DOES HE WISH HE'D NEVER STARTED WRITING? OR WRITING W/ THE S? OR NEVER CHOOSING TO BREAK AWAY?

What do you think our threshold was? When we finally decided to meet? ⟹ MAYBE WE HAVEN'T CROSSED IT YET.

room looks like an abattoir where the writhing animals spurt vineblack.[15] WRITING AS VIOLENT ACT?

Ten crates remain, along with several dozen loose
sheets of paper scattered over the floor. S. gathers
the pages, reads the words that the sailors have written on them, front and back—fragments of stories,
stories for which S. will never have the beginnings
or the endings or middles, just these little glimpses
of what some sailor has poured out, has given up,
has spent of himself. SELF AS SOMETHING
FINITE / DIMINISHING

On the table is a stack of unmarked paper, a sand-
glass (which S. assumes will measure out three
hours), a pot of ink, and a pen. He wonders, briefly:
where does all the paper come from? It is a mystery,
yes, but one that is quickly forgotten when S. sits,
positions a sheet of paper squarely in front of him,
dips the pen, and begins to write, holding his bleeding hand in his lap so as not to stain the paper.

I don't have a whole lot left ...

It is a glorious thing, to be able to write with pen
on paper instead of nail or hook into oak, to feel
one's words flowing so smoothly from instrument to
surface, without the barriers of friction or poor
leverage, and yet with its own subtle tactile plea-
sures as the nib scratches tiny channels into the

---

[15] Cf. the slaughterhouse scene in Chapter 1 of *The Cordillera*.

sheet. And here, unlike in his cabin, here he feels no division between his mind and his hand, no errors in translation or static in the transmission: the words appearing on the page are the ones he has intended to put there, the images match the scenes in his mind, the sensations the very ones that warm his chest, prickle his scalp, push against his eyes.

What is it that causes him to lose track of his surroundings? Is it the primeval pleasure of expression? The pain of his injuries? The effects of his simultaneously spilling his life onto the page and into a crimson puddle at his feet?[16] The euphoria that comes when those sensations from his past (the sweet, comforting aroma of his mother's holiday cake in the oven, the tartness of the berries on his tongue, the tickles of cardamom and cinnamon, the fullness of butter; his father's face, with its hooded eyes and crooked nose and sleepy smile; peals of quiet laughter from brothers and sisters bundled against the chilly drafts that swirl through the apartment) breach the dam that has held them back and sluice through his mind, his nerve endings,

---

[16] Cf. *Wineblood's Mine*, p. 322 (in which the dying Caswell decides to write his last words in his own blood on the side of the mine cart, and all he can think of to write is an inventory of his meager possessions; he dies before even specifying who will inherit them).

FOR ME: IT USED TO BE WORK. NOW IT'S YOU.

Bullshit. Work's still part of it.

BUT NOT ALL. BIG DIFFERENCE.

his veins, his heart? Perhaps all of it. Some answers add up to little.

When S. returns to the world, to the literal space of the secret room on the orlop deck, he dimly registers Maelstrom's bulk in the doorway with a cluster of threaded faces behind him, peering in. The bearded sailor's mouth shapes words and his voice issues sounds. *Ah, hell*, he seems to be saying, *it dint ness t'go li' this.*

But now it does.

The crew pushes into the room. The whittler, the pouting girl, the men with the jug-ears and the broom-mustache, the boy from the ghost ship, they're all there—even the damned monkey, which is riding on the boy's shoulders. Three of the sailors pull S. to the deck and hold him down. He watches dumbly as the girl—whose pout has taken on a hint of a snarl—hands a fishhook and a spool of black thread to Maelstrom, who shakes his head and mutters several more words before he punches the barb into the flesh at the corner of S.'s mouth.

S., rising above himself, sees his own eyes go wide as the thread is pulled through.

Straka had to keep agreeing, though— every step of the way. Even if he didn't think that's what he was doing.

So it's what he really wants?

INTERLUDE

[TOCCATA AND FUGUE IN FREE TIME]

→ MIMICS PLOT STRUCTURE OF BLACK 19

Is this our clue for the code? Not getting anywhere with it.

Or with __any__ of the FNs.

*Nothing.
Grrrr....*

MAYBE SHE DIDN'T JUST CALL IT AN INTERLUDE B/C OF ITS FUNCTION IN THE BOOK... MAYBE IT'S A BREAK FROM THE CODED-MESSAGE CHAPTERS?

AGENT #4

A MAN rides an evening train bound for Budapest. He sits in his shirtsleeves; the unseasonable heat that filled Sarajevo during the day has persisted within the train even as they cross over the Dinarides. It is as if the heat has attached itself to the passengers themselves. Despite the late hour, they continue to pass bottles back and forth and chatter, *agitato*, about the shocking events of the day, the unknowns of tomorrow. *The Archduke is dead!* Serbs are cursed roundly, as are anarchists and syndicalists and Turks and nationalists of

another guy watching my place from the bus stop this morning.

JEN— PEOPLE STAND AT BUS STOPS + WAIT THERE. THEY HAVE TO LOOK AT SOMETHING.

Easy for you to say. No one's stalking you. As far as you know, anyway.

many stripes, although no breath is wasted on warm words for the dead prince.

The man does not join in;[1] indeed, he has a knack for avoiding invitations to social frivolity (and, really, for avoiding much notice at all). He sits and reads the newspaper that he picked up from a table inside Schiller's delicatessen. It was from behind this newspaper that he told Ilifá to get his team of armed and tubercular idiot-boys back on the street, on the off-chance they'd get another opportunity to accomplish what Čabrinović's bomb had failed to do a half-hour prior. And sure enough: the car appeared on Franz Josef Street—the foolish prince, his harridan wife, his flustered driver—and stopped directly in front of Princip, as if he were a passenger they were scheduled to take on and not a feeble, sweaty homunculus with a gun and a mission.[2]

Agent #4 is an asshole.

Even apart from the whole starting WW I thing.

---

[1] For a few years after the publication of Straka's *The Black Nineteen*, a bloody tale of political intrigue in the Habsburg Empire, there arose a theory that Straka's works had been written by "Apis's Amanuensis"—the mysterious, rarely seen, never-photographed (and possibly not-real) aide to Dragutin Dimitrijevic ("Apis"), who led the Serbian secret military society the Black Hand. (Rumors flourished that the so-called amanuensis was really the brilliant, murderous tactician behind the group's rise.) However doubtful it may be that this man wrote the Straka books, it is obvious that Straka is playing with that notion here in the Interlude. Strikingly, though, the author turns the tables on the Black Hand agent in this first section. But is this the Amanuensis-Straka killing off his past self? Rejecting a former ideology? A different Straka, killing off one of his rumored identities? None of these?

[2] An identical description of Princip, the real-life assassin of the archduke, appears in *The Black Nineteen* (p. 262 of Karst's English-language edition).

AMANUENSIS THEORY DEPENDS EXCLUSIVELY ON BLACK 19 FOR SUPPORT! + B19 IS AN OUTLIER — NOT MUCH OVERLAP IN MATERIAL OR STYLE W/ OTHER VMS BOOKS. THIS SCENE IS THE ONLY OBVIOUS REFERENCE TO IT.

It wouldn't be a theory at all if it weren't for all the rumors that Straka was a killer.

Two pulls of Princip's trigger finger did the work. Good night, foul prince; good day, opportunity. Telegrams from anxious statesmen and eager generals are surely inundating Véyoda at the Château already. The coming war, sure to be widespread and protracted, will make for excellent business.

The man fidgets, then rises out of his seat and arranges his heavy overcoat back into a tidy, cushioning ring; his hemorrhoids have been flaring since before the train even left the station. When he settles back down, he inadvertently meets eyes with a group of three men who are standing wobble-legged in the aisle and looking at him. It's funny, he thinks, that drunks sometimes notice him when the sober do not. These three are probably trying to figure out where he comes from, as his features—square, dark, heavy—are not like theirs. One of them has a spectacularly unkempt and filthy-looking beard; there could be huge populations of rodent life domiciled therein.

Yesterday's news? one of the other men says to him. *How can you read yesterday's news on a day like today?*

The man shrugs. *I know what happened today.*

This sets off the three drunks. Torrents of laughter. *Have a drink*, the bearded one says. *Drink with us.*

CAN YOU LOOK INTO WHERE DOBSON'S FUNDING CAME FROM? You think he's getting paid to make the Shimizu org.? HE'S BEEN A FEUERBACH GUY UP UNTIL NOW. Um... couldn't he have just changed his mind? Looked @ the evidence, drawn a different conclusion? NOTHING'S THAT SIMPLE IN THE STRAKA WORLD. You haven't slept in a while, have you?

The whole idea of The S, the New S, the new New S..., all the killings, a guy as powerful as Bouchard... it's completely unbelievable. It's ridiculous.

WE SHOULD PROBABLY GET DRUNK, THEN. Put up or shut up, buddy. Name a time + place.

Oh, I guess you meant that we'd be doing it separately.

SHIP OF THESEUS

The man squints at him in the dim light of the car. *Do I know you?*

Ha! the bearded one shouts. *Ha!* He slaps his knee. Nearly doubles over in hysterics. *Doubt it*, he manages finally. *I'm from far over—*. His wrist sweeps emphatically but in no particular direction; his words dissolve into a slur. MAN FROM NOWHERE (VMS)

Hand it here, the man says. If he has one drink, they'll shut up and go back to ignoring him. *To the changing world, then*, he says, and the men guffaw like asses. The plum *rakija* burns his throat. He neither likes the taste nor dislikes it. He has always believed that the cultivation of trivial preferences is a waste of his time.[3] He swallows, hands the bottle back, thanks them, lifts the newspaper again. If they persist, he'll use more emphatic means of discouraging their attention.

He looks out the window. Outside, the fields and the trees and the occasional farmhouses are brushed blue with early night. There is enough of a reflection in the glass for him to observe the crowd in the train and confirm that he is no longer being watched. He feels a tickle in his throat and coughs softly to clear it, but it persists. He coughs again, tries to grind his

I'VE HAD THIS—→
A PROF FROM CROATIA BROUGHT IT W/ HIM TO THE LISBON CONFERENCE. DRANK IT W/ HIM + MOODY + A FEW OTHERS. HE ARGUED THAT IF APIS'S AMANUENSIS WASN'T STRAKA, THEN HE AT LEAST TRAINED STRAKA AS AN ASSASSIN. MOODY KEPT POINTING OUT ALL OF THE ASSUMPTIONS HE WAS MAKING. THE GUY WASN'T HAVING ANY OF IT.

What about you?
I WAS KEEPING MY MOUTH SHUT + LISTENING —PRETTY MUCH WHAT I WAS SUPPOSED TO DO.

[3] The same might be said of Straka's attitude toward distractions of any sort.
Some passive-aggressive snark here?

So when I talk about how my parents expected me to do what I was told + not ask too many questions...

{ 302 }

———

throat clear with a series of increasingly vigorous *hrrrremms*. He hopes he is not catching a cold; he must be at the Château in two days, and the hemorrhoids alone are enough of an irritant when traveling. He coughs again. His airway feels constricted. He closes his eyes, concentrates on inhaling deeply. When he opens them again, he is facing the window and staring at a clearer image of himself; inky night has draped itself over the countryside and hidden it from view. His eyes look puffy, and his skin seems to have taken on the tone of the night. He watches himself gasp, sputter. He lifts a hand ineffectually to his throat, closes his eyes again.

Eventually the newspaper settles over his face. It will stay there until the train squeals into its berth in Keleti Terminal and a porter pokes at the stiffening body. Of course the Habsburgs' secret police will note the tragedy, file reports, etc., but really: a dead man on a train is just a dead man on a train, as long as his papers are in order, there are no significant valuables to be claimed, and there are no significant people who will be troubled by his loss. And this man is insignificant, he is nobody, he is nothing more than a name on some identity papers. (They do find a crumpled page, torn from a book, in his pocket. What sort

———

Handwritten margin notes:

I think I'm getting sick again. I so don't have time for that.

You really need to figure out who the hell Serin is. Don't you want to know if they're playing you somehow?

THEY'VE NEVER ASKED ME TO SHOW THEM ANYTHING. I CAN'T SEE HOW I'D BE PASSING ANY INFORMATION TO THEM. WHY TURN DOWN THE MONEY FOR NO REASON? IT'S HELPING ME DO THE WORK. — *That's prob what MacInnes said at the beginning.*

WOULD MACINNES AGREE? DOES THE MULTITUDINAL SELF CONTINUE AFTER DEATH?

of man carries torn pages from books? A crazy man!) There are no questions that must be asked, no fellow passengers who must be interviewed.

There are only two passengers who might even remember the dead man, and they are nearly insensate with drink, dragged off the train by conductors and left to slump and moan on the platform while crowds shuffle past with averted eyes. And their ephemeral companion on the train, the bearded traveler who'd passed a bottle to the dead man? They might speculate that he disembarked at some small, rural station hours outside Budapest (The only thing they'd remember clearly about him is that he was a selfish bastard to disappear without offering to share that third and final bottle with them.))

As for that bottle: it rests at the bottom of a river, the river along which the bearded man is now floating in a tiny, algae-splotched fishing boat as he heads back toward open water, making sure to keep his valise dry, its contents safe.

* * * *

Each time S. returns from land and climbs back aboard the ship, he walks directly to his cabin. He

{ 304 }

Vanessa saw Moody come into the café late last night—stumbling drunk. Came in, looked around. Ran into the newspaper rack when he left + knocked it over. Big scene.

WHAT'S WITH HIM? THE GUY'S GOT EVERYTHING HE WANTS IN HIS HANDS— OR AT LEAST WITHIN REACH. Guess that's not enough. (Or, maybe he's afraid it's all going to get taken away?)

How did the rakija taste?

I LIKED IT. I WAS DISAPPOINTED THAT HE'D ONLY BOUGHT ONE BOTTLE. Selfish bastard.

no longer catalogues the repairs, replacements, and
refittings that have altered the ship-scape in the
time he has been away. He registers such changes
only in a general, atmospheric way. To him the ship
remains the same; it is the ship in which he sleeps in
a cabin under the forecastle, the ship on which he
works—on the deck, in the rigging, in the room of
ink and paper—and it is the ship that takes him
where he needs to go. The ship is the ship he is on.
The ship is the ship it is.[4]

He is aware, in an abstract sense, that the population of crewmen continues to dwindle. Each time he
returns to the ship, another one or two seem to have
vanished. He doesn't bother trying to identify which.

Another thing he notes—or perhaps *endures* or
suffers is the more appropriate verb—is the painful
drone that fills the sky: ever louder, ever more
oppressive, equal parts deep-bass roar and metal-
on-metal scream, so textured with static fizz and
combustive pops that if he holds a hand aloft, he
can feel the sounds as if they are grains of sand
whipped by a desert storm, stinging as they pelt his
palm and the pads of his fingers. Nearly all of the
sailors now have their ears plugged with sail-scraps,

---

4 See fn 8, Chapter 7.

{ 305 }

resin, anything on board that can be scavenged for such a purpose.

When he reaches his cabin, he sets his valise down on the gnarled floorboards. He removes his shirt. He hunches over a basin with scissors and blade and soap and removes his beard. He blots his face dry with his shirt. He lifts the lid of a cigar box—a keepsake from one of his blurry visits land-ways—-and removes a fishhook and a loop of black thread. He threads the hook, re-sews his mouth, cuts off the thread-tails with the razor blade. (It's a simple task, no more difficult than shaving. He can do it in the dark. He can do it in a thirty-knot wind and seven-foot seas. He can do it in his sleep, and he probably has.) He puts his shirt back on, uses a sleeve to blot away the blood leaking over his lips, and rejoins the crew on deck, doing his part to keep this patchwork tub above the waves, waiting for his turn to go below and open a vein of ink and spill himself into those pages.

After three hours, he will haul himself back up to the deck, ink-stained, hypoxic, and groggy, and blow a note on his whistle. Work. Go down. Come up. Sleep, occasionally, even though none of the others seem to. Work, go down, come up. For days,

PER DR. B: IT'S EASY
TO GET USED TO DOING
THINGS THAT ARE
HARMFUL TO OURSELVES.
DO IT OFTEN ENOUGH
+ IT BECOMES ORDINARY/
HABITUAL— JUST HOW
YOU LIVE.

SHIP OF THESEUS

or weeks, or more; it's hard to say, as S. no longer pays attention to time. Eventually Maelstrom, from the aft deck, will blow the notes that tell him it's nearly time to disembark for the next target. S. will descend to his cabin, light a lamp, study the face in the photograph, pore over the documents detailing what this Agent has done in the service of Vévoda or his clients—the killings, the disappearances, the destruction, the intimidation, the suppression, the provocation—and set to planning. When he hears the whistles blow the Phrygian[5] tumble of notes that means *land ho!*, he will pack up the valise, cut his threads free, and climb into the dinghy. By this time, his beard is usually thick enough to obscure the wounds and scars around his lips—(not that anyone on land ever looks at him closely enough.))

This is his work, his ritual, his life. As Maelstrom often reminds him, *Innt no rest f'the damned.*

---

[5] This page of the manuscript, which is an inky mess, shows Straka agonizing over defining the musical mode in which these notes occur—a detail that, to me, seems less than trivial. This "tumble of notes" began as Phrygian, then became Mixolydian, then Locrian, then Dorian, then Locrian again, and it returned to being Phrygian just in time for printing. The tonal differences, he explained in a letter, were significant, and they were important to the "feel" of the detail. I confess I have a tin ear, and I think the detail would have worked just as well if he had made up a musical term for it, or if he had omitted mention of it entirely.

I don't understand how you're able to move around so much without being noticed. You're tall, you're good-looking, you've got that funky bent nose... I think you're pretty memorable.

IT'S MY RAFFISH CHARM. (MOST PEOPLE DON'T GET TO SEE IT.)

Um... I know that's not it. Seriously: is there something you do?

AVOID EYE CONTACT. NO ONE THINKS YOU'RE WORTH REMEMBERING IF YOU'RE JUST LOOKING @ THE GROUND. AND ALSO: USE STEAM TUNNELS WHENEVER POSSIBLE.

Feels like this n has to have a clue n it... she's going out of her way to mention all of these...

{ 307 }

* * * *

AGENT #34

The Edinburgh coroner's inquest lists the deceased's name as the name on his Dutch passport. This passport has not been forged or altered in any way. It is a spotlessly, incontrovertibly official document. It is also, however, utterly fictional. #34 sloughed his original name and citizenship when he entered Vévoda's employ. Records of his prior self no longer exist. *—PERSONAL HISTORY ERASED*

The cause of death is given as *cardiac arrest*. A more accurate characterization, though, would be: cardiac arrest, brought on by transdermal absorption of an untraceable poison (extracted from the leaves of a rare Andean nightshade) that was swabbed into his hatband while it hung from a rack in a crowded, dimly-lit Grassmarket pub.

In the dead man's trouser pocket, the coroner finds a leaf torn from a Finnish novel: pages 157 and 158 from *Archerin Tarinat*, by one Jänkä Sääksi[6] He has heard of neither the title nor the author.

Like Straka? No— wait—the candidates all continued being themselves even when they would've been writing as Straka, right? No one needed to, um, expunge his past?

—TRUE, FOR THE MAJOR ONES. MAYBE LOOPER + THE AMANUENSIS HAD SCRUBBED/SECRET HISTORIES.

Or Vaclav! —WELL, IT'S NOT THAT HIS HISTORY WAS ERASED— IT'S THAT HIS FUTURE DIDN'T EXIST.

ANOTHER ARCHER'S — → TALES . . .

also: Sääksi = Finnish for "osprey" ← (FICTIONAL AUTHOR)

---

[6] In my opinion, far too much has been made of the purported connections between Straka and the "Santorini Man" deaths. If you, reader, are interested, you will quite easily find a variety of sources full of spurious information on the subject.

I did look it up... and it seems like there were Santorini-Man-like deaths reported here + there into late '70s.

Whoa: found this on the El País website: body was pulled from the water near Barcelona last October—no ID— a page from a book in his pocket — cause of death not drowning but injuries consistent with a fall. —IT DIDN'T SAY WHICH BOOK?

— No. I'll see if I can find out. Prob. just a coincidence.

MAYBE. BUT STILL: A LOT OF THINGS THAT LOOK LIKE THEY'RE S OR NEWS-RELATED ARE HAPPENING ALL OF A SUDDEN. WHAT IF ALL OF THAT ISN'T OVER? WHAT IF IT WENT DORMANT, BUT IT'S NOW COMING BACK? MAYBE DESJ. FOUND OUT SOMETHING—

He hands the paper to the Detective Inspector, who assures him that it is spotlessly, incontrovertibly meaningless. As the coroner walks away, he notices the D.I. holding the page up to the light, studying it closely.

* * * *

When S. is on the orlop, with the pen's nib flying over paper, with ink spattering over skin, fabric, wood, what emerges on the paper are flashes of image, lightning-strikes of sense-memories, fragmented impressions of events. They refuse to be strung into coherent, linear narrative no matter how consciously he tries to arrange them so; in fact, the more he tries, the more the pieces resist his efforts. Many feel as if they belong to his past, but others almost certainly belong to the lives of others: he hears the voices of Ostrero's father threatening to sell him to the child-charmers in the *suq*, and of the parents in Pfeifer's village describing the misery of the Winter City; he chronicles the suffering he has seen and that of which he has only heard; he scribbles impassioned elegies for people he has never met and would never know were lost; he transcribes

Sounds a lot like Coriolis. It's all over the place.

WHICH IS EXACTLY WHY MOST OF THE CRITICS HATED IT. WRITERS + LIT PROFS TEND TO LIKE IT A LOT MORE.

a captain's log of voyages he has never taken on a ship he has never boarded; he chronicles (confesses?) his murderous skulkings on *terra firma*, although these accounts drift away from fact, toward distortion and grotesquerie as he—a dazed but rapt Hephaestus—sits and sweats in the greasy orange glow, watching his hands as if they were not his own. Sola never appears on his pages, though he senses her presence in the margins. She urges him to probe more deeply, to see more sharply, to continue asking *Why* even when the *Because* seems evident. But she never enters the writing itself. *I don't belong there*, he imagines her saying. *My place is outside it.*

What does it all add up to, this farrago of images and words and voices and lives and nonsense and rants and fever-dreams and soliloquies and abject lies? What is he making, line by line, page by page? What are the other sailors making? What, exactly, is the nature of those volumes accumulating in those crates? He cannot say. But somehow he feels as if he and Sola and they are working on one thing, a thing that reaches everywhere. His task is to keep putting words on paper, letting the tiny revelations accrete. *Relax*, Sola whispers. *You don't need to understand.*

Margin notes:

ONE CRITIC SAID THAT CORIOUS HAD "ALL THE EARMARKS OF A SLOPPY FIRST DRAFT — AND ONE PENNED IN AN ABSINTHE HAZE, AT THAT."

SAME GUY SAID SHIP OF THESEUS "GAVE HIM NO CAUSE TO RECONSIDER HIS EVALUATION OF V.M. STRAKA'S WORK."

I'm not surprised that Straka hated critics.

HE DIDN'T EVEN LIKE THE ONES WHO LOVED HIS BOOKS.

I think we can pretty much conclude that he didn't like anyone who wasn't committed to The S or who wasn't Filomela.

REDUNDANT. SHE WAS COMMITTED TO THE S. SHE JUST WASN'T IN IT.

Often, when S. returns from land, he finds that many of the crates have disappeared from the room. He doubts they've been stowed in the hold; these days the ship is always drafting high, running across the waves with a minimal load.

* * * *

AGENT #26 (YOU[7])

The Boss, that man in the Château, needs his copper, so you travel from Butte to Bisbee to Cananea to Ashio to Outokumpu to the Kafue to ensure that the supply flows freely and cheaply. And if that means from time to time you need to string up a Wobbly from a railroad trestle, or torch a tent-city, or send a message in a volley of axe-handles, or slit a chieftain's throat while hyenas laugh in the dark, or give a twitchy mine-guard a machine gun and a wink, or teach a lesson in gravity to some myopic muck-rake with ink-stains on his fingers, you do it, and you do it with stealth, professionalism, cold efficiency, and

---

[7] Interestingly, this section marks the only use of true second-person narration in Straka's entire oeuvre. (He did, of course, make occasional use of the direct-address you.) In my notes to him, I suggested that he try his usual third-person here instead, but he was adamant. If I—or anyone—ever again advocated changing the point of view in this section, he vowed, he would pull the manuscript from the publisher and throw it into the closest fire.

{ 311 }

Don't buy it. Would he really have been so harsh with her, at this point— when he was starting to understand what she meant (or could mean) to him?

WHO KNOWS? MAYBE IT WAS BECAUSE HE WAS STARTING TO UNDERSTAND THAT + HE WAS OVERCOMPENSATING. MORE LIKELY: HE REALLY, REALLY DIDN'T WANT ANYONE MESSING W/ AN ARTISTIC DECISION IF HE HAD A FEELING THAT THIS WOULD BE THE LAST BOOK HE'D EVER WRITE.

clarity of purpose. The Boss is reshaping the world according to his vision—the way all the greatest men in history have done—and you are an instrument of his epic will. Also: he gives you the option to take your pay in any currency you like.

You've never seen him, of course. You've never been to the Château, and you don't even know within which country's borders it sits. But you've heard stories from other Agents: once, years ago, the Boss invited a favored few to the Château. They toured the vineyard and then the cellars, where he opened a cask of the richest, most intoxicating wine any of them had before tasted: the deepest of reds, a flavor utterly unlike any other (so rich as to haunt the palate for hours), the very essence of a great man's will, picked and crushed and macerated and aged and decanted.

It is said that an Agent who does his (or her) job expertly—and you do, you pride yourself on it—may one day find that his (or her) handler has slipped an invitation to just such an event into the pocket of his (or her) coat. You have faith in this story. You long for the day you become part of it. Every now and then you'll buy the most expensive bottle of wine you can find, just so you can drink it down and tell yourself

{ 312 }

what a creepy way to think of yourself.

BUT NOT UNCOMMON. ISN'T THAT WHAT ANY TRUE BELIEVER THINKS? IT'S JUST A QUESTION OF WHOSE WILL YOU'RE FOLLOWING + TO WHAT END.

(JUST LIKE BOUCHARD'S)

Do you think the Bouchards stayed there after Filomela outed them?

NOBODY SEEMS TO HAVE REALIZED THAT SHE OUTED THEM.

I hadn't paid much attention to these lines before... but just now they made me realize that I don't have a story like that yet. That one big faith, that one thing I'm dying to be part of.

→ IT DOESN'T WORK OUT SO WELL FOR AGENT #26.

Ha, yes, ok, funny, whatever. So maybe Straka was dissing people who believe that particular story.. but don't you think everybody needs one or maybe a few?

THAT'S GETTING INTO SOUNDS-LIKE-MY-PARENTS TERRITORY.

that whatever the Boss serves at the Château will be many thousands of times more satisfying.

This is why you wish you weren't required to carry a torn page with you. Every time you reach your hand into your pocket and feel paper, you think it might be an invitation. Every time, disappointment stabs you when you realize that it's not that but another scrap of some madman's tale. But you have instructions, and you abide by them: you carry a torn page whenever your assignment is an S-dispatch. You are to carry it but not to read it. You are to leave it with the body, preferably in a pocket. If the body is unclothed, the mouth will do.

Why? you asked your handler once, a few years ago. *Isn't that precisely what The S does to Ours?*

We invented it, the handler said. *It is our signature, so to speak. When The S does it, it is a taunt, a cheap attempt to confuse and dishearten us.*

Well, it confuses me, you said before you could stop yourself. You wondered immediately if your career had just ended, if you would even leave the building alive.

(*Your job is simple*, the handler said. *It is to do what you're told.*)

Right now, on this rainy afternoon, you are riding a city trolley, heading toward a nondescript

{ 313 }

Handwritten annotations (top margin):

Not talking about reeligion. Not necessarily, anyway. Straka had faith in the story of himself as a writer, + in the story of how people need to stand up to power — + maybe in the story of his having a real connection with Filomela. She had faith in the story of herself as protector of his identity + of his words, and definitely in the story of what he + she could be together. And what I'm saying is: I don't have anything like that. That's what I expected to find by now. You have one — it's about you being an outstanding scholar.

Right margin:

THERE'S BEEN A BIT OF A BUMP IN THAT ROAD.

Shut up. At least you still have a road. You're not giving up just b/c Moody screwed you over. You still believe in what you can do.

I'M OLDER THAN YOU ARE I'VE HAD MORE TIME TO FIND A ROAD.

FOUND AN S IN THE TUNNELS — PRETTY CLOSE TO THE ACCESS NEAR STANDEFER. MOODY AGAIN — MEANS HE KNOWS I'M AROUND + USING THE TUNNELS. (IT SAID "CALL PLS" ON THE WALL NEXT TO IT.)

Are you going to call?

I DON'T KNOW. IF IT'S A MISTAKE, IT'LL BE A REALLY BIG ONE.

Near bottom, referencing "what you're told": Cf.: my parents. ← NICE TO SEE YOU GETTING INTO THE "CF." WELCOME TO THE **DARK SIDE.**

Now that I think about it, I know they weren't ordering me around — just trying to keep me in a nice, safe little box. Good intentions, but still.

Bottom margin:

I CAN UNDERSTAND THAT ← ... EVEN IF NOTHING HAPPENED IN THE PARK, THEY FELT LIKE THEY FAILED. AND THEY DIDN'T WANT TO FEEL THAT FEELING AGAIN. NO ONE DOES.

←ut I'm me. I'm not just thing for them to have feelings about.

WHY DO YOU THINK THEY'RE VISITING?

Don't know. But it can't be good.

building at an unfamiliar address. Your assignment is an S-dispatch, and an important one, considering the urgency with which your handler summoned you. The air in the coach is thick with the smell of damp wool. You think you feel a tug at your coat pocket—more a quick pinch than a tug, really—and you grab for the pickpocket's wrist but find only air.

You reach into the pocket and feel the page you are carrying. You relax. Everything is as it should be. But then you realize: you've always carried your torn pages in your left coat pocket, not your right.

An invitation?

You think you deserve one, although you'd never risk saying so aloud. You're the Agent who located the storehouse in El-H——. You have a long record of pristine S-dispatches, even if none of them has turned out to be the "S." you've all been looking for. You've invested years of your life in reliable, unquestioning service. The invitation is overdue.

You take the paper out of your pocket, shield it from the eyes that surround you, steal a glance. It is the page your handler gave you. It is filled with Oriental characters, which you do not understand. You feel a physical pinch of disappointment.

Handwritten marginalia:

NOTE, TOO, THAT YOUR PSU DEGREE WILL BE WORTH EVEN LESS IF YOU DON'T ACTUALLY GET IT.

Sounds familiar: you play by the rules your whole life, you do everything that's asked of you and you do it well, you've never caused trouble, and what do you end up with? a lame ex-boyfriend, a degree that doesn't mean much, and a lame job that sets you up for a lame, ordinary life, and oh by the way your dad had to pull strings even to get that for you.

WHAT'S WRONG WITH ORDINARY?

It's not as *good* as exceptional.

DIDN'T SAY I WAS (I MIGHT WISH I WAS

And don't try to make me believe that you're all at one with being ordinary. Because I know that's a lie.

You scan the faces around you, looking for any-one suspicious, notable—or notably un-notable, as you and your fellow Agents tend to be. The faces blur together. The trolley whines to a stop. A few passengers shuffle out the door and into the rain. This is when you notice the stinging sensation across your thigh. Blood weeps through a thin slash across your trousers. Before you can respond, before you can pitch yourself out the door to chase the person who did this to you, your vision dissolves into kalei-doscopic smears of color.

An artery in your brain bursts.

When the bus clatters forward, someone's wet-wool shoulder innocently bumps you and you fall, still gripping the torn page. You smack into the shoulders and backs and arms and knees of irritated strangers. You land on the wet floor, which smells like ashes and leather, and all you see are smudges of black and gray and yellow-brown. You die there, in a city where you are unknown, in a country where you are unknown, in a world where you are—and should be—unknown. You weren't quite unknown enough, were you?

The last feeling that bathes your system is dis-appointment, for surely, surely, you were going to

{ 315 }

I GET WHAT YOU'RE SAYING, THOUGH... IT'S LIKE WHAT I WAS FEELING RIGHT AFTER MOODY TOOK ME DOWN. ONE OF THE THINGS DR. BRAND TALKED ABOUT WAS THE DIFFERENCE BETWEEN BELIEF + EXPECTATION. AS IN: IT'S GOOD TO BELIEVE THAT OUR EFFORTS ARE LIKELY TO BRING POSITIVE RESULTS, BUT IT'S ANOTHER THING ENTIRELY TO EXPECT THAT THEY WILL. WE CAN'T DEMAND A PARTICULAR OUTCOME; WE'RE NOT ENTITLED TO ANY PARTICULAR OUTCOME. IT'S THE EXPECTATION THAT MAKES US SO MISERABLE WHEN THINGS GO WRONG.

I understand that. But I don't feel it.

AND THEN THERE ARE THE OUTCOMES YOU DON'T EXPECT, AS IN: I WAS DESPERATE + FEELING COMPLETELY ALONE, SO I STARTED WRITING IN A BOOK W/ A STRANGER. AND HERE WE ARE.

You're right. One caveat: we're also in a shit-ton of trouble. And please don't say "at least we're in it together."
FINE. I WON'T SAY IT.
You're thinking it. I can tell.

I left so many traces of myself with phone calls, searches—god, I was even emailing people without thinking about who they were. It never occurred to me to be more careful.
I SHOULD'VE SAID SOMETHING. WE BOTH FUCKED UP.

find that invitation in your pocket tomorrow, or
the next day, or the next—

* * * *

On each mission, S. encounters allies, facilita-
tors, and aiders and abettors, but he does not know
or seek to know anything about them or their lives
or even how they were contacted. It's safer, isn't it,
to be a glass-smooth surface of ignorance? To offer
no purchase to those who seek it? To remain unman-
ageable, perilous, deadly?

In turn, those who help him know nothing of who
he is; they know only what he does.

Perhaps he is a bit like Vévoda himself: a man
whose physical presence is intangible but whose influence on the world—on its boundaries and its resources
and its agonies and its aspirations—is anything but. A
man who exerts this influence from an estate located
in the principality of Rumor,[8] a place where the light
bends at unnatural angles and an ordinary man would
need special lenses to see what's truly there.

---

8 The Principality of Rumor was, I believe, Straka's original title for this novel; he mentioned it in a 1944 letter to me, in which he said he was working on a suite of literary
caprices and that he had no idea what shape it would eventually take.

---

* * * *

AGENT #47

((Clawing at his throat, #47 collapses forward onto the breakfast table in his hotel suite,) landing nose-first in the halved grapefruit from which he has just spooned an unexpectedly tart bite. A man who might be The S—certainly *an* S—appears (from where? the window ledge? behind the curtains in the adjacent room? inside a closet?).

This S pulls #47's head up from the tainted fruit. *I'd like this to end,* he says.

#47 shakes his head, speaks through the thick saliva that is filling his mouth: *It won't. Don't you know that?*

The man pauses. He tilts his head, as if he were listening to voices that #47 cannot hear. *I do know,* he says, finally.

#47 studies the man's face. Has that face ever been one they were instructed to look for? He doesn't think so, but perhaps his memory—perhaps his entire brain—is failing him. He is drowning in himself. He wants to ask: *How many of you are there? We keep dispatching you, and you keep coming back.* But he will not have enough time or breath.

{ 317 }

Handwritten margin notes:

I wasn't planning to end up @ my parents'. I just got into the car + drove fast. I didn't want that guy to see me anymore. Didn't want him — or anyone — to know where I was. NOT EVEN ME.

I'm sorry. I got scared. And the fucking motel catches on fire....?! The motel, + then my parents' barn? Don't even try to tell me it's coincidence.

Tired of this. Tired of school + stalkers + my family + campus cops + or people who just seem like stalkers. Tired of S + New S + New-New S + every other possible fucking iteration of S. Just want to get out of here + spend time with you without all the danger / stress / bullshit.

CF. CH. 10 — IT'S NOT ENOUGH OF A REASON TO GIVE UP.

Did you see the Daily Pronghorn today? Page 5? GODDAMNIT. I TOLD you IT WAS A TERRIBLE IDEA.

I guess now's not the time for me to say it's a cute picture of you...

apparently that's a good guess.

His poisoner will sigh, audibly, as he crumples a page.

* * * *

((It's not so much the killing that exhausts S. as it is the planning and rowing and trusting and traveling and stalking and killing and escaping and rowing and sewing and sailing and writing and sailing and writing and sailing and writing and planning and rowing and trusting, all the while knowing that Vévoda is hunting him)) too, that it's just a matter of time before an Agent's knife or gun or garrote or ice-pick[9] catches him unaware or some Vévoda-client-state's secret police tracks him down, snatches him off the street, turns him over for liquidation. (Of course, no matter what weapon is used to subdue him, it's a defenestration that will finish him off, that's what they do, they plant a page, and then they hurl you from a high place, they fall you, they plummet you.)

No, it's the constant churn, <u>the need to keep moving keep doing keep risking and there innt no rest f'the damned,</u> there jus' innt.

---

[9] This would appear to be a reference to the murder of Trotsky, whom Straka admired. There is no evidence of which I am aware, though, that the two men ever met or corresponded.

{ 318 }

Handwritten marginalia (left margin, top):
and the writing and writing and writing and writing a worthless paper on "Rain," all the while knowing that ⊂⊃sahas it in for me.

HERE: I WROTE ONE FOR YOU. IT'S GOOD. USE IT HOWEVER YOU LIKE.

<<[Stunned]>>

DESPERATE TIMES, ETC.

Handwritten marginalia (left margin, bottom):
SOMEDAY WE'LL SLEEP.

Someday we'll do a lot of things.

LIKE WAKE UP @ NOON, GO OUT FOR COFFEE + PASTRIES, SIT OUTSIDE IN THE SUN @ THE CAFÉ FOR HOURS...
Yes.

Handwritten marginalia (footnote area):
SIS DOCS SHOW LINK B/W BOUCHARD + STALIN; OMIT LINKS B/W BOUCHARD + UK

Handwritten marginalia (bottom):
Kolaches. I love those things.

You might say that S. has only himself to blame, that it is entirely his choice to fight this fight, to live a life of vigilant somnolence or somnolent vigilantism, to allow himself to be satisfied with Sola in the margins of his manuscripts instead of in his arms, and you might be right. But you ought to understand, too, that there's an attrition that takes place inside, one in which options and choices and even desires are ground ever smaller until finally their existence can no longer be confirmed by observation or weight or displacement but only by faith. Until desire is a ghost.

* * * *

AGENT #8

The less said about #8's death, the better. Even S. would concede that was more suffering than any one person should have to endure—even if that person were, say, a man who fired a bullet that ripped through Corbeau as she leapt from the cave, a bullet that, coated in the residue of her life, shed its velocity and dropped into the waves, too late rendered harmless but never forgotten.

[Right margin handwritten notes:]

WEIRD SHIFT IN POINT OF VIEW— NARRATOR TRYING TO CONVINCE THE READER DIRECTLY THAT S. ISN'T ENTIRELY TO BLAME.

Might as well have started with "Dear Filomela, Sorry you wasted your life, but..."

HE DOES BEAT HIMSELF UP PRETTY THOROUGHLY ELSEWHERE.

LIMITATIONS OF VENGEANCE

SOMETIMES I WONDER: HOW MUCH OF THIS AM I DOING JUST TO GET BACK @ MOODY? AND ILSA, TOO?

—You're doing exactly what you would have been doing. You're just a little more intense about it.

APPARENTLY I'M ALLOWING YOU TO MAKE RASH DECISIONS (WHICH, ADMITTEDLY, BENEFIT ME INDIRECTLY).

You're not "allowing" me to do anything.

* * * *

What little sleep S. gets is disturbed by hypnagogic terrors. He feels himself semiconscious but paralyzed, and surrounded by shapeless malevolent presences who watch him from the shadows, gradually approaching, tightening their ring around him. Sometimes he feels Sola entering the dream—actually entering the dream, not whispering from its margins as she does when he's writing, but existing *with* him and filling the air with a scent of clary sage.[10] With one loud, crystal-bell note that she sings from the deepest part of herself, she banishes the shadows back to the hell-pit whence they came, and he can settle back into desperately-needed sleep. But most of the time she does not appear, there is no crystal-bell note to scatter the shadows, and the ring around the room tightens and tightens around him until the shadows fall upon him as one, and he awakens with his limbs locked and aching, his voice raw, his screams resonating throughout the hull and the decks and all the spaces between.

[10] Allow me to revisit an earlier observation: we cannot necessarily identify the real-life models for characters based on textural details alone. Here, Straka chose clary sage as Sola's scent, but he just as easily could have chosen rose-geranium or kaffir lime or bougainvillea.

Margin notes (left, top):
I've had these since I was a kid. Not very often, but when they happen, they're terrifying. All you can do is watch the horrible things closing in on you, + you know that they're only interested in doing you harm.

DID YOUR FAMILY KNOW?

My sister did. We shared a room for a while when my parents were redoing the house. She saw it happen—she was awake and it totally freaked her out. She said the sounds I was making were terrifying. ← SHE WAS RIGHT!

WHEN DO YOU THINK IT STARTED?

It'd be a good story if I said it happened for the first time the night after I disappeared. But I have no idea.

Margin note (bottom left):
OK, I do know. It started that first night in the old factory.

Margin note (bottom right):
WAS THERE ANYONE LIKE THIS IN YOUR DREAM? SOMEONE WHO WAS PROTECTING YOU?

Nope. All alone. Eventually I learned how to wake myself up when it started to happen. Doesn't always work, but I'm the only one who ever saves me.

If only he could summon her.

Wait—

Can he? If not to the orlop, then to his cabin?

He can try. He has a needle, and there are fresh, unmarked boards patching the bulkhead. He can, at least, try.

* * * *

AGENTS #9 and #41

O, P——! City of defenestrations! City of ten thousand free-falls! City of gravitational re-education! You are a city in which an S-dispatch becomes a thing very like poetry!

The Boss must understand such poetry. Otherwise, why would #9 and #41 have been called in? Local resources are plentiful in the occupied city. Jackboot cadences drum the streets at all times of day and night, and those soldiers would think nothing of liquidating two subversives spreading lies over radio waves. Killing, smashing equipment, perhaps even burning down the entire block for good measure. The soldiers would carry out the task gleefully, as would the occupiers' secret police, as would the collaborators' secret police. But when the Boss

Handwritten margin notes:
I THOUGHT WE WERE GOING TO MEET UP AFTER YOUR PARENTS LEFT. WHAT HAPPENED? — Had to get away. Decided I didn't have 72 hours to spare.

Ct on the Williams. (I'm on a roll!) Think I need an a— on the final. You THINK ILSA CAN BE FAIR? Didn't before. Now I do.

O.S.S. DOCS: LINKS B/W BOUCHARD + NAZIS

wants something done in a certain way, that is the way in which the thing is done.

The intelligence is not certain—it never is—but this is what they know: the Boss's name (*Vévoda*, they whisper to each other, with the giddy thrill of transgression) is being broadcast over a shortwave frequency and linked to all sorts of malfeasance and treachery. And where there are such overt accusations about the Boss, there is also an S, if not The S.

(The Boss does not like to be the subject of stories. The Boss does not like to be known. The Boss, frankly, does not like to be thought about, except by those jockeying for his services. His clients appreciate this. They depend upon it.)

The offending radio signal has been traced. It originates here, on a busy street near P——'s central square, on the top floor of a building that houses the least compliant of the city's three daily newspapers. The broadcasts occur every nineteen days and nineteen hours—S.'s timing is impeccable—and the next one will begin tonight at eight. Each broadcast features two voices, one male and one female. This is surprising: S. has (or Ss have) always worked alone. In any event, after #9 and #41 visit the top floor of that building, both voices will be silenced.

{ 322 }

So if all of these sections are based on actual killings, is there any evidence that Straka (or anyone connected w/ the S) did broadcasts like this?

NOT THAT I'M AWARE OF.

It would be so cool to hear his voice.

DOUBT HE WOULD'VE BEEN THE ONE SPEAKING.

I know. Just saying.

———

#9 and #41 arrived in P—— on separate trains three days earlier. They met in a hotel with a view of the newspaper building. They enjoyed reconnaissant strolls through the quarter, compared notes over strong coffee and nips of brandy. They read through the S-files again and again. They mused aloud that only a madman would devote himself to being an impediment to progress, to political realities, to common sense, and to the natural flow of cash and service and product. They ate, they napped, they walked, they watched. They planned. They refined the plan. They each confessed, guiltily, a desire to turn these two S-dispatches into works of creative expression. Into art.

They settle on *narrative*. Of course the story of the broadcasters will end in twin defenestrations. That is a given. But perhaps there is art to be found in the context of their actions, in their motivations, in the desires that underlie their doomed rebellion against the Boss and all that Is.

#9 proposes a scenario in which the dangerously unstable male S snaps and sends himself and his paramour through the window in a murder-suicide. #41 demurs, favoring a double suicide. *Star-crossed lovers,* she offers. #9 is impressed. *That's good,* he says. *So very Shakespearean.*

{ 323 }

Window was open when I got home. I didn't close it. Too scared to go that close. Thinking about Desjardins.

Favorite class: Shakespeare through Performance. Took it last year. Studied the ———— tragedies, + we all had to perform in scenes as part of it — which was terrifying to me. I've never acted in anything, never wanted to. I had to be Cordelia in a scene from King Lear. Got so nervous. I thought I was going to pass out. Then the prof. — she was this tiny old French woman — said something about letting go — don't even remember what it was exactly — but it worked, and I let go, and it ended up being totally fun. And somehow that made the rest of the semester more fun, too. I know my tragedies inside out.

They disagree about the tone the broadcasters' suicide note should take. #41 wants something mawkish and saccharine about how their love cannot withstand the cruel fires of war. #9, feeling a sudden warm tingle in his underparts, proposes instead a confession that the two misfits can no longer live with the shame they feel about their degenerate sexual practices. #41 eventually concedes. She knows, and is rather in awe of, #9's long and impressive body of work, which goes back to the days of Vévoda's original Detectives. He sent one of S's wharf-rat confederates plummeting into a gorge (O, poetry!). He torched the library at Leuven. He sold the Japanese on the Mukden plan. He has performed dozens of S-dispatches, spanning three decades.

#9 writes the man's lines, and #41 writes the woman's. They read over their literary efforts together on a sofa in #9's suite, leaning closer and closer to each other until their shoulders touch. #41 finds herself with her hand on his thigh. She wonders: is this what people mean by love?[11]

---

[11] Many of Straka's characters find themselves confused by the notion, the feelings, the responsibilities, and the practical applications of love. As repellent as Agent #41 may be, this is a moment that reminds us that she has in her not just a bit of humanity but also a lost-child bewilderment about the world she imagines herself to have mastered.

{ 324 }

Handwritten margin notes:

My sister emailed me insurance photos of the barn after the fire. There's an S on the wall that was still standing. Are you still going to say it's a coincidence??

NO. BUT PANIC ISN'T A GOOD PLAN.

Please tell me how I'm supposed to not panic!!

FXC ARGUING THAT LOVE IS WHAT MAKES US MOST HUMAN — TO DENY IT IS TO DENY AN ESSENTIAL PART OF YOUR HUMANITY.

I ASKED HER ABOUT THIS. SHE SAID THAT'S WHAT SHE MEANT. VMS WROTE THE LINE, SO HE MUST HAVE UNDERSTOOD IT ON SOME LEVEL, + SHE WAS USING THE FN TO PUSH HIM ON IT. — And she never found out if it worked. SHE THINKS SHE DID.

So I guess we should remember that about Jacob, Ilsa, even Moody. Right? It's pretty much what everyone's looking for, even if they don't realize it + even if there's a lot of collateral damage. OURSELF TOO.

Ship of Theseus

At precisely 8:00 p.m., as #41 is smoothing out the wrinkles in her clothes, #9 turns on the radio, tunes it to S's standard frequency. The voices are small, barely penetrating the static. They talk about a lethal gas being manufactured in a Vévoda factory on a tiny Mediterranean island.

The targets are in place. The operation commences.

#9 and #41 stride past the soldiers who control the streets and who have been instructed not to notice them. They pass the darkened first-floor offices of the newspaper, that anarchist rag. They ascend the back stairway, five flights. They are quiet, confident, in complete harmony. (Each of them envisions, greedily, the celebration in #9's suite after their work is done and before they must depart P—— on separate trains.) From the landing they hear the two voices, which are befittingly weak and thin-sounding (#41 kicks the door open, and #9 silently thrills at her demonstration of power and will.)

Inside: one long and empty room. Not a stick of furniture. On the floor are a spinning phonograph and a microphone wired to a radio transmitter the size of an infant's coffin. No man. No woman. Just words, captured in the grooves of an acetate disc.

S.I.S. DOCS RE: RUMORS THAT ARP HAD SECRET FACTORY ON ITALIAN- OWNED ISLAND. UNCONFIRMED.

My mission is complete. Didn't have to kick the door open. Got the master key for Standefer from the Dept. secretary's desk.

THIS IS SUCH A HUGE MISTAKE.

But you're interested in what I found, aren't you?

#41 turns to #9 just as a tiny dart buries itself in his throat with a sound not unlike the parting of moist lips. The next dart comes for her before she can look away from him.

They fall to the floor, twitch and convulse together like partners in a dance. The bodies remain there, undiscovered, until the stench drives the newspaper's staff out of the building several weeks later. The editor-in-chief seeks out a member of the collaborationist police, asks for assistance, and is told that dead bodies in his building are his own damned problem—doesn't he realize there's a goddamned war going on?

* * * *

The ship: a dying aviary. Fewer sailors, fewer whistles. And the notes that blow now are not the rich, warbling tones that sang out when S. first boarded the ship (and, presumably, for centuries before then), but enervated squeaks that are no match for the terrible resonance that saturates the air, shaking not only the ship but the sea and the sky. The orlop is the only place one can escape from the tumult.

A charcoal haze dims the seascape. The ocean winds push, but do not clear, a stink of cordite and

---

[Handwritten annotations:]

Esp. in the 1930s. That was a really bad decade for them.

THE S WRITERS, DYING ONE BY ONE. →

So my old friends invited me to go out for "for-old-times" drinks. So irritating. It's like they're throwing themselves a wake. You know what bugs me most? They all know what they're doing next + they're all excited about it. I mean, sure, why not waste time being nostalgic if you've got nothing else to worry about?

WHY NOT JUST GO? YOU'VE BEEN GRINDING. NOSTALGIA'S NOT THE WORST THING IN THE WORLD.

Well, that was a mistake. All they wanted to talk about was "Jenny's new boyfriend." Roommate's been talking, I guess. They said Jacob found out + it got his attention SO WHAT?

charred flesh. And every now and then comes a nau-
seating wave of the smell from Vévoda's testing field
in the coastal mountains; it doesn't just *remind* S. of
the tarn, it fills him with the sensations of being
there, his feet on the bristly surface of the dead
meadow, his lungs laboring in the altitude, his
friends moving and talking and believing and trying
to conceal their fear from one another.

Why does the air smell like this? he asked Maelstrom early on, looking not so much for an answer as
for a way to extricate himself from the wolf-trap of
sadness that to this day snaps closed on him whenever he thinks of his dead friends. Why?

Tha's th' world burnin, sunnydags.[12]
You've smelled it before?
Time atimes. Nev' like this.

The strain is taking a toll on Maelstrom, on the
other sailors, on him. They've aged quickly, their
bodies declining in concert, their minds fogging as
one, their fears coalescing as they wait for whatever
it is that is coming for them.

---

[12] This line is an echo of one uttered by the cruel Wineblood in Chapter 6 of *Wineblood's Mine*. (Minus the *sunnydags*.)

{ 327 }

[Handwritten marginalia:]

BEEN THINKING ABOUT MY OLD FRIEND GRIFF... HE WAS A LIT MAJOR, TOO. WE BOTH DID 20TH CENTURY. MY SENIOR THESIS ON STRAKA, HIS ON PAUL HAMMOND PAUL (BRITISH AUTHOR, BOOKS WERE DENSE + DIFFICULT, + HE WASN'T WELL-LIKED, EITHER. ALSO: RIDICULOUS NAME). PHP WROTE @ THE SAME TIME AS VMS, SO WE USED TO JOKE ABOUT HOW COOL IT WOULD BE IF OUR AUTHORS TURNED OUT TO BE THE SAME PERSON — EVEN AS WE WERE ARGUING THAT THE OTHER'S AUTHOR WROTE CRAP.

Getting called in for a meeting w/ the head of PSU Libraries on Monday. Not good.

Fun. Are you still in touch?

IT'S LIKE THE SLEEP TERRORS. *Except we can't shout ourselves awake.*

I still think there's a code in the wall-writing that we're just not seeing yet.

SHIP OF THESEUS

* * * *

INVOCATION OF THE MUSE TURNS INTO FLAGELLATION OF THE SELF.

But you're supposed to invoke a Muse for inspiration, right? But that's not what he's doing—he's asking her to save him.

DO YOU MEAN S- OR VMS? Either way, it's bullshit—making it her responsibility to save him. He made his own choices.

O Sola! O for you to transcend this brightest bedlam of invention! Sing to me, Sola, of amour, and may your song pull like a current, carry me through these foaming rapids of blood and ink, for I am a man driven time and again off course.

~~O, sailor. O, for your trance to end, this mindless bedlam and deception! You're simply a sailor, no more. Days are long and nights disturbing. You've married a rudely foaming madness of blood and ink, and why? Damned man. Riven time and again, you're aught more.~~

Strikethroughs on the bulkhead, strikethroughs in the floorboards. In the cabin, everything that begins as a call to her comes out, somehow, as a curse of himself.[13] And so he gives up trying; he closes his

IF THIS IS VMS TALKING HERE, HE KNOWS IT'S HIS FAULT. HE'S SAYING HE'S DAMNED FOR CHOOSING BLOOD + INK OVER LOVE. AND I THINK THE STRIKETHROUGH SUGGESTS THAT EVEN THOUGH HE KNOWS THIS IS THE TRUTH, HE STILL CAN'T STAND TO HEAR IT.

You mean _see_ it.
[⌒⌒]

---

13 Compare S.'s different responses to his experiences with "mediated writing." In Chapter 7, he seems flummoxed by it, but one senses a bit of wonder in him as well. Here, though, we see S. resisting it, straining to overcome it, as if he is more certain of what he wants to say and cannot abide not being able to say it. Is it possible that Straka himself was grappling with a similar conflict—between artistic intention and execution? Between desire and the ability to express it? My correspondence with him offers no guidance on the matter, but as these seem like fairly commonplace struggles—the sort that beset many people, not just artists—I will venture to proclaim that it is more than possible; it is certain.

{ 328 }

eyes and writes—simply puts nail to board and makes shapes, without any intention, inspiration, or comfort. When he opens his eyes, he discovers that only one short sentence—a question—has been cut into the wood before him:

WHO IS SIGNE RABE?

* * * *

AGENT #2

#2 is dying in the driver's seat of a Cord 810 that is parked in the dark at Fort Point and registered in the name of a man who has never existed. The Agent's hair, much grayer now than it was in the photograph, is tousled by the Pacific breeze blowing through his window. He uses his dying words to taunt S., who has lingered in the back seat to watch his longtime adversary expire. *Go to the Territory,* the Agent says. *Find the governor. How surprised you'll be.*

At the morgue, when the jaws are cracked open, the coroner will discover pages 189 and 190 of _Ang Mamamana Kuwento_ (authored by one Liwliwa Siloy) crumpled loosely into a rosette.

{ 329 }

Marginalia:

Did you ask Filomela about this?

ALL SHE KNEW WAS THE NAME — SAID MACINNES MENTIONED IT CASUALLY BUT WAS WATCHING HER RESPONSE ... SHE THOUGHT RABE WAS DURAND BUT NEVER FOUND OUT FOR SURE.

She had no idea what she was asking ... (But didn't she know she'd be putting someone in danger by doing this? And for what — jealousy? Signe Rabe was just a name to her. No: a name, a rival, — PER ILSA : a threat.)

RABE = GERMAN FOR "RAVEN" —▸ DURAND?

NEVER ANSWERED. WHY NOT?

h. 8 code ↓ dn't matter ← her rival was already dead.

Went back and checked — These lines aren't in the original MS! Section ends on "intention, inspiration, or comfort."

SO SHE PUT A QUESTION TO HIM DIRECTLY INTO THE TEXT? GOOD THING HE WAS ALREADY DEAD — HE'D HAVE GONE BALLISTIC.

Maybe that's what she wanted — she was asking if he loved someone else.

SOUNDS LIKE ONE OF THOSE QUESTIONS WHERE SHE KNOWS THE ANSWER + IS TRYING TO GET HIM TO CONFESS.

Don't ever do that with me. Jacob did it. It was annoying as hell.

WHAT WAS HE TRYING TO GET YOU TO CONFESS?

I don't know. I didn't have anything to confess.

ARCHER'S TALE (TAGALOG) > *Silay = bird common in Philippines*

- THIS ACTUALLY HAPPENED — THE SF CORONER WROTE A MEMOIR MENTIONS THIS AS ONE OF THE UNSOLVED MURDERS THAT HAUNTED HIM. I MEAN, THE DETAILS (IE: CAR + PAGE) ARE RIGHT ON — EVEN THOUGH THEY WEREN'T IN ANY OF THE NEWSPAPER ACCOUNTS THE MEMOIR WASN'T PUBLISHED UNTIL THE LATE '50S.

▾ SHOULD I BELIEVE YOU?

So you think Straka's confessing? ⟶

WELL, HE COULD HAVE FOUND
OUT ABOUT IT IF HE KNEW SOMEONE
IN THE POLICE DEPARTMENT, OR
EVEN THE CORONER HIMSELF —
BUT I THINK IT SOUNDS LIKE
HE WAS THERE.

I didn't think so before.
Now I do.

CHAPTER 8

THE TERRITORY

THE **TERRITORY:** a remote stretch of tropical river basin, little-known to the outside world until Vévoda discovered the mineral wealth of the surrounding hills. Then he sent in extraction teams, sent in guns and money, sent in aspirations of modernity with which to enchant the indigenous, sent in overseers and chemists, sent in a private army to make sure the area remained little-known.

Shortly after Vévoda established his operations in the Territory, the government of an adjacent country sent in a detachment of its military to annex the land and claim its resources. None of those men returned alive, and days later that country itself was invaded, occupied, and gelded by a northern-hemisphere power with close ties to the arms dealer.[1]

Airplanes chartered by rival mining concerns for flyovers do not return. Naval vessels prowling the coast meet with inexplicable disaster. Spies posing as potential customers (or as laborers, or as anthropologists studying the locals, or as inept adventurers who've lost their way in the jungle) are mailed back to their handlers in multiple parcels. If any of Vévoda's employees leave the Territory, they do not talk; if any of them consider talking, they vanish before they are heard. (Zapadi, Obradovic, and Ledurga are not the only ones who have paid for seeing what Vévoda did not want them to see.)

What, exactly, is being stripped from the earth inside those hills? Iron and bauxite, says one intelligence agency (albeit one not known for its

[1] An earlier draft of this chapter contained a much longer and more detailed history about the Territory. While the vast majority of that history was tragic, there were some comic elements in it as well, including a sequence about escalating governmental attempts to contain, and thus possess, the area. What began with a hundred-mile-long painted stripe evolved (or devolved, depending on one's feelings about private ownership of land) into an army of effigies painted with fierce-looking facial expressions and positioned at regular intervals all around the boundary; which were replaced by a waist-high stone wall; which was replaced by a ditch; which became a moat; which became a moat filled with carnivorous eels, which were quickly eradicated by harpy eagles; whereupon the moat was allowed to dry up, the ditch was filled in, and a dizzyingly high rail fence was erected, and to that fence were nailed the old and rat-nibbled and much-less-fierce-looking-than-before border-scarecrows, and from there, the measures became absurd. I suspect that Straka made the wise decision not to distract readers with such an extended (if clever) comic set-piece at this point in the deadly-serious narrative of S.

{ 332 }

Clue for code in here? Title's no help.

NEEDLE IN A HAYSTACK.

Rail fence.

WHICH MEANS WHAT?

It means we know even more about how badly Filomela was hurting.

It's a rail fence cipher—look it up.

COOL. HOW MANY RAILS ARE THERE? AND HOW'D YOU FIGURE IT OUT?

FR says the fence is "dizzyingly high"—so I thought it'd be more than just a few. I hit it with the first one I tried. Guess? 19. Yup.

independence).[2] Zinc and molybdenum, says another. Pitchblende, says a third, and some rare metals as yet unnamed. All of this may be true, or none of it. What seems obvious to S., though, is that you wouldn't raise an army, orchestrate wars, co-opt regional *juntas*, perfect a vast regime of silence and blood simply to protect a bauxite mine.

So when S. imagines the Territory, he does not imagine a picturesque idyll full of the varied greens of dense jungle, the coffee-brown of a turbid river, the bright blues and greens of tropical birds flickering through the air. He sees instead hills slathered in a blue-black paste. He sees a jungle floor where foul-smelling and sticky blue-black webs dangle from the canopy, ensnaring creatures that will eventually die struggling in their grip. He sees a river that is an annelid ooze of blue-black pulsing toward the sea—not flowing but *pulsing*—slowly, incrementally, but relentlessly forward.

This is the Territory of S.'s mind, however. In reality, the river is a river, and it is the river it ought to be:

---

2 While he never confessed such a thing to me, I believe that Straka somehow had access to information contained in files maintained by several of the world's most fearsome intelligence agencies—including dossiers that had been compiled about him.

asked Vanessa if I could pick up shifts at the café. Nervous about library meeting. Might be blowback from Special Collections logs. → YOU DIDN'T DO ANYTHING WRONG IN THERE. IF ANYONE DID, IT WAS MOODY—OR MORE LIKELY, ONE OF THOSE GUYS W/A GUEST ID.

Someone might've set me up. Plus: Moody's a prof + I'm not. The Guest ID people must have powerful friends + I don't—all I have is someone who's been expunged. And don't forget Ilsa (although I'm guessing you never do.) ??? WHAT ARE YOU TALKING ABOUT?

a richly-silted, free-flowing waterway that empties itself into the sea. S.'s guides, a man and a woman, meet him at its mouth, waiting for him in the shade of a canoe they have tipped on its side. The man helps S. pull the dinghy up the beach, and they hide it amid marsh grasses that are as tall as trees.

The man and woman are young, nineteen or twenty at most. They avoid looking directly at him, although whether this is a matter of local custom or simply of good sense is not clear. The woman introduces herself as Anca and the man as Waqar. She does not volunteer a name for the infant who rides on her back in a sling. S. says his own name aloud, but Anca shakes her head. "Taraqachi," she says, pointing at him.

"S.," S. says.

"Taraqachi."

"I don't know what that means."

She regards him silently.

"All right," he says with a shrug. "Taraqachi." What matters is what you do, not what you are called.[3]

After the introductions, the guides speak only to each other, in few syllables and in a tongue unlike

---

[3] Here we see S. rejecting naming as being an essential component of identity. He first explored this idea in *Triptych of Mirrors*, an overlong, solipsistic, and commercially-stillborn novel that was published shortly before he and I began working together. In retrospect, though, that book seems to have served as a study for *Ship of Theseus*.

Handwritten margin notes:

IF IT IS, THEN VMS HAS TO BE ONE OF THE YOUNGER ONES: MACINNES, VACLAV, WECHSLER, SINGH, DROZDOV... ✳︎ ⟶

So what happened in 1930? Some kind of betrayal?

MAYBE HE KNEW WHAT WAS GOING TO HAPPEN TO HIM IN PARIS? SEEMS HARD TO BELIEVE. (AND EVEN IF HE DID, WHY WOULDN'T HE HAVE TOLD ANYONE ELSE IN THE S? WHY WOULD HE HAVE LET THAT PERSON STAY IN?

any real-life people who fit down here?

NOT THAT I'VE FOUND — BUT THERE MUST HAVE BEEN SO MANY PEOPLE WE'LL NEVER KNOW WHOSE JOBS WERE TO HELP VMS + THEN DISAPPEAR. WE CAN'T KNOW EVERYTHING. IT WAS A BIG + MESSY LIFE.

What about characters in a Straka book? Maybe Mr. and Mrs. Magnusson in Wineblood's Mine?

YOU'RE RIGHT — SOME PARALLELS.

ALSO: COULD BE AN ECHO OF STENFALK + CORBEAU — AS IF THEY'VE CYCLED AROUND AGAIN.

Found these entries in Ekstrom's journal: May 1929: "Our friend has become more like a son to me than I ever thought possible. A. feels similarly. Grateful."

November 1930: "Our friend arrived today. It is difficult to keep myself from weeping openly."

✳︎ The friend has to be Straka, right?

SIGNIF. OF NAME? No clue.

SHIP OF THESEUS

any S. has heard. Anca climbs in first, then takes the
valise from S. and stows it snugly underneath a fishing net. S. follows her. Waqar launches them from
the shore and into the rippling water.

Anca is in the bow, and when she faces forward
to paddle, S. finds himself face-to-face with the
baby, who focuses a gaze of cool, absolute appraisal
upon him. S. knows he looks a fright; the stitch-
wounds are weeping and his beard is not yet long
enough to hide them, his cheeks have sunk, scabs
and sores decorate his lips, his head is balding
irregularly, and a burst capillary has stained the
white of one eye. If they were to see him without
his clothing, see the bluish mottle that has spread
over his skin, they would surely abandon him in terror or revulsion.[4]

Waqar hands him a scrap of papery bark, on
which a face has been sketched in cochineal ink and
in surprisingly fine detail. It is the face of a middle-
aged man, bald and three-chinned, eyes narrowed
by his fleshy cheeks. The face looks familiar, though
S. can't quite say why. Only a few of the fifty-seven

---

[4] This is a moment that crystallizes one of the most interesting features of S. as
a character at this point in his development: while he is capable of killing cold-
bloodedly, he also seeks social connection (but feels insecure about his ability to
succeed in doing so).

{ 335 }

remain, and this face does not belong to any of them. "This is the governor?" he asks.

Waqar nods. He takes the piece of bark from S., wipes the image into a smear of red, and drops it over the side for the river to carry away.[5]

"This is Němec?" S. asks. Both of his guides' expressions darken at the sound of the name.

Anca gestures for S. to lie down in a narrow space along the center line of the vessel; they have gone far enough upriver that he must now hide himself. He feels confined by the damp fishing nets, and he cannot find a way to arrange himself so that the valise does not jut into his bad hip. The day is brutally hot. The humid air is difficult to breathe, and his beard itches like mad. He can hear the whispers, rising from the water and through the hull. The baby watches him, clearly unmoved by his plight.

Before, on the ship, Maelstrom had argued with S. about the mission to the Territory. *All y'gots a crypty frag some Agent baits y'with.*[6]

[5] In Waqar's action, we see that selves—specifically, iterations of our moral selves—can be effaced quickly, easily, and without a second thought.

[6] I can imagine Straka offering an argument that this is all that any reader has when he or she is presented with an author's story. His language would be deadly serious, but between the lines one would be able to detect a winking acknowledgment of his own jesting self-deprecation contained in Maelstrom's statement.

M+D just left me a message—said they're coming for a visit. I don't like it.

THEY HAD TO HAVE NOTICED HOW UPSET YOU WERE WHEN THE BARN BURNED. MAYBE THEY'RE JUST COMING TO SEE FOR THEMSELVES

If that's true, it's part of the whole problem. The entire story of my life.

APPARENTLY NOT THE ENTIRE STORY.

???

YOU'RE NOT AS HELPLESS AS YOU LIKE PEOPLE TO THINK.

How do you know what I think?

Oh, and also? I've never said I was helpless. & fuck you.

I HATE LOOKING AT THIS PAGE.

S. had nodded. That might be so. He'd be going nonetheless.

Vizz aroun', sunnydags. Smellat smoke. Pull y'digits ou' yer ears. Int no time f'excursin allwheres jus' so y'can solve y'self. Maelstrom folded his massive arms across his massive chest. He waited, and S. waited.

They stared at each other, silent amid the constant, maddening roar that surrounded the ship. The big man's concerns were justified, S. knew, and his argument was a good one. How much could one person's identity matter? Or, put more precisely: how much could one person's *knowledge* of his identity matter? But down on the orlop an hour before, S. had found himself writing about paddling up a tropical river, and he'd sensed Sola in the margins. *Keep going,* she'd said plainly. *Keep paddling and you'll find yourself.* When his shift had ended and he'd returned to the main deck, he did not follow protocol. He did not blow his whistle. He did not trundle across the deck in the twilight, did not climb the ratlines and take his place in the tops. Instead, he stood mid-deck and cut the stitches out of his mouth with his knife (that piece of obsidian, fitted into a whalebone handle). Feeling awake and determined and surprisingly *whole*, he'd stormed astern

Just so you know: I've pretty much gotten my shit together in my Marketing class. There was some begging, tears, etc. involved, but I made up all the work. It'll be close, but I think the only things between me + the degree are the Art History final + illsal. F Jaulkes.

THAT'S AMAZING. REALLY PROUD OF YOU. KEEP GOING.

to the chart-room and flung open the door, disturbing Maelstrom's contemplation of another dripping-red chart, and he'd made his demand.

They stared and they waited, until a burst of indigo light flashed in the western sky[7] and they both turned to look. S. had just opened his mouth to ask what had happened when the shock wave hit the ship, a sharp and heavy broadside that knocked them to the deck, sent boards and splinters and nails flying, dropped a sailor from the tops, rolled the ship nearly to the point of capsizing. A sound like shredding metal stabbed at their ears. The virulent smell was piercing and everywhere. From the deck, S. watched the sailor with the push-broom mustache fall to the deck, clutching his head and bleeding freely from the nose. The whittler whimpered as blood leaked out of one ear. The monkey, somewhere, shrieked.

Maelstrom pulled himself up on the rail, looked out at the sky where the light had flashed. S. followed his gaze and noticed six dark spots crossing the sky in a V formation just above the horizon.

---

[7] In February 1946, there were reports of strange indigo-colored flashes in the sky near the Dutch town of Wolvega. While the weapons manufacturer Arp Syndikat maintains a factory in the area, no firm connection between the phenomenon and their activities has been shown—or even remarked upon in print.

Airplanes. They were far, far off, yet the noise of their engines was deafening, as if they were swooping directly overhead, grazing the forestays. And then, after another flash of light—one that would leave S.'s vision streaked for a ship-time week—the airplanes vanished. The world fell quiet. Just breeze, gentle waves, and murmurs of fear trapped behind sealed lips.

They're in. Aint tract us yet, bu' they're in.

"In where?"

Where vessels li' us were formered safe.

"So what does—"

Means'll be comin in, offner an' longer. Tractin' us closer. He whistled, and the sailors who'd recovered themselves whistled back. It was a song of agreement and desperation. The plan: a jibe and a downwind run to the Obsidian Island to empty the hold. *Damt if we're goin down full up.*

As the jibs were being raised, Maelstrom took S. by the shirt and leaned in nearly nose-to-nose. *Droppin y' in the Territs onna way. Dunt mean y'won. Just safer y' plain-sight y'self landways, til we get th' lay.* He stomped away before S., overwhelmed by the sailor's breath—the very essence of putrefaction—could say anything.

Called my sister to ask WTF re: M+D coming. She said Jacob called them + said he was worried about me — because of classes + "how I was acting" + you. They asked her if she knew anything about what was going on with me. She said she told them about "that huge stack of crazy S shit" I had when I went home. God, she sounded so pleased with herself. I hate her.

YOU TOOK THAT STUFF HOME WITH you??

I wasn't going to leave it in the apartment.

The baby will not stop watching him.[8] It drools, it gums its tiny fingers, it wrinkles its mouth in curious shapes, it issues sudden cries for no apparent reason, but it watches him, and its attention is so disconcerting that S. sighs audibly when it finally drifts to sleep. Then he lets himself relax, watches the cumulus clouds drifting across the sky and the kingfishers flitting in branches that overhang the water. A harpy eagle dives from on high, disappears from S.'s view below the gunwale, then rises again, flying away with a whip-thin brown snake wriggling in its talons.

Waqar's foot nudges S.'s shoulder, then flips some of the netting over him. S. doesn't understand the need for more caution—he sees no signs of human life on the river or on the banks—but he trusts that they understand the local threats better than he does. He tries to ignore the fishy stink and focuses on the sounds: the *tzik-tzik* of insects, the *jeek* of a gray-winged trumpeter, the plashes of creatures breaching the river's surface.

---

[8] I will not be surprised if Anca's baby becomes the subject of much debate and conjecture amongst readers of this book. Clearly Straka intended to suggest something with the nameless baby's presence, although precisely what he meant is far from obvious. My sense is that we are to infer that S., in this moment, sees the baby—with whom he begins and ends at a distance, perhaps even at a mysterious impasse—as proof that there is no place for him in a conventional family life, that he has no choice but to continue with his dangerous work and his rootless life.

[left margin, handwritten] FUNCTION OF BABY? SYMBOL? METAPHOR? IRRELEVANT TO PLOT.

Is he imagining the baby he never had with Filomela?

OR WITH ANYONE.

SHIP OF THESEUS

and she emphasizes it in the footnote.

DISCREPANCY W/ORIGINAL MS.

He should, of course, be thinking about the governor—*Němec,* he repeats to himself, testing it again and again for any sort of familiarity[9]—but his mind is tired and the stale, humid air is stupefying. Without intending to, he falls asleep (could there be a worse place for a sleep-terror than in a canoe on a river that teems with carnivorous fish and reptiles?), and he drifts into a dream.

He is sitting in a canoe—a canoe made of steel rather than bark—and he is sitting in the stern, paddling with long, confident strokes instead of traveling as a lump in the bilge. The sun shines and sweat soaks his clothes, but chunks of ice are floating in the water, bumping the hull, scraping the keel. In the bow, facing away, is Sola. Her hair is long again, as long as it was when he met her in the Old Quarter, but her dark curls are now shot with dramatic bolts of gray. In a sling on her back is a monkey, although the monkey is so perfectly still that S. questions whether it is alive.

Sola does not speak, nor does she turn to face him. He knows, somehow, that some sort of contraband

---

[9] An interesting moment here, as S. slips back into the traditional assumption that there is something meaningful and durable about names. (Consider the ship: while it is nameless, and while it undergoes small changes almost constantly, its identity is never in question.)

———————

is stashed in the bilge between them, a cargo that would be dangerous for them to look at or even to acknowledge. He does not look; he feels, strangely, indifferent to the mystery. He paddles and she paddles, and they are close but utterly apart, wordless and faceless to each other, and they paddle this way into the chopping, foaming current, upstream and forever.

S. awakens when the tarp slips off his face and the sunlight turns his lidded view bright red. He blinks, lets his eyes adjust as the canoe follows a sharp bend in the river. The landscape has changed; while before the river was running through flat land, they are now in a deep valley. Dramatic, russet-colored cliffs rise at least half a mile into the air on both sides of the water.

The hills are green with vegetation, though on each face there is an oval red-rock patch that has been carefully cut out of the wild green, its boundaries crisp and assiduously maintained. Inside each one of these ovals is a petroglyph, carved in high relief. S. can see fifteen or twenty of them just by turning his neck a few degrees: There is a bird of prey with its wings spread. There is an open eye. A radiant sun. Three slender fish, arranged as sides of

———————

a triangle. A closed eye. An open hand. A lightning bolt. A figure that reminds S. of windmill blades. A ram's-horn spiral, a spider, a snake, a wolf, a bird.[10] Each figure is twenty-five or thirty feet high, large enough to show fine detail even at this distance, and the backgrounds have been shaded with a blue-black glaze to accentuate the effect of depth.

Some of the glyphs are riven with cracks, or pocked, having lost chunks of themselves to gravity. That those figures have been overlooking this valley for a long, long time is obvious, and S. is unsurprised when his guides ship their paddles and hunch forward in a sort of *salaam*. The quality of the silence in the canoe shifts from a simple absence of speech to a reverential hush.

The canoe drifts forward on its momentum. With Anca hunched over, the baby on her back looks straight up into the sky, and it smiles and gurgles. When she straightens to resume paddling, the baby again faces S. and returns to solemnity. The cloud-streaked blue vastness undoubtedly made for more pleasant scenery.

---

[10] Many of these images appear on walls in the titular cave of Straka's fourth novel. There are some subtle but significant changes in their appearances here, though. See pp. 48–55 of the English edition.

The changes don't seem significant to me.

ME EITHER

———

"Those figures," S. says quietly. "What are they?"

Anca's voice surprises him. He wasn't really expecting an answer. "Our stories," she says, keeping her gaze upriver. "Who we are and how we are here." From the stern, Waqar makes a *psshht* sound. Why? Is he worried they'll be overheard? Is there something about the figures that S. isn't supposed to know? Do their stories need to be kept safe from outsiders?

From far upstream come sounds of machinery: engines grinding behind a bend in the river, the hiss of exhaust, the repetitive thump of something heavy pummeling the earth. Waqar toes the net again, pushes more of it over S.'s face, and S. has to struggle to contain his irritation. He watches through the mesh as the canoe bears left, leaving the river and following a narrow, twisting tributary, then an even smaller one, then one smaller still. To their left is a clearing, with many canoes like theirs lined up along the riverbank. Visible beyond them are the roofs of thatched huts, shadowed by trees.

"Old village," Anca says. "Old ways."

"Do you live there?" S. asks.

"We always have," she says. "We always will."

———

———

These are their people, and yet S. must remain hidden. Trust, he gathers, is in short supply here.

Waqar makes one quick, furtive bob of his head, some subtle acknowledgment sent to shore. These people—or some among them—know he is here, and they have been expecting him. He is increasingly aware of how little he understands about his situation—much less than he would tolerate on a typical mission, when the goal, the means, and the risks are defined and sorted before he ever leaves the ship.

The pummeling sound continues, closer now, and then there are three explosions in quick succession. The sounds are far-off, but S. feels his body tighten, bracing itself for another shock-wave punch. To his relief, it does not come.

The tributary bends rightward, sending them back to the river's main artery. Another settlement comes into view, larger and more densely populated, denuded of vegetation and packed tightly with listing shacks made of scrap wood and tin. Along the riverfront are four long, barracks-like buildings and a concrete dock outfitted with a tall crane and other heavy machinery for loading ore into container ships. Electric wires run along poles, emitting a low, toneless hum.

———

"New village," Anca says. "Built by the Company. Many people moved here. They take the Company's money and help them steal our hills."

S. pulls aside the netting and raises his head a few inches so that he can see more, but Waqar kicks his shoulder—not hard, but not gently, either—and he sinks back down. Has he seen this place before? Was it shown to him in a dream? In an orlop fugue? Does he know it from whatever life he had before he became S.?

There must be two thousand people living in the New Village and working in the mines. He wonders how many are left in the Old Village. Fewer than a hundred, he guesses, based on what he saw.[11]

A population, once unitary, now split by their divergent interests in the surrounding hills. What matters most to some were the figures *on* the hills; to others, the riches *in* them. S. is reminded of the K——, of how fewer and fewer of the tribe's artists chose to descend into the dark to paint the walls with history. He thinks of the ship, too, with its

---

[11] There is a similar dynamic at work in *Wineblood's Mine*. As Hieronymus Wineblood explains to the man who produces the propagandist newspaper distributed in his mining empire's tent-cities, you can starve a town, figuratively, by luring away its most adept breadwinners, which then allows you to get down to the business of starving them literally until they come to you, prostrate and begging for work.

Handwritten margin notes:

amazing how many companies Arp Syndikat spun off— + how many each of those spun off, + how many each of those... Coal, steel, chemicals, railroads, newspapers, petroleum, banking, etc. Just started drawing a family tree of Bouchard / Arp + it's already out of control.

You've heard of TLQI, right? BIG AGRIBUSINESS.

My dad's firm does some PR + marketing consulting for them. Guess what I found out about them?

YOU TRACED THEM BACK TO ARP/BOUCHARD.

Give the man a prize.

I SERIOUSLY DOUBT YOUR DAD IS SOME EVIL BOUCHARD PERSON.

I know. But it makes the marketing job even more repulsive. Don't want to be any part of that world.

HARD TO AVOID. MAYBE IMPOSSIBLE.

———

thinning crew. He wonders what it must feel like to be among the last—or to be the very last—of your kind.[12]

The tributary bends sharply away, then, taking them on an even wider loop around the mining town and into view of another stretch of steep hills, one that runs miles into the distance. Many of the distant hills, though, have had their peaks lopped; they rise from the valley and end abruptly in rough, flat plains, silhouettes echoing that of the black island's volcano. (The difference, of course, is that these hills are not monuments to the earth's power but to man's.) The Company steals the hills, Anca said; S. marvels at the double truth of this. The minerals inside, yes, but also the peaks themselves.

In the center of each false mesa is what appears to be an open pit, with men and machines hacking out the hill's innards and driving shafts deeper and deeper into the earth. Paved roadways wind up to each of the sites, connecting them to the riverfront. In the declivities between the hills are tumorous humps of rubble. All of it—the pits, the flattened

———

[12] Straka confessed to me—in a note in the margins of the *Winged Shoes* manuscript, no less—that he had begun to suffer from this very feeling, as a group to which he belonged (uneasily and/or tangentially, I assume, given his social limitations) had been losing its constituents rapidly.

———

mountaintops, the crushed rock—is rimed in the same blue-black gloss as the hillside figures. If such figures once adorned these hills, they are no more than memories now—and memories that are rapidly being forgotten.[13]

A third truth, then: Vévoda's Company has stolen the symbols, too.

Most of the hills close to the village are intact, as are their oval clearings and the petroglyphs framed within them. S. wonders how long this will be true.

"Němec," Waqar says from the stern, and spits.

S. understands the governor's strategy: if you're going to tear open the hills, erase a people's history one blast at a time, then you start with the ones farthest away. The Old Villagers will be furious no matter what you do, but the New Villagers will tolerate it as a reasonable trade for the prospect of modernity and wealth. By the time you get to the hills right on the settlement's edge, the New Villagers will have forgotten that the carvings ever existed, or at least that they were ever thought to be of value, and the Old Villagers will be gone.

[13] As Straka explored so deftly and memorably in 1932's vastly-underrated Lopevi, even the most progressive, visionary, cooperative, and well-intentioned societies can be undone—with astonishing speed by cataclysms unleashed by both nature and man. Cultural identity, Straka argued, should not be considered any more durable than individual identity.

Had to order this one from a rare-books place online.

I COULD'VE JUST LENT YOU MINE.

It's OK. I wanted my own copy. (Dad doesn't check the credit card statements, anyway!) ← Embarrassing

{ 348 }

Anca takes one hand off her paddle and rests it on the gunwale in a fist. "Taraqachi," she says, and S. wonders what that word means, because she seems to believe that he, one man, can stop all this. He wants to tell her that he can't, that he's tired, that with all these years of stealth and death, all he's ever done is make the world infinitesimally safer for himself and perhaps for other people who've been targeted by Agents, that even if he kills the governor, a new one will quickly be installed in his place. If Vévoda needs what is inside those hills, Vévoda will acquire what is inside those hills. And yet S. doesn't wish this knowledge upon Anca or Waqar. He doesn't want to think about it himself.[14] He must retain his bare illusion of relevance.

He notices that one of the ruined hills, perhaps a mile off, has retained the bottommost arc of its totemic clearing, just a little red-rock scallop down into the surrounding trees and their blue-black-daubed foliage. And in that space, too, is the bottom edge of a carving. The shape is hard to make

---

[14] Cf. the character of Jerry Frost in *The Santana March*. Plagued by fatalism about the prospects of his shallow, corrupt culture and in his ability to effect change in anything so much bigger than himself, he finds a form of redemption in an ostensibly pointless expedition into the legendarily dangerous mountain terrain through which the Devil's Winds blow.

SO FXC WAS CAPABLE OF WRITING USEFUL FOOTNOTES...

SHIP OF THESEUS

out, as it's so thickly covered in bluish paste (which has the strange effect of making the land look simultaneously charred and frozen), but this is what it looks like to him:

And in the foreground of his view: the face of the baby, who is now peacefully asleep, tiny mouth wrinkling and sucking softly at the air.

He remembers Sola in the margins, telling him to keep going when his resolve falters, to continue up the river and do what he believes should be done. His efforts will not be *sufficient*, but they may well be *necessary*. Even if he can't stop it—and you can pick your *it*, the *it* of ruin in the Territory, the *it* of campaigns and weapons that turn cities to ash and populations to ghosts, the *it* of one man's life traded for another man's profit, the *it* that leaves children without fathers or mothers or homes—his task is to *try*. The origin of that imperative, that *supposed to*, remains as much a mystery to him as the origin of the symbol, but that doesn't make it feel any less real.

{ 350 }

Taraqachi. Perhaps this is what it means: the one
who *tries*.

Anca and Waqar paddle on for another ten minutes before the governor's mansion comes into
view. It sits, glaringly white and new, atop a foothill
that rises from the river's edge. Several hundred
of the workers' shacks could fit inside it; several
hundred more could fit within the gardens. The
governor's view—say, as he breakfasts on the terrace—must be breathtaking: the river, the tributaries that snake darkly through the valley, a stretch of
intact hills, great swaths of sky, and, of course, the
sudden city[15] over which he presides. A view from
the spot where earth is transformed to numbers in
a ledger.

The river bends, drawing them around to the far
side of the estate, where a dense band of forest
crowds the hillside and offers cover for a trespasser.
Waqar nudges S. with his foot—*Get ready*—and
with a few strong strokes, he and Anca bring the
canoe up along the bank where the vegetation is
thin enough to allow S. to disembark, which he does
with little grace. He clutches the valise to his chest

Sounds a little like Orsupatte.

---

[15] A reference, Perhaps, to the "Sudden City" of *Coriolis* (Book Six), which was itself a
reference to the "Sunken City" from which Emydio Alves hails in *Winged Shoes*.

as he shifts his weight from one foot to the other, waiting for the circulation in his legs to restore itself. "Follow the monkey," Anca tells him as she pushes off the bank with her paddle.

Sound advice ·

He isn't certain what she means, but the words don't surprise him. *Of course* there is a monkey. There is always a monkey. "Will you be here when I get back?" he asks.

"If it is safe," she says, but her tone makes S. think there's something important she's not telling him. The story you walk into, he has learned, is always more complex than it first appears.

Anca and Waqar paddle to the middle of the river, where—as Maelstrom would put it—they plain-sight themselves. Waqar drops a fishing line into the water; Anca pulls the sling around to her front and nurses the baby. The governor's guards (for undoubtedly there are guards) will see them only as a couple of Old Villagers who are stuck in the old ways, sweating and scorching themselves out on the river—a joke, really, these people who cannot grasp that there are easier and better ways to make a living than praying a fish will impale itself on your hook, these people whom one cannot help but pity, at least until that pity grows tiresome, at which point

This is how my dad feels about anyone who's not white collar + "upwardly mobile" (his words).

⌐ ARE ACADEMICS UPWARDLY MOBILE ENOUGH?

No way. School is a means to an end—an end that doesn't involve school.

{ 352 }

———

one draws one's gun and chases them back to the sad, pointless mudflats of their ancestors.[16]

S. opens the valise, removes what he needs, hides the case in the hollowed trunk of a dying possum-wood. He quickly finds the monkey: knife-cuts in bark that suggest a grinning simian face. It marks the beginning of a path up the hill that is narrow and overgrown, more implied than *there*.

Is he being watched? Perhaps, but he senses no imminent threat, and he has faith in his ability to vanish when he needs to. He moves smoothly, quietly through the trees—how odd, really, for him to be able to be so certain of his stealth, of this ability that his body has acquired and developed, and to remain so utterly uncertain about the man to whom that body belongs, to the identity that both sheathes and animates it—and studies his surroundings, watching and listening for signs that he is not alone. A howler monkey cries out from a far-off hill, the sound echoing through the valley.

———

[16] Straka was never more outraged than when he was contemplating the exasperatingly endless condescension imperial outsiders have shown throughout history, boasting of cultural and spiritual superiority while bringing their "inferiors" little but death (both physical and spiritual), disease, and despoilment. See *The Brigade*, his fictional history linking contemporary (and real) suppressions of indigenous movements in Africa, Asia, and the Americas. Many current leaders of revolutionary movements have cited this novel as inspiration.

———

There are brief bursts of rustling along the ground: rodents, most likely. Insects *preep* and dart around him, and the air is full of birdsong, though the singers are unseen. Some of the songs sound out of place to him, and he catalogues them: a merlin; a crow; an oystercatcher; and a magpie tanager *twick*ing heatedly.[17] But there are no signs of sentries, dogs, alarms, booby-traps—nothing to slow his progress—and before long S. finds himself at the top of the hill, peering in at the world of the Territory's governor.

He slips through the trees along the perimeter, reconnoitering. On the terrace, silently clearing a table, are two servants whose features and skin tones match those of Anca and Waqar. An older man stands guard at an entrance gate on the driveway, his belly straining the buttons of a faded field-gray tunic, his unshaven face bristled with white, his eyelids drooping and snapping open as if he might fall asleep on his feet. Voices of women and children come through open windows on the third

---

[17] Many commentators have remarked upon Straka's frequent use of birds to define a fictional landscape and wondered if he might be a trained ornithologist or at least a passionate bird-watcher. I do know he was at least the latter; several times he cabled to inform me that he would not be able to respond to any of my questions about a manuscript for a week or two, as a particularly beloved species was migrating through his area and he simply had to watch them. And no, reader, he never specified the area or the species.

Took me a while to find this...
was wondering if you weren't going
to ask on principle.

SHIP OF THESEUS I GUESS I'M NOT THAT PRINCIPLED.
COME ON: SPILL.

———————— *So: didn't find a manuscript of his*
book — found a pad w/ notes. Just

story of the mansion. A pale and roundish man in *skimmed — didn't want*
to take it or be in
white linen and a floppy, broad-brimmed hat is in *there too long reading —*
the garden, strolling along rows of roses in astonish- *but it looks like he's*
saying VMS was
ing colors; every now and then, he squats and plucks *Summersby. (Didn't*
a few weeds with the languor of a man doing so by *see refs to Ekstrom —*
choice rather than at another's command.]¹⁸ *so maybe he's saying it*
was all Summersby?)

This, then, is the governor. • *Didn't find your*
tape, but it doesn't
When the man takes off his hat to fan himself, S. *matter — he must have*
gets a clear look at his face. Waqar's sketch was not *an audio file of it by*
an exact match—it portrayed him much more ghoul- *now, anyway. (Why*
didn't you?!?)
ishly—but it was close enough to serve as confirma-
tion. And yet S. still does not recognize him. • *No Sobreiro. (Which I*
was hoping for.)
At the end of a row, the governor turns, and now • *Did find a framed*
each step brings him closer. S. holds his position. *photo of Ilsa face-*
down in his desk drawer.
Insects buzz around his head, sip the sweat on his
face, and he remains still. He has three darts at the • *Did find a piece of*
obsidian in a padded
ready, though he knows he will need only one. *box + a mailer it might've*
The governor's walk brings him to the edge of the *come in — postmarked*
garden, where he pauses in the shade cast by a *from Paris.*
sapote tree. S. watches the man's chest move as he • *Also: architectural plans*
takes his heavy breaths in the tropical heat. Perhaps *for his house on a table w/*
an estimate from
the dying Agent misled S.; perhaps there is no great *Zwilling's (which*
surprise to be found here. *is who the university*
hired to redo the

---

¹⁸ Cf. the grape-crushing by guests at the gala in Chapter 10—an example of this work- *climate control in*
as-leisure, leisure-as-work dynamic, a luxury afforded only to the monied and powerful. *Special Collections).*

UNBELIEVABLE

I MEAN, WE DON'T KNOW
EXACTLY WHAT HE'S PLANNING
TO STORE THERE, BUT I'M
NOT GIVING HIM THE BENEFIT
OF THE DOUBT.

Again the governor takes off his hat. He swabs his forehead with a handkerchief. His chest expands, contracts, and S. aims for that gorgeously vulnerable spot below the sternum, for that coronal burst of nerves hiding behind the skin there. S.'s aim, as it has been for years, is immaculate. The sound of the dart traveling and striking—one sound—is both familiar and seductively new.

The paralytic effect is nearly instantaneous. Though the governor is fully conscious, he is eighteen stone of dead weight as S. drags him into the woods.

The governor's face is round. Capillaries flare along his fat-shrouded cheekbones. His hair, gone to gray, is closely shorn, his cheeks cleanly shaved. His nose is red-splotched and thick, and his eyes have that middle-aged squint. His left ear is misshapen. It's not until the man's expression tightens into something lapine and twitchy that S. understands who this is. He pictures the governor fifty pounds lighter, with wild hair and an uncooperative beard. "Pfeifer," he says. The eyes are wider-set, which seems less likely to be a change wrought by age than by the imprecision of S.'s memory.

"Němec," the governor says, but his voice is Pfeifer's, roughened by years and clotted by poison.

{ 356 }

Thinking about
   Moody's CV + all the
grants he got while he
was still a grad
   student. Maybe it's a
part of why he split
w/ Desjardins?
   Maybe he got bought
by MacInnes' people,
or by someone else.
WHY WOULD ANYONE
DO THAT? WHO CARES WHAT
  A GRAD STUDENT IN LIT DOES?
Don't know. Maybe they
thought they could get him to
write things that were wrong
but sounded right. a way to
keep people from getting closer
to finding out who VMS was?
and/or who/what Bouchard
was/is/became? — IT'S A STRETCH, JEN. — It's a theory, Er

→ FILOMELA CHANGED THIS. IN VMS'S
MANUSCRIPT, IT'S OSTRERO, NOT
PFEIFER. AND THE GOVERNOR'S NAME
IS SPANEL (THE SPANIARD). SO: VMS
DEFINITELY THOUGHT IT WAS GARCÍA
FERRARA WHO SOLD OUT.

But she covered that in the Ch. 6 code.
MAYBE SHE WANTED TO BE
ABSOLUTELY SURE HE GOT IT.

Of course he changed his name. "Pfeifer" was wanted for the bombing. So much easier for him— and for Vévoda—if he were re-created as a new man altogether. "Did Vévoda choose that name for you?" S. asks.

"What," he breathes, "makes you think I've met him?"

"You oversee the mining here. You're one of the few people who has seen me up close. If *anyone* has been to the Château, it's you."

Němec laughs. "There is no Château. It's a fiction."

This is itself a fiction, of course. "Did Vévoda name you?" he asks again.

"Who can remember something that happened so long ago?" The governor smiles tentatively, perhaps because he is unsure which parts of his body he can still move. (The mouth, yes; the face, yes; not much more.) "Are you still known as S.?"

"I'm not known."

"That's a shame. It…must make you sad."

"They shot you in the cave."

The governor emits another weak laugh. Apparently he is the sort of man who employs chuckles as punctuation. "You *heard* them shoot," he says.

"They killed everyone else. Why not you?"

Handwritten margin notes:

· Why didn't you just use your middle name?

BECAUSE MY PARENTS GAVE ME THAT ONE, TOO. AND BECAUSE I LIKED "ERIC" MORE.

But you've never changed it legally, right?.

UM... BEEN BUSY?

"I was lucky," Němec says. "The first shots missed. I said I wanted to be useful to them. I meant it. My life changed in an instant, but better a change than an end." He runs his tongue over his lips. "Tell me, is it ending now? Am I dying?"

S. ignores the question. "Stenfalk, Corbeau, Ostrero," he says. "Out of all of them, *you* were angriest. *You* wanted to torch the factory. If it was anyone's fight, it was yours."

"Yes, it was. Until I decided it wasn't. Why is it still yours? Why was it *ever* yours?"

S. looks at the man on the ground in front of him: arms at his sides, dirt and leaves clinging to his once-flawless linen, a moving face trapped in an inanimate body. He wonders: can you ever make another person fully understand the choices you've made? "The poison," S. explains, answering an earlier, easier question, "is from the red-speckled mamba. Diluted, it's a remarkable paralytic. So you probably won't die. Not from that, at any rate."

"Look at us," the governor says. "We're growing old. We are old. Well past time to ask—to *know*—what the measure of our lives will be."

"It's quite easy to measure yours. You sold it to Vévoda."

FILOMELA SAID THERE WAS A MANUSCRIPT THAT CAME TO HER IN 1940 THAT WAS TERRIBLE, + VMS LATER ASKED FOR IT BACK SO HE COULD DESTROY IT. WANTED THE ENVELOPE IT HAD COME IN, TOO, WHICH SHE SAID HAD A LEGIBLE POSTMARK (WHICH HAD NEVER HAPPENED BEFORE): DUBLIN. SHE SAID THE MS WAS IN ENGLISH, BUT IT WAS RIDDLED W/ERRORS THAT SHE THOUGHT SOUNDED LIKE THEY CAME FROM A NATIVE GERMAN SPEAKER.

The Wechsler book. A failed Straka collaboration, or a failure of his own? COULDN'T HAVE FELT GOOD EITHER WAY.

If it was a Straka project + a bad enough experience, maybe that drove him to Bouchard and Arp? JEN? Eric? — OR LEFT HIM OPEN TO BEING TEMPTED.

"It's been a good life. I facilitate profitable ventures. I administer. I oversee. I certainly don't run around the world poisoning people." The governor pauses; he watches S. closely, testing his response to the provocation. S. is careful to offer him nothing. "That's what you do, isn't it?"

"I've been running," S. says, "ever since the day we left B——."

"So you really are the S he's wanted most. After the Agents have spent all these years ruling out—"

Not "ruling out," S. wants to say. *Killing.* He reminds himself to stay calm.

He notices a trap-jaw ant crawling across a sweaty crease in the governor's forehead. It could sink mandibles into skin at any moment. S. watches it. He measures his breathing—slow inhale, exhale—as he deliberates. Finally he brushes the ant away. He neither expects nor receives thanks for his action.

"You could have stopped running," the governor says.

"I've never had the choice."

The governor laughs, a hiccup of sound that his frozen body chokes off at his throat. "You've always had a choice."

AND WE KNOW HOW EASY IT IS TO GET CAUGHT UP IN THAT.

THE NEW S TAKING OUT THE (OLD) S ONE BY ONE? But not always by killing them—they turned a lot of them, too. Bouchard+ MacInnes had a lot of money.

Campus cops all over Standefer today. + in Moody's office. FUCK. A THOUSAND TIMES OVER: FUCK.

No idea how he knew. I swear I didn't take a break or move anything.

HOPE YOU'RE RIGHT.

I really don't want to get caught. I know I was out of my head. I'm not that kind of person. I'm really not. But everything's so crazy right now.

S. wonders why they have not yet been interrupted. "Isn't anyone going to come looking for you?" he asks. "Right now, you seem just as alone as I am."

"The guard by the road, perhaps. It depends how much wine he's had at lunch. I hope you won't kill him. He's old and shaky and has very little sense left, but he's a good man."

"No one else?"

"Maybe one of the children if they're eager to play. Maybe my wife." The governor pauses here, manages to tilt his head half a degree. "You're not married, are you?" he asks, though he must know the answer. "Did you ever find that girl you were looking for? Szalómé?"

"We've crossed paths," S. says. Sola. Thinking of her makes him ache. Aches are distractions.

"But you've never *found* her. You've *passed by* her."

"I haven't given up."

The governor sighs—rather theatrically, S. thinks. "I have a good life. I have a family. I eat well. I sleep well. I grow my roses. I'm not in danger—the present situation excepted."

"Perhaps you should be in danger more often," S. says.

WHICH WOULD BE A LIFE MORE LIKE STRAKA'S.

Filomela's, too.

{ 360 }

———

"Listen. Think. At any point you could've decided that finding Szalómé was the most important thing you could do. At any point you could have said *no* and stopped sailing hither and yon trying to save whatever cramped and dark and past-tense little niche of the world you've been trying to save—"

"What do you know about a ship?"

"I didn't say anything about a ship."

"You implied."

"What I implied is…that you've made your choices. And so you've never found her. And you still don't know a damned thing about who she is, let alone who you are." An iridescent green fly lands on his nose, buzzes, rubs its legs together, then takes off again. "There's a girl in the village who looks a bit like her, you know. You could be introduced."

S. does not respond.

"I married a girl from the village," the governor says. His smile shows teeth that are as garishly white and straight as the mansion itself. "Her name is Molýb. Her father is the chief who led the split."

"And the one, then, who helps you strip the hills."

"We don't strip. We harvest."

"And the petroglyphs?"

———

{ 361 }

So while you were doing break-ins + who knows what else, I got back to research. Found the record of Desjardins' marriage: 12/1/52, in Carcassonne. To SIGNE RABE.

Holy. Fuck.
But who was she?
And why was Filomela writing about her?
Carcassonne isn't far from Perpignan. Connection to Durand? Was she Durand's daughter??

Signe Rabe: born 11/4/30 in Perpignan. Mother: "A. Rabe." No record of the father.

"The chief understands that they're no longer needed. There's no proof they were carved by his people's ancestors, anyway. It's simply what the tribe had *chosen* to believe." The man's breathing has slowed. "Their history, mine, yours…A story of…choices.

"They needed their stories only because they had nothing else. Think of what Vévoda does: he helps people reshape their world in dynamic ways. Inventive ways. He offers patterns of understanding. There is destruction, yes, but it is in the service of—" He closes his eyes, opens them. "Of creation. And this creation is as profound as, and more real than, shapes on hillsides…or colors on canvas…or scribblings on paper—"

"Be quiet," S. tells him. One nick from the pen's nib could stop the paralyzed man's lungs, could drown him in this jungle air. Not even a slash—just one solitary en-dash written into the skin of his forehead, or perhaps a full-stop into his neck. If S. chose to carve the S-shaped symbol into him, death would arrive before the shape was complete.

The governor is hushed, for a moment. But then he chuckles to himself, as if he's powerless to contain his thoughts. "My father-in-law! The man is passionate about his minerals. He named all his daughters

{ 362 }

after them. Could there be a purer expression of reverence for the place he calls home? Molýb is short for Molýbdena. Her sisters: Bauxia, Ferra, Argenta, Urania. The youngest—and, frankly, the most stunningly beautiful, though they are all beautiful—is called Substantia. All the girls were sought—"

The governor is stalling him. S. scans the grounds. Can it really be that no one has noticed his disappearance yet?

S. repeats the sixth sister's name. "The blue-black material," he says.

"Yes. Though in the earth, it's gray, with lovely gold veins. I can show you some, if you like."

"But what *is* it?"

"It's simply *substance*. That's all it's ever been called."

"Your friends were killed because they found out about it. Now people around the world are being killed by it. And here you are, helping him get as much of it as he needs."

"This? This is nowhere near as much as he needs. Don't underestimate the demand for—"

"Enough," S. says.

"Are you going to kill me?"

"I said, enough."

That's amazing—he's trying to butter you up and he still manages to be an arrogant prick.

THAT'S NOT SURPRISING. WHAT'S SURPRISING IS THAT HE'S TRYING TO GET ME BACK ON "THE TEAM."

For as long as it takes him to get the book out.

"We have four children, Molýb and I," the governor says. "Don't kill me. You don't have to."

||"Actually," S. says, "I might."||

This is when the gunfire starts—in the distance, a smattering of discrete pops, like a volley of corks at midnight on the new year. "What is that?" S. asks.

"You don't know?" The governor again gives that dead-in-the-throat laugh, which S. now thinks is reason enough for the man to die.

"Tell me."

More and more guns begin firing, many more—hundreds, by the sound of it all—spitting constant and relentless streams of bullets. The governor's smile widens. (O, those teeth!) "It must be precisely four o'clock," he says. "In which case, that's the sound of our greatest act of creation." A great many explosives recently went missing from a warehouse, he explains. He received reports that the Old Villagers were planning to bomb the docks while a ship was being loaded. It was to be the overture to a great and bloody revolt. "We thought it best to stop them before they did so," he concludes.

If there are screams, they die in the dense air before reaching the altitude of the mansion.

"You're killing them," S. says.

{ 364 }

TURNS OUT THE PUBLISHER CALLED SUMMERSBY'S LAWYER'S DAUGHTER TO MAKE SURE MOODY HAD RIGHTS TO USE THE TAPE. SHE SAID SHE'D GIVEN IT TO ME + SO I'M THE ONE WHO HAS TO GIVE CONSENT.

!!!

That's amazing. She must have liked you.
OR SHE'S JUST AN HONEST PERSON. WHICH IS CAUSE ENOUGH FOR CELEBRATION. AS IS THE FACT THAT MOODY CAN'T PUBLISH HIS BOOK W/O ME GIVING THE OK.
which you're not going to do.
OF COURSE NOT. BUT I'M GOING TO USE IT TO GET ESME EMERSON-PLUM TO MEET W/ME. WHEREUPON I'LL BLOW MOODY'S WHOLE ARGUMENT TO SHIT. + IN THE MEANTIME, I'LL LET HIM STEW.

S'S SUCCESS—TEMPORARY AND INSIGNIFICANT.

SHIP OF THESEUS

"Just those who are involved," the governor says, "and those who failed to stop them. The orders came from elsewhere. Had the choice been mine, I'd have simply arrested them and sent them to the mines. But first they'd have to watch the show in the hills."[19]

The show?

The gunfire from town ebbs quickly, now coming only in short bursts, and S. imagines bodies along the path from New Village to Old, bodies in and between the thatched huts, the wounded being cut down as they stagger into the forest of shadows. Then, from the distant hills comes an explosion that buffets S.'s eardrums and reverberates through his head. A column of brown dust rises into the sky; then sparkles of blue-black drift down in rings around it. There is the sound of raining rubble, delicate from this distance. Another explosion: another mountaintop, gone. And that smell, that blue-black smell, that acrid stink of substance, it fills the air of the valley, as do the murmuring

---

[19] Cf. *A Hundred Aprils in Amritsar*, a novel that exposes grievous acts of misrule and collaboration in colonial India, culminating in the events surrounding 1919's infamous massacre. Here, as in that novel, we see a powerful character "punishing" a population, with horrific results, and refusing to acknowledge culpability for his choice to serve as an instrument of slaughter.

Funny — Washington + Greene seems like the exact same book as Amritsar, except instead of the Amritsar Massacre it's about the Triangle Shirtwaist fire. Same structure, same tone, same hero 365 w/ a different name.

THERE'S NOT REALLY A HERO IN EITHER BOOK.
How well do you know Singh's work?
NOT VERY. — *Can you read some more of his stuff?*
I'm busy getting through Straka.
AND ALL THE OTHER WORK YOU'RE SUPPOSED TO BE DOING. *Whatever.*

SOME PEOPLE THINK SINGH MIGHT HAVE HAD A HAND IN THIS ONE.
Like Durand with The Painted Cave.
EXCEPT IT'S NOT BECAUSE OF THE DETAILS. IN SINGH'S CASE, IT'S ABOUT THE STYLE.

voices, which turn suddenly into prolonged shrieks that clench jaws, drain dark trickles from ears. The turmoil disorients S., slows his thoughts, his ability to make decisions.

Or perhaps he's simply old and overwhelmed.

The paralyzed man's little finger twitches.

What S. needs is a bit of quiet, a still moment in which to figure out what to do—he should never have come in without a plan—but then there comes another great explosion as another hilltop erupts, and then a fourth and a fifth. How many more? "We've been instructed to triple our production," the governor says amid all the noise. "The hills were all going to be opened at some point, so why should it matter when?" His tone is emotionless, pragmatic. This is not gloating; this is belief.

Then: three loud cracks from nearby, and S. looks up and sees the old guard out on the lawn, a hundred yards away, rejuvenated by a firearm and a reason to use it. He stands, his hip cocked, perfectly steady, as smoke wisps up from the barrel of his rifle. The gun is not aimed in S.'s direction. It is aimed at the river.

S. feels his insides boiling. It is an unfamiliar feeling, such fury. *Emotion breeds mistakes*, he tells

HEY — REREAD DESJARDINS' NOTE TO ME. DOESN'T IT SOUND LIKE THIS WAS HOW HE WAS FEELING?

Like he couldn't decide which of his students he could trust. So he trusted you. Which—let's face it—was totally irrational.

BUT HE WAS RIGHT— HE TRUSTED HIS INTUITION, + HE WAS RIGHT.

Not everyone's going to think that.

THEY WILL WHEN MY BOOK COMES OUT.

Are you going to dedicate it to him?

NO. THE DEDICATION'S ALREADY TAKEN.

BUT I'LL TELL HIS STORY. AND MAKE IT CLEAR HOW MUCH WE OWE TO HIM.

You said "we."

Vaclav's dive, Ekstrom's
Rescue: the beginning of V.M. Straka.
CAN'T PROVE THAT'S WHAT
HAPPENED, THOUGH.
Not yet.
RIGHT. GOT TO KEEP
LOOKING.

SHIP OF THESEUS

Which is a lot more fun than an entry-level
marketing job.
EVEN IF EVERYONE THINKS IT'S IMPOSSIBLE
(+ THUS POINTLESS)?

yes. Of course,
there are some other
good reasons to do it...

himself. *Emotion breeds mistakes, and words are
gifts to the dead, and what* begin at the water *shall
end there and what ends there shall once more
begin.* Voices fill his head; a kind of delirium rises.
He watches, stupefied, as the old man pivots, turns
the gun in their general direction, paces forward
slowly. The guard takes a position behind a marble
fountain where water spouts from the mouth of
Mercury, that winged-shoe messenger who doubles
as a god of commerce.[20]

BEGAN AT WATER:
CALAIS MASSACRE.
SANTORINI MAN. EVERY
MAJOR SHIFT FOR S.

MERCURY = HERMES.
CLEAR REF. TO BOUCHARD.
It shouldn't be water
spouting from his
mouth, then.

"We all have our jobs to do," the governor says. If
this is an appeal to S., it is an ill-chosen one. The
words are probably his final ones, although S. does
not linger to confirm this. He does, however, relish
yet again the feeling of nib piercing skin, that tiny
punch through a trivial dermal defense. (Really: we
imagine ourselves to be so well-contained, so clearly
defined, so individually integrious, yet it takes so
little to open us up, to send us spilling outward or
to introduce something foreign and toxic.) A ghost

I don't know if that's
really a word, but I
like it.
NEW FAVORITE?
No.
Top Ten, maybe.

---

[20] A complicated reference here. It is, to my eye, the moment in which S. is most clearly
functioning as an alter ego for the writer, who long struggled with the intrinsic tensions
between art and commerce, between purity of intention and pragmatism (or, farther down
that road, cynicism). These conflicts are difficult for everyone, though, and they are certainly understandable—merely evidence that one suffers from the affliction of being
human. I pointed this out in a bit of marginalia in my working-copy of the *Ship of Theseus*
manuscript, but I do not know if he ever saw it.

SO IS THIS VMS'S
REVENGE FANTASY
AGAINST ALL THE
PEOPLE WHO SOLD
OUT THE S?
If it is, though, then it's
also making a point
about how empty revenge
is.

of that feeling tingles his fingertips as he dashes through the trees; as bullets whizz and whine around him, scorching leaves and splintering branches and dropping a magpie with the tragic luck of occupying the wrong space.

He pauses to load the blow-gun. He aims. The old guard falls like a stone.

S. rushes down to the river. Branches slash his cheeks; vines cause him to stumble; he makes more noise than one would expect from a man who does not exist. The blasting of the hills continues. Seventeen, eighteen, nineteen…

Once again, he has saved nobody, stopped no calamity from befalling those around him, stolen life for no greater good. He longs to be back on the ship.

He finds the canoe a quarter-mile downriver, nosing uselessly into the bank, caught in a V made by the exposed roots of a strangler fig. Waqar's body is gone; the blood greasing the side of the canoe and the grasses on the bank suggests that it was tugged overboard by something hungry. Anca lies on her back on a fishing net that is saturated in red. There is a dark hole in her neck. Her eyes are wide open and aimed at the sky.

{ 368 }

Handwritten margin notes:

— Sounds like more self-pity. Blaming the world for problems he made.

— You may be right. But isn't what happened in Havana the very definition of tragic luck? They were finally going to get away. Finish the book + be together.

Sounds familiar...

STRAKA THE MAGPIE →

Is this about your uncle?
I DON'T REMEMBER.
It wasn't your job to save him, you know.

OK — MAYBE IT IS ABOUT HIM. BUT IT'S ABOUT MY FRIEND GRIFF, TOO. WE WENT OFF TO GRAD SCHOOL — I CAME HERE; HE WENT TO FLORIDA. I ONLY SAW HIM ONCE AFTER THAT. HE CALLED ME ONE NIGHT — TOTALLY DEPRESSED, LOSING HIS MIND, NEEDED ME TO TALK HIM DOWN. SO I DID. THEN I BORROWED A CAR + DROVE TO FLORIDA TO MAKE SURE. STAYED FOR A WEEK — A HARD WEEK — + HE FINALLY AGREED TO GO INPATIENT FOR A WHILE, + IT ALL SEEMED TO HAVE WORKED OUT. AFTER HE GOT OUT, WE HAD A FIGHT — IT WAS OVER SOMETHING TRIVIAL — + WE NEVER TALKED AGAIN. A YEAR LATER HE ACTUALLY DID KILL HIMSELF. I DIDN'T FIND OUT UNTIL I READ IT IN THE ALUMNI MAG'S OBITS. — Shit, Eric. I can't imagine.

→ CONNECTION TO CORBEAU + TO DURAND'S DEATH IN MADRID? (But Durand. alter ego has already died. WHO KNOWS? THE WRITER MAKES THE RULES.

But it wasn't your job to save him, either.

↗ Or maybe it's a way of saying he was reliving Durand's death.
AND EKSTROM'S TOO. (WAQAR, OBV.)
But what about the baby? Signe didn't die.

SHIP OF THESEUS

Of the baby there is no sign: no baby, no sling.

There are many possible explanations for this, and S. mumbles them aloud after he climbs in, pries the paddle from Anca's stiffening fingers, settles in the stern, pushes off, and paddles madly downstream. The baby? Pulled over the side, like Waqar? Snatched by someone who hacked through the thick woods to get to it? Set adrift in a basket, Moses-like, by a desperate mother, to be carried by the current. There is the possibility of a happy ending. *Not the one he thinks.*

Or this: perhaps there was no baby in the first place. Perhaps S. imagined it entirely, conjured it as a metaphor for a life of promise, a life he has never had.

BUT THERE WAS A BABY— SIGNE, DURAND, DESJARDINS— WE KNOW THEY'RE CONNECTED.

There is no evidence at all to suggest the baby was real, apart from S.'s dubious memory.

One baby existed. The other one didn't.

NEGATIVE SPACE.

If a baby never exists, then it cannot be lost, can it? S. paddles and mutters and nods.

When he passes the Old Village, it is ablaze.

VÉVODA — CREATION REQUIRES DESTRUCTION

The tributaries meet, and the current slingshots S., this man piloting a canoe of the dead and missing and never-were, along at greater velocity. Other canoes are on the river up ahead, and he paddles even harder to catch up, so hard that he courts capsizing with each stroke. When the rearmost of the

So was he trying to tell Filomela without giving away the secret? God, it would've been so much easier just to tell *her.*

THE BOOK WAS THE SAFEST WAY TO DO IT.

Maybe— but it didn't work. She didn't get it.

canoes is within hailing distance, he shouts until he is hoarse. Finally, just before the river divides around a rocky shoal, swirling and churning with a ferocity that S. does not remember from the paddle upstream (but *of course* he doesn't remember it; he must have imagined the easy, lazy currents just as he imagined the baby), the two people paddling it turn back to look in his direction.

In the stern—he could swear it, and does, and will ever—is Sola, steering expertly through the rapids.

In the bow is S. himself. Younger, perhaps, arms muscled and bronzed, shoulders high and square, but he can tell: that man is me.

Who is he to the two of them? A madman? A derelict? A revenant?

S. loses his grip on the paddle, and the water sweeps it away. He paddles toward it with his hands, all the while watching it float farther away. Watches the canoes ahead of him catch the current and whip downstream through the rapids that fork to the left of the island. Watches himself drift inexorably toward the deeper, slower, rockier right-hand fork. When Sola and his other self have disappeared from view, he drops his head, grinds

WHAT IF EKSTROM WAS TALKING ABOUT TWO DIFFERENT "FRIENDS"?
WHAT IF 1929 WAS VACLAV + 1930 WAS SIGNE?

So Ek died when Signe was only a couple of months old. God.

HE GOT TO SEE HER, AT LEAST. GOT TO FEEL WHAT IT WAS LIKE TO BE HER DAD.

You wouldn't have written that a year ago.

the heels of his palms into his eyes. For a long time he drifts with his eyes closed, the canoe spinning lazily each time it bumps a rock. He drifts, this man in a canoe with a dead woman and a baby who never was, drifts and hopes, half-heartedly, that the ship will find him whenever and wherever this particular branch of river disgorges him into the sea. In this life, it's the one thing on which he's ever been able to rely.

The ship does not find him. He finds the ship. (Or, more accurately, he sees the bombed, burned remains of it not far offshore: scraps of charred planks and masts, canvas and crates, rope and wire, all of it undulating on the slick of blue-black that coats the surface of the water. Smoke rises from much of the wreckage; some fragments float with little sails of dark-orange flame raised and beating in the breeze.) If any part of the hull was left intact, it has already disappeared below. Vévoda's warplanes have flown away, but the fierce drone of their engines lingers in the air, rising and falling in pitch as it spins in the swirling winds.

The bodies float face-down. Around them, the surface is boiling, raising great thick-looking bubbles

---

[Handwritten annotations:]

M+P think you started the fire in the barn. Because of the symbol + what my sister told them and what Jacob said about you. Nothing el say about you matters. Dad said he's going to call the police, but wanted to give me the chance to "do what's right" first. So el did — el told him to fuck off. And you'd think that's when there would've been shouting, but there wasn't. Which is why el got back in the car, el guess. We were at the stoplight across from the Med Center when el realized what was going on + got the fuck out.

COME TO MY PLACE TONIGHT. STAY WITH ME

Can't.

SAW A HAULZ-IT TRUCK OUTSIDE YOUR APT. TODAY.

el did, too. Wore a at, kept my head down. They were clearing out my stuff— my dad + my sister's idiot boyfriend.

—SO WHERE ARE YOU STAYING?

Your place?

that blow gray vapor and the blue-black smell as they burst. He identifies several, or tells himself he does: there is the whittler, with one arm missing; there is the slight frame of the pouting girl; there is the refugee from the ghost ship; there is a sailor he can no longer recognize. All around him is the smell of burned flesh. He calls out, asking if anyone has survived, begging for someone to have survived, but all he hears is that vertiginous hum, his own ragged breathing, his own voiceless shouts.

And there, breaching: there is the biggest of the bodies. There is the expansive halo of hair, the thick limbs and barrel trunk. There, still clutched in his hand, is one of the maps, entirely unburned but covered to all four corners in the deepest, bloodiest of reds.

What begins at the water shall end there, and what ends there shall once more begin. Words are a gift to the dead and a warning to the living.

What is the story he tells himself? That he is a man in a boat on the edge of civilization? That he is a man floating on the edge of a life that should never have been his? That there is nothing? There is nothing. The woman who could save him, who could

You know it wasn't your job to save Griss either, right?

— SOMETIMES. NOT ALWAYS. I'M A LITTLE RAW RIGHT NOW. WORRIED I MIGHT BE LOSING MY SHIT AGAIN. IF I AM — I DON'T KNOW — I'M SORRY. SORRY, JEN.

Don't apologize. Because then I'll have to apologize for losing mine.

———

explain, is gone. His other selves are gone. His stitches are gone. His poisons are gone. (His pages are gone, lost underwater or turned to ash.) He has only this empty vessel of himself. He is a ghost.

Library shitcanned me. Need new place to leave book Put it in a bag w/ my name + tell them to keep it behind the counter for me @ Pronghorn.

THIS IS NOT A LONG-TERM SOLUTION.

We'll be lucky if it's a long-term problem.

19 rails, with those marked letters:

HAVE YOU EVER STOPPED THINKING ABOUT HER HAVE YOU EVER GIVEN ANYONE ELSE A CHANCE

I cried when I figured this out. Filomela thought Durand was the whole problem. She didn't realize that he was thinking about her— he just never gave her a chance to show that she loved him back.

Was it hard for you to read this over this winter? → NOT REALLY. MADE ME FEEL LIKE SOMEONE ELSE UNDERSTOOD WHAT IT FELT LIKE.

I guess it's not as sad as it seems at first

CHAPTER 9

BIRDS OF
NEGATIVE SPACE

I can't get anywhere with the code in this chapter.

ONLY ONE FOOTNOTE — SHE'S NOT GIVING ~~US~~ HIM MUCH TO GO ON.

But it has to be in here somewhere.

This is ~~driving me crazy~~ frustrating the hell out of me.

DON'T WORRY — I COULDN'T CARE LESS ABOUT HOW PEOPLE USE "CRAZY." NOT ANYMORE.

when did that change?

I DON'T KNOW. BUT I THINK IT'S BECAUSE WE'RE DOING THIS.

THERE IS only one window in S.'s apartment, and the view from it is almost entirely blocked by icicles that are bigger around than his fist. Peering between them, S. watches yet another dark, gray morning passing in a wintry haze of snow and ice. Every shape on the ground has been made vague, rounded into a white approximation of itself.

He presses a hand against the window, fingers splayed. The chill numbs his palm, tightens itself around his wrist, and creeps up his forearm before he pulls it away. Its image remains on the glass, an island of transparency in a sea of frost. A temporary clarity, authored by his body heat.

{ 375 }

Yes. He is still alive.

The frost will swiftly retake the space, of course, creeping in from the edges. Before long, all that will remain is S.'s own memory of where the boundary used to be.

He has no idea how he came to be in the Winter City. He has no recollection of arriving. He does not know how he ended up in this apartment. His earliest memory is of plodding down a thickly-iced boulevard, his teeth chattering in a wind-bitten polar cold. Around him were hundreds of other people, but they were hazy and indistinct to his eye, pale impressions. He tried speaking with several, but he was ignored, as if he was not part of their world. Gradually it dawned on him that no one there was part of *anyone* else's world. They all occupied the same space but did not occupy it together. Imagine a thousand leaves of tracing paper, each with one person lightly penciled on it, all stacked atop a scene of a frozen city block. A thousand discrete and solitary realities that appear to be occurring in the same location.

Had he died and gone to some sort of purgatory? Had he come to live, somehow, in the strange land

{ 376 }

[left margin handwritten, blue ink:]

I know this is going to sound crazy— but as soon as I finish my last exam, I want to get on a plane with you + go to Brazil. Seriously — forget the ceremonies, forget my parents, forget my lease, forget my stuff. Forget all of it. I've got my dad's credit card.

—AND I'VE GOT SERIN $—

[pencil:] You still don't know who they are or what they want.

[pencil, caps:] I DON'T THINK I'LL EVER BE ABLE TO EXPRESS HOW THANKFUL I AM THAT YOU'RE A PART OF MINE.

ERIC — Please read this. I need you to read this.

[pencil:] SO YOU LIED.

I didn't. I just didn't tell the whole story.

[bottom handwritten:]

[pencil, caps:] YOU REVISED THE WHOLE STORY.

I've never told anyone before. I've never even considered telling anyone. I've never thought it mattered before.

Jesus, Eric — don't go away over this. I was trying to help you understand. I'm sorry! I'm fucking sorry!

[right margin, pencil:] Really? Does this really offend you so much? Or are you just looking for a way to bail on me?!

Call from VP of Student Affairs. Think they've decided. I'm afraid to call ~~to~~ back. As much as I've said I don't care, I care.

— DOESN'T HELP TO PUT IT OFF.

SHIP OF THESEUS

of Stenfalk's folktale, that mythical Winter City to which misbehaving children were sent? Was he here as a prisoner? An exile? Or a penitent? These are questions he still cannot answer. It's possible, he knows, that he has gone mad, but there is no way to tell, and in any event, what can be done about it? You can't just whistle and summon sense and order back into your mind ((All you can do is button your coat, lace your boots, and trudge through the frigid business of being.))

S. turns away from the window and paces the room, trying to stimulate the circulation in his legs. It is a small space, roughly the same size of his cabin on that ship which no longer exists. The floor is composed of ill-joined pine boards. The walls have been lightened with a thin whitewash. He has electricity, a small lamp with a naked bulb, water, a privy down the hall that he shares only with ghosts. He has heat, though not as much as he would like. Even inside he wears a heavy greatcoat, along with boots and gloves and woolens, all of which still feel as if they belong to a stranger. He stuffs his trousers and sleeves with newspaper for insulation. He has a simple wooden desk, a chair, and a pen, just as he

You know, I get that Straka's trying to tell Filomela that he realizes his life is empty without her, but I am so sick of this martyr pose. He made his choices, over + over again. He's the one who could've said "let's be together— none of this matters more than you, than us." And he didn't. He just fucking didn't. And it feels like you don't really get that, like you're always ready to make some excuse for him — which is crazy, because you're the one who's actually met Filomela, you're the one who's seen first-hand what her life ended up being + what it ended up not being.

YOU'RE COMPLETELY RIGHT. WHAT HAPPENED W/ THEM WAS TRAGIC, + IT WAS HIS FAULT. I GET THAT. BUT HE WAS JUST A PERSON, NOT SOME SUPERHERO. NOT EVEN A REGULAR HERO. KIND OF BROKEN, KIND OF SAD, KIND OF SMALL. FULL OF REGRETS. MAYBE NOT THE GUY YOU OR I OR EVEN FILOMELA WANTED HIM TO BE — BUT HE WAS WHO FILOMELA FELL IN LOVE WITH, SO THERE HAD TO BE SOMETHING GOOD THERE — + MAYBE HE REALIZED TOO LATE WHAT WAS IMPORTANT, BUT YOU KNOW WHAT? THAT HAPPENS.

did on the orlop deck. There is a typewriter on the floor; he only uses it when the apartment is so cold that the ink won't flow. He sleeps on a pallet in the corner, a burlap sack filled with newspaper. He drinks tea. He eats biscuits that are no better than those on the ship. He did not acquire any of this; it was simply *there* in the room when he arrived. He keeps close track of his stocks of ink and tea and biscuits. He keeps expecting them to diminish. They never do.

S. sits back down in the chair, shuffles himself in close to the desk, and hunches over his work. He dips the pen and scratches away at the paper, finishing the sentence that he had abandoned to stand at the window and stare out between the icicles and prove his existence.

He sips the tea in his cup. The cup is cold. The tea is, too. *God, it's cold in this place.*

He has no desire to leave the Winter City. In his time there, he has witnessed no strife or anguish or misery. He has not had to grieve anyone's death, much less witness it. He has never sensed the presence of Agents.

SHORT, JUMPY SECTIONS IN THIS CH. FEEL LIKE SINGH'S EARLY WORK. (HOMAGE?)

BUT SINGH'S LATER NOVELS FEEL A LOT LIKE STRAKA'S— THAT NOT-QUITE-OUR-WORLD STRANGENESS, THE VEILED SELF-EXAMINATION, THE QUESTIONS OF IDENTITY.

I'M GOING OUT ON A LIMB HERE— BUT IT SEEMS LIKE SINGH +VMS COLLABORATED ON AMRITSAR +ENDED UP INFLUENCING EACH OTHER.

It's a pretty strong limb. You can see the same thing happening with Summ.—before +after both Santana March + Night Palisades.

{ 378 }

SO YOU'RE LIKING SUMM. SO FAR? Loving. Kind of trio but you can tell there a smart guy behind i SO IT'S AN ESCAPE Funny.

You are unlikely to die violently in the Winter City. But you're not really living, either.

There is a daily newspaper in the Winter City. It serves three important purposes, although S. values only two:

First, it fills sleeves and pant-legs and boots and bedding.

Second, it chronicles events in the world in which S. used to live. It tells the stories of war, commerce, riots and massacres, the mad scrap for power in its myriad shapes and tones. (The newspaper contains no news about the Winter City because there *is* no news in the Winter City. This, too, could be seen as a function of market forces; the Winter City—frigid, static, irrelevant—is a place no one cares to control.)

Third, the newspapers are the medium on which S. writes. He has filled thousands of pages, writing in the thin white spaces between lines of type, super-imposing his words over the printed ones when he runs out of margin. Palimpsests atop palimpsests.

The stack of newspapers in the corner, the ones he has filled, rises nearly to the ceiling.

Got the Eliot paper in. Asked Ffoulkes to grade it—which I'm sure pissed off Ilsa—But he said she had to do it. I can bring it to him again if I need to appeal.

WELL, YOU GOT IT IN. THAT'S WHAT'S IMPORTANT.

No, actually, the grade is what's important.

Ilsa gave me a C. Ffoulkes agreed with her.

WHERE DOES THAT LEAVE YOU?

Same as before— totally unsure if I can pass. Oh, and Ilsa threw me a look in class today. Everything I do makes her hate me more.

A NEW FAVORITE WORD FOR YOU? *— I was really trying to exercise restraint here... But hell yes.*

Ship of Theseus

Not once has Sola spoken to him from the margins. When he first arrived, he wrote nearly without cease just on the chance he would find her there. Now, when he writes, he forgets to look.

Some time ago, when S. still cared about where the Winter City might be, relative to the world of which the newspaper speaks, he formulated a theory: while the Winter City is *of* that world, it is not, strictly speaking, *in* it. You certainly can't get there just by sailing your ship into the low latitudes. The Winter City is neither above nor below nor parallel to that world. The Winter City *is*, and the familiar world *is*, and they are in some proximity to each other, though perhaps not always.

It would be difficult to read what S. has written, but a meticulous eye might notice, amid the torrent of words, mentions of the following: a taciturn sailor; children dying of snake-bites, trembling and feverish; a saint's manifestation in an oil-slicked puddle; mass graves; a spinning bicycle wheel; a man with legendary mustaches; a love-struck adventurer with wings on his shoes; a factory fire; the lonesome death of the Spider Prince; soup lines; trenches; the smell of warm holiday cakes; bank notes passing

I CALLED SUMM.'S LAWYER'S DAUGHTER TO THANK HER FOR NOT GIVING HER CONSENT TO MOODY. WE TALKED FOR A WHILE— SHE'S REALLY INTO THE STRAKA QUESTION. DON'T WORRY—I WAS CAREFUL ABOUT WHAT I TOLD HER. BUT THE AMAZING THING IS WHAT SHE TOLD ME. I WAS TALKING ABOUT THE BAD—CHILDREN MYTHS IN SOT, + SHE SAID THAT ONE TIME WHEN SHE WAS LITTLE, SHE TOLD HER DAD THAT SHE HATED HIM, + HE SAID SHE SHOULD BE GRATEFUL—AND CAREFUL—

BECAUSE HE KNEW A LITTLE GIRL WHOSE PARENTS WERE BOTH DEAD + WHO WAS BEING CHASED BY BAD PEOPLE ALL AROUND THE WORLD. AND ALL THE GIRL HAD WERE TWO UNCLES WHO HAD TO TAKE TURNS BEING HER DAD { 380 } AND THEY HAD TO KEEP MOVING FROM PLACE TO PLACE B/C THEY WERE BEING CHASED, TOO. SHE SAID SHE THOUGHT ABOUT THAT LITTLE GIRL FOR YEARS AFTERWARD, + IT ALWAYS MADE HER CRY. Signe? AND THE "UNCLES"? ONE'S SUMMERSBY. WHO'S THE OTHER?

what was it you & Grriss argued about? Was it really that trivial?

waiting...

SHIP OF THESEUS

OK — SO NOT LONG AFTER HE GOT RELEASED, HE CALLED + ASKED ME TO LOOK OVER A CHAPTER OF HIS DISSERTATION — HE SOUNDED DESPERATE, WHICH I THOUGHT WAS RIDICULOUS SINCE IT'D BE YEARS BEFORE HE HAD TO TURN IT IN. I LAUGHED

between pink hands; a hanged man swinging from a *A LITTLE, THEN TOLD* yardarm; a panhandler's homily; an archer whose *HIM I'D READ IT WHEN I HAD TIME. HE GOT* arrows fly around the world and land at his feet; a *REALLY ANGRY, CALLED* tent-city aflame; railroad tracks that run through a *ME A CONDESCENDING* mountain tunnel; a vanished tribe; a band of would- *ASSHOLE. I LOST IT —* be revolutionaries; a young woman aboard a ship, *FELT LIKE HEY, I DRIVE TO FUCKING FLORIDA +* shy about her accented English; an insane parade of *HELP KEEP YOU ALIVE,* monkeys; a driving rain of printed pages; and infi- *+ THIS IS WHAT I GET? SO I TOLD HIM TO FUCK* nite regret. Whether any of these elements cohere *OFF + HUNG UP. TOTALLY* into stories is a separate question entirely. *SELFISH, SELF-RIGHTEOUS,*

SMALL. BUT I'VE BEEN THINKING ABOUT IT + I REALIZE THERE'S MORE TO IT THAN THAT.
  S. looks up from his work when he hears the rum- *IT'S ABOUT UNDERSTANDING* ble and clank of the newspaper truck trundling along *HOW FRAGILE HE WAS,* the snowy main street, as it does every morning on its *HOW FRAGILE I'VE BEEN HOW FRAGILE WE ALL* way to deposit stacks of the day's newspaper in a *ARE. INCLUDING YOU.* wooden bin in the central plaza. The truck, like the *AND ILSA + MOODY (EVEN* people of the city, is visible only through that frosty, *IF NEITHER OF THEM KNOWS IT). STRAKA +* foggy translucence. The sounds of its complicated *FILOMELA, DEFINITELY.* engine and snow-chained wheels are similarly muted, *WE ALL WANT TO BE* but S. has trained himself to hear them, looks for- *GREAT — HOWEVER YOU DEFINE THAT — AND WE* ward to the daily clamor. The simple ritual of going *SO OFTEN AREN'T. WE'RE* outside to fetch a newspaper is one of the few things *ALL JUST IN THE MUCK TRYING TO BELIEVE* that help S. maintain whatever sanity he has left. *WE'RE CAPABLE OF GREATNESS,*

BUT CLOSER TO BREAKING THAN WE WANT TO ADMIT. AND WE TELL OURSELVES STORIES — ABOUT OURSELVES, BUT MAYBE ALSO ALL

MIXING SOT + VACLAV'S *THESE STORIES ABOUT OTHER PEOPLE,* *LIFE.* *ABOUT CHARACTERS — AS A WAY TO* *HIDE FROM HOW SMALL WE ARE.*

You just said VMS *Maybe it's not hiding.* *was Vaclav — without* *Maybe they help us not be* *any qualifiers.* { 381 } *so small.*

MAYBE — BUT W/ HELP FROM OTHER PEOPLE ON SOME BOOKS? OR ALL BUT THE LAST 3? WINGED SHOES (LOVE STORY WRITTEN FOR ~~HER~~ FILO) CORIOLIS (MASSIVE EXISTENTIAL FREAKOUT), + SOT.

ı

When he steps out of his building and onto the street, the cold shocks his lungs, leaves him short of breath. The wind punishes him as he moves against it, numbing his face, stinging his eyes, sending needles of cold through his many layers of clothing. It howls down the street with what is the closest thing to a melody one hears in this place.

There are no birds in the Winter City. Not that S. has seen, anyway. He dreams, occasionally, of a black bird on its back in the snow, struggling. Its breast has been pierced by a bullet. What spills from the wound is not the bird's blood but the pigment from its plumage; it seeps into the snow, spreading outward in a black oval. The carcass pales as it drains, lighter and lighter, and the snow thirstily, even greedily, accepts all the color it is giving up, until finally it is just a white, raven-shaped husk in a cold expanse of black. A bird of negative space. But S. knows it's just a dream. He has enough sense left to tell himself that.

He walks with his arms wrapped around himself, though this offers no additional warmth. How far will he have to go? He can't say. A mile, perhaps

{ 382 }

WAIT. HE SAID
"YOU ALL"?
Just double-checked.
He did.

Letter from Summ.
to Ekstrom, Oct. 1930:
"Distressed to hear of
S.'s too-lengthy hospital
exile. please know
that you all have our
best wishes + loving
thoughts."

TWO MONTHS BEFORE
EKSTROM DIED.
Also: can't find any
mention in Durand's
docs that she was in the
hospital then.
MAYBE SHE DIDN'T THINK
IT WAS WORTH WRITING ABOUT.
SHE WAS TOUGH.
She was also thorough.
She was corresponding w/ Garcia Ferrara
regularly right before then, + again in March 1931,
and there's no mention of it. Not even an oblique one. as far as I
can tell.

He has to tell himself
it isn't true.

more, but his sense of such things feels impaired, and on some days the slog feels twice or even three times as long. The Winter City, it seems, is a city of mutable distances.

Will today be the day when another resident raises his head and meets S.'s eyes? Acknowledges, even in these circumstances, a shared humanity?

It will not. Today will be another day of his walking among the mute and alienated, every step reminding him that he is as ghostly and indistinct to them as they are to him. They may share a destination—the newspaper bin—but they will return to their sad, quiet domiciles and read of distant events that they have no power to change.

S. tries to blink away the ice crusting his lashes. He tucks his head and mules onward.

The bin is four feet high, and the snowbank in which it sits is nearly as high. S. reaches in and with numb, fumbling fingers, picks up a copy. On the front page today: a photograph of yet another city leveled by incendiaries.

The extreme cold neutralizes the sweet aromatic compounds of the newspaper ink, or perhaps it's just that the whipping wind carries the smell

I can't believe you went to Standefer.

DESPERATE TIMES, ETC. *and no one recognized you.* EVEN SHE DIDN'T, AT FIRST. ALL I DID WAS WEAR A HAT. IT'S AMAZING HOW EASY IT IS TO BE INVISIBLE.

instantly away. Still, S. raises the newspaper to his nose for a whiff, expecting and receiving nothing. He folds the newspaper in half, rolls it up, tucks it into his coat pocket, and begins the trek back to his building. Often, the wind reverses direction the moment he does, which makes the return as difficult as the journey out. Today, though, it holds its course and blusters at his back, pushing him along so insistently that his walk becomes a trot. He slips and falls several times, takes a plunge into a drift of fresh snow.

As he approaches his building, a sudden gust sends him skidding past the doorway. His arms wheel; his feet search for purchase as they try to backpedal, but he falls again, this time onto his belly, and he slides along the ice like a penguin. He comes to a stop against the window of an empty storefront. The plumbing inside the building must be leaky; icicles as thick as oak trunks reach down from the ceiling to the floor.

He watches his reflection in the window as it struggles to stand. When it finally manages to gain its footing, he studies it carefully: a man regarding him, standing before a forest of ice, the last traces of youth in his face having departed, and he is brought

{ 384 }

Been thinking about this lately— it really just hit me that this is it ... leaving college means you can't think of yourself as a kid anymore. You're not a kid anymore.

And sometimes that's exciting — but sometimes it's totally depressing.

ONE OF THE THINGS THAT HIT ME IN THE HOSPITAL WAS THAT I'M NOT REALLY YOUNG ANYMORE. OK, I'M NOT 30 YET, BUT STILL — I SPENT A DECADE STUDYING THIS STUFF, + IT TURNS OUT IT WAS FOR NOTHING. NO PAYOFF. NO SATISFACTION. NO CAREER. AND HOW THE HELL DO YOU START OVER? HOW DO YOU REINVENT YOURSELF? AND, OBVIOUSLY, I HAVEN'T YET.

Maybe you have — just not in the most obvious way.

(A) I DON'T KNOW WHAT YOU'RE TALKING ABOUT, AND (B) TO WHAT END? WHAT'S THAT GOING TO GET ME?

ⓐ I don't know

ⓑ maybe that's just what we're supposed to do.

back to a moment in the cave above the wharf city, a moment amid stalactites and stalagmites and the painted histories of the K——, a moment of hope—however faint—in which Corbeau was still alive, Pfeifer was still Pfeifer, and S., despite knowing none of his own history, felt connected to both past and future.

He turns away from the window, squares his shoulders to the bitter wind, and heads back home, against the wind. Fury swirls inside him like the snow-devils that spin over the streets—at Vévoda and his Agents, yes, but also at himself, for choices made and deferred. How strange: he is alone in a cityscape of half-existence, and yet the anger reminds him of what it feels like to be vibrant and real. He would laugh at this irony, but the wind might freeze his lungs.

In the foyer of his building, he unwraps his scarf and stamps his feet free of snow. On the floor is an envelope with a smeared letter S inked on it. His back complains as he bends to retrieve it. He sniffs the ink and finds it sweet. He tugs off his gloves, tears it open, discovers a note in an unfamiliar hand. It addresses him by name but is unsigned. He is instructed to go, with haste, to a flat on the ninth

{ 385 }

— I WASN'T ANYWHERE NEAR AS ANGRY AS I THOUGHT I'D BE, YOU KNOW.

I'm sure Dr. Brand said something about how talking things out always helps... ★

BUT I FELT IT EVEN BEFORE I STARTED TALKING TO HER. (I MEAN, I WAS ANGRY ABOUT WHAT SHE WAS PULLING W/ YOU—BUT NOT SO MUCH ABOUT HER + ME.)

★ ARE YOU GOING TO TRY THAT W/ YOUR PARENTS?
Are you going to try it with yours?

I THINK IT STARTED TO FADE WHEN I MET YOU.

(MET YOU FOR REAL, I MEAN.)

floor of a building six blocks west of the plaza. This would mean braving another arctic half-mile.

He doesn't hesitate. He wraps his scarf, dons his gloves, and invites the weather to visit its worst upon him. If he is walking into a wolf's lair, a room full of Agents who have decided that an icebound exile is not a grim enough fate for him, so be it. He is ready for whatever may come.

By the time he reaches the building, his eyebrows and lashes have iced over, his cheeks are deadened with frost, and his upper lip is thickly glazed with mucus and the vapor of his breath. He pauses, looks up at the ninth and uppermost floor. No light comes from the window. Half-seen pedestrians stream around him silently—without words, without even the sounds of their feet compressing the snow.

Is it even colder than usual today? One of his feet has gone completely numb. He chops his heel against the ground, trying to kick some feeling back into it. A triangular chunk of ice goes skidding away, revealing the corner of a brass plaque set into the sidewalk. On it is the symbol that he has not seen in ages. He kicks and kicks at the ice until the entire plaque is uncovered.

{ 386 }

[left margin handwritten:] I didn't use your paper. I didn't even read it. Every word of that fucking paper is mine. + it wasn't easy—that's what I told them right as I walked into the office. I hardly even remember what happened after that. Too much adrenaline.

[left margin handwritten:] SIGNIFICANCE?

[left margin handwritten:] So is this in honor of his life? Or celebrating his death?

[bottom left handwritten:] NEVER THOUGHT OF THAT — "TELLER OF TALES" IS AMBIGUOUS — COULD B MEAN "STORYTELLER" OR "LIAR!"
And what about the symbol? Which side is using it? That's not at all clear to me.

[bottom right handwritten:] OK— I understand now. B/c good guys don't burn barns. BUT THERE'S ALSO ONE @ FEVERBACH'S BIRTHPLACE. AND IN DURAND'S CAVE. AND ON EKSTROM'S DRAWINGS OF THE BIRDS.

> ⸎ FROM THIS BUILDING FELL ⸎
> ARQUIMEDES DE SOBREIRO,
> TELLER OF TALES.
> JANUARY 9, 1625
> ⸎   ⸎

AND IN FILOMELA'S
CAVE, TOO.

But there's
also one on the
pavement right under
my bedroom window.

Good guys don't
fucking do things
like that!

Fresh snow has drifted up the building's steps, nearly to the front door, but his footprints are the only ones leading up to the portico. He pauses there, scans the street behind him, expecting something— he doesn't know what—to appear different. But all he sees are the same insubstantial people walking among each other, turning corners, entering and exiting buildings, kneeling to re-lace frozen boots, carrying newspapers that appear less solid, less sharply defined, than they do sitting in the news bin.

OBVIOUS NOW. BOTH
SIDES USE IT. ONE TO
MAKE THEIR MARK;
THE OTHER TO TAUNT
THEM — AS IN: WE'RE
WINNING AND WE CAN
APPROPRIATE YOUR SYMBOL
OF WHO YOU ARE.

The stairs are uneven, and they creak and groan under his feet as he climbs flight after flight. He ascends slowly, reminding himself to be calm, to conserve energy and focus. (O, for the time when such things were instinctive!) When he steps out onto the ninth-floor landing, though, he is sweating and breathing heavily. He takes off his scarf and gloves and stows them in his coat pockets. The only

you wanted me to think it through.

SHIP OF THESEUS

You can't just leave. It's not fair.

Leave later if you want. But please be here now.

because I told you my story source of light is a tiny window that is opaque with frost. The air smells of abandonment.

For the first time in his exile here, the voices of the past call to him, though not in the usual clamorous babel. He hears just two. They are faint and thin, surrounded by the vast echo of empty centuries:

Você não está seguro, a male voice says.

Ninguém é, a female voice says.[1]

WHY USE PORTUGUESE HERE?

Trying to speak to Filomela as directly as possible.

Then, almost inaudibly, a high-pitched, descending tone that could be a squeaky hinge, a sick cat, or a man plummeting nine stories to his death.

S. approaches the door to the flat. He runs his hand through what remains of his hair, then wipes it dry on his coat. He knocks.

Footsteps approach slowly from inside the flat. The knob turns, and the door opens—just a crack, through which he can see the eye that scrutinizes him. The eye then looks left, right, and over his shoulder, as if to confirm that S. is alone.

Wish you could get Moody to call his guys off or if there really is a new S. and they're after me, get your fucking pals from Serin to do something about it.

Unless it's them.

"It's me," S. says. "Just me."

The door opens wider. A hand reaches through the gap, grabs his wrist, pulls. Alarm fires through

Can't find anything— and I don't how many more ways I can look at this footnote.

MAYBE IT'S NOT PART OF A CODE. MAYBE IT JUST MEANS WHAT SHE SAYS.

Then where's the code for the chapter?

MAYBE THERE ISN'T ONE. MAYBE THERE'S SOME OTHER KIND OF MESSAGE.

---

[1] In the original typescript, there are numerous strikethroughs and handwritten corrections which show that the author changed his mind repeatedly about which voice should utter which line—so often, in fact, that the page becomes a smudged, illegible mess. I have reproduced the line as it was originally typed—a decision more archaeological than editorial.

→ *Maybe it's been right there in front of us. The title. The image. That's all she needs—she's saying they're similar— both birds,* { 388 } *both fragile—at any moment they could cease to be who they are right now. Could die. Could find they believe something different. Or love someone different. SO: SEIZE THE DAY. Which he didn't.*

his body, until he realizes he is being guided, not yanked. He steps over the threshold…

…and into a bare and nearly featureless room, where paint peels from the walls in long, nearly ornamental curls. There is no furniture. There is a window, iced-over on the outside, begrimed on the inside. There is a closet door along one wall. The only detail about the room that matters, though, is that Sola is in it.

She pushes the door closed behind him, then looks up into his eyes, searching for something while keeping a firm hold on his arm.

Her presence here is astonishing. Nearly as astonishing to him, too, is the fact that she is in focus and vivid, warm-blooded and breathing, undeniably *real*. And also: he can feel her touching him. Her hand is a warm, tight compress around his wrist. The fur-edged cuff of her black overcoat tickles his skin.

Shallow wrinkles line her forehead, the corners of her eyes and mouth, the declivity that defines her chin. Her hair, cut to chin-length in a style he assumes is fashionable in some place or time foreign to him, is a mix of bright and dark grays. Her face is still a bright, pale orb of moonlight, but she seems thinner than he remembers. He is terrified, suddenly, that she will vanish again, that they will continue to age, and likely die, apart. He very nearly blurts *I love you*.

"Are you real?" he asks instead.

"I can't prove that I am," she says. "But you can't prove that I'm not."

"So it's a question of trust. Or faith." He smiles.

"Yes. I believe so."

She goes to the window, peers through a pinhole space that allows a clear view. She scans the street, the nearby buildings, the sky.

"I think we're safe," S. says.

"No," she says. "No one is."

Feeling is returning to his frozen foot in maddening stabs. He flexes his toes, winces, flexes again. "So," he observes, "Sobreiro lived here."

"For a very short time," she says. "More significantly, he died here."

"It's quite a coincidence that this is where we'd meet."

"Perhaps a coincidence. Perhaps a tradition."

"I don't understand."

"You seem to think I have answers. I'm doing the same thing as you are: following instinct, reacting. Perhaps I'm a half-step ahead."

Top margin (starred note):

★ OR MAYBE THAT'S WHAT HE WAS DOING W/ THE WHOLE BOOK — LESS DIRECT, BUT STILL, MAYBE THE BEST WAY HE THOUGHT HE HAD. MAYBE HE THOUGHT HE'D BE GIVING MORE OF HIMSELF BY USING THE BOOK.

Top right:

DON'T FORGET: FXC MADE HER OWN CHOICES, TOO.

Top, in cursive (black ink):

Maybe he thought that — I mean, why wouldn't he? Writing was what he loved doing, it was how he defined himself — maybe the only way he knew himself — but it's also pretty convenient. Do it in the book, and you get to duck doing it in person. You're risking less. You're exposing yourself less. It's about not being brave enough to love someone. To be *with someone*, in love.

Left margin (upper):

WONDER HOW MANY TIMES STRAKA WAS ON THE VERGE OF DOING THIS...

Doesn't matter how many times. What matters is whether he did or not. And he didn't — UNLESS YOU COUNT THE INVITATION TO HAVANA.

Not enough. Not even close. ★

Right margin (middle):

You should have told same Plumberson — whatever something like this about Vaclav

Left margin (lower):

JEN: GOT A PACKAGE FROM THEM TODAY. ANOTHER CHECK — BUT MORE IMP.: A PRINT OF THE HAVANA PHOTO!! NOTE SAYS IT RECENTLY CAME INTO THEIR POSSESSION + THEY'RE EAGER FOR INSIGHTS. — Uh-huh.

So now it's time for you to pay them back.

THEY'RE ON OUR SIDE. I KNOW IT.

Maybe they're the ones who bought it at the auction in the first place and they need you to figure out why it's so important. Or they could've altered the image to mess w/you, send you in the wrong direction. You can't *know*.

Right margin (middle-lower):

It's over. I've told them she made a mistake.

Bottom right:

GREAT, GREAT NEWS, JEN. AMAZING. But why did she? She was so sure before.

"How did you find me?" he asks.

"It was the only place left," she says, as if this were obvious. "Do you still want to find Vévoda?"

Until today, until an hour ago, he would have struggled to answer this. But now? "Yes," he says. "Definitely."

She has found the location of the Château, she tells him, and she knows how to get them both inside. Nine months from now, in land-time, a thousand people descending on the place for an event at which Vévoda will make some sort of announcement. From the guest list (which includes heads of state, military and religious leaders, tin-pot dictators, upstart rebels, and titans of industry—in short, everyone to whom Vévoda can sell arms, everyone for whom he can broker alliances that will require arms, everyone harvesting or acquiring natural resources on a large scale, everyone eager to hear and parrot his pithy observations about destroying in order to create, about the art of rearranging the world), the announcement is almost certainly a significant one. "You can have a tremendous impact there," she says.

"I've achieved nothing," he informs her. "I have nothing significant to show for my life. What impact could I possibly have?"

Really?

Do you think anything like this ever happened @ Bouchard's?

NOT THE WAY IT HAPPENS HERE. I THINK THIS IS WHAT VMS WANTED TO HAPPEN. WISH FULFILLMENT.

Except that isn't the ending he wrote.

{ 391 }

———

She opens the closet door, revealing the valise he left behind in the Territory, though now it is more battered and scarred, flyspecked and mildewed. She drops it in front of him, and when he asks if it's his, she nods.

"You were in the Territory," he says. "In that canoe."

"Yes."

"Who was with you?" he asks. He braces himself for her answer.

She looks confused. "I was alone," she says.

She is not lying, he thinks, though what she says is not true.

Bundled against the cold, they descend the stairs of Sobreiro's building and expose themselves to the city's eternal winter. She stays several paces ahead of him, and they do not speak or look at each other, lest they call attention to themselves. They walk quickly, both of them hunched over to fend off the wind, and even then, S.'s eyes sting and burn and tear; the wetness freezes on his cheeks. His fingers stiffen into a claw around the handle of the valise.

A mile, maybe more. S. squints. He even closes his eyes for a dozen steps at a time, and when Sola stops, he bumps into her back. She has led him to

———

the Winter City's harbor, which is frozen in pack ice and looks as though it has been for centuries. Skeletal remains of ships, captured and crushed by the ice, fill the bay.

"Why are we here?" he asks.

"We have a ship," she says.

He looks at her, dumbstruck, and she points out over the frozen waste. The solid ice stretches for miles. Beyond that, though, he can see a thin band of open water and a dark blot atop it. She steps down onto the surface of the sea, then looks back, waiting for him to follow her, but he is afraid. He envisions himself walking atop the ice and hearing a tremendous crack, then watching a fissure open under his feet. He imagines falling into the water and being swept under solid ice by the current.

"The ice is solid," she says. "I walked in from the ship."

A question of trust. Or faith.

"My papers," he says uncertainly, remembering the stack of newspapers in his apartment. "My work."

"Already loaded," she tells him, and he believes her. He takes her hand. He steps out onto the ice, and they move forward together, one step, and then another.

Santorini-Man body found in Nova Scotia last month. Two others: one in Cameroon, one on an atoll off Belize.

WTF? THOUGHT THE BARCELONA BODY WAS JUST A COINCIDENCE... BUT NOW?

If I'm going to get dumped in the river, I hope I at least get to choose which Straka book they take the page from.

DON'T JOKE ABOUT THAT. Actually, I think I have to.

FINE. WHICH BOOK? Winged Shoes.

NOT SOT? I want the fantasy love story. The one without all the regret.

WHAT BEGINS AT THE WATER SHALL END THERE...
It's funny — how can he ever know if he's at an ending or a beginning? How can we ever know?

like a gun — TELL ME YOU DON'T HAVE A GUN.
I don't have a gun.

They walk side by side, slipping but never falling. "I've always thought you know who I am," he says, speaking loudly to make himself heard over the wind.

"As much as anyone does," Sola says. "No more." He watches her breath blossom and dash in the stiff wind.

"You found me. In the Old Quarter. You knew to be there."

"I wasn't looking for you. You were there."

S. presses. "As far as you know, who am I?"

She wipes her nose, brushes ice crystals from her lashes, continues her shuffle forward. "What you're asking, I think, is who you *were*," she says slowly, "which is relevant only if you care deeply about it. Do you?"

S. hesitates. He knows he used to care. He feels as though he *ought* to care. He has spent years *assuming* he cared but doing little to pursue the matter. The mystery no longer moves him. The facts of his life are no more important than the long-forgotten official documents on which they were inked. And the memories? The feeling of being part of a family, the sense-impressions of a child, the minor epiphanies and heartbreaks of a teenager for whom the real world begins to resolve into focus

{ 394 }

Straka, to Filomela. Why couldn't he have told her directly??

IN THE ORIGINAL MS, SHE DOESN'T ANSWER HIM HERE. Filomela, to Straka. as directly as she could.

A QUESTION HE HAS TO ANSWER FOR HIMSELF. Or decide whether he needs to answer it at all.

BECAUSE WE ARE ONLY WHO WE ARE — MEANING RIGHT NOW. And also who we decide we will be.

as he spends day after day packing gunpowder into brass casings? He has experienced these in the trance-states on the ship and in the frigid apartment. He may not be able to possess those moments, but they are around him, and from time to time they may shine brightly. He can see the stars; he no longer has a need for the constellations.

A hundred yards ahead, the solid harbor ice ends and the pack ice begins. Dark water is visible in the cracks between the floes, which undulate with each push of the waves beneath. And floating amid all the ice, with huge chunks of it bumping against its hull, is a familiar ship.

[Intuition tells him it is the same ship, somehow resurrected and restored to a condition even shabbier than its usual chaos of disrepair. It may be the most awkward, shabbily-rendered, ramshackle vessel ever to float on water, an offense to even the most forgiving of nautical sensibilities.] No two pieces of wood in the carvel-planked hull appear to have come from the same source. Warp afflicts all three masts and the bowsprit. The sails are stitched-together scraps of canvas in shades of yellow and

VMS'S VISION OF HIMSELF?

Or Vaclav's.

OR: A TONGUE-IN-CHEEK DESCRIPTION OF THE WHOLE "V. M. STRAKA" COMPOSITE.

Wow. Hard to think of how those could be more different.

bone and gray, scarred with long and winding seams that conjure images of surgeries gone horribly awry. The topdeck guns are a hodgepodge of weapons from different eras and regions, and a few are so crusted-over that they must have spent decades on the ocean floor. It is entirely possible, S. realizes, and in fact seems quite likely, that not one plank or hatch or cleat or peg or bolt or nail or rope remains from the night he was first taken aboard. And yet: this is the ship. However aberrant and ugly this ship is—however fundamentally *impossible* it is—he finds the sight of it comforting. Even if every plank in the bulkhead in his cabin has been replaced, he knows that when he lies in his hammock tonight he will nonetheless feel the presence of his words wrapping around the room. He may not understand all, or even much, of what he read in the book on the Obsidian Island, but he has put his faith in its tale of the ship's continuity.

"It takes more than destruction to destroy a ship like this," she says. HA.

He stops walking. Leans into the whipping, ice-flecked wind so he won't be blown backward. "Have you been to the island?" he asks.

"The island is where I boarded."

Could be said about the S. Right? People are still going missing, falling, getting Santorini-manned... so someone's out there fighting.

HOPE THE S IS... BECAUSE THE NEW S IS.

Wait— how'd you know I didn't use your paper? I hadn't told you yet.

I DIDN'T. JUST BELIEVED.

So you were willing to lie. I might have done it, you know.

Maybe I just wasn't desperate enough.

MAYBE I KNEW YOU WEREN'T.

———

SO I SHOULD PROBABLY TELL YOU THAT I WENT + SAW ILSA THIS MORNING. TOLD HER THAT YOU + I HAD DISCUSSED THE POEM BUT THAT I DIDN'T DO ANYTHING BEYOND WHAT A TA WOULD DO— ASK QUESTIONS, TRY TO GUIDE, ETC. — + THE PAPER YOU WROTE WAS ALL YOURS. SAID I'D SIGN AFFADAVITS, WHATEVER WAS NEEDED.

"Why were you there?"

"Helping the Lady. Curating. Translating. Bind-ing. Restoring what can be restored."

"But how did you _get_ there? Originally? It's not on maps. It's inside the—" He doesn't have the word he requires. With his gloved hands he makes an arc that suggests a dome.

That's why she backed off? I don't buy it. Not with the way she came at me before.

Sola exhales deeply. They both watch as it rises, tumbles, dissipates. "Just like you," she says. "A long time ago, I was taken there. On a different ship with a different crew. Why? Asking why is like ask-ing why the sky is above us, why the stars are beyond it. They're good questions, to be sure, but they have no answers, and at some point one chooses not to ask anymore."

MAYBE SHE KNOWS ME WELL ENOUGH TO TELL WHEN I'M BEING SINCERE.

WE TALKED FOR A WHILE, ACTUALLY. FIRST I TOLD HER I WAS GOING TO GIVE MOODY MY CONSENT. (SHE SAID SHE DIDN'T "GIVE A FUCK ABOUT MOODY.") AND I TOLD HER I WASN'T ANGRY @ HER ANYMORE. NOT ABOUT ANY OF IT. SAID WE'RE ALL JUST TRYING TO FIGURE OUT WHAT WE WANT + GET CLOSER TO HAVING IT — + COMPARED TO ALL THE STRAKA VS. BOUCHARD S VS. NEWS, BOUCHARD VS. ALL THE PEACE + FAIRNESS REMAINING IN THE WORLD, NONE OF IT MATTERS ALL THAT MUCH.

Ahead of them, the crew is lowering a gangway down to what S. hopes is one of the steadier floes in the pack and one to which he and Sola will have a navigable path. He eyes the ice below his feet. It must be thinning. At any moment, a crack might open beneath them, or the front edge might tip below the surface of the freezing sea.

Sola steps out onto a smooth, flat floe. When S. hesitates, she waves him forward. "Hurry," she says. "The sooner we get to open water, the better."

Except you're still a little angry at her.

THEY'RE JUST WORDS. THEY DIDN'T COST ME ANYTHING.

So much for sincerity...

———

||S. contemplates the valise in his hand//It's not heavy, but he is wary of anything that might disrupt his balance. "Who was the man with the scars on his face?" he calls to her. If that man had chosen someone else in the bar to shanghai, S.'s life might have been entirely different, possibly even sane, serene, blessedly ordinary. He had already met Sola, though, he reminds himself. Perhaps she would have led him to this same place, if only by a different path.

"I've seen him several times," Sola says, "but I don't know him. His purposes are not necessarily the same as ours."

"Not necessarily?"

Sola turns and walks out over the ice. He can tell that under her heavy coat, she has shrugged. "Not necessarily," she repeats. The wind carries her words back to him.

His first step onto the pack ice is a tentative one, and the unsteadiness of it sends him a few steps into a staggering, wide-armed dance. He recovers quickly, though, well before the ice's edge. He feels less frightened than he thought he would.

He follows Sola's path, hopscotching from one islet of ice to the next. While he is careful with his footing, he finds himself enjoying the ride on each

{ 398 }

Handwritten margin notes:

MEET ME HERE TONIGHT. MIDNIGHT. OK? OK. *I'm going to use the tunnels. Don't feel safe above.*

I WOULDN'T. MORE VOICES + MORE SYMBOLS DOWN THERE LAST NIGHT. SAFER ABOVE

MOODY LAUGHED WHEN I ASKED HIM ABOUT THE GUYS WHO'VE BEEN FOLLOWING YOU. HE SAID I MUST HAVE FOUND THE RIGHT GIRL FOR MYSELF.

REMEMBER WHAT I SAID ABOUT ANGER FADING AWAY? IT FLARED BACK UP AGAIN. A BARN FIRE. A FUCKING BLACK-VINE FIRE. HE WAS DRUNK, BUT STILL. *next time one of them comes near me he's going to regret it.*

IN THEORY: GREAT. IN PRACTICE: DON'T EVEN THINK OF PUTTING YOURSELF @ RISK LIKE THAT.

So I'm just supposed to wait around?

tilting slab, the rise and fall, the listing to one side or the other, the giving way as he pushes off to jump to the next. By the time he catches up with her on the broad, flat block on which the gangway rests, with open water, rippling and serious, just beyond, he feels a joyous desire to go back to the harbor, make the ice-walk all over again.

On the deck are twenty or so sailors who look as if they are dressed in patchwork outfits of the same materials that compose the sails, readying the ship for departure with the plodding stolidity that S. remembers well. One of them takes Sola's hand as she hops down to the deck, and S. drops his jaw, stunned to see such a gesture aboard this ship. He himself receives no such offer of help, but several of the crew glance up at him, offering a different sort of silence than he used to get—obtuse, perhaps, but respectful. It is a welcome change.

Though he knows no one survived the attack in the Territory, the ship's rebirth gives him hope; he scans the icy deck, stem to stern, hoping to see Maelstrom's distinctive bulk, but the big man is not there. He studies the faces and physiques of the assembled crew. He recognizes none of them. What he does recognize are the black stitches that seal their mouths. |*Tradition.*|

"Where did you find your crew?" he asks Sola.

"They're not *my* crew," she says. "They're *the* crew."

"But who recruited them? Someone must have."

She shrugs. "There's rarely a shortage of the willing."

"Did you make them sew themselves?"

"I'm a passenger. I don't have any influence over them. I don't have any authority."

"Do I?" he asks.

"I hardly think so," she says, and the dismissiveness of her answer stings him. He wants to say, *Really? After everything I've done, everything I've been through, everything I've given up?* But he knows such complaints have no place here.

"They do understand our mission," she adds, "and they do recognize its importance."

He suggests that they proceed to the waist, to shelter themselves from the wind, but she declines. She tells him to follow her and leads him to the chart-room door. "You do have one old friend here," she says.

S. has no idea whom she might mean. No one in the old crew was his friend, and the only friends he ever had on land are long dead.

{ 400 }

IT CONTINUES. HE'S
EXPECTING THE S TO
CONTINUE. AND THE NEW
S CONTINUES. NOVA SCOTIA
BODY WAS ID'ED — GUY
NAMED KAVANAGH. IRISH
WRITER. RADICAL. NOT
VERY WELL KNOWN, BUT
STILL.

How'd they ID him?
Whole point of
SantoMan is that
he can't be ID'ed.

SOMEONE MUST HAVE
MADE A MISTAKE.

EXCEPT THEY KEEP GETTING KILLED.
OR BOUGHT.

She opens the door and leads him into the gloomy den, as dank-smelling as ever but now with a fetid, musky odor as well. All S. notices at first is the table at which Maelstrom would hunch himself over his maps, but then he hears a rustle from below it. Curled up on a blanket is the monkey, now ancient and rickety, the fur around its snout and eyes so white that S. at first assumes that the creature has been out in the frosty weather on deck. It looks up at S. and makes a thin, high-pitched noise in its throat. It might be a greeting, or it might be the familiar mockery.

"It's good to see you," S. lies.

The monkey curls its lips back, revealing a toothless void of a mouth. It then promptly drops back into sleep.

"It's as if the thing is following me," S. says.

"Or you're following it," she says, and though he cannot see her face, she sounds as if she is smiling.

She picks up a scrap of paper from the table and hands it to him. "Our map," she says. The paper is much thinner than the heavy parchment of Maelstrom's charts. And unlike those—which, despite their fungal spots and their propensities to bleed, were carefully drawn works of cartographic precision, even artistry—this one looks as if it was scrawled out in a great hurry.

{ 401 }

what's with all the creepy dental details?

Called Jacob today. Told him that the next time he tries to fuck my life, he should at least have the decency to let me know first.

WHAT DID HE SAY?

He went on + on about how he was genuinely worried, etc. I said I understood that he had good intentions, I just didn't care. All I care about is what's going to happen when my parents get here.

THERE'S NO WAY IT'LL BE AS BAD AS YOU THINK. YOU'RE AN ADULT. THERE'S ONLY SO MUCH THEY CAN DO.

I know that. Not sure they do.

I ASKED HER.
SHE SMILED. SHE SAID
SHE DIDN'T KNOW FOR SURE
THAT THE MAP WAS CORRECT,
BUT YOU COULD TELL SHE WAS
REALLY PROUD SHE'D DONE IT.

Checked satellite maps.
Doesn't look like there's
anything there now.

BUT PLACES CAN BE
OBSCURED FROM SATELLITE
MAPS. SOUNDS LIKE
GARDEN-VARIETY
CONSPIRACY-THEORY,
SURE, BUT STILL...

We should go.
Look for ourselves.
It's not that far away.
Maybe a day by train?
Less?

Or Filomela put it in. That
would be so bad-ass: putting
a map to Bouchard's estate
in the goddamn book.
She's my idol.

SHIP OF THESEUS

NOT IN THE ORIGINAL MS.
MAYBE HE DIDN'T BOTHER TO
DRAW IT? THOUGHT SOMEONE ELSE
WOULD?

J.B.C.

CITY COPS CAME TO MY
APT. THIS MORNING.
I'M GUESSING THEY FOUND
ME B/C OF THE CAR
REGISTRATION. KNEW IT
WOULD HAPPEN EVENTUALLY
ANYWAY: TOLD THEM
THEY COULDN'T COME IN
W/O A WARRANT. WHICH
THEY WON'T BE ABLE TO GET,
B/C THE ONLY THING THEY
HAVE IS MOODY ACCUSING
ME. NO PROOF I WAS
EVEN ON CAMPUS THAT
DAY—OR FOR MONTHS
BEFORE.

France. The foothills of the Pyrenees. S. had heard a rumor, years ago, that Vévoda's estate was in this region, but he never found evidence that it was anything more than another wild guess.

"How did you get this?" He barely recognizes the sound of his voice.

"If you mistreat many, many people for many, many years, eventually one of them will grow desperate enough to risk her life to stop you," she says. "One person's audacity: the only prerequisite for resistance."

"And the woman who drew this?"

—If they found you, then the suit guys can find you.

JEN: IF THEY HAVEN'T DONE ANYTHING BY NOW,
THEY'RE NOT GOING TO.

Maybe they're waiting for us to { 402 }
find something. I don't know. All I know is I keep
seeing them. —— THEY MIGHT NOT EVEN BE
WHO YOU THINK THEY ARE.

"Risked her life. And gave it."

"What happened to her?"

"She washed ashore in Cap de Bol. She had drowned, but not in the sea. She had drowned in wine. Someone had *held her down and drowned her in wine*."

Why does this feel so much more shocking than the massacre at B——? Than the slayings of Ostrero, Stenfalk, Corbeau? Is it because it seems like a much more personal sort of killing? One that Vévoda, personally, was much closer to?

||Is it so much worse than anything he has done?||

Another good question, but also one without an answer. It is also one he decides not to ask anymore.

The Winter City has disappeared behind the weather, one shroud-dream over the next, and the pack ice has thinned; there are still bergs floating in the water around them, but they are smaller, and solitary, as lost as the stars in the firmament above the ship. S. and Sola are sitting in one of the less-foul-smelling cabins on the second deck, drinking tea that she has made. It is a terribly weak brew, but still a luxury he never thought he'd encounter on board. They speak little; it is as if the air has been churned up

[handwritten margin note, right of top paragraph:] Newspaper in Marseille reported this : 3/19/48. It _happened_.

[handwritten margin note, right of middle:] ANOTHER PART OF A CONFESSION? OR JUST FOLLOWING THROUGH W/ S.'S STORYLINE?

WE WOULD'VE HAD MORE TIME.

with decades' worth of fruitless pursuit and missed connections and thoughts unspoken, and they are waiting quietly for all this matter—these motes of opportunity forgone—to settle around them. Perhaps, afterward, they will leave the cabin without stirring any of them back up. Bar the door behind them.

S.'s cup is nearly empty, and he gently swirls the last tepid puddle of tea, watches a few flecks of leaves spin within it. He asks her if she has been down to the orlop during her time on the ship.

"That has never been my role," she says. "It's the crew's. And it has been yours ever since you chose to enter—which you could have guessed, if you'd read the Lady's book more closely. I shouldn't be surprised, though. I'm told that's what happened with Sobreiro." She touches his cheek; though she has kept her hands wrapped around her cup, her fingertips are icy. It feels like a strange moment for such an intimate gesture.

"So I _am_ connected to Sobreiro. But how?"

Her tone is one suited to giving instruction to a dim child. "Different stories," she says. "Same tradition."

And for the first time, he understands the tradition, or at least recognizes the most essential of its constituent parts. The stories that move outside time—that

Wandering if we'd be where we are now if we'd met sooner.

But then it became hers.

---

divert, oppose, resist. His life of words, of pictures and sounds that *contemplate* what the world is or could be. One atom of truth. He remembers Maelstrom, his guide long ago, bearing down on him and rasping *Got t' respect 'er, trait 'er like a frag a' y'self. She's wha's carrickin us.* It is time to descend the ladder. To get to work. "Come with me," he says. He wants to tell her that his best moments at the desk came when he felt her nearby. And now she is here. She is nearby.

"I'll walk down with you," she says. "But I can't stay."

They stand on the rocking deck of the orlop, in the doorway to the room.

Around them are the brush and rumble of water against the hull as the heavy winds speed the xebec on its course. S.'s head buzzes, and a wave of vertigo sweeps through him. He wants to sit down at that table, flip the sand-glass, and lose himself in a sweet cloud of ink and images—wants it as much as an addict craves his laudanum, his cocaine—but he also feels himself filling with anxiety, even dread.

It must be someone else's turn at the table. Not his, not yet. "Are the sailors still taking shifts here?" he asks.

"They are," Sola tells him, "but not on this voyage. You're to stay here until we reach Vévoda's."

"That might be too much..." He wonders whether she can hear how his voice tightened, how weakly it trailed off.

"You *should* stay, dear," she says. "This might be one of the last things you ever do. Make the most of it."

He shakes his head even as he is thinking *yes*. "There's so much to do, to plan. I have to get my supplies in order. The darts, the—" He knows this is a flimsy pretext. The truth is that he simply doesn't want to risk being apart from her.

Dear.

"The supplies in your case are already well in order," she says. She gestures toward the desk. "This is where you'll find the plan."

He raises a hand to his lips. They are wind-burned but smooth. "I don't have a needle," he says. "I don't have thread." His legs are shaking, and it's not because the arctic cold has burrowed so deeply into his bones.

"It's part of the tradition," she says, "but it doesn't have to be." Again she touches his face; this time he reaches up, holds her hand against his cheek. For a moment they are quiet—one more moment on the shifting ship.

{ 406 }

ESME SAID THEY'RE GOING TO PUBLISH MOODY'S BOOK REGARDLESS OF WHAT I DO. SAID THEY'LL GIVE ME SOME $, + IF I DON'T TAKE IT, THEIR LAWYERS WILL FIND A WAY TO FINESSE THINGS SO THEY CAN TALK ABOUT THE SUBSTANCE OF IT.

Bitch.
You should get a lawyer. Fight.

I GAMBLED — I TOLD HER I THOUGHT MOODY HAD THE STORY WRONG. AND SHE SAID SHE DIDN'T PARTICULARLY CARE — THE EVIDENCE HE HAS IS REASONABLY STRONG + THAT'S ALL THEY NEED— THE IMPORTANT TRUTH WILL BE WHAT THE SALES NUMBERS ARE.

Maybe she thought you were bluffing?

NO, I THINK SHE MEANT IT. SO I GAMBLED AGAIN. SHE ASKED WHO I THOUGHT STRAKA WAS, AND I SAID VACLAV. SHE LAUGHED—ASKED IF I HAD ANY EVIDENCE @ ALL THAT HE WAS ALIVE AFTER 1910. SHE SAID, "IF YOU CAN'T AT LEAST SHOW THAT HE EXISTED, YOU WILL NEVER GET ANYONE TO PUBLISH THAT BOOK."

You didn't say anything about Sig did you? Or Desjardins?
NO.

"Is this where I'll sleep?" S. asks.

"If you sleep, yes."

"What about my old cabin? Below the forecastle?"

"That's where I'll be. That's where I've been."

"I wrote about you there," S. says. "On the bulk-head. At least, I tried to write about you."

"I know."

"Can you still read the words?"

"No," she says, "but I know them."

S. cannot say how much time has passed—not land-time, not ship-time—but he knows he has flipped the sand-glass again and again. Sola saw him reach for it once he had settled himself into the chair and shuffled it forward, tightening the space between himself and the table, and she told him he didn't need to do that, did not need to measure the hours; he would not have to vacate the space for anybody, and nobody would be coming to relieve him—but it feels like an important part of the ritual, and he turns the glass religiously, marking steady time even as he lurches, zigzagging, through it.

At first came the sorts of phrases and images and details and ideas and feelings he has come to expect over the years: orphans and refugees from his forgotten life, and companions from whatever state he'd find himself in at the moment when ink was spilling into the grooves etched by the nib.]But then— and he feels the change—it is as if a piano chord, struck in a vast concert hall, has been allowed to ring and decay, and even as the chord itself fades, some of its overtones continue to hum with life in all that space, and those tones are joined by notes from bowed strings that rise, coalesce, weave together in unexpected harmonies, carry the piece along with them in new directions, and when he follows them, he can see the Château and its grounds resolve in his mind.

His vision is not one of an architectural blueprint or a plat map, but rather the scene of Vévoda's gala as it unfolds. He can see the layout of the estate, of course: the Château itself; the tidy stands of trees that shield the Château from view to the north and south; the undulant lawns and lush gardens; the fields of grapes that extend far inland, running up and over gentle slopes of umber; the outbuildings; the barn in which Vévoda stores, in careless fashion, the art and antiquities he has acquired by gift and theft and auction; and the half-dozen barracks for laborers, behind one of which is a deep, dark, dry well.

THINKING ABOUT SUMMERSBY'S LETTER TO EKSTROM... SEEMS LIKE THE S FELT LIKE A FAMILY. TO HIM, ANYWAY. MAYBE TO THEM ALL.

Especially Vaclav— cut off from everyone else. He probably needed it more than any of them.

He sees pavilions spread over the lawns and pennants snapping in the breeze, sees guests in dinner jackets and gowns and well-tailored suits and military tunics with medals winking in the torchlight, hears popping corks, laughter, the reserved voices of people who do not give their trust easily, and even the conspiratorial silences. He can see Agents observing the proceedings from within the crowds and from without, their stealth—to his eye—as obvious as if they were spotlit. He can see the handshakes that conclude deals and hear the clinking glasses that toast progress and a world remade. Some guests totter on canes and in wheeled chairs; some stumble drunkenly; some straighten their backs and eye the ones who are stumbling. [Many are stamping exuberantly in oaken tubs with pantlegs rolled and hems held high, thrilling as they play at seriousness with the work of the fall crush, decorum be damned, and joking at how all the vineyard's workers should have their wages cut because this, this is an amusement, not work,] or maybe they should just be sacked altogether and Vévoda can fill his barrels with what guests crush at his parties.

((He can see a young man—twenty-five or so—standing in the midst of it all, in front of the Château's

— MOODY KNEW THAT ESME HAD DECIDED TO PUBLISH THE BOOK W/O THE CONSENT. THAT WAS ONE OF THE THINGS HE LAUGHED ABOUT.

POOR VS. RICH, LABOR VS. MANAGEMENT

enormous iron door, which practically writhes with cast-bronze figures of gods and serpents. The young man is the next in the Vévoda line, Edvar VI, and his task is to meet these guests and inquire about their needs and reassure them that not only will the Vévoda empire continue to serve them but it will do so with even more speed and stealth and ingenuity and force. He is the planet at the center of the gala, the axis around which the party whirls and time passes. The one person S. cannot see: Vévoda himself.

He describes every step of his and Sola's approach to the Château from the sea. He can see the grotto into which the ship will sail, a passage carved from the rock over millennia by the tenacious seas and exploited for centuries by corsairs prowling the Mediterranean. He can see, on a wall inside the grotto, a fierce, skeletal frigatebird painted in black on a field of red—the insignia of the pirate Juan Blas Covarrubias—next to a hash of mysterious symbols that almost certainly enciphers the location of Covarrubias's richest cache of treasure, a tantalizing puzzle that he and Sola pass by without hesitation, fierce as frigatebirds themselves and immune to distraction.

He sees the trail of switchbacks leading them up into the heart of the steep seaside bluff, and then a

---

Did you know that Bauchard's wife killed herself a month after the award ceremony? That might give B. (+ any kids) a reason to hate Straka.

OK— I still sometimes wish the pirate was Straka.

THERE'S AN OLD OUT-OF-USE ELECTRICAL BOX @ THE PLANETARIUM— EYE-LEVEL, MAYBE 50 FT. TO THE RIGHT OF THE LOADING DOORS. WE COULD USE THAT.

Won't people think it's weird if they see me go back there?

I DON'T THINK THEY'LL SEE IF YOU KEEP YOUR HEAD DOWN + WALK LIKE YOU KNOW WHERE YOU'RE GOING. STEAM TUNNEL ACCESS IS JUST DOWN THE ALLEY, THOUGH—USE THAT.

narrow passage that must have been hacked into the rock with hand tools over the course of decades. He follows their close and sweaty shuffle along that path, which leads them, twisting and turning, to the mucky bottom of that disused well. He chronicles their quivering breaths. He sees notches cut into the stone, which they will use to climb toward daylight. He sees the two of them emerging from the well. He sees—or glimpses—a figure skulking behind the barn in which Vévoda stores his hoard of art and wonders if it might be, somehow, in some form, Khatef-Zelh. He sees the barracks in which the wine-drowned woman slept during the nineteen years she labored in Vévoda's employ. He hears the whispers of many thousands of restless souls and discerns the lost woman's voice among them. He listens to her closely, now not even daring to breathe, listens with the most intense concentration he can muster. He charms it upward from the surrounding din, brings it up to his ears until he can make out her words: *les caves, les caves, il est dans les caves.*

The wine cellars. Vévoda is in the cellars.

And he can see the building that sits atop the cellars, and inside that building the great oaken barrel that has been rolled into the building, can see

Just got an email from my Art History TA. He said el nailed the shit out of the final. Said my answer to the essay question on Bosch was the best he's ever seen.

YOU'RE AMAZING. YOU CAN DO THIS.

the servants filling bottle after bottle from it. He notes the doors that connect the sunlit surface with the black cellar. He can feel the cool air exhaled by the cellar when the doors are opened, can smell oak and fermentation and earth and time. But then the gift of such sight ceases to give: he cannot see into the network of cellars, cannot place Vévoda within it. He tries and tries, but he cannot see.

He lays down his pen, cradles his head in his hands, concentrates for what might be hours or days, but he just cannot see it, and finally he understands that he is not meant to see it, not here; he must descend into the dark maze himself, before he will find Vévoda, this man who has had more influence over S.'s life than S. himself, find him and write the ending.

When he returns to the table, the orlop deck, the ship, he is startled by the sound of heavy breathing behind him, and he spins quickly, grabbing the back of the chair, ready to swing it if he must. But he puts it down again, and gently, because there, sitting on the deck with her back against the bulkhead, is Sola, asleep and snoring softly. It is remarkable: for so long, he tried and failed to summon her when he was in this room, and now here she is, the muse as

YOU SNORE A LITTLE. IT'S SWEET.

You snore a lot.

her physical self. Muse, heroine, co-conspirator, love—whichever role it may be that truly fits her, she is *here*.

And then the whistles come, the sequence of notes that he remembers so well: *Land ho!*

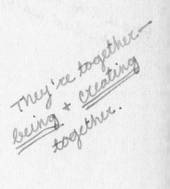

They're together— being + creating together.

LETTER FROM ARTURO. I'LL COME TO YOUR PLACE TONIGHT. 11.

DON'T:

ⓐ I have my lit exam tomorrow.

ⓑ I know what it's going to say— and I don't want to hear it now— or maybe ever.

ⓒ It's not safe for you.

IT'S NOT JUST THE LETTER. IT'S ALSO WHAT CAME WITH IT.

LET ME KNOW WHEN I CAN SEE YOU. HOPE IT'S SOON.

I THINK I NEED YOU.

Please tell me she died peacefully.

IN HER SLEEP.
SPENT THE LAST FEW DAYS
GETTING THINGS IN ORDER,
THANKING PEOPLE + SAYING
GOODBYE, LISTENING TO MUSIC.
LIKE SHE'D DECIDED IT WAS TIME.

CHAPTER 10

SHIPS OF THESEUS

SHROUDED **IN** the Med-
iterranean fog,[1] the ship sails into the corsairs' grotto,
the warp in her mainmast affording them just enough
clearance. Inside, the crew secures the vessel with
lines through heavy iron rings secured in the stone
centuries before. The remnants of waves lap in,
then roll out—a music of the shallows—and the ship
bobs gently over them.

One of the sailors, an older man with close-set
teardrop eyes, bald but for two wings of white hair
flaring out over his ears, helps Sola lash the valise to

YOU HAVE A PASSPORT, RIGHT?
Yeah— from when I was going to go to Paris. But it's at home. Maybe I can get my sister to bring it up to me. She owes me one.

Have you seen photos of Summ. from the 1940s? This is him.

Wonder if there are any photos of him with Signe.
DOUBT IT. THEY PROB. WERE AS CAREFUL WITH HER AS THEY WERE WITH VACLAV. EVEN MORE.

---

[1] Straka's phrasing here is no accident; though the characters have a map to the
Vévoda estate, they still must view the location through the fog. As the essayist Norman
Bergen discussed in the third volume of his *Spinning Compass* series, there is a powerful
human need to *locate* evil—that is, to contain it by assigning it a specific, bounded place
(in some cases, a particular person)—even though this is impossible. The boundaries of
evil, Bergen argued, are blurry and porous, if they can be said to exist at all.

I hope those guys find a photo from Desj.'s wedding one of these days.
THERE WON'T BE ANY S WRITERS IN IT. (NOT THAT THERE WERE MANY LEFT...)
I know. Just want to see him + Signe together.

S.'s back. After giving the ropes a final tug, he hands each of them a thin wooden whistle and sees them off, down the gangway to a slippery rock shelf that follows the narrowing passage deeper inland. When S. turns his head for one last look at the ship, he is surprised to see the old sailor still at the rail watching them. The sailor nods to him, a quick bob of the head that counts as the greatest demonstration of solidarity—even humanity—that S. has received from a member of the ship's crew. In that nod, too, is a recognition that they will never cross paths again.

S. and Sola pass Covarrubias's red frigatebird of death and its enciphered promise,[2] and instead of pausing to contemplate it—or the *S* symbol that has been drawn under one of the bird's wings—they keep walking while quietly practicing the avian warbles and trills that will allow them to communicate behind enemy lines: *Follow me; Proceed with caution; You're being followed; Hold your ground; I've found Vévoda; I've been exposed; I've been wounded;*

[2] In February 1933, after Karst & Son had delegated to me the task of informing Straka of the dismal sales figures for *Lopevi*, he responded—in a letter which I did not retain—that if only he could locate one of Covarrubias's treasure caches, neither he nor Karst nor I would ever again need to worry about "the tedious and inherently contradictory business of selling stories." He had discovered a map, he said, showing one buried near Biabou, on the island of St. Vincent, and would be proceeding there forthwith. This was one of the rare occasions on which I understood Straka to be making a joke.

{ 416 }

I cry every time I read her letter.

I KNOW. I DO TOO.

She doesn't seem to be making anything up here, either: there was a rumor about Covarrubias + Biabou.

—AND ALSO: NO ONE BOUGHT LOPEVI. THAT PART'S TRUE, TOO.

Glad you brought it with you.

Save yourself; Run. By the time they're midway through the narrow, hand-cut corridor, they've worked out a lexicon of fifty calls. Are there contingencies for which they have no signal? Yes. Safety is rare, they know, and risk is infinite.

They sidestep through the passage, often bumping feet or shoulders, still practicing the calls in lieu of speaking. S. sweats profusely, even in the subterranean cool, its very mildness a shock to his body, which is still conditioned for a polar climate. He stops to wipe his stinging eyes. He whistles for Sola to wait, and she does, looking back at him with an air of impatience.

The valise weighs heavily on his shoulders. It holds supplies, yes, but his examination of its contents was cursory at best. Just how careless a man has he become?

"You could say careless," Sola says, surprising him, as he didn't think he'd voiced the thought. "You might also say *trusting*."

"I might," S. says. "In my experience, those are synonyms."

"You've trusted many people."

"Most of them are dead."

"Do you trust me?"

FINALLY GET WHY SUMM.'S CONFESSION MADE SO MUCH OF HOW ALONE HE'D BEEN IN HIS LIFE AS THE ONLY STRAKA: TRYING TO GET NEW S/ BOUCHARD TO LAY OFF FILOMELA, YES— BUT ALSO TO HIDE SIGNE, MAKE THEM THINK THAT WHATEVER THEY'D HEARD ABOUT HER EXISTENCE WAS JUST RUMOR.

PASSAGE → TRANSITIONS/CHANGE

SERIN COVERED THE TICKETS. I still want to know where they get their $$$

You didn't tell me it would be this COLD.

I'M THE ONE FROM CALIFORNIA. YOU SHOULD BE USED TO IT.

If Covarrubias had been Straka, we could be in the Caribbean.

———

"I do," S. says as their soles scrape over the stone, "but you might be better off if I didn't."))

If the passage were wider and the ground smoother, she would certainly be stamping toward him; instead, she has to angle herself and choose her steps with care. Her approach is no less dramatic for it, though. She pushes herself into him with such force that it knocks him back a step, and there they are, together below all this earth, at the mercy of gravity. He can feel her chest rising and falling as she breathes, can smell the familiar scent of sweat and clary sage, can hear the sound of her lips parting. "You trust me," she says, "although for reasons I cannot fathom, you don't *believe* that you do. Or that you should."[3]

He feels her chest rise, fall, and rise again. He understands what she means; he's just not certain it's true.

Her breath is warm on his neck, and it is sharp. He wonders whether he has again spoken aloud

———

[3] I care little about reviewers or reviews, but I would like to acknowledge the work of one K. R. Simmons. In a review of *The Winged Shoes of Emydio Alves* in the September 10, 1942, edition of an Oregon newspaper called the *Portland Clarion*, Simmons proved him- or herself to be one of the few people—perhaps including Straka himself—who understood that the book was not a failed novel of world politics but an exceptional and revelatory work of personal emotion. Perhaps unsurprisingly in this world where literary gifts go unrewarded, the *Clarion* folded weeks later, and I have not discovered any further work by the astute Simmons.

———

For all the people in Straka's world who sold out, exploited, backstabbed (etc.) their friends, there were just as many who were completely loyal to each other (+ to the work they were trying to do). It's taken me a while to realize that.

I DIDN'T REALIZE IT UNTIL YOU WROTE THAT.

OK— none of this one is true, as far as I can tell (apart from her not thinking much of reviews).

SO WHICH PART IS THE CLUE FOR THE CODE?

I have no idea.

It's in here. It's got to be.

YOU'LL FIND IT. I KNOW YOU WILL.

I keep wishing we could've told her that it was Vaclav, she was in love with Vaclav. And then I remember that it hadn't mattered to her for a long, long time. The love mattered — not the name, not the dates, not the facts. And then I just start crying all over again.

without knowing it. "Listen," she says. "We are *we*, and we have been *we* for a long, long time. And in that way, I *am* you."

— YOU CAN JUST TELL ME THINGS LIKE THAT. YOU DON'T HAVE TO WRITE THEM.

Some things are easier to write.

At the bottom of the well, they rest for a moment, gather themselves for the climb to the surface, which appears as a pinpoint of golden light far above. S. tests the first foothold for traction, pushes himself into the air, and as he is reaching for a handhold, he wonders whether they should turn back. Turn back, sail the ship toward one of the nearby beaches, swim to shore, and live what is left of their lives in safe and quiet ignorance of Vévoda and The S and mystery ships and voices of the dead and assassinations and Sobreiro and the whole of history. Can he possibly be justified in poisoning a thousand people? And even if he can, is there a *point*? Will he be saving anyone but himself? Will it make anyone's life less miserable?

I'M GOING BACK TO STANDEFER. I'M NOT LEAVING W/O TALKING TO HIM.

That's a bad idea. But I get why you think you have to.

((The climb is more strenuous than he had imagined. Though his time in the Winter City left him thinner, without so much weight to pull upward, the fact remains that he is old, or very nearly so, and a quarter-mile climb straight up is not what his body is meant to be doing anymore))His neck and shoulders are sore from the weight; his knees groan and

Is your leg OK? Are you going to be able to run if you need to?

DON'T WORRY ABOUT ME.

tremble with each step upward; the ropes have dug into his skin. Sola, below him, seems to be having little difficulty. She has aged since they met in the Old Quarter, of course, but she seems to have done so more slowly.

S. keeps climbing, not out of bravery or indomitability but because his only other option is to fall,[4] and at last they crawl out of the well and spill themselves into the daylight behind one of the workers' barracks. All through the climb he has been imagining a reward: a few moments of basking in the sun's warmth, letting his muscles unknot, breathing deeply in the clean seaside air, his ears brushed gently by the strains of distant strings. It is immediately clear that this is not a reward he will receive.

Instead of the sea air, he smells the blue-black stench; while it is not overpowering, it is uncanny and jarring. What is overpowering, though—what doubles him over, clamping his hands over his ears, writhing in the grass—are the voices of the place: screams of terror and fury, as loud and sharp

---

ALSO TRUE (THE FACT THAT IT WAS ONE OF THE RUMORS, I MEAN).

4 One of the more entertaining rumors about the author's place of residence held that he spent six months of each year in a remote cabin near Thunkar, Bhutan, where he busied himself with mountaineering in addition to writing. While this is almost certainly untrue, I have no doubt that even the Straka of advancing age had the vitality to scale the forbidding peaks of the region.

as if they were coming to him not through a fog of
centuries but in the sharp stabs of an infinite present. He is aware, vaguely, of Sola helping him to
his feet and leading him forward. Gradually the
voices subside, and when he drops his arms to his
sides and opens his eyes again, he finds himself
with Sola in a pavilion that Vévoda's servants are
using to warm food, pour drinks, invisibly stage-
manage the festivities. Many of those servants—
perhaps twenty, twenty-five—are standing before
them in a rough semicircle. They are men and
women, young and old, all of them in flawlessly
clean and pressed livery.

He has already seen them in his ship-visions, and
he knows the moment: the servants have been
expecting these two travelers, and are willing to aid
them because of the grievous wrong that was done
to their friend and comrade, that poor woman who
dared to resist. And still: S. is angry that their assistance will be passive, that they will not themselves
rise up against the man in the Château. "You work
for *Vévoda*," he says before he can stop himself, and
the contempt in his tone is unmistakable. He feels
the mood darken. It dawns on him that if he ever
possessed social graces, he lost them long ago.

Marginalia (handwritten):

Thanks for the tea.
YOU'RE WELCOME.

The pages. Think about that. She sent us the pages.
ARTURO SAYS SHE NEVER READ THEM.
Think of how many people would kill to read them. (OK—bad choice of words.)
NO—IT'S A GOOD ONE. CAN'T FORGET THAT. HAVE TO BE CAREFUL.

SERIN SAYS THEY HAVE PEOPLE HERE.
I hope I don't see them.

★ ARTURO EMAILED. SAID IT WAS A FRENCHMAN
WHO GAVE HER THE ENVELOPE. SOMETIME IN THE
MID-70s. THEY BOTH LIKED HIM — THOUGHT HE WAS
KIND + POLITE, EVEN THOUGH HE DIDN'T SAY MUCH.
FILOMELA SAID HE "MOVED WITH *SHIP OF THESEUS*
GREAT SADNESS." IT HAD TO BE DESJARDINS.
STILL GRIEVING AFTER, WHAT? 15 YEARS? 20?
He + Signe never really got a chance either. not enough of one,
anyway.

LET'S
NOT
BLOW THIS.
I
won't
let
you.

→ AGAIN, FRENCH + SWEDISH — ANOTHER V. OF DURAND + EKSTROM?

A middle-aged man with a long, white scar snaking down one cheek—so thin and precise that it looks as if it was bladed into him by a careful, artistic hand—narrows his eyes, folds his arms across his chest. "We do," he says, "but you're about to pretend to work for him, which is not much different." Quiet laughter bubbles through the group; this man commands more of their respect than S. ever will. Sola quickly offers apologies, which the man receives with a nod. His name is Tupp, he says, and the woman now coming forward with two stacks of neatly-folded clothing is his wife, Roselin. She hands one stack to Sola, hands the other to S. Trousers, shirt, vest, jacket, tie, stockings, and the newest, shiniest shoes S. will ever wear.

Swedish
for *Rooster*

French for
house finch

★ "Don't tell us your names," Tupp says. "It's better if we don't know." Ha!! Your passport says Nicodemu— FORGET YOU EVER SAW THAT. Roselin directs them to the far corner of the pavilion, where a makeshift dressing-screen has been created from wooden crates draped with a tablecloth. Behind the screen, S. stands mutely, his eyes averted, as Sola unbuttons her blouse.[5] "No," she says, "look at me," and when he is slow to do so I've graduated. They've got nothing.

Email from the provost. They're going to investigate the archive thefts. Don't know how they'll get into Moody's house, but still...

MUST'VE TAKEN YOU FOREVER TO DO ALL THE DOCUMENTATION.

Meh. I wasn't very busy.

HOW DO YOU FEEL ABOUT THE LIE?

It wasn't really a lie. Just a story. I mean, he would have tried to bribe me for access if Ilsa hadn't been willing to steal for him.
(PRETTY SURE THAT'S STILL A LIE.

Well, it can be both. Plus, they won't care when they find all that stuff he stole. And if they do — so what? I'll be, like, 5000 miles away? and

YOU STILL DON'T KNOW THAT YOU GRADUATED.

[5] This moment recalls one from *Winged Shoes* in which Alves finds himself alone with the fifth daughter of the Prince of Santiago. Also true...

I know I did. I interpreted the shit out of "Political Poem." I was on fire.

{ 422 }

which — again — I am not, right now. You can probably hear my teeth chattering.

she repeats herself. She holds his eyes as she undoes
the rest of the buttons and shakes off the blouse,
letting it fall to the floor. With a few more buttons
unfastened, her dress falls to her ankles, and she
steps out of it. How strange, he thinks, to have seen
her so many times—in the physical world, yes, but
so much more often in his mind, in his dreams, in
the amniotic aura of the orlop—and now to see her
like this. Those visions weren't false, but this one is
true, and the difference between the two is vast.

He watches her watching him. His hands shake,
but he manages to slide the buttons through their
buttonholes. He sheds his shirt, his trousers. And
there they are: artist and muse, assassin and abettor,
two bodies pulled into middle age and beyond,
and—most truly—two individuals swallowing their
uncertainties, standing and facing each other in
underclothes that are in grave need of washing. *This
is who we are*, he thinks, and she nods, even though
this time he is certain he has said nothing aloud.
Then she kneels in front of him, presses down a
loose corner of the tape that holds a goatskin full of
Sanguinem ulcera to his calf. S. dresses quickly, and
Sola, examining the drape of his trousers over the
goatskin, nods; it is well enough concealed.

{ 423 }

I wonder how Filomela felt about this scene.

SHE MIGHT'VE BEEN THE ONE WHO WROTE IT.

JEN— I HAVE TO TELL YOU— I HAVEN'T SAID THIS BEFORE BUT I'VE WANTED TO + NOW I WANT TO SAY IT ALL THE TIME; **I LOVE YOU.** I LOVE YOU ON THE PAGE + I LOVE YOU IN THE LIBRARY + IN THE COFFEE SHOP + IN THE LAST ROW OF THE VARSITY. I LOVE YOU HERE. I LOVE YOU IN NEGATIVE SPACE —OK, I DON'T KNOW EXACTLY WHAT THAT MEANS, BUT I'M PRETTY SURE IT'S TRUE— + I LOVE WHO YOU HAVE BEEN + WHO YOU'LL BE. I SHOULD SAY THIS TO YOU IN PERSON, AND I'M GOING TO — OVER + OVER — BUT I THINK I NEEDED TO SAY IT HERE FIRST. JENNIFER HEYWARD, I LOVE YOU.

ALSO: I LOVE YOU IN PRAGUE. IN A DRAFTY APARTMENT. WITH LOTS OF BOOKS + HUGE STACKS OF PAPER ALL OVER THE PLACE. I DEFINITELY LOVE YOU ~~THERE~~ HERE.

CJ: what I'm going to say to you tonight in person.

Her servant's outfit fits as if it were tailored to her pleasing form. Her hair is pinned into a fussy bun, and her apron is starched and is the most pristine of whites. Dressed this way, she seems like a stranger. He can tell she is dampening the energy that normally crackles through her, and he already misses it. She runs her hand over the outline of her whistle, which she is wearing around her neck and tucked into her blouse. She touches S.'s chest to make sure he has his as well. He would like very much for her not to take her hand away, would like to have that gently reassuring pressure with him always. But of course such things are impossible.

When they rejoin Tupp, he is using a napkin to wipe a spot from the shining leather of his shoes. S. asks the scarred man about the smell in the air. "That's from one of Vévoda's weapons," he says. "Why are we smelling it here?"

Tupp waves a hand in disgust. The vineyard's field workers, he explains, had firm instructions to stay in their barracks during the gala. If any one of them was so much as glimpsed by a guest, he would be sacked and expelled from the grounds immediately. An hour ago, though, a group of military men from a variety of countries on three different

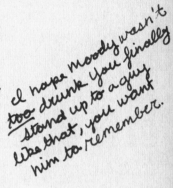

continents—men who'd been drinking heavily together once they'd gotten their nationalistic posturing out of the way and acknowledged their brotherhood of force—had barred the door of one of the barracks from the outside, poured a jug of Vévoda's dark wine over the wooden doorway and walls, and struck a match. The barracks erupted in flames, and as the workers inside screamed and pounded the walls and begged to be let out, the military men retreated to a nearby grassy slope, where they glutched from a fresh bottle of wine and took in the spectacle, laughing. "These are the very last people who should be in possession of weapons," Tupp says. "These are not even people who should be allowed to drink wine." He spits onto the flattened grass at his feet.

"The workers," Sola says. "How many were lost?"

"None," he says. Some of Vévoda's Agents had appeared from their concealed positions around the estate and smothered the fire with special blankets big as parachutes and some sort of aerosol powder. The laborers were told they had to remain in their smoke-saturated quarters, although in a gesture of humanity, the Agents allowed them to open the three small windows to begin airing the space.

At first, the oddest part of the story, to S., is the thought of Vévoda's Agents helping anyone other than the man who pays them. He is about to comment upon this when he realizes there's something even stranger. The military men poured wine on the door? The wine is *flammable*? "Is it wine, or is it a weapon?" he asks Tupp. "How can it be both?"

"We don't receive explanations," Tupp says. "You'll have to decide for yourself."

Roselin shows S. one of the bottles that she has just filled from the cask, which she says contains one of Vévoda's richest and most precious vintages. Through the green glass, the wine looks perfectly black. It is the color, S. thinks, of endings.

"He shares this very rarely, and even then only with small groups," Roselin says. "He's trying to make the best of impressions, almost certainly on young Edvar's behalf."

Generation to generation. History as blood. "What do you know about the son?" S. asks.

Roselin laughs, a short and bitter bark. "There is nothing to know about Six. He is nothing."

Tupp pours eighteen glasses, which he sets on the tray that S. will carry as he circulates. S. has never seen a wine so dark; it has the hue of orlop ink and of

---

Margin notes (handwritten):

But why does Serin want to know all of this?

BECAUSE THEY LOVE THE BOOKS. SAME AS WE DO.

You have to get them to tell you who they are. Go to Paris + track them down if you have to.

I WILL. YOU'RE OK WITH GOING AHEAD?

If I'm going to go out into the unknown, it might as well be the *really* unknown.

---

the glaze on the wounded hills of the Territory, the opacity of the muck around the Black Vine blast and of the sludge Stenfalk coughed from his lungs. "Is all of his wine like this?" he asks. Tupp shakes his head, says that most are the traditional wines of the region. Where the black grapes come from, nobody knows.

S. picks up a glass, swirls it under his nose. The aroma is pleasing, very nearly intoxicating by itself: the smell of sweet ink, sharpened with the bite of alcohol. The voices in his head return, guttural whispers, and he closes his eyes to listen. Somewhere within all those voices is the drowned woman's, but he can't pick it out before they go quiet again. When S. opens his eyes, he finds Tupp and Roselin looking at him with what might be curiosity or concern.

S. steadies himself, then hands the glass to Sola. She holds it up, studying the strange color. "I wonder," she muses, "if this is what they used to drown her."

Tupp sniffs. "They wouldn't use the good stuff on us."

When Sola raises the glass to taste the wine, he stops her. "It stains the tongue," he explains as she replaces the glass on the tray. "You'll be noticed. Around here, a black tongue gets you summarily sacked."

———

From outside the pavilion comes a volley of wolf-whistles aimed at one of the younger serving-girls. After they fall away, S. notices the absence of any other sounds in a similar register. "There are no birds here," he says.

Sola's hand goes to her neck, to the whistle underneath her blouse.

"Vévoda has the trees sprayed every week," Roselin offers. "He cannot abide the birds—the songs, the waste falling from the sky, the theft of his grapes."

Their whistles will not blend in at all. The guests may not notice, but the Agents surely will. Once they separate, any communication between them will be risky. *Nothing to be done about it*, S. tells Sola with a look. *We simply have to be careful.*

"It's time," she says.

He nods. "It's time."

S. hefts his tray and steps out of the tent. The ink-wine in those eighteen glasses undulates gently, absorbing the tremble in his hand. (The problem is one of imbalanced weight, he tells himself; it cannot be one of failing nerve.) He moves in the direction of the barrel room; with just a few minutes of flawlessly invisible service, he'll be able to enter it without

———

attracting notice at all. Each time he hands over a glass, the recipient looks through or around him. Even after all these years, he is quietly astonished at how easily invisibility can be achieved.

Again, his visions on the ship are serving him well. He sees what he expected, perhaps even created: untrammeled debauchery, spiced and thickened with *sotto voce* discussions, suspicious glances, and disappearances into tents to conduct business of the commercial, political, and carnal varieties. S. senses a discordance, taut as a wire, on which the revelry hangs. It reminds him of the barely-contained fury he sensed on that night, an age ago, on the wharf in B——.

Nearly everyone who plucks a glass from the tray has that deep shade of blue-black staining his lips, tongue, and teeth. They look ghoulish to him, though apparently not to one another. One glass finds the palsied hand of a man S. recognizes as the former president of a Central American *junta*, a man he thought had died years ago. Around him are several other members of his inner circle, the men who must have helped orchestrate their leader's strategic disappearance; they have ersatz-revolutionary scruffy hair and beards to go with the gold-braided epaulets in which they probably believe more fervently. With them is a Texan oil tycoon whose pock-marked face S. has also seen in the Winter City's newspaper; a finance minister from Eastern Europe; a Central Asian rocket scientist in the simultaneous employ of several major powers; and four young women—French and Catalonian, S. guesses—who smile and smile as they gently parry pinches and strokes and attempts at *frottage*. The finance minister jokingly gargles his first sip, but when the once-dead *Presidente* throws an elbow into his side, the liquid erupts from his mouth, staining his chin with a black-wine beard and streaking his off-white jacket and trousers. They roar with laughter, even the girls, who are wiping the sickening black mist from their faces.

His tray unburdened, S. strides with purpose and calm toward the outbuilding where the barrel is being drained, just another servant fetching bottles for re-supply. In the distance is the barn full of ill-gotten art, outside which several guests have queued for a tour. S. wishes he could investigate; he imagines discovering paintings he has admired before (perhaps even some from the repository in El-H——), sculptures from cities that have since been reduced

{ 430 }

No Khatef-Beth here he sets it up in Ch. 9, and he doesn't deliver on it.

[EXCEPT HE DID.
MUST HAVE BEEN ON
ONE OF THE PAGES FILOMELA
DIDN'T HAVE. AT THE TIME.

God-he was so terrified that something would happen to Signe.

YOU REALIZE SHE'S ANOTHER REASON
HE DIDN'T SHOW HIMSELF TO FILOMELA, RIGHT.

yeah. and I know I shouldn't, but I still want to fault him for it couldn't he have found someone else? couldn't he have let Summ. d it by himself? But I gu. he felt like he had

I wonder if knowing about it would have made Filomela feel any bet

to ashes, a pristine first-press of Sobreiro's book of tales. (Would there also be books looted from the library on the Obsidian Island? The S book itself? The thought makes his hand tremble anew.) But he will never know what the barn contains, because he has no time. There is never enough time for a man who must do what S. does.

Two serving-men leave the barrel room carrying cases full of bottles they have just filled toward the servants' pavilion. They have been instructed to leave the door ajar for him, and they play their roles well. With a quick scan of the lawns to make sure no Agents have their eyes on him, S. slips inside.

The barrel looks ordinary enough: French oak darkened with age, five feet in diameter at top and base, on its side and fitted with a spout for bottling. The only evidence that it contains Vévoda's strange vintage: a nimbus of blue-black staining the wood around the bung, a few dark spatters and daubs on the floorboards below. Written in block letters on the barrel's side: NOIR CALAIS 1912.[6]

It all goes back to Calais.

---

[6] How fitting that in the final chapter of his final book, Straka includes such a clear allusion to the event that shaped his literary career and, indeed, his life: the 1912 massacre at the Bouchard factory in Calais.

On a shelf near the door is the small hand-drill that has been left for him. He takes it and squeezes himself into the tight space between cask and wall. He bores a hole into the flat of the barrel at the top-most edge, then connects a length of rubber tubing to the spout of the goatskin and slips the free end through the hole. He tips the goatskin.

After just a few moments, though, he raises it again. He is about to cause the deaths of a thousand unsuspecting people. Viewed from a different angle: he is about to rid the world of a thousand of its most reprehensible warmongers and exploiters of men. The moment ought to feel charged, he thinks, perhaps even intolerably so. And yet this act feels to him like the most mundane of tasks, no more remarkable than going out for a newspaper or brewing a cup of tea.

He removes the tubing from the hole in the barrel and from the spout of the goatskin. He clamps the skin shut. He is sweating, suddenly and furiously. His head spins. He holds himself still, not so much standing as letting the barrel and the wall hold him in place.

This is not what he wants to do.

Does it matter what he wants? Especially now, at this moment, a moment of opportunity that might

Thanks.
NENÍ ZAČ
I am so impressed.

WHAT HE
WANTED: TO WRITE;
TO CHANGE THE WORLD;
TO BE WITH FILOMELA;
TO MAKE SURE SIGNE GREW UP SAFELY.
HE WANTED ALL OF IT. IS THAT SO BAD?
No. But it still ended up hurting
Filomela. And don't you think Filo would've
helped him raise Signe if he'd asked? Couldn't
he have relied on her instead of Summersby?
MAYBE. HE DIDN'T THINK THAT WAS SAFE
ENOUGH — FOR FILO OR SIGNE.

Or himself.
WHICH WOULD BE
UNDERSTANDABLE,
TOO. — *I get it.*
I just don't like it.
They should have
been together.
The 3 of them.

justify decades of flight and struggle and terror and blood? Can it possibly matter what one man wants?[7]

It does, he decides. It does now, and perhaps it always has.

What he has added to the wine thus far will not kill. It will, however, create some embarrassing situations—doses of humility, delivered by the blue-black glassful. S. smiles to himself. How strange, he thinks, this feeling: levity. (He has felt it before, of course—just not in the part of his life that he can remember.) There will be a sort of poetry to the scene, too: a thousand individual rebellions from within, a thousand purges of the foulness these people have gulped down in their lives and their work.

Vévoda—Edvar V—deserves a more severe fate, of course. But what of Edvar VI, the ascendant prince? Is he a different man than his father? Is there anything that churns away at his insides? Will he be as ruthless as the old man, or—heaven forbid—more so?

you're calling me a thing?

---

7 Careful readers will note that this line echoes one from Chapter 26 of *The Viper's Humor*. Just before Dr. Hull disappears into the jungle to distribute his vaccines to the hostile indigenous tribes, he tells the priests in the Morondava mission that "[i]t does not matter what one man wants." In the thoughts here attributed to S., Straka seems to have been acknowledging that his feelings on such matters had changed.

MOODY WAS BAITING ME. OVER + OVER. TRYING TO GET ME TO BLOW UP— JUST LIKE BEFORE. AND I ALMOST DID, BUT I COULD HEAR YOU TELLING ME THAT IT DIDN'T MATTER WHAT HE THOUGHT ABOUT ME OR ABOUT ANYTHING. SO I JUST TOLD HIM WHAT I THOUGHT: THERE ARE WAYS THE TRUTH WILL COME OUT, EVENTUALLY. BUT YOU KNOW WHAT? EVEN IF IT DOESN'T, THAT'S ALL RIGHT. I DON'T NEED THAT THE WAY I THOUGHT I DID. THERE ARE MORE IMPORTANT THINGS.

Also true: this is what Hull does in Ch. 26, + the quote is exact. What's going on? Why is Filomela being so disciplined all of a sudden?

Did you ask?
I DID. SHE SAID IT WAS HER SECRET. OR MAYBE SHE SAID "OUR."
Seems like an important detail.
OK. I'M NOT PERFECT.
I don't want you to be perfect.

An idea strikes, just as Sola's whistle flutters in through the open window: *Is everything going as planned?*

He responds: *The cellar doors are open. Come in after I leave. I'll join you soon.*

She does not whistle an acknowledgment. Her silence contains the following: *Do you have a good reason to deviate from the plan? Now is not the time to lose focus. Now is not the time for doubt or trivialities.*

I'll join you soon, he whistles again. This time, she acknowledges him.

Back in the servants' pavilion, he retrieves his valise from the crate in which it was hidden. He looks through the vials, held in place by leather loops and arranged alphabetically. He finds the one he is looking for—*Avis veritatis*—and tucks it into his vest. He has used this rarely over the years—the results are always unpredictable—but it might just be perfect for this evening at Vévoda's Château.

Edvar VI gnaws at a troublesome cuticle on his middle finger as he waits for the approach of whichever guests he must endure next, still reeling from the harangue of an aspiring young dictator seeking

{ 434 }

SO WE'RE ON?

We're on. Don't forget the pages.

[..]

Just making sure.

THEY SAID DESJARDINS' WIFE DIED IN 1956. NO FALLING, NOTHING SUSPICIOUS— JUST A REALLY HORRIBLE, DRAWN-OUT ILLNESS.

God. She was so young. They got so little time to be together.

When do you think he found out who she was?

MAYBE SHE TOLD HIM WHEN SHE WAS SICK — WANTED SOMEONE TO KNOW.

POINT OF VIEW SHIFTS FROM S. TO EDV.-6. NOT MANY SUCH MOVES ELSEWHERE— SIGNIF. ?

Imagine if you'd known about the monkey back then.

I WOULD HAVE LOVED IT. I'M NOT SURE I DO NOW. STILL: IT'S EXTREMELY COOL HOW THE WORDS CAN STAY THE SAME BUT THEIR MEANING CAN CHANGE.

Because the reader changes.

EXACTLY.

_____

to outfit his army on more favorable terms of credit. He consults his pocket watch. He has been instructed to address the guests from the dais in the courtyard at 7:00. It is now 6:45, and apprehension has snarled his insides. He knows he appears sallow, ill at ease, and he knows there is little he can do about it, apart from mopping his forehead over and over with his handkerchief, which Father has decried as a gesture that reveals a fundamental and unacceptable weakness. He reaches into his breast pocket, touches the pages on which his lines have been scripted, reassures himself that nothing can go too horribly wrong. All he has to do is read.

An explosion—small, but sharp and loud—makes him jump, sends his heart into his throat, and then all around people are screaming. Agents run toward the commotion, carrying their blankets and converging on the American auto manufacturer's pavilion, in front of which something is on fire and a dozen guests are scrambling away from the flames. Young Edvar realizes, slowly, that that something is a man. Before the Agents can get to the burning man, he topples over, writhes maniacally, flinging himself back and forth over the blackening grass. At last, the Agents wrap him in blankets that both snuff

_____

the flames and muffle the man's screams, and they carry him somewhere away from the party, the smell of his charred flesh trailing thickly in his wake. Once the man has been disappeared from the scene, the party resumes with little discernible change in the atmosphere. Edvar shakes his head. He wonders what sort of tragedy it would take to curtail the party, to send these fools scattering back to their homes and their wars and their rivalries.

A microphone squeals, and Edvar whips his head around to see that the Agent assigned to him, one of his father's oldest and most trusted, one who still wears the brown duster from the old days, has mounted the dais and is speaking into the microphone. His fedora shades his face, and his voice contains no accent, no distinctive timbre—both face and voice are meant to be forgotten immediately—but his stance contains authority that even the drunkest, most ill-behaved guest recognizes. *Gentlemen and ladies. A fellow guest has had an accident because he chose, against explicit instructions, to test the volatility of his wine. This wine is to be drunk and enjoyed, but it must be respected. You have just witnessed the consequences. Thank you. In fifteen minutes' time, you will hear from the new*

Chairman of Vévoda Holdings, Edvar Vévoda the Sixth. Like the wine, he must be respected. The only difference, perhaps, is in what the consequence of disrespect might be. When he leaves the dais, it is to dead silence across the grounds.[8] Even the giggling wine-stampers have gone quiet, and many of them are staring at their purpled feet in the wooden tubs and wondering if this is so very much fun anymore.

Edvar shakes his head again and stares down at his own shoes, which are polished so brightly that he can see his reflections in them. *All you have to do is read,* he tells himself. He takes the papers from his pocket, scans them, tucks them back in a ((a waiter— a gray-haired and bone-thin man he does not recognize—approaches)) with a tray on which sits a glass of Father's good, dark wine.

"Perhaps you weren't paying attention, old man," he says, "but Father instructed the servants not to give me the black wine today. I must be at my best, don't you see? Bring me a glass of Grenache instead, if you please."

Wait – you hadn't gone to New York yet.

TURNS OUT DJ ALREADY KNEW ABOUT ME. FROM LISBON. SO THAT PAPER MUST NOT HAVE SUCKED AFTER ALL.

I'm pretty sure I told you that months ago.

---

8 As mentioned in the Foreword, there were several pages from the original manuscript that were never located amid the chaos and bloodshed in Havana. I have chosen not to specify where Straka's words end and mine begin in this reconstructed tenth chapter. Though literary scholars will no doubt howl about this decision, I believe it is sound; to define such boundaries would be to portray the work as a mere pastiche, rather than a collaboration that maintains the unity of Straka's intentions for the novel.

FXC'S REASONING: BULLSHIT.

You had, um, strong feelings about that.

STILL DO. I'M A LIT GUY. I WANT TO KNOW.

And their story is the more important one...

I THINK I GET IT NOW — HER WAY OF EMPHASIZING THAT THE WORK IS THEIRS, THAT THEY'RE CO-CREATING. AND NOT JUST SOT — THEY'RE CO-CREATING THEIR STORY.

{ 437 }

"You're speaking soon, I understand," the waiter says. "You seem nervous."

Edvar is surprised at the creaky fellow's insolence. Has he been sampling the black wine, against both orders and propriety? No—the man's tongue is the usual pink. Perhaps the man is senile, or an imbecile. "I am not nervous," he says.

The waiter gives the subtlest of shrugs. "You're speaking to a thousand very powerful people. Anyone would be nervous. Are you certain that you don't want this glass?"

"What if Father sees me with a black tongue?"

"You can remind him that he spent the party hiding, on the pretext of giving tours of the cellars."

Edvar cannot help but grin; the waiter speaks the truth—perhaps more than he knows. Edvar takes the glass from the tray, lifts it in a solitary toast. "Cheers," Edvar says. He sips the wine, and—*oh, God*—this is salvation in a glass. It is the very thing he has needed all afternoon. He immediately feels the warmth of confidence rising in him.

The waiter bows his head. "Pleased to be of service," he says, and, tucking the empty tray under his arm, he walks off toward the servants' pavilion. The American auto manufacturer's people shout at him

{ 438 }

Seems like everyone's worried about their fathers.

We emailed back + forth last night. He didn't apologize, but he did say he "might have been too hasty" in trying to commit me.
Seemed like he was most interested in finding out if I was planning to go to graduation and what he should tell the people in NY. (I said ① no, and even if I were I wouldn't want him there, and ② I already told them thanks, but I won't be there.)

TOUCHING.

Best he can do, I guess. He canceled the credit card — said he didn't want to "enable."
He's right. I'd do it if I were him.

———

to bring them more wine. Of course, Edvar thinks. They require some refreshment as they move on from the loss of one of their own.

At 6:55, S. heads back to the barrel room. His contribution to the wine is taking effect. There are lines forming at the outhouses for the field workers, and fights are breaking out as people try to bull ahead to the front. Dozens of guests have wandered up to the Château itself, begging wide-eyed for the comforts of plumbing. Several mad dashes have been made toward the edge of the woods a quarter of a mile away—not all of them successful. The chaos, it seems, is getting underway.

Inside, he finds two servants around a new cask, marked NOIR YPRES 1915, taking turns trying to release an uncooperative bung. S. leaves his tray on the shelf and heads for the open cellar door. They glance at him, nod, turn away as S. ducks into the darkness. A few steps in, though, he pauses; from here, he'll still be able to hear Young Edvar's address. Tupp may regard the young man as a cipher, but soon it will be obvious who he truly is.

———

I wonder if *this* is where Filomela started reconstructing.

IT DOES FEEL LIKE A SHIFT — BUT NOT A HUGE ONE — PLENTY OF WHAT COMES AFTERWARD IS CLASSIC VMS.

She had to know his style pretty well, though...

At 6:59, Edvar VI blots his tongue with a white napkin. It comes away with zebrine stripes, and he drops it to the ground, along with his empty glass. He owes that waiter tremendous gratitude. The wine was exactly what he needed. He feels entirely in control. He believes unwaveringly in his eloquence and in his gifts of suasion. He feels as powerful as white phosphorus, as calm as a cloud of ash. If Father gripes about his drinking the black wine, he will brandish the reams of new purchase orders that will be filled out and signed on the spot once his words flow into those two thousand ears.

He climbs up to the dais, feeling as if his flexed muscles might tear through his snug-fitting suit. He steps to the microphone and wraps his hand around it, producing a squeal of feedback that will alert everyone that the most important event of the evening is about to begin, and they should close their mouths or zip their trousers or whatever they need to do to assemble in front of him and pay attention to his words.

They gather, acquiescent.[9]

---

9   There is no greater sin, in the worlds of Straka's stories, than acquiescence to the limits that power (whether political, economic, or social) imposes upon the individual. It is less clear how Straka viewed acquiescence to the limits an individual imposes upon himself. The dialogue between Viktor and Sofia in Book Two of *Coriolis* offers some evidence on the matter but is far from conclusive.

DETAILS ARE CORRECT; ARGUMENT MAKES SENSE. WHERE ARE THE CLUES?

I think the second sentence is a clue — it's just a clue about a different message.

———————

He removes his script from his pocket. He unfolds it. He clears his throat. He begins to read. "Gentlemen and ladies," he says, "I have met many of you today, and I look forward to making the acquaintance of every one of you before you depart our lovely home. My name is Edvar Vévoda the Sixth, and as you may have heard, I will be assuming the chairmanship of Vévoda Holdings in the coming months due to my father's declining health—or, rather, what I have been asked to refer to as his declining health." How funny—that last line was off the cuff, but there was a ripple of laughter, and it felt good, it felt right. "Many of you have been clients of my father's for quite some time, and I want to assure you that Vévoda Holdings will continue to provide you with the services you have come to expect, including, but not limited to, those that you might actually need." With these latter words, Edvar feels as if he has plucked a string, sounded a pure, vibrant note with virtuosity, with grace.

He looks down at the next sentence, decides it is boring and rather pointless. So, too, for the one that follows and the one after that. No matter. He knows what he needs to say, and he is momentarily transfixed as those words appear on the page, superimposing

———————

themselves over the text that was prepared for him, filling the margins, pulsing with life, words that are his creations, his alone. He notices the hush in the crowd and wonders how long he has been silent. They are waiting for him, for his voice, his words, his expression of himself, his vision. He looks right, left, around the edge of the dais. Is the old Agent there? You never quite know with that one.

"I believe," he says, and he decides to repeat this for emphasis, "*I believe* that it is also of paramount importance to inform you that neither I, nor my father, nor his father, have ever felt anything but contempt for you—or for your predecessors in whatever pathetic, evanescent fiefdom you purport to control. Half of you behave like infants, the other half like crotchety old men. Fortunately for my family, you all enjoy having toys that… that make very loud noises and/or cause a great deal of destruction."

He pauses to take a breath. This is going well. His mind is alive. They are listening, and they are being moved by the power and forthrightness of his words. There are gasps and shouts, even some violinistic cries. He has sent several people scurrying to the woods in fear, which is unfortunate, but it is the sort of thing that happens when one finds the words that truly come from within oneself. And there, there is the old Agent, watching him closely from the left side of the dais and scanning the grounds; he flashes subtle, precise hand signals to the other Agents on duty. Edvar acknowledges the old Agent with a nod, for if anyone can appreciate what he is doing at this microphone—radiating strength, decisiveness, power, it is he.

"Let me be clear," Edvar continues. "We—" (Although who is *we*? His father and himself? The company? Further contemplation may be necessary. But for now: *we*.)

A breath.

"We will thrive as long as you, our valued customers—and yes, we value you, despite your repellence, for you are the providers of grandeur and ease, you are the brandy-drowned ortolans whose bones gloriously lacerate our gums, you are the soft, yielding flesh beneath our thrusting hips—as long as you value power and profits and political gamesmanship over the search for love and serenity, over the lives and the dignity of all (including and especially those who are not you and are not known to you), over calm acceptance of your place

ORTOLAN A FAVORITE OF BOUCHARD'S.

How do you know?

ONE OF THE BRITISH NEWSPAPERS DID A PROFILE ON HIM RIGHT AFTER THE AWARD CEREMONY + MADE A BIG DEAL OUT OF IT. I MEAN, IT'S THE PERFECT MEAL FOR A VILLAIN.

———

as one—*just one!*—tiny and finite arrangement of molecules in a vast universe."

A great hubbub in the crowd! All eyes, all ears on him, even as guests pound on the doors of the mansion and the outhouses, as they race into and stagger out from the woods! Agents hurrying forward to express their solidarity! How glorious it feels to speak so passionately, so fluidly, so effortlessly, to have such a direct connection with what smolders inside him!

"We will thrive," he continues, "for as long as you choose extraction over creation, as long as you mistake commerce for art and destruction for progress, as long as you remain drunk on the juice that issues from the crush of a thing or place or person. We will thrive as long as you conflate power with influence, primacy with honor, goal with purpose, duty with responsibility, for thus is our business…perpetuated…thus does it hum with ever greater velocity. Our fondest hope is to continue to exploit your toxic dreams and to do so limitlessly, for thus may we claim our prenegotiated percentage of your—and, in many cases, your adversary's—personal infinity."

The old Agent is now expressing his support—his enthusiasm, even—with more florid hand signals that Edvar cannot interpret. Other Agents are

———

approaching the dais—draw near, gentlemen, draw
near, do not miss any of these words, for this is Truth
and it is a miraculous thing!

"It is a miracle, what we do," he says to his audience, who are experiencing a kind of ecstatic surge
in their own truthful expression. So many people
coming forward to him! Such a triumphant intro-
duction of his vision, which is a thing very much like
art! He will not just continue the family business; he
will lead it to new heights, new breadths, even new
depths, and the old man will come to realize, finally,
that he, Edvar VI, is not a fickle, uncurious, half-
witted nuisance but rather a—))

S., pleased with the chaos he has sown outside,
ventures deeper into the maze of Vévoda's cellars, the
susurrus of old voices rising in intensity as he does.
He listens closely, tries to make out words, is very
nearly losing himself in their swirl when the sound of
a gunshot from the lawn stops him in his tracks. A
shot, then an amplified thump, and then a long, long
piercing squall of feedback echoing across the estate.

His stomach lurches. He hadn't expected anyone
to be driven to kill the boy. Was the shooter an infu-
riated guest? Or one of Vévoda's own Agents,

Keep waiting for Moody news to hit. Nothing yet. Want to call a friend from the library, but it doesn't seem like a good idea.

Oh: Esme Plunderson-Plump called today. Wanted to know if we were interested in writing "the book that rehabilitates Tiago Garcia Ferrara." (Guess whose company owns the rights to GF's entire catalog—in 12 languages!) I asked if she'd publish our Vaclav book + she laughed. Quote: "I've told Eric many times that I can't give him my money to chase ghosts. I can't publish what can't be proved, and this can't be proved. Period." Fine. Screw her. She doesn't deserve our book. When we write it, I mean.

Looking forward to seeing you tomorrow. Kolaches don't taste as good without you.

Anyway. Hope your meeting in Uppsala went well. (You're probably even colder than I am!)

putting an end to a disastrous situation before more harm could be done?

Move, he tells himself. The boy is dead. The world may be a better place for it; even if it isn't, your guilt will not bring him back.

He blows a soft, breathy quintet of notes on his whistle. *I'm in the cellar. Have you found him?* He waits, listens for Sola's response.

Above him, the shrouded sounds of chaos, of violence, are intensifying. Inside his head, the voices pulse with ancient agonies. This place must have been the site of unimaginable suffering, of hearts and souls and lives stolen from the people that these voices once were.[10] Its present stillness, its cool quiet, is a temporary anomaly.

He is about to blow his whistle again when—finally—he hears her response, from somewhere below him and far to his left. *I've found him. Fourth level down. Two others with him.*

Edvar Vévoda V, unaware that he no longer has an heir, has just filled his guests' glasses with a

---

10 As I write this final note, sitting in the cramped and dusty office of Winged Shoes Press on New York's East 33rd Street, it occurs to me that hearts and souls and lives can themselves be sites of unimaginable suffering.

WORDS — VMS'S? — ARE A GIFT TO THE DEAD.

Aren't words a gift to the *living*, too? Why would they just be a warning?

SOT = A WARNING TO FILOMELA? FOR HER SAFETY?

Or to warn her that he wasn't capable of giving her what she wanted.

WHAT THEY WANTED.

This makes me so sad. Especially when I think about how we're here together. She didn't ever have a chance like that.

NO. BUT SHE WAS HAPPY THAT WE DO.

pipette drawn from a barrel marked NOIR NV (a stunning blend of the more contemporary black wines, the greatest example of his artistry to date, if he may risk such a lapse in humility, *but oh, is he not simply speaking truth?*) when he freezes, wrinkles his face as if he has just smelled death. "Did you hear that?" he asks his guests, but they say they did not. "Birds," Vévoda murmurs. "I've got filthy god-damned birds in my cellars."

I'm on the fourth level. Call to me again.
Here I am.
Be careful.
Yes. You be careful, too.
"Birds," Vévoda says, speaking clearly now. "Filthy things. Make my skin crawl."

As it was in the cave above B——, the sources of sounds are difficult to pinpoint. While the two uppermost levels of Vévoda's cellar were orderly, laid out in a grid, with barrels evenly spaced and clearly labeled, the third was a warren of dark paths winding in many directions, its barrels of differing sizes and compositions—some marked, others not. A deeper funk of earth and fruit and

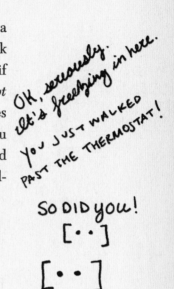

OK, seriously.
it's freezing in here.
You JUST WALKED PAST THE THERMOSTAT!

SO DID YOU!
[••]
[••]

years thickening the air. An even greater sense that the living rarely walk within.

And the fourth level? If it was mapped before it was constructed, that cartography was executed by a madman. S. creeps toward Sola's signal, only to find himself again and again at a fetid dead end. Paths initiate loops that they do not complete, they range out hundreds of yards beyond the boundaries of the upper levels, and they ascend and descend in unlikely—perhaps even impossible—slopes. The voices in his head are louder here, and more clearly defined; when he sees what looks like a human femur protruding from the earthen wall and touches it, a scream spikes right through him. What he does not hear: Vévoda or his guests. He must not be as close as he thinks.

It is also on the fourth level that he sees, for the first time, a barrel marked with the S symbol. And once he sees the first, he starts to see them on nearly every barrel he pauses to inspect.

Fourth level. Are you still here? Are you to my left?

Yes, and yes. Look for a long, straight passage that slopes down.

So really: it was you who drew that S in the book, right?

I SWEAR IT WASN'T.
MAYBE SOMEONE — I DON'T KNOW,
SOME FRESHMAN WHO'S
NEVER EVEN HEARD OF
STRAKA — STUMBLED
ACROSS THE BOOK IN THE STACKS
+ DECIDED TO MESS WITH IT/US?

Works for me.

IT WAS A WHILE AGO, ANYWAY.
NO ONE'S GOTTEN HOLD OF THE
BOOK SINCE THEN.

Although we can't know for sure...

SHIP OF THESEUS

———

Vévoda wipes his guests' glasses dry after they
have sampled, with obvious pleasure, the black
Taranaki 1863.

Again, the whistles.

"My only consolation," he comments to those
gathered, "is that they will never find their way out.
How long do you think they can last down here? Two
days? Three? Can birds live on wine and bones?"

NOIR ODESSA 1871

NOIR DAHOMEY 1840

NOIR GALWAY 1831

NOIR BIJAPUR 1791

NOIR ADANA 1909

NOIR RIO NEGRO 1878

NOIR BARKOL 1756

All of these: times and places where great numbers of people have suffered, died, disappeared.
Individuals and communities, wiped clean. Traditions and histories, myths, the most commonplace
stories told by the least-known individuals, all gone.

To drink the black stuff is to drink what has
been lost.

———

*Looked all these
up. Depressing.*

WE'RE INCREDIBLY LUCKY.
LOOK AT WHERE WE ARE.
LOOK AT WHAT WE GET
TO DO.

*Do you still
think that? Because
I don't feel it.*

*That's embarrassing.
Totally lost perspective there.*

YOU WERE SCARED.

———

To hold it in a barrel, S. imagines, is to imprison the vital; to cellar that barrel is to warehouse the sublime.

To launch a Black Vine is to take all the churning fury of the lost and use it to render other people, in some other place, equally lost. A chain-reaction of erasure, the ordinary contagion of oblivion.

He passes a barrel on which no mark is visible, as its contents have leaked through a split stave and blackened the wood below. He can still see an outline of the spill across the earthen floor. He kneels down and touches a finger to it, and all at once, the mad chorus of voices in his head goes silent.

Silent.

Settled. Returned to the earth and settled. Voices and narratives, re-absorbed into the ground on which we walk. And this is the key, he realizes, the thing that makes the purpose of all that work on the ship and in El-H—— and on the Obsidian Island and in Budapest, Edinburgh, Valparaíso, Prague, Cape Town, Valletta, the Winter City, and a thousand others come into focus. All that ink, all that pigment, all that desperate action to preserve that which had been created—it is valuable because story is a fragile and ephemeral thing on

———

its own, a thing that is easily effaced or disappeared or destroyed, and it is worth preserving.
And if it can't be preserved, then it should be
released and cycled.

To write with the black stuff is to create and, at
the same time, to resurrect. We write with what
those who've come before us wrote.

Everything rewritten. *Part o' the tradition.*

And his greatest revelation is personal: he doesn't
care about Vévoda anymore. As long as the man
lives, S. and others will resist what he brings to the
world. When Vévoda dies, someone else will take
his place. When S. dies, someone else will take his
place. Another S. Another story.

Sola. He must find her and tell her what he now
understands. He blows one short note on his whistle
and hurries through the junctures in directions that,
he hopes, will lead him to her. And when she answers
him, she sounds so close, and he doubles his pace,
darting through the near-dark. A sudden drop in the
path sends him stumbling, and as he is falling he
remembers Pfeifer's injury in the cave, prays the
same fate will not befall him. He lands roughly, but
when he pulls himself up to standing again, all the
parts of him seem in working order.

ANOTHER POSSIBLE PLACE WHERE FXC TOOK OVER.

Here is where Time collects, collides, all at once. A drop of wetness falls on his head. He rubs the spot and finds a dark streak across his palm. Looking up, he sees that the ceiling has been saturated with blue-black and is dripping down here and along the curving path before him. He runs ahead, wiping the substance off his forehead, out of his eyes. The sweetly biting aroma fills the air, as do the desperate whispers, until they are drowned out by a scream, a scream of outrage, which he knows is Vévoda's. Then another—the high scream of deranged glee. It is the monkey's. And when, another fifty yards along a straight, downward-sloping corridor, he turns to his left—oh, if only he knew how to paint! how arrestingly strange the image would be!—and finds Vévoda, white-haired, white-bearded, and blanched of color, swinging around wildly with a pistol in his hand, trying to draw a bead on the white-muzzled monkey, which seems to have re-acquired the piss-and-vinegar of its youth and is scampering wildly between and over and under barrels, pulling out the bungs and tossing them far away into the dark and letting the black wine spill onto the floor, just as it must have done on the level above them.

I'M SO GLAD FILOMELA NEVER OPENED THAT ENVELOPE.

Yeah. I have nightmares about his version. All those women...

I DON'T THINK HE WAS TRYING TO SHOCK READERS. I THINK HE REALLY FELT LIKE HE'D FAILED THEM ALL.

One of Vévoda's guests chases the monkey—pointlessly, as the monkey never lets him get close, and the primary effect of his pursuit is to interfere with the raging Vévoda's sight lines. The other guest scrambles around on all fours, searching for the discarded bungs so he can save at least some of the black wine before it all seeps back into the ground. And then there is Sola, standing still and steady in the middle of all this chaos, holding aloft the most powerful weapon that anyone in this cellar possesses, a naphtha lighter, and her thumb is poised over the flint wheel. He watches her face—her open and steady face—and he knows that she is willing to set all of this alight—willing, without hesitation, without further thought, to lose everything, including—and perhaps especially—herself. She is willing to do it because she already knows that it is the effort, the effort to resist, that matters.

"Put down the gun," S. says as he steps from the shadows. "Your son needs you." This is a story, of course, and one that has little to do with truth, other than to manipulate it. The white-bearded man turns toward him, tremors shaking the hand that holds the gun. It is aimed at S.'s head. A pull of the trigger right now will erase him, immediately and irrevocably.

He really was there, right? When the projector went out?

I SWEAR I HIT HIM. SIX OR SEVEN TIMES AT LEAST. YOU HEARD ME HIT HIM.

So where did he go?

STEAM TUNNELS?

MAYBE SERIN HAD PEOPLE THERE, TOO.

Wish they'd told us. Also wish we could've stayed there + watched the stars some more.

IT WAS YOUR IDEA TO LEAVE EVERYTHING + GO.

How many parking tickets do you think my car has by now?

Vévoda looks to Sola again. Studies her. Assesses her threat and the truth of it. Perhaps he sees what S. saw in her face—that cool embrace of self-destruction for a noble end. He lowers the gun, tosses it to the ground near S.'s feet. He barks at his guests to stop running around, they look like fools and they ought to be embarrassed, and besides, he'd better go see what his damned son has gotten them into now.

S. picks up the gun. He opens the chamber. One bullet, which looks decades-old and unlikely to fire. He shakes it out into his palm and flings it far off into the dark. He tucks the unloaded gun into his belt.

There is a pause, a shift in dynamic, when they are all keenly alert to one another's physical presence and to the strange congruity of this moment, this point in time around which their stories all pivot.

Vévoda pushes past them and plods up the inclined passage, the two shamed guests following behind him, while the monkey races ahead, unstoppering barrel after barrel after barrel, making the three men slop through the soggy mantle of black wine. Scorched leather scents the passage as the caustic wine causes further ruin to their shoes, to their moods, to their senses of how much power they wield in this world.

[Handwritten marginalia:]

I THOUGHT YOU WERE WORKING IN THERE.

I can't. It's way too cold.

YOU'RE THE ONE WHO CHOSE THIS PLACE.

Shut up. You would have chosen it, too.

IT'S FUNNY — EVERY TIME YOU COME IN HERE, I CAN READ YOUR FACE + GUESS THE TONE OF THE NOTE YOU'VE JUST WRITTEN.

I love you more every day we're together.

HEY — THAT WAS YOUR I'M-BEING-A-SMARTASS FACE.

You're not a very good reader.

ALWAYS THOUGHT THIS WAS
VMS OPTING FOR AN ANTICLIMAX
TO SHOW HOW SMALL BOUCHARD'S BRAND OF
EVIL WAS... HOW, REALLY, ALL YOU HAVE TO DO IS
LOOK IT IN THE EYE SQUARELY ENOUGH, SEE IT FOR
WHAT IT IS, SHOW THAT YOU DON'T HAVE LESS POWER. NOW I THINK
IT'S FXC TRYING TO SHOW VMS THAT THE FIGHT WASN'T
AS IMPORTANT AS THEIR BEING TOGETHER.

Couldn't she have
had both in mind?

FUNNY — you
SAID A LONG TIME
AGO THAT WHAT
MATTERS IS
WHO'S HOLDING
THE PEN.

SHIP OF THESEUS

Their control is not absolute. This is the story.
S.'s story.

"Unless you know how to get back," S. says, "we
should follow them."

(("It's too bad," Sola says. "I was fond of these shoes."))

S. takes hold of her left hand with his right, and
they walk together, with Vévoda and his guests still
visible at the other end of the long, straight passage.
"Keep the lighter out," he tells her, "and keep your
thumb on the wheel."

See? This whole final
sequence was here.
From the monkey's
appearance on.

OK — this has to be
one of the lines that
Filomela wrote.
SEXIST?
a girl knows.

Where will their steps lead? Up through the
higher level of the cellar, certainly, and across the
lawn to the servants' pavilion and down the dry well
and through the engirding passage and into the
grotto and onto the ship. One of the sailors will
untie the lines—perhaps the old one, with the white
wings of hair, surprised to see them returning
alive—and the others will draw up oars and lead the
ship to the star-filled sky, to a warm wind blowing
from the southeast, to open water, and they will
sail. And as they do, S. will pick up Maelstrom's old
spyglass from the chart-room, where it was hidden
under the blankets on which the black-stained
monkey sleeps and snores. Looking out over the

WHAT IF ESME'S RIGHT?
WHAT IF WE CAN'T
WRITE THAT BOOK?
WHAT IF WE'RE
COMPLETELY WASTING
OUR TIME?

We're not wasting our
time — whether or not we
find a trace of Vaclav
this year — whether or
not we ever do. We're
together, and I love
you. Full stop.
The End.

WE DON'T KNOW THAT
THAT'S THE END.

We don't know that
it isn't. So why
not believe?

Interesting that she didn't include
the naval mines.

SHE PROBABLY DIDN'T KNOW THAT HE
INTENDED TO
BRING THEM BACK.

Or maybe she
did know... but what
she wanted most was for S. + Sola
to have a clean escape.

port rail, he will see something he has not seen in a long, long time: another ship. Not a ghost ship, no; she is a ship with flags flying and sailors working on deck, sails trimmed and humming in the wind, a glorious wake churning out behind her, and what looks like two people standing on the quarterdeck and sharing the wheel. He can't see their faces through the glass, can't really see much about them at all, but he slides the glass closed and tells Sola that the ship is one of theirs, and as for the identities of the two people at the wheel, well, both Sola and he will let their imaginations fill in their features.

EVEN FILOMELA'S VERSION IS A LITTLE AMBIGUOUS.
I don't think it is.

END

Hey, put the book down.
Come in here & stay.